D1521163

Misterioso

BOOKS BY GILBERT SORRENTINO

Fiction

The Sky Changes
Steelwork
Imaginative Qualities of Actual Things
Splendide-Hôtel
Flawless Play Restored: The Masque of Fungo
Mulligan Stew
Aberration of Starlight
Crystal Vision
Blue Pastoral
Odd Number
A Beehive Arranged on Humane Principles
Rose Theatre

Poetry

The Darkness Surrounds Us
Black and White
The Perfect Fiction
Corrosive Sublimate
A Dozen Oranges
Sulpiciae Elegidia: Elegiacs of Sulpicia
White Sail
The Orangery
Selected Poems 1958-1980

Criticism

Something Said

Misterioso

Gilbert Sorrentino

Dalkey Archive Press

Portions of this work have appeared in *Conjunctions* and the *Stanford Humanities Review,* to whose editors the author makes grateful acknowledgment.

The author thanks the John Simon Guggenheim Memorial Foundation for financial assistance granted him upon the initiation of this work.

Library of Congress Cataloging in Publication Data
Sorrentino, Gilbert.
   Misterioso / by Gilbert Sorrentino.
   I. Title.
PS3569.07M57   1989   813'.54—dc19   89-7707
ISBN 0-916583-43-0

Partially funded by grants from The National Endowment for the Arts and The Illinois Arts Council.

Dalkey Archive Press
1817 North 79th Avenue
Elmwood Park, IL 60635 USA

Printed on permanent/durable acid-free paper and bound in the United States of America.

For with men and women, with men's men and women's men, with men's women and women's women, with men's and women's men, with men's and women's women, all is possible, as far as can be ascertained, in this connexion.

—*Samuel Beckett*

Perhaps a question will open the way to resolution, for instance: Why does this old A & P supermarket, with its wooden floors, narrow aisles, and overabundance, or so some think, of house-brand canned goods and bakery products, display, as if carelessly forgotten atop a binful of Granny Smith apples, a seemingly well-read paperback copy of *Absalom! Absalom!*?

"That was made into a movie, I think," a well-dressed woman, in her hand a box of jelly doughnuts, says. She is smiling, but close observation reveals that the smile is an involuntary rictus. Everybody has problems. "On the 'Academic Playhouse of the Air'?" Silence attends upon her question, the kind that invaded the streets of John Keats's little town. "Or did it win an Academy Award, or something?" Back comes the silence, or perhaps the silence returns.

Nobody in the market either wants or is able to answer her question. Perhaps no one believes she cares about the famed novel in one way or another. Evidence: a copy of the latest paperback best-seller, *Accidental Bodies,* is in her shopping cart. "Put this one in your beach bag, packs a shattering wallop of steamy sex!"

The Ace of Diamonds is protruding from between pages 150 and 151 of *Absalom! Absalom!* ". . . cling to above the maelstrom of unbearable reality—The four years . . . are gone, leaving us immobile, impotent, helpless; fixed, until we . . ." Of course you remember it.

She hopes that it's better than *Acquisitions,* a book that she has started three times but just can't get into. Too thick, anyway. Who can *read* it?

There are many people who don't even pretend to read it, and for such as these, a wire rack near the express checkout register contains magazines which promise stories of action. There is *Action,* "Holocaust of Death at the Indy 500," *Action at Sea,* "Death beneath the

7

Arctic Ice," *Action Monthly*, "Rape and Death Stalked State Trooper Kimberley Butz," and *Actionworld*, "Death Is Their Mistress—The Green Berets." "To tell you the truth, my husband reads these sometimes," she says. "I think he likes the ads in the back for dirty books, machine guns, and big knockers on the girls." The young woman giving out samples of cherry-cheese dip nods and smiles into what she takes to be a smile.

"Isn't it the truth," she says. Her smile slowly fades, a well-worn but useful fade, as close observation reveals to her that her interlocutor's smile is an involuntary rictus, which shows no sign of fading, slowly or otherwise.

"She'll get herself in a jam if she smiles at some horny guy like that," the sample woman says in the direction of *Absalom! Absalom!* and the Granny Smith apples. Neither apples nor book replies. For the most part, things are silent.

Some few miles away, in a suburb of the city in which the A & P is located, a middle-aged woman sits in a weathered Adirondack chair placed on a lawn in the shade of a large plane tree. We don't know the name of the suburb.

"Agapa," the woman says, looking up from a novel whose title cannot be discerned. Is it too much to hope that it is, perhaps . . .?

"It's *Sanctuary*," she says. "The old version. I like it better."

This woman, whose name is as yet unknown, is a . . . wait a minute. The name of the suburb is Agapa, and it is not unlike any of the other suburbs contiguous to the northern boundary of the city. An attractive vegetarian couple, for instance, lives right here, on Rensaeller Street.

That's Rensellaer Street.

The woman wears a golden charm on a slender chain about her neck. She may be unaware that the charm is the seal of Agares, Master of Tongues and Crocodiles, a bad hat. Tied snugly around her attractively mature body is an apron with the word *Agfa* across it.

Agfa, so a representative of the company, or firm, kindly writes, makes supplies of every kind for the photographic industry. It is apparent that all camera enthusiasts know this, judging from the volume of outraged mail received.

"Ah Lady," a priest is saying, "cries tears of blood when people like to peruse over dese magazines' ads for sexual aids, pornographical degrading materials such as large female bosoms, an' guns of all descriptions. Duh stories are not so big wit' her either." No one in the market pays any attention to him, since he is in mufti, and his accent is obviously "put on."

Karen Aileron looks distractedly out the window, a tofuburger sizzling in the skillet on the stove. She's put on some weight, but her legs are still good, her bosom, thanks to *Actionworld,* still firm, and her white teeth, well! They flash now as she smiles to herself, thinking of the movie she saw a couple of nights ago—*Aini, the Destroyer!*—and the wonderful love scene in the cabin of a 747. She sighs and wipes her hands on her Agfa apron as she turns to check her tofuburger. Satisfied, she smiles in a friendly way, and says, "Hi! I'm Karen Aileron! I used to attend to aerial wishes, stratospherically svelte amid soft drinks and tiny liquor bottles. But here in my comfortable flat, I dote on simple meals, good thoughts, and fantasy guys. Hi!"
    "I hate it when two people wear the same clothes," the rictal woman says to the checkout clerk. "I mean it's not impossible for two people to be wearing the same clothes, I guess. It's just that I hate it, I don't know, I can't explain it." The checkout clerk, not being of a literary turn of mind, glances, with a quick raise of his eyebrows, at the boy who is bagging groceries. The latter looks blank.

The woman in the Adirondack chair is of the opinion that she might as well be living in Akron, for, in the early afternoon, an Albanian woman of indeterminate age passes by, as she has for the past month. Her looks and clothes are more or less nondescript. More or less.
    However, knotted tightly about her neck as a kind of ascot, she wears, or sports, what the woman in the Adirondack chair is certain is a pair of filthy ice-blue bikini panties.
    Why, though, *Akron?*
    Allen, a waiter with bunions, callouses, corns, and ingrown toenails, whose public discourse is usually limited to variations on "Hi, I'm Allen, your waiter, and I'll be gleefully serving you this evening," suddenly says, "Hi, I'm Allen, and I prefer the Alps." He winces as he bangs his foot against the base of the service bar. "Fuck Akron."

Some do prefer the Alps, some, perhaps surprisingly, Akron, while others look to more exotic purlieus—the Gobi Desert, the Serengeti, the Amazon Basin. The latter, for instance, is a sediment-filled structural depression between crystalline highlands. Geologically speaking, it is known as a fylfot.

"I'm nobody's dummy," Allen simpers a moment prior to toadying.

The woman in the Adirondack chair, as we are about to discover, is a sculptor, who at one time enjoyed a small renown. Of *Amber Glass,* one of her last works, a small wooden figure of Olive Oyl, she notes, "I want to deconstruct the notion of female comic-strip characters as figures of contempt." What the hell. She is reading *Sanctuary* in order to take her mind off a suit, filed by the owners of the Ambers, a semi-pro baseball team, who contend that she is using their copyrighted name without permission or authorization, thus subjecting their organization to ridicule and scorn. Considering the level of the Ambers' play, this is quite a feat.

"Is nice things about America, also and Americans," the Albanian woman says, in a rich yet amusing accent. "I learn these thing in studied of American Revolution in citizen class." She goes on and on, to such an extent that Amon, Who Vomits Fire, is tempted to singe the bikinis right off her neck, but desists, for private, probably depraved, reasons.

"Why the hell is this copy of *Anal Fancies* carelessly tucked in among the action magazines?" Andy says. He is an unprepossessing young man who hangs around the soup.

"I wouldn't let a dog read that trash," the rictal woman says, or fumes. She neglects to add that which we suspect, that she owns a well-thumbed copy of *Annals of Sapphism: Womanlove,* unfortunately now out of print. Forty-two full-color photographs depict two young women, possibly college-educated, exploring the forbidden pleasures of female eroticism.

Probably out of print because the text deconstructs the very notion of the phallus. Well, not precisely a *text.*

Has it been mentioned that the woman in the Adirondack chair, "the sculptor," owns a puppet, dressed as a French maid, called "Annette," and another, clad only in leopard-skin briefs, called "Mr. Anthony"? They are the gifts of an old, somewhat perverted acquaintance,

"Queenie" Antilles, sometimes known to close friends as "Cunty" Uncles. *She* has a few stories to tell! Such amazingly lifelike puppets are painstakingly crafted by hand in old Antoine by canny craftsmen to whom craftsmanship is more important than speed or handsome profits. Observe their bent, grizzled heads encircled by wreaths of pipe smoke.

"I think they're made by some*body* named Antoine," the sculptor says, suddenly laughing gaily as she remembers a couple of things.

Then perhaps they're made in the rustic hamlet of Apple Pie?

"Perhaps," the sculptor says. "But I think they're made in Après-le-Bain by the renowned puppetmaker—I should have earlier mentioned it—Antoine! Or *have* I mentioned it?" She returns to *Sanctuary,* singing contentedly to herself in an untrained yet pleasant alto.

"How funny she sing 'Is It Lonely for You This Evening?' " the Albanian woman says. She stops to stare rudely.

"Get the hell out of here!" the sculptor implores her. "And besides, you foreign bitch, it's 'Are You Lonesome Tonight?' "

"I not is," the Albanian woman modestly rejoins, to general hilarity.

As the rictal woman leaves the A & P for the oppressive heat of the streets, she is knocked sprawling by Grace Armstrong, a ridiculous figure in "sweat" clothing, or "sweaties," who is just finishing her daily jogging stint. She bears little resemblance to the sluttish young woman of the good old days. She says, to anyone who will listen, that this exercise keeps her sane, an exaggeration of the first order.

"Running, actually," Grace says. "It keeps me sane. I really prefer to call it a 'regimen.' "

Jack Armstrong, a man who suffers, as can well be imagined, from the monicker he bears not proudly but with the calm resignation and sad visage that has done many things, finishes writing the final paragraph of a story. He is, finally, pleased. Critical comments: remarkably perceptive, packs a satisfying wallop, steamy and exotic sex. Jack is rummaging among some books on his desk, or riffling through the pages of same, for the perfect epigraph for his story, one that will display not only his erudition but his sensitivity to walloping prose. A sensitive depiction of the lower stratum, learned, but not annoyingly so, Mr. Armstrong has chosen the perfect epigraph, packs a probing wallop. He settles on one from the work of a writer he disgustingly, at least some think, calls "Arthur." Just "Arthur."

". . . je vous détache ces quelques hideux feuillets de mon carnet de damné." Jack seems a complete schmuck. But wait. "Arthur" enters Jack's study, actually his bedroom, his hair tousled and greasy, his knobby wrists protruding from the sleeves of his too-short *la jaquette* or *la veste,* his slate-blue trousers wrinkled and rumpled. Around his neck is a filthy *la corde.* His eyes are the clearest, most piercing blue that Jack has ever seen. In a soft voice, heavy with contempt, he says, "J'ai seul la clef de cette parade sauvage." Jack turns upon him that which is crudely known as a shit-eating grin. We've all seen it.

By the way, that's Rensselaer Street.

Grace Armstrong is a student, as many of you will have guessed, at the Art Students' League, where she is working on a small semi-geographical canvas called *Asbury Park.* "And a real disaster it is," her instructor adds. She is now on her second year of work on this picture, and is known to the other students as "Mrs. Asbury Park." The anger and humiliation that this sobriquet causes Grace may be the reason behind her daily stint of jogging. Or it may be because of something that happened *in her youth!*

"Actually, it's a regimen of running," Grace says, scraping off another layer of paint. It's bad work, all right.

A flyer offering the services of Mrs. Louise Ashby, Healer, Reader, Advisor, Seeress, Prophet, details, in a testimonial from one G.A., the beneficent and salutary powers of Art. It reads, in part . . .

But now it must be reported that the priest has come across the copy of *Anal Fancies* slipped between two copies of *Actionworld.* He is astonished, disgusted, repelled, and aroused by the cover photograph of a young man and woman in anal coition. "My God," he says, "dey look like dey like it."

. . . "people were talking about me and I was drinking too much alcoholic beverages and gambling away all my earning, and, finally I lost my suitcase. My husband left me for a bimbo and I had nowhere to turn until I heard of MRS. ASHBY, one visit to her and today I am a student at a famous Art School and working happily on a genuine oil painting . . ."

This is a familiar if crass testimonial.

It is not generally known that the demon Asmoday, Familiar of the Cur from Hell, spends a month each winter at the world-famous ski resort of Aspen, Colorado, where, on almost any given day during the "season," one may see famed film stars, famed writers, and rich, powerful people who are famed in many diverse walks of life. As they enjoy themselves much like regular persons, they as firmly insist on their treasured privacy.

"I am, as you may well imagine, disguised during my sojourn in the brooding mountains as my good buddy, Astaroth, Angel of Unearthly Beauty, a luscious broad with a knockout figure and a lot of bad threads."

"I much admiring American jargo," the Albanian woman says. For her, as for so many who grease the wheels, prime the pumps, stoke the fires, and unfailingly "take it on the chins," Aspen, Colorado, is but a fantastic dream, a lambent Xanadu. The sculptor is safely in her house, fearful that the unwanted figure lurking in the road beyond the bed of phlox may never go away. She may be right. Time will tell.

Léonie Aubois pours the last ounce of vodka from her 1.75 liter bottle into a glass with an oranges-and-lemons motif etched into its outer surface. Some call such vessels "Depression glasses," make what you will of that. A pot of Campbell's Vegetarian Vegetable Soup simmers on a burner of her hot plate. She rises from her torn, stained armchair, totters, staggers, and falls to the floor. "God damn them all," she says. On the wall, a tear-off calendar reveals that this day is August 29, 1982. There are two pieces of reading matter—outside of the calendar —in the room: "Autumnal Aspen Leaves," a poem on yellowing newsprint, Scotch-taped to the wall above the dirty, rust-stained sink, which poem begins:

> O Empress in your trembling golden gown,
> Chilled in the Autumn winds that swirl and gust—

and an offprint of an article from an unknown journal of ideas and opinions, "The Avant-Garde: Finally Dead?" by Nora Avenel, reportedly a horny cultural journalist. These are depressing items.

"And God damn that bitch too," Léonie says, and begins the drunken weeping that is by now second nature to her. She could use a bath.

The jelly doughnuts are a homely touch designed to reinforce the market's probability, its, how shall we say? credibility. To strengthen further the much-desired pilosity of just about everything, we may modify the generic term with a brand name, casually and naturally affixed, to wit: ". . . in her hand a box of Jane Parker jelly doughnuts . . ."

"I like much this jaybarger jelly donuts," the Albanian woman says. Note her modern, time-saving spelling of the substantive.

Yet among those who distrust the veracity, even the usefulness of the anecdotes thus far presented as facts, are the priest, who doesn't understand why *he* is chosen to have an unseemly erection caused by his shocked glance at the photograph so glibly mentioned, the sculptor, who trusts nothing beyond the confines of her suburban property, and a certain "B," of whom we know nothing, and who has intruded rather brusquely. "B" may be either a man or a woman. It's impossible for us to get a good look, attendant as we are upon the Albanian woman's culinary opinions. No sparrow falls, as they say. The Albanian woman, by the way, seems pleased, convinced that everything so far offered is exemplary of life in America. She may well be right.

The A & P, incidentally, is in direct competition with two other neighborhood markets, Rudy's Superette and Crown SuperMart. Because of this unseemly situation, the A & P management is increasingly chagrined to discover that it is more and more difficult to fob off tainted meat and rotten produce—most especially, bananas—on its customers. By means of unspeakable midnight obeisance to Baal the Cat, King of the Invisible, the management is about to close a deal to sell out to Baby Brownie, owner of a chain of cinema centers, which Mr. Brownie calls "CineCenters," subtlety being his trump card in the exhilarating and aggressive world of the entertainment business. True to his code, however, a code that no expert has been, as yet, able to crack, Mr. Brownie, or "Babe," as his wife calls him in those all-too-few moments of marital passion that they occasionally share during their rare and jealously coveted country weekends, likes to listen to Bach, especially, one, or two, might say predictably, *The Art of Fugue.* While enjoying this acclaimed masterpiece, written by the great composer at the age of four, the entertainment czar invariably reads aloud from *Bad Girl,* the spicy novel of some years past, bound specially for the Brownie library in pale-blue vellum, a favorite skin, or whatever it is. Three of his children, Wotan, Natty, and Elmo, are, sadly, permanent residents of the Bahamas, where they are, unfortunately, rather unsuccessfully attempting to cling to a questionable sanity. A fourth, adopted child, Balte, probably lost to business forever, hangs around the mayonnaise in Village Victuals on Baltic Street. Literati know that this slobbering albeit repulsive idiot served as the model for Max Champagne in the justly neglected novel *Baltimore Chop.* Bam, his friend, a towering wreck of a man, in plaids, who steadfastly refuses to comply with the Mann Act—he is a graduate of a famous Ivy League school—never lets Balte Brownie forget this youthful indiscretion. From the next aisle, where he hangs around the Hispanic food products, he laughs immoderately, making what he fondly believes to be the sound of popping champagne corks.

Then, to lighten things considerably, there is the joy of Banana Amaze, which the rictal woman makes for her busy family at least once a week. It keeps her, so she claims with a smile, "in touch." This is a dessert, not to be confused with Banana Split—a pedestrian confection which requires little preparation—that is perfect for those evenings when a festive atmosphere is desirable, and is also an excellent conclusion, or *rondo,* to hearty winter fare. The recipe follows:

Banana Amaze

1 3-pound chicken, cut into serving pieces	1 envelope of ruy Lopez
Salt and freshly ground pepper to taste	2 cups of Kobayashi
3 tablespoons chicken fat or valerian	1 cup each Kronecker and Schur products
2 large mastiachi peppers	4 milk-chocolate bars, plain or tinctured

4 ripe bananas, peeled and cut into 2-inch pieces

1. Sprinkle the chicken pieces with salt and pepper to taste. Tenderize by beating with hammer, being careful not to cut the skin. (Traditionally, the chicken is wrapped in vellum and buried in loose materials overnight.) Heat the chicken fat or valerian in a heavy skillet and add all the chicken pieces, skin side down. Cook until golden brown and turn the pieces. Add the mastiachi peppers and the bananas.
2. Cook for approximately 3 hours over low heat. Add the ruy Lopez and cook another 15-20 minutes.
3. Remove everything from the skillet to a hot serving platter and add the Kobayashi, martingales, and Kronecker and Schur products to the skillet. Cook over high heat, stirring to dislodge the blackened, charred particles that adhere to the pan. When the Kronecker and Schur products turn a dark brown and curl at the edges, return the chicken, peppers, bananas, and ruy Lopez to the skillet.
4. Add the milk-chocolate bars, cover the skillet, and cook for 10 more minutes. When the chocolate has melted, serve immediately, with a large, unpeeled banana for garnish.

Yield: Four servings.

We don't understand why this recipe, which may be found in *Get It on in the Kitchen!,* is attributed to a "Mrs. Banjiejicz," and described as a "Polish holiday favorite." Our doubts are reinforced by a recent letter from one of our many admirers, Mr. Barbatos, who understands the behavior of nervous birds, collects "modernana," and is an authority on peppers and their use in national cuisine. Mr. Barbatos writes:

Sirs:

I am reading some sort of thing as you *well know* and can't help but "laugh" along with you at the notion that Mrs. Banjiejicz talks about "Banana amaze" as a Polack people "favorite" since anybody who knows anything about peppers knows that mastiachi peppers are decisively unknown to the swell Polack people. Mastiachis, known to the people of Michoacán as *chilis de penes,* are completely unknown to the great Polack people. I don't think that Mrs. Banjiejicz knows anything about peppers.

Sincerely, etc., etc.

Letters like these usually occasion numerous replies, and Mr. Barbatos's is no exception. Here is a reply from Betty Barker:

Dear Sirs:

The unsigned letter that criticizes Mrs. Banjowic's recipe for Banana Amaze is an example, a telling type, of the type of mentality that we let run loose in this once-great city, where I got robbed the other night outside of Village Victuals of a potatoe which I paid for by a huge thug in a plaid suit. When I was a student at Barnard forty years ago, I remember, *very well,* a lot of girls. Since then, I've tried my hand at writing and am the author and publisher, at my own expense, among other well-received books, of a historical romance novel in free verse, *Baron Darke of Eagle House,* of which Valerie Menses was occasionally heard to comment, "it packs a romantic wallop!" and also *A Batch of Stuff,* a collection of adult musings on Life which also did not sell very well because of ineptness in distribution methods by mockies. So you see that I am not exactly anybody's fool.

But enough about my accomplishments, for I just want to state that your ignorant correspondent knows very little about the Polish, when he says "mastiachi peppers" are something that the Polish don't know anything about. After all, His Eminence himself is a Polish person. At Barnard, I knew a lot of girls and often, we'd eat Banana Amaze at somebody's house, often *Polish,* after "cramming." Once I remember we traveled all the way to Greenpoint to somebody's house on the subway and, if you know where Barnard is and Greenpoint also, you know that this is a long subway ride. Does your correspondent think that I and my girlish college friends all of whom are now middle-aged and with children of their own, from Barnard, would travel all the way to somebody's house in Greenpoint by subway if we didn't know that there we could get Banana Amaze? I also have it on an authority's word contained in a highly regarded newspaper column that the Polish element in Greenpoint grow mastiachi peppers in their backyard but that they simply call them "Peppers." I think you should be ashamed to print letters from foreigners who don't know American customs.

Yours truly, etc., etc.

Finally, a Mr. Bathin, the proprietor of the Pale Horse Inn, writes:

Dear Sirs:

You might be interested to know that while browsing carelessly through a local bookstore, I became angry to see the exchange of letters on the subject of Banana Amaze. I think that it is all *stupid* because how is a reader like myself to make up their mind about who is right in this culinary argument when we do not even know about these so-called peppers? It is obvious that you know very little of the writer's task which a well-known author says is "to inform the long look with all that is in our power." I would be proud to serve such an author at my Inn, one that *Town 'n' Country Notes* reviewed in a favorable 2-Stars light. As far as you people are concerned, you are lowlife.

Respectfully, etc., etc.

Evident, we hope, is precisely the sort of thing we have to put up with as we try to inform a long look, with all that is in our power, with this and that.

One of the powerful looks so informed is to be found in "Baye Tree," a delightful yet thoughtful romp excerpted from an otherwise essentially self-indulgent fiction, which Charlotte Bayless, an extraordinarily libidinous woman, especially favors. Leave it to Charlotte! At present, Charlotte is right here in town, doing God knows what, although she may be on the verge of rude expulsion from her otherwise fulfilling job. She still likes what she calls "mayonnaise sandwiches," which may explain the faint, secretive smile that plays about her generous mouth as she yawns, stretches, and wonders just what kind of day *this* is going to be. Frank Baylor, "Father" Frank to the seedy acquaintances he pathetically calls his friends, knows nothing of this smile; still, he wages his lonely battle against the gonorrhea that renders his life a living nightmare and a waking horror. Yet the insidious disease also brings home to him some powerful moral truths. Too late! Because of his half-forgotten romance with the church, Frank prefers "Beacon," another excerpt, to "Baye Tree," doubtless because of the vague yet penetrant aroma which clings to the multifarious items therein assiduously detailed. And commented on. At some length.

Yet both Frank and Charlotte have time, wrested at great personal expense of spirit, to indulge their taste for current news and gossip, however malicious. For example, they are currently agog at the unexplained presence of *Anal Fancies* in the A & P—Charlotte, agog because of the priest involved in the burgeoning debacle. This is called the recognition factor, or, more professionally, the Empathy Syndrome. They also follow the sex-for-ducats scandal involving Beauchamp, a white-haired ex-hostler, and are enthralled by the memoirs of Edmé-Pierre Beauchesne, which read as freshly as if they had been penned yesterday. These "jottings" are amazingly attuned to past events chillingly like those contemporary and corrosive occurrences which assert themselves ever more powerfully into the weakened—the *already* weakened—foundations of a true cultural sophistication; indeed, the historical *connaissance* implied by Beauchesne to be "dilatory at best," might well be a mirror image of our own dilatory *connaissance,* one that threatens America itself, perhaps fatally. Time will tell.

Then too: Beaumont and Halpin to Begin New "Geriatrix" Porno Line; "Beautiful Dreamer" Stolen from Stravinsky Melody, Researcher Claims; *The Beautiful Sun* Gets Final Production O.K.; *A Bed of Poses* "All Lies," Attractive Blue-Blood Whore Asserts; Miner X. ("Beat-Off") Beely Makes *Guinness Book of Records;* Olga Begone Goes on Acclaimed Aluminum Diet.

There is no end to the tidbits which Charlotte and Frank snap up. After all, *they live in this world,* and *you're a long time dead.* Or so they believe.

It is Beleth, the Terrible, who casts the ancient spell of malediction which compels "Ben," an otherwise nice young fellow with a penchant for rhumba rock and cerise bikinis by Jockey (women are often beside themselves at the sight of his manly equipment), to hang around the eggplants. From this vantage, he hears the jubilant shouts of unemployable pals echoing through the air. "Ben" has tried mass, to no avail; novenas to St. Jude, *nada;* benediction, incense and all, *rien.* His girl, a pert gamin known as "Muffie" to her Bennington friends, no longer enthralled by his threatening bulge, now shops alone, repressing her sobs as best she can, at Saks, Bergdorf's, Tiffany, and Gucci. Her remark, "Eggplants? Oh come *on!*" is, you might agree, like as a knife in the young man's heart and crotch. "Ben," however, seems able to do nothing about his jeopardized love, although he misses Muffie's lackadaisical sexual enthusiasms. Occasionally, though, Berith, the Red Soldier of the Lie, and one of Beleth's closest confidants, causes him to dream of sweet, silly Muffie energetically fucking a tugboat. Miner X. Beely, at this intelligence, is struck dumb with envy.

Bermuda, at this time of year, is beautiful, with its several tans, shorts, green stuff, oranges bright, and fawning menials. The sculptor thinks of this as she peers out at the Albanian woman, who is now lying on her lawn, *Sanctuary* opened over her face in an inverted V. The sculptor recalls the man, precariously existent on that sunny isle, who dresses as a maid. Cute as a button, good legs, nice face but for a hairy mole. He calls himself Berthe, is learned, but not annoyingly so, and says, to anyone who gets near him, that this ancillary enterprise keeps him sane. Men who are too forward quickly learn of his prowess, for he packs a sure wallop! Gossip amid the flowering shrubs and lethargic jalousies insists that he is a nonproductive painter and sculptor, yet he is often seen in the company of Edward Beshary, crass, grizzled mogul who brooks no nonsense. When E.B. isn't vulgarly and openly compromising Berthe's reputation, he is on the phone to Beverly Hills with endless talk of deals. Suffice it to say that Berthe has no friends.

There is, purportedly, a long monograph in the *Enfer* division of La Bibliothèque Nationale concerning Beshary's perverse exploits while an assistant professor at Bennington, before, as he might say, he wised up. An interesting sidelight on this, courtesy of Mr. Beely, is that the *Enfer* division is remembered as the employer of the famed French poet and wit Guillaume Apollinaire, who labored amid its musty erotics as curator. Apollinaire's true name, Kostrowitski, strikes Beely as Polish, and Betty Barker assures us that in the poet's beloved "Annie," the "rosiers" referred to are mastiachi peppers. If this is so, Miss Barker asserts, the line in which this word occurs should be translated: "Her mastiachi peppers and her vests don't have paste buttons." "Proof enough?" Miss Barker queries. It is something to think about.

It is probably unwise to speak of Apollinaire and "Annie" and "her," i.e., "cette femme," who walks alone in the garden, lest such names arouse the interest of Bifrons, Disturber of the Dead, a dread spectre for whom Bermuda, for instance, is but as the crackling of thorns under a pot. Nor is he interested in such publications as *Big Apple,* now in its twenty-second year of surveying the arts, and as shiny, provocatively controversial, and just plain dumb as ever. Along with regularly featured essays, such as the controversially provocative "Minimalist Fiction: The Real Thing—Or Just Words?," there are the controversial ads for such products as "Big Yank": Now hit that FANTASTIC spot you've heard so much about on NATIONAL TV for new heights of

ECSTASY! This baby is EIGHT INCHES of amazingly LIFELIKE sculpted latex especially designed to hit that SPOT! Perfect for COUPLES or the SINGLE WOMAN. With stand and convenient harness. Perfect for travel. $59.95. Bifrons doesn't cotton to this sort of copy.

Jay Bindle, no longer "Heeb" or "Hoib" and rarely even "Jay" to anybody, sits in his apartment watching a game show on television. It is not controversial but it is provocative. Craftsmanship is more important than speed or handsome profits. Should he open a can of hash? Should he make himself a peanut butter sandwich? Should he go out for a cheeseburger and risk death or injury? Should some other rough fate be his lot? Suppertime will soon draw nigh and the shades of night will, subsequently, he feels, fall.

"I could use some of that cherry-cheese dip, honey," Charlotte Bayless calls to the sample woman. "Honey? Say, *honey?*" Although her present distance from the A & P is not considerable, she may as well be in Binghamton, famed for blond families, or for that matter in the mansion that now stands deserted on Biscayne Bay, a mansion which figures importantly in this tale of greed, lust, and disaster. It stands empty, save for the rats which contentedly inhabit it. Rats are easy to please: some chow, fresh water, and a place to hang their little hats. Things ain't what they used to be on and about the golden sands, even though a small revival of yesterday's gaiety is to be attempted with tonight's opening of an exact replica, right down to the busboys' filthy aprons, of the Black Basement, a once-notorious café of an earlier and more innocent time, previously detailed. "We want to make the Black Basement the friendly, vital place it used to be years ago," Jimmy Blackhead, the owner, grins. "The dominant theme will be, of course, blackness. I've always had a thing for black, there's something exciting, but not annoyingly so, about it." Mr. Blackhead looks wildly about, his eyes calmly taking in every detail of the feverish last-minute activity of the workers who are methodically putting the finishing touches on the bar and dance floor. "For instance, we'll have, like, book jackets from books that have black like as a dominant theme, blown up to *enormous* size on the walls." He gestures toward breathtaking replicas of the

jackets for *Black Hose and Red Heels, Blackjack* (whose unforgettable husband-and-wife team, Mr. and Mrs. "Jack" [John] Black, have
created a whole new sense of insouciant style among the charming and
rapacious young), and *Black Ladder* (a play, actually). An interested
observer wonders how he manages to *find* these old jackets, and Mr.
Blackhead fields the question politely. "Well," he laughs, "there are
certain bookshops that . . ." His voice trails off as two carpenters
plunge to certain serious injury from a scaffold. When asked if Black
Ladder Books, the famous "home away from home" for Biscayne Bay
literary types, might be a possible supplier, Mr. Blackhead pales and
quickly calls attention to the replica of *Blackout,* a collection of short
stories once described as "life in our time." "I think the room packs a
distinctive literary wallop," Mr. Blackhead concludes, moving off to
supervise the harassment training of a waitress in an alarmingly short
skirt specifically designed to reduce her worth as a human being and
make male customers act something awful.

From the reviews of *Black Hose and Red Heels:* "A sophomoric
display of cynical attitudes toward life and its beguiling wonder." "No
amount of provocative intelligence can mask the misogyny and just
plain contempt for humanity and the animal kingdom here disguised as
'sophisticated' humor." "Life in our time? Don't make me laugh!"
"Intelligent satire like that of Swift or Abbagnano is one thing, but this
amounts to no more than adolescent nose-thumbing." "A piece of
fucking shit!" "Precious, pompous, and nasty, yet I was sexually
aroused." "Packs the same sort of fetid wallop as the Marquis de
Sade."

"Joker," sometimes "Joan" to the men he plays cards with, is dead at
last. Records reveal that his name was Keith Blague. A manuscript of
poems is found among his meager belongings. It is entitled *Songs of
Forgetting* and signed "William Blake," clearly an attempt to deconstruct the notion of the poem as a personalized object of admiration.

Blammo, a fervent youth whose face would stop an eight-day clock,
wrenches himself away from the cereal aisle, and relays Charlotte's
request to the cherry-cheese dip woman. "Oh *please!*" she cries. "Does

that bitch think I'm her personal maid?" Has it been mentioned that she has knockout legs? Blammo returns to the cold cereal. What is a "maid"? he wonders.

We've held off speaking of Sol Blanc, palsied and balding, who directs Blanche Neige Press with his double, Saul Blanche, original founder of the small but daring house. Both read excellent literature incessantly and bewail the market conditions that compel them to publish books that are, well, crap. They rarely complain of Turpin's Syndrome, the debilitating disease, popularly known as *un oeil qui dit "zut!" a l'autre,* that afflicts them both. "We think it's the toilet seat in Rudy's Superette," Saul says, glancing up from Adams's *English Domestic or Homiletic Tragedy, 1575-1642.* He smiles, but close observation reveals that the smile is an involuntary rictus, one of the symptoms of the dreaded illness.

"Rudy's is a fucking pigpen," adds Blast, the stock boy. "I'm going over to hang out at Village Victuals as soon as I can. Now *there's* a toilet seat. Clean? Hey!" Blast may be referring to the Village Victuals on Bleecker Street, since the Baltic Street store prohibits all but official employees from using its rest room. Rudy (not his real name) knows of the difficulties that indiscriminate toilet-seat use can cause. "Was I or was I not the night manager at Le Bleu de Ciel for fifteen years? It's those two kikes' own fault." He wipes a smidgen of chicken fat, or *schmaltz,* on his brother Blightie's attractive all-cotton form-fitting shirt. Blightie grimaces, but says nothing, for the freedom that a life of letters bestows will soon release him from his brother's tyrannical usage. Even now, he is in the middle of a piece he calls "Blind Bums," an affectionately humorous yet intelligently satirical report on a partially sighted softball team in St. Augustine. He is also the author of *Blinding Clarity,* an unpublished novel. A letter from "Blinky" Blinque (Professor Raoul Blinque of Harvard, the excellent university) states that "*Clarity* is the best unpublished manuscript outside of my own— *The Deconstruction of the Charnel House Motif in the Fiction of Daniel Defoe*—that I am aware of." Blightie, whose real name is Paul, bides his time. Rudy, as usual, is not wholly approving of his brother's literary efforts. "A lotta shit!" he notes.

Karen Blonde, an interested reader, writes: "Hi! I'm Karen Blonde, but call me Blondie, O.K.? I'm often a brunette when I'm up among the flawless azures but down here I feel that there's nothing like subzero temperatures and dried cowshit for the complexion. Hi!" Sir Bloom, forgotten till now, manages to get hold of this missive, and, redolent as it is of Miss Blonde's steamy sex, he relaxes on a really nice-looking chaise longue and begins a gratifying bout of self-abuse. "This is the life," he thinks. And why not? Does he not study the lives and mores of the Bloomsbury circle, from which his name mysteriously derives, in the spare moments snatched from a busy life, perhaps his own? You bet he does.

Blow, an interesting, depressed person with an awareness of life in our time, is not coping very successfully. He thinks that he is in possession of information which proves that his conception occurred behind the bandstand of the Bluebird Inn, a small roadhouse specializing in foxtrot contests. What is the basis for this unsettling *idée fixe*? His reading of a poem in a twenty-three-year-old issue of *Blue Filter*. It is not the celebrated Determinate Meaning of the poem that convinces him, no, but the equally celebrated Indeterminate Meaning that "does the trick." It, however, just *may* be that the Objective Correlative is the cause of his present unhappiness, but we cannot blame *that* on John Crowe Ransom. He has enough to answer for.

"I don't appreciate the *mot*," Ransom says, "and charitably ascribe it to an irresistible desire to be rather a 'wise guy'; yet the arena of the verbal arts is littered with the bodies of wise guys, my own being conspicuously absent. Wise-guyism damages one's professionalism, and one should never speak impromptu in one's professional capacity, as I once said to heartfelt plaudits." In the Blue Ruin, a febrile nightspot dedicated to dancing, drinking, and various forms and shows of gaiety, the patrons are, so it appears, unimpressed with the savant's remarks. He packs up his personal, annotated copies of *God without Thunder, The World's Body* (revised), *The New Criticism, Poems about God, Chills and Fever, Grace after Meat, Two Gentlemen in Bonds,* and *Selected Poems,* and leaves to save a civilization *worth* saving from the barbaric hordes. Many of his poems are about the headstrong virility of youth and the slow, dark wisdom of age.

For a change.

The Blue Ruin, located within easy walking distance of all major hotels and the new convention center, was at one time the celebrated Blue Rune, a workingman's tavern which film stars, when film stars were film stars, were wont to frequent, incognito, of course.

"It was called Blue Runes, corrupted white-eyes," an impassive fake savage, Chief Blue Wind, says. "And if white flag of surrender not on pole (indicates wooden pole) by time stick (indicates stick, actually a tree limb) burn (indicates burning end of stick) to here (indicates spot roughly halfway down stick) . . . all *die!* For the earth is our Big Mother and we wish to be one with her womb and that is why, like, we burn stick and carry on about white flag and abject surrender. Also buffalo! Right! Are you hip that my squaw even now passes through your exhausted suburbs, disguised as a old Armenian broad?"

"This guys is a old and meaning broad!" the Albanian woman says proudly. She's mowing the lawn! Can she be mowing the lawn?

In spite of Blue Wind's threats and the imminent danger they pose, Sir Bloom, to add spice to and otherwise enhance his autoerotic pleasure, dons a costume described in the Kinky Klothes catalogue as the "Blushing Nun." Although it is cruel to say so, and surely unworthy of Swift and Abbagnano, he is rather fetching in this homely garb. Garb, it should be pointed out, of indeterminate meaning. Most of the members of the Board of Directors, on which he sits, want to get rid of him, although it is only fair to add that two of them, the Earl of Bodoni and Mr. Stanley Boils, men of vim, demur. There is, currently, a lot of trouble on this board. In a *Bookwatchers PreViews* roundup of recent books on hardball business practices, Daniel Boone, the tough-minded Wall Street analyst, exposes the infighting that takes place whenever these powerful men gather to determine who will garner "the big bucks," "the heavy bread," "the real money," etc., etc.

You can tell them by their subdued ties, tiny penises, and bony wives.

"Daniel Boone," he grins powerfully, "is not, of course, my real name." He toys with a gold paper clip and complacently proffers his tie. "I was born in Boonton, originally called Boonetown after Cheech Boone, the blue-blood arbitrager so much in the news lately." Boone leans back and complacently sucks on a massive phallic symbol disguised as a "cigar." "So it all just came together for me," he chuckles complacently, his sinewy mind never still.

"Perhaps I should switch to the 'Bo-Peep' look," Sir Bloom says, "since Blondie's letter is now but a sodden lump in my sweating palms, or, actually, palm. Looking at myself in the mirror (indicates mirror) in this lubricious act, it's hard to believe that I pretend to regular-guy status at the annual Born Again Employees' Picnic. Privately, I'm but a hulk that is a shell of what was once a man." He continues to abuse his sacred temple (see *Poems about God*), still slightly irritated at his impulsive decision to lend his "Boss Lady" outfit to a mid-level executive, a whiz kid who not only plays polo and tournament-level squash, but who is presently *designing his own house.* Although soft-spoken, on the Street this dynamo is known as Botis, or "the Viper." Yet he can tell a sudden off-color joke to the mailboys, who adore him, and regularly picks up the check at his club.

"I'm currently brushing up my French by reading *La Bouche métallique,*" he notes, serious now. "A marvelous book, filled with subtle tips that only the humanities can offer the hard-driving executive." He toys with his DuPont lighter. "You're surprised that I read enlightened and serious fiction in a foreign language?"

"I like *Madame Bovary* myself," Sir Bloom pants. "Especially the lyrical, yet icily malicious Charles Boyer translation. *That* is imposing entertainment!"

Bra, the engaging and sprightly young woman who aspires to an acting career as Tabitha Bramble (her real name), is having a quiet argument with her new friend, Lucy Brandon. They stand by the peanut butter machine in Crown SuperMart.

"I got bigger knockers than you possess," Bra says.

"No, I fear that my jugs are much the larger," Lucy replies.

"Go to! *These* are tits, my pal," Bra insists.

"Even the untrained eye can see that my melons take the palm," Lucy suggests.

Rudy would never stand for this sort of disturbance in his Superette. "It's a goddam shame," he says. "Always happens in those stores with the *loose* stuff, you know, the stuff in bins and barrels. Put that sorta shit in your store and you get all kinds. Imagine these two broads demeaning, denigrating, derogating, and insulting their own sex with talk of 'knockers' and 'jugs'!"

But hold, gentle Rudy! Can we fairly indict Tabitha and Lucy for this conversation? Are they not but helpless pawns in this sprawling, lifelike canvas? Or on it? We could start over, as did the painter Braque, who started over more than once. Perhaps a revisionist approach, taking into consideration the sociopolitical climate in which the concept of "breasts" thrives, might be effective.

"I find it interesting," Tabitha remarks to her chum, Lucy Brandon, "that in countries such as Brazil, home of the Amazon Basin, which is, as you know, a fylfot, the words 'knockers' and 'jugs' still have currency."

"That is on account of Brazil is a hotbed of *machismo* and they do not give a fuck about us broads," Lucy frowns. "They are a bunch of *cacahuates.*"

"And yet," Tabitha replies, "recent studies suggest, and so forth, et cetera."

"Of course," Rudy says, "I draw the line at paying chicks the same as guys, they get their periods and these mood things and they could kill you or hit you with a lamp or an iron. I saw it in a magazine."

"I still prefer the Alps," Allen the waiter says. "What care I for knockers?"

Allen's last remark, by a chain of associations too hackneyed to detail, leads to an uncharacteristic digression. Does anyone remember George Brent in a long-lost film, *Carom*? It is based on an unpublished novel in Zola's Rougon-Macquart series, *Le Bricoleur.* Brent plays a poet engaged in the writing of a great epic which he calls "The Bridge." Unfortunately, he has accidentally contracted leprosy in the South Sea Islands. Alice Bridgenorth, a wanton and debauched chanteuse, falls in love with him, despite the muslin mask he wears to hide what we all know is his decaying nose. She loves him for his mind.

In the sculptor's small yet excellently selected and judiciously arranged library, there is a copy of the once-famous but now out-of-print and sadly neglected anthology *Bridges: Poets Express Their Love.* One of the selections, from a longer poem, "Spanning the Azure," by Gilberte Brie, contains a section of some seven lines which are identical to those lines spoken by George Brent in the climactic scene of the film, one in which the poet renounces billiards and cheap sex to devote himself, in the few years remaining to him, to the completion of his opus. The sculptor often finds solace in this poem, particularly in the couplet

> Broadway! It is thee I chose!
> Thou art my only Broadway Rose.

Hard to believe that George Brent played a role like that. George Brent's with the moustache, right? Played in a lot of Bette Davis flicks?

"Not one single Native American was cast in that movie," Blue Wind says. "For that and for certain other slights my squaw, resplendent in decadent lingerie intended as a symbolic reproach to the white-eyes, even now stalks the streets of your bourgeois suburbs so as to scare the shit out of ladies with blue hair."

"I need an Alka-Seltzer or a Bromo-Seltzer in order to listen to a ruffian like that," Betty Barker writes. "Believe me, at Barnard I knew a lot of girls who were perfect ladies and not one of them had blue hair."

Not too far from the locale in which this discussion of the cinematic arts is in progress, in the Bronx to be exact, the once wildly abandoned Dorothea Brooke, tired now of attending to her plants, throws down her trowel and heaves a sigh. She so heaves for it is time to turn, for an hour or so, to the pages indited by her namesake, Rupert Brooke, perhaps the best-known and -loved of the younger Georgians. Her eyes fall on one of her favorite poems:

> Just now the lilac is in bloom,
> All before my little room;
> And in my flower-beds, I think,
> Smile the carnation and the pink;
> And down the borders, well I know,
> The poppy and the pansy blow . . .

Dorothea puts the book down. "I think," she thinks. Her hands fly to her face, all pink. She commences to sob. She sobs. "O seasons, O castles," she cries, for some deep, hidden reason. Suddenly the trowel disgusts her! "Well I know," she knows. Dorothea, raised in Brooklyn and a graduate of Brooklyn College, wishes, as she fills up a watering can, her cheeks wet with tears, that she could have those carefree student days back, those days spent so happily in a little Brooklyn Heights furnished apartment. Her roommate, Brown, kept her on her literary toes. For example, one day Dorothea says, "Look, Brown! Smile the carnation and the pink."

"Dotty, I don't know how you can read that slop by Elizabeth Barrett Browning and those other terrible drudges. 'Let me count my days,' indeed!" Dorothea is hurt, but all ears.

"What about 'Patterns,' Brown?" she suggests.

"Are you kidding me or something?" Brown answers. "Listen to *this*, it's by a young guy who shows enormous promise. 'I was screaming inside, my eyes frantically trying to signal this like a lighthouse whose keeper has run amok.' If that's not worth all the 'Patterns' you can come up with, I'll kiss your ass."

The reader with a long memory will recognize in that snatch of prose the hand of Anatole Broyard, now a book-person-essayist-commentator on themes literary. His work is eagerly awaited by many people, whose eyes, now and again, frantically try to signal this.

"I understand that there are expatriates in, like, Brussels even, who await," the demon Asmoday says, feeding arms and legs to his large cur.

"We await him and his work at Bryn Mawr," a young woman says. "What do you think of my jugs, by the way?"

This is the sort of cheap joke which was avoided by both Swift and Abbagnano. Right?

As right as the poppy and the pansy!

Ted Buckie-Moeller is going through his expense-account vouchers, changing here, padding there, trying to make a few extra bucks. Is he chewing on his pencil? Check. Is he waiting to see *Black Silk Stockings* on the Playboy Channel? Check. Is he thinking of telling the new super that he can keep his goddam bike any goddam place he goddam well pleases? Check. He angrily starts again on the first bill, a lunch check for two at the Bluebird Inn. That's what started the old ulcer up again, that goddam lunch! He should have stuck to photography. Maybe.

Bud opens his fly and heads toward a group of women stocking up on the Village Victuals special on paper towels. Tall and flabby, he rarely parts his hair. He hates his hair, and takes no notice of his personal appearance. He *hates himself!* "I deserve a better break than being an uncontrollable exhibitionist even though I rarely if ever commit serious sex crimes. I'm not like, you know, a sex *fiend.*" He is almost upon the women, his eyes signaling his intentions, were the women to look, like a demented lighthouse.

"Buddhism," Father Frank suggests, "might conceivably be of some assistance to Bud—may I call him Bud?—in his attempts to integrate his sexual drives with those of the community as a caring human being with special needs. Or one could be a priest, but *not* like the one who's looking at that dirty magazine. Roman Catholicism, well-handled and attractively presented, increasingly packs a timely wallop!"

"Well, boys, we are now fair deep in the mountains above shining Budd Lake."

So does a chapter of Elizabeth Barrett Browning's favorite novel, *Buddy and His Boys on Mystery Mountain,* begin.

"Buddy," said Dick Witherspoon, "now that we're a far piece from the heartless, roaring city, what was the name of that feller who threw your father from one of the beetling crags hereabouts 'count your dad owed him several thousand dollars he refused to pay him?"

"Ned Blutwurst," answered Buddy, in considerable dismay. "What's the reason for such an odd query, Dick?"

"Wa-al, nothing really," Dick chuckled through divers flying wood chips. "I thought I remembered the blasted rogue. He drowned in Budd Lake some few years since, they say, I reckon I believe, if I recollect aright."

"So the rumor was bruited," Buddy laughed joyfully. "I immensely like those wood chips flying from your busy penknife."

"Just what would a feller mean by a few years since?" Dick rejoined, a look of sly cunning on his athletic face.

"I do not know, Dick," Buddy replied in incredulous amazement. "But you are tarnation perceptive."

Then, with visible relief, he quickly put the steaming grub on the rough table, and the two chums, their manly good looks heightened by the leaping flames, fell to with a hearty will.

"There is nothing quite like sizzling pork and beans and a light but nourishing salad for a fellow after a day's tramp through the mountains high above Budd Lake," Buddy said, a slow smile infecting his face like the beacon from a lighthouse.

"This is the life," Dick replied mysteriously. "Too bad your old dad is dead as a doornail and can't no longer acquaint you with woodland lore afore he used ter settle down comfy-like with his pipe by the fire."

Buddy, touched by his friend's clumsy attempt at velleity, and not a little worried by the facial pallor caused by his use of noxious tobacco which it was his habit to smoke and chew, said nothing, but stared into the flames in momentary confusion.

"Say!" Dick whooped. "That was some feed! If I could eat ramshackle like that ever once in a while yer wouldn't hear a word of complaint out of *this* young feller! Nosirree!" And with that, Dick pushed his rude chair back from the rough-hewn wooden table.

"The air here on Mystery Mountain is what puts a keen edge on a fellow's appetite," Buddy blushed. "I submit that the worst victuals in the whole wide world would taste mighty good up here."

"Go on!" Dick joshed excitedly, banging his calloused palm on the rough wood of the rudely hewn table. "You take the cake as a cook, Buddy," he continued, and now, how 'bout a song? That old one, 'Big Bullies 'Mid the Fishes'?"

Buddy glanced about, his clear blue eyes seemingly troubled. "Sounds capital to me, old chum, but I thought that tonight . . ." His voice trailed off, the shadows dancing wildly on the cabin's rough-hewn ceiling the while.

"Yes?" Dick grinned knowingly, tamping down the " 'baccy" in his mellow valise.

"Well, I thought it might be vouchful to read aloud, by the light of the glowing grate and this smoky oil thing, from *Sonnets from the Portuguese.*"

Dick, his dark eyes frantically signaling affirmation, nodded eagerly. "I do believe that would be fine. They are passionate though careworn verses, yet one can nowhere detect in them the loveless smirk of the depraved pornographer."

"Mrs. Browning's body, if I may use such a word, was her sacred temple," Buddy solemnly agreed. He began then to read, in a quiet but manly voice, the beautiful words weaving a spell of enchantment throughout the mysterious dimness of the crude shelter. The other boys, weak from hunger, had long since cried themselves softly to sleep, although they *had* drunk their fill of the crystal-clear spring water that is Mystery Mountain's bounty.

"I love thee to the level of everyday's most quiet need, by sun and candlelight, you guys," Mrs. Browning says. "Each one in a gracious hand appears to have a gift for mortals," she further allows. "I feel great affection for these honest lads. How do you feel about it, Bob?"

"Let them fight it out, friend! Things have gone too far" is the surprising reply from the garret.

A curious occurrence: Dr. Rex Buer, he of the golden hands, and known to all who have had the good fortune to be cared for by him as "The Healer," is on a mission for the redoubtable Buildings Department, the organization whose awesome responsibility it is to make the poor disappear in seemly fashion. Dr. Buer's task, this sultry day, is to care for a Bulgarian of advanced age. The Dragon of the Dead, the fearsome Bune, possesses the soul, spirit, and body of the work-gnarled Dimitrov Plovdiv. On his way to Plovdiv's small but immaculate apartment, which boasts a fairly decent but much-reduced reproduction of *L'assassin menacé,* which canvas Bune forces old Plovdiv to worship, a curious occurrence takes place. Marion Bunt, on her way through the streets to buy something to settle her stomach, accosts "The Healer," and makes him a number of torrid sexual offers, e.g., Howdya like to —— me in the ——?; Can you use a good ——job? Dr. Buer accompanies Mrs. Bunt to her apartment, trembling with excitement. It's been a long time since he —— anybody in the ——, and almost as long since he's had a ——job, or, for that matter, any kind of a job. In the bedroom, "The Healer" has a massive coronary as Mrs. Bunt playfully throws her perfumed half-slip in his face. So "The Healer" dies, unable to heal himself!

Although the characters are not fully realized, their very *humanity* is attractive.

The above-noted anecdote is thought to be part of the text of a long *sirventes,* "The Burglary." Although the text is lost, there is, if memory serves, no mention of a burglary in the poem. Is the title, then, a metaphor? A metonym or synecdoche? An analogue? A symbol? An instance of parataxis? Yes? Or no?

"Did he actually say 'if memory serves'?" Lord Bury asks, bursting in unceremoniously on Sir Bloom to show him a new book on Lytton Strachey, or by Lytton Strachey. Whatever, it is of abiding interest, for one can never learn too much about Bloomsbury and its brilliant circle of varlets. But Lord Bury's news must of needs wait, for Sir Bloom, rather like a lighthouse whose keeper has run amok, has reached the point of orgasm, a *jouissance* that not even this notable literary intelligence may detain. Thus doth the body make morons of us all.

"It's quite amazing, old chap," Lord Bury says. "Quite amazing. You look, in *your* 'Blushing Nun' costume, quite the way Lady Bustier looks in *her* 'Blushing Nun' costume. Ripping!" he exclaims.

Marcella Butler is waiting for the man she wishes, sort of, to be her third husband. Well, not really. He is late and she's alone. She knows that he won't come and that he won't call, for he is no longer interested in her. Dinner grows cold, the candles burn down, her new pumps pinch her feet as evidenced by a glance toward said pumps and a faint grimace. On the refrigerator is a stick-figure drawing, on oaktag, of what looks to be a little boy, his head all teeth. Body, arms, legs, and head are in red Crayola, teeth in black. Underneath this figure, in ragged, awkward letters which pitch wildly to right and left, is the message I LOVE GRANDDMA. This declaration is in red, green, and orange Crayola. Marcie looks at herself in the hall-closet mirror. Her hair is the wrong shade of brown, dull, *Jesus,* dull. Her skirt is too short, her blouse too tight, *Jesus.* Her lace-patterned black stockings are ridiculous. And the heels. The heels! They remind her of Mrs. Scheh and *her* heels, Mrs. Scheh, the math teacher who went crazy. Mr. Olsen and Mr. Andrews were math teachers too. They went crazy too. She should put on a girdle, although she hates them, but her hips, her thighs, *Jesus.* Who the hell does she think she is? She knows that he won't come, and if he should, he will probably be wearing those slacks which are unsettlingly close in color to that shade once called "electric blue." *Jesus,* she doesn't even like the man, really. Isn't that right, Grandma?

In truth, the death of "The Healer" is detailed in "Butts on the Beach," one of the interlinked stories in *Cameras Work,* by Josh Cabernet [Ka-bur-NET], a writer of whom, so it is threatened, we have not heard the last. Who has made an auspicious debut. Who is delighted and surprised by the wonderful reception accorded his first. On which a small publisher had the courage to. Whose photograph is seen here and also there. Who although a lawyer. Who hopes the screenplay will do his. And yet who has faith in. After all, isn't he a? Who is, yes, thinking of a. Who is a little, well, scared. After all, Dickens. Conrad. Who wonders if. Who doesn't really feel all that. Who is, yes, tired, but gratified by the marvelous. Who is thankful to his wonderful agent and her. Who fully agrees now with his quiet but convincing editor about the suggested. Who is sure that the book is just about as good as. Who, yes, thinks. Who has strong opinions but doesn't think that. Who isn't really sure that. Who thinks people today want books that this and also that that. Who thinks that his generation is. Who knows that courage and hope are. Who feels that the best advice is simply. Who affirms that informing the long look is.

Of *Cameras Work,* Michelle Caccatanto, with her customary uncial pertinence, writes, in part: "Josh Cabernet has given us an impressive and gritty collection in his *Cameras Work,* a series of connected stories which reveal a sophisticated intuition of the small despairs and triumphs of lower-middle-class domesticity. . . . The stories, although sympathetic and compassionate, are tempered by Mr. Cabernet's observant, cold, yet not pitiless eye. Learned, but not annoyingly so, the author . . . proves convincingly that 'old-fashioned' craftsmanship is more important than . . . fashionable obscurantism. . . . Characters are so convincingly etched that we feel as though we are participating in their lives. *Cameras Work* supplies a subtle bas-relief of a grey world which the more fortunate among us cannot even imagine."
She says that to all the boys.

Insofar as we may now determine, the dessert called Banana Amaze does not exist. Apologies—and kudos!—to all those readers whose attempts to create the dish are even now terminating in tears and blasphemy.

Then too: Famed Author's "Caddy" Named after Favorite Bar, the Cadillac Lounge; Unrepentant Eulogist's Poem "Calafawnya" Again Denied Coveted Prize; *The Caliph* No Cure for Summer Theatre Doldrums; *The Caliph* and *The Caliph Lorzu* Both Fakes, Expert Claims; Caliph's Walk Newest "In" Club for Publishing Rebels; Callipolis Voted "City of Beauty or Goodness"; Calvinist Accuses Cambridge Don of Stealing Baseball Cards, Strapless Bras; Camels and Chesterfields No Longer Welcome in Health-Crazed Canada; Cannes Ga-Ga Over "Cans" This Summer.

The Albanian woman is hot and sweaty after her chore, and, distraught because of the absorbent inadequacy of her impromptu neckerchief, reveals that she is Frieda Canula, a superintendent's wife. Threats by the much-disliked Carruthers Brothers and the imminent danger they pose are unable to dissuade the bedraggled varmint from telling everything to anyone who happens along.

"Is Carruthers the brothers seizing husband for exposing same in 'Cartel,' smashing wallop-read in *Albanian America*. I take saddened walk with good-lucks muffler (indicates neck region) and halt when in window I glimpse into I see idol of Albanian Lard Goddess. Is like special *vernissage* just for Frieda."

As she speaks, her warm eyes abaft, suburbanites, including an attractive vegetarian couple with an enlightened interest in caffeine-free beverages, roughly jostle her. Jerry Casey, who is a picture of health despite his grey hairs, hands her a bar of Castile soap.

"A wordless reproach," Casey smiles, and turns his face toward his condo, settling nicely into the poisoned landfill. "Another wordless reproach," Casey smiles again, as he knocks Mrs. Canula sprawling with a nifty hook off a jab. "You don't stop them now and they'll be here with their bongos and soiled underwear by the thousands." Thinking better of his largesse, he retrieves the bar of Castile and places it in his pocket, where it rests, silently. Things are silent, mostly.

"He pack a wallops!" Frieda says from the border of pinks.

A faint sound of cheering issues from the sculptor's house. And why not? But who is she? *Really?* Can she be a Catholic? Does it matter? Is this maybe a metaphor, or what?

All we know is that "the . . . pinks" probably belong to Rupert Brooke.

Cedric, a name that suddenly thrusts itself upon us, such are the mysterious and ineffable workings of the isomorphic synapses, doesn't ring the old bell. Yet here it is! in all its nominative substantiality. Rather than clutter this report with people who will not pull their own weight, what do you say we get rid of him with vaunted celerity?

O.K.

Cedric, poor man, is found dead in Central Park, often called "the Jewel of Parks," "the Emerald of Parks," and "a really terrific park." A Certificate of Death is made out for one "Cedric Doe."

Ce Soir, a haunting scent which recalls the long, slow twilights of the Serengeti, is still notorious as the *parfum* favored by Jeff Chandler, a film star who untimely died. Emmanuel Chanko, on whose face the sun oft falls golden, despite his embarrassment at being known as "Puppo" or "Peepee" Chanko, considers him a comic genius "not inferior" to Charlie Chaplin. Many disagree with Chanko, to wit: "A confusion of entelechy with fantasy yearnings." "Get the fuck outta here!" " 'Puppo' is a *cetriol'.* "

Now we have a *Charles* to deal with. How may literature be created when. . . ? O.K. Central Park again? Under a bush. "Charles Doe": Into the ground with him. And another Charles! What the—?

Mistaken identity?

Good! He's not Charles but somebody else we don't have to care about.

A statue of Arthur Rimbaud is to be found in Charleville, his place of birth. Rimbaud is well known for the famous gibe, directed at Paul Verlaine and his crude yet understandable manifestation of uncontrollable sexual desire: "If you only knew how fucking silly you look with that herring in your hand!" Leads to shooting in Brussels three days later, Verlaine's anger reaching its zenith when Rimbaud taunts him by calling Charles Baudelaire, one of Verlaine's saints, "Good-time Charlie," or variantly, "Up-to-the-minute Charlie." Charlotte Rochambeau, a whore of a certain age whose speciality is the knotted-silk-kerchief trick, takes the wounded Rimbaud to Charmaine's, where they dine sumptuously on chaudrée aux fruits de mer, poulé sauté beauséjour, bavette de boeuf sauce chasseur, haricots verts au citron, pommes de terres duchesse, tomates grillées à la Provençale, pain rôti aux herbes, salade de cresson et endives, and banane étonnement. Excellent wines, tedious to detail, give each course the indefinable perfection which lies at the heart of all great dining experiences. Rimbaud is notably enthusiastic about the dessert. "Hein!" he exclaims. It is not generally known that Mlle Rochambeau goes on to write a *récit* based on the amours of Rimbaud and Verlaine, called *La Sottise*, rendered into English as *Chattering Fools* by Rodney Chatz.

Luba Checks throws the deadbolt on the Yale lock. The police lock is next, then the chain. Lo! two slices of rare roast beef, a hard roll, a small jar of Hellmann's mayonnaise, a translucent pink spheroid—perhaps a tomato?, a small bottle of Perrier. The article on the crisis in Israeli morality in the *Magazine.* Lifts her skirt to her waist, slips out of her shoes and pulls her pantyhose down and off. Depressing deli items, ho! await her, as does the latest article on the crisis in Israeli morality in the *New York Review of Books.* Waiting also: the latest article on the imminent demise of organized crime after the arrest of 487 top mobsters, and a front-page review of *The Inner World of Lytton Strachey.* Television. Long hot soak in small shallow basin jokingly called a "tub." Luba takes out her partial upper plate. Takes out her partial lower plate. Takes out her contact lenses and puts reading glasses on. Disgusting deli fare. Blouse open, then off, then into the bathroom sink with the pantyhose. On the coffee table a postcard from her daughter in Seattle on welfare. "Thanks for the check. It will come in handy for the baby. Dorrie." Luba puts an ice cube in an Old Fashioned glass, fills it to the top with Bombay. Can it hurt? Puts on a terrycloth robe and sits down with her gin. She's a long way from her salad days as Lyubinka Czechowyczy. Who isn't? Unconfessed to the boring but kind friend from work with whom she spent the afternoon is the fact that she would very much like to get laid. Then, and, you know, like right now.

Chester leaves the baths, shaken. While there, he is sexually active with a young man whose name is Chester. He has a drink with a young man who introduces himself as Chet. He is sexually willing but physically unable to perform with a young man who is surprised to learn that his name is Chester since his name is Chet. This Chet is a waiter, well, not *actually* a *waiter.* Another man, his own age, asks for a cigarette as he is dressing, and mentions that his name is Chet. Chester doesn't even want to think about their haircuts and moustaches, uncannily alike. He is just too old, too goddamned old for this. And why is that *woman* smiling at him?

It should be made clear that the woman who smiles at Chester is not the same woman who is sprawled on the street in front of the A & P. She looks a bit like her but looks, as Aristophanes says, can be deceiving. Of course, he said it with more panache.

Far below, at the mouth of the secluded valley, barely distinguishable amid the gorse flickering in the sunlight, a Chevrolet stands abandoned in the shade of the ancient yews. Farther on, beyond the small farmhouses whose chimneys even now send up their wisps of dried-conifer smoke, which latter betokens the slow labors of the placid women preparing luncheon, the University of Chicago dominates the great shale bluffs that overlook Chinatown and its self-absorbed throngs of Chinese, jabbering their unpronounceable gibberish in the packed and fetid streets. Chinatown!

Chooch sighs, and then, alerted by the thrashing of heavy boots in the dense furze behind him, hides his video cassette of *Chorus Orgy* in his soiled bedroll. Just in time! For at the edge of the clearing, a tall young man, his blond hair and beard matted with gooseberries, thorns, briers, chicles, and nightshade dust, stands regarding him with curiosity. His plaid mackinaw and worn moleskins bespeak, more eloquently than could any words, the fact that he is a Christian. The young giant strides toward Chooch, his huge right hand extended in greeting. Chooch forces a smile, then extends his own right hand, glad that he'd had the presence of mind to conceal the film, one which might well have maddened the hardy wayfarer. They shake extended hands firmly, their eyes locked in mutually homophobic embarrassment, while all about them the forest murmurs its inscrutable message, i.e., "krik-kk, krik-kk, krik-kk."

"I'm Knute," the newcomer says. "Secretary of the Christian Conservative Student Crusade." His piercing eyes instantly pick out the ruined Chevy far below. "Hmm. Seen any yids pass this way?" His smile is cold and Chooch weighs his reply carefully.

"No yids in these feral parts," he replies evenly, his face impassive. "Saw a couple of young women in innocent gingham, from the Christian Student Union, I think they said." It is, he realizes, a mistake.

As Knute's face darkens, Chooch helplessly recalls the Christmas, long ago, when his drunken father destroyed the Christmas tree they had joyfully chopped down together, more or less. He had had Knute's face—pitiless and vengeful. Is Knute, too, a drunkard? Is Knute perhaps his father? Probably not, and yet . . .

A cloud drifts over the sun and the windy crag grows suddenly grey and cold.

"You say young *women?*" Knute sneers. "What's gingham?"

It may fairly be said that the above fragment, allegedly part of a story by Jack Armstrong, exhibits neither remarkable perception, such as what we could never forget it, nor exciting wallop, which each phiz bedizeneth, and nowhere may any particle in it be construed as displaying steamy and exotic sex, to which all mortals bend the natural knee, or knees.

"And how!" the priest says, still uneasily hovering about the magazine rack.

The fragment, in point of fact, seems hardly irrefragable. To speak with whitest candor, it is very poor work, and reads like a bad parody. So shrewd readers often proclaim!

"You got the wrong story!" Jack protests. But Jack doesn't know that this is an occurrence in no way uncommon or remarkable. "The wrong story" seems to be, to paraphrase Chrysippus of Soli, our burden and our cross.

Buddy Cioppetini, known as "Hoagie" or "Doggie" in the nondescript ginmills he frequents, is bald. Yes, and to add insult to injury, he has misplaced his Chevy, in connection with which the words "crick," "holler," "draw," "gulch," and "fen" keep coming to mind, but none of them rings the old bell. He stolidly continues, then, to shine his old shoes, his good old shoes. "What," as George S. Patton said, "the heck." Suddenly he remembers that on the front seat of his car lies his dog-eared, worn, and much-annotated copy of *Homo Ludens.* Without it, there is no telling what he may consider doing.

Perhaps—just a thought—perhaps, like our literary friend, the lighthouse keeper, he will run amok?

Civil War Songs of the Northern Armies: "Sloggin' inter 'Bammy"; "Have *My* Beans, Sojer"; "Jeff Davis Is Tarnation Mean"; "Embraceable You"; "Fuck the Dangèd Rebs!"; "Lady of Spain"; "What Is This Chickenshit?"; "Hardtack in Heaven Tonight, Cap'n"; "Babalu."

Florence Claire, once an actress who still gets an occasional laxative commercial, each a wonderful opportunity for her to "hone" her "craft," does anonymous book reviews for *Virginia's Beat,* an "important journal" ancillary to the "publishing" business. She is currently putting the "finishing touches" on the review of a new book of "poems" by Pamela Clairwil, another sometime actress, whose photographs of shattered people sitting next to garbage cans, etc., etc., "grace her pages." Florence changes the phrase "slipshod writing" to "automatic writing." It has, she feels, the perfect soupçon of literary ambience she seeks. She likes the phrase, and vows to use it in the future whenever she decides, for one reason or another, not to, uh, well, not to read, uh, well, not actually read all, uh, of an assigned book. In this determination, she joins the prestigious guild. Meanwhile, she *must* attend to that nagging chancre.

"That's really a bit terribly much!" the population of Clappeville says. "It is one thing to use fiction as a means of retaliation on those one feels have wronged one, yet quite another to descend to the vile and the base!" They say these fairly complex sentences in unison. Chant them, really. And there are a *lot* of people in Clappeville. Got its own croissant shop. All the residents are clearly perturbed by this egregious breach of etiquette.

This is the town which put "Clarinet Polka" on the map. There you go!

Elects mayors named "Clark," always. "Clark," inverted commas intact.

Claims that Buddy Clark's recordings sport bebop orchestrations. They are enthusiastic about this one, although we doubt the truth of the statement. A flatted fifth does not a bebop make, to paraphrase Bartók.

"Cleanthes of Assos is best known for his *Hymn to Zeus,*" a solitary voice cries. All turn about nervously. "It is a song cycle what tells the musical story of the early Stoics and the beat is shifted to the splash cymbal, said beat accented on one and three!" Silence. Clubfoot Pete, Clappeville's police officer, a figure in a tattered suit, eerily blue, clumps through the crowd, looking for the offending hipster. Many feel, though of course do not say, that this voice of musico-philosophic rebellion is that of the owner of the Club Zappe, a roadhouse which specializes in fox-trot contests, as does the Bluebird.

One begins to see the intricate yet asymmetrical weave in the pattern, no? "But what are patterns for?" Dorothea Brooke cries.

The Bluebird is mentioned at least once or twice in *Seize My Ravaged Heart,* a frivolous novel which is obviously the product of . . . Florence pauses . . . "automatic writing." "Florence is pretty dumb," experts ascertain.

In Colma, however, surprising developments unfold. A group of locals, calling themselves The Committee Against the Committee on Committees, is convinced that the reason that their town is home to every cemetery in Northern California is that it lies within the infamous "fog belt." But what to do? A series of amazing adventures follows. Liaisons, drunken picnics, messy divorces, God only knows how many leftovers! Threats and imminent danger. The despairs and triumphs of middle-class life, e.g., wide ties, e.g., crudités. All against a background of intrigue and inflamed passions. Deviled eggs! An occasional good read. Pleated gabardine trousers. The dead are, as usual, unimpressed, although a few do pretend, give them credit, a polite interest.

Karen Complexion on being modern: "Hi! I'm Karen! You might think a flight attendant is all business, but when I'm groundside, jogging and working out with that *special* microchip whiz, I know how important well grooming and competent grammar could be. Take it from me, *hair on most sections of the body is unwanted.* Oh, hi!"

As is often the case, *Complex Resolutions* and *Complicated Webs* go unread. *Compost* is a magazine no longer extant. Yet how gently the editorial hand guides the prose to its lapidary finish! They have nothing of the crass, no, it is all relaxed clothing and the exhilaration of cupidity. Even the heartland is enthusiastic, witness the cultivation of understanding therein regarding short fiction, enjoying now a revival of sorts.

"People have little time for long books now, but they do feel the need for worthwhile literature," says the attractive, perfectly coiffed president of Concrete Proposals, a garden-pool company, or something about fronds or something. "The mood is upbeat," the attractive, modishly attired executrix mutters, scratching one of her things the while.

The ladies of the Condom League agree. Yet they look surreptitiously at their neatly folded white gloves and nervously adjust their little veiled hats. As usual, something is going on under the table. Ladies!

Louis Condy, children's-book author, and now a resident of a resurgent Coney Island, considers thoughtfully: "Now that I'm getting on in years and feeling good about beating that bum sodomy rap, I have little patience with talking worms and kids who want to know what the milkman does." He holds up his new manuscript for inspection. "So I'd have to agree with the grout-theory people, yes." Condy has a touch of the rampant buboes, a nagging disease which slows him down some. "Was Christ always mad?" he concludes in an upbeat mood.

Speaking of Christ, a delegation from the Confraternity of the Most Precious Blood is dispatched to the A & P. A certain citizen, known mockingly to the neighborhood as "Mr. Congeniality," is thought to have dragged his unspeakably deformed foot to a public telephone to register his protest against an "embarrassing priest." The priest, now back at dairy products, is trying to "do something" about his obstreperously tented trousers. It is, perhaps, his great trial.

Allen decides that Connecticut, after all, will be just paradise. Chet will be along, dearest Chet, who, Allen recalls, often tells complete strangers that he is not *actually* a *waiter.* If only they can once again rent the little cabin that looks across the flame-touched gorse fronds and the copious furze, alive with golden glitterings, to the peaceful shimmer of the Connecticut River, whose slow current carries the still-living dreams of rangy pioneers! If only.

O lost! And cry the wind, brief ghosts!

Through his tears he spies Connie, a perfect bitch if he ever saw one, seat herself in his section. Sullenly placing a tumbler of tepid water on her table, he says, "Hi! I'm Allen, your waiter." Connie, her eyes frantically but not annoyingly signaling a desire for friendship, orders a "Consensus," two slices of anchovie Pizza topped with sharp melted Cheddar and lightly sautédé Raddishes on a bed of crisp Iceberg Lettuce, with Savory pickles and fresh golden Pommés da Terre Franchais.

"Obvious that the joint knows nothing of real cuisine," Mr. Bathin says in a telephone interview. "Pommés da Terre Franchais is an item should be atop the Pizza. These people will eat anything." He hangs up and the operator sticks the interviewer with the charges.

"Cuisine mighty fine chow is," Frieda Canula says through her banjaxed mouth, proving that, although in pain, yet hath she her mind entire. But now, bearing down upon her, the sculptor, her face pale with fury, her eyes rolling wildly, like those of a frantic, screaming leper in a lighthouse, brandishes her copy of *Sanctuary,* a prop by now half-forgotten in the turmoil of things. Frieda staggers back in fear and awe, for she takes the sculptor to be, quite understandably, the Lard Goddess. "I'll give you 'chow'!" the sculptor screeches.

Are we to discover, at last, whether or not *Construction in Metal* is a translation of *Les Constructions métalliques*? Rimbaud knows, but is dead. Gary Cooper, although he regularly crosses the void, won't say. Craig Copro, Captain, USAF, is forbidden to speak to anyone, confined, as he is, to the Bachelor Officers' Quarters on Corfu, "island of exhilarant foliage," for an infraction involving a cute bus driver, a secretly drugged assistant professor of petroleum engineering, and a pair of jump boots. Karen Cornfield? Busy, as usual.

"Hi! I'm Karen Cornfield! Busy as usual while in the clouds which stream delightfully, I have little time to entertain questions on matters literary, and when I'm down on good old *terra firma* I just want to be, well, *slinky* for that special heart surgeon! Despite books and the overtly homosexual types who seem to be involved with them, I think it's pretty important to be, well, just a woman. That's why I fabulously scent."

Corrie Corriendo, never fully realized, packs up some old clothes to give to the poor. Rusty old things, really. She clanks over to the window to gaze at the traffic far below, fingering the while her grey-blue aluminum wig. She catches the reflection of her face in the pane, and steps back, startled. So it comes at last to *this*. Yes, she is discarded now, thrown away like an old steel sneaker by those she thought her friends. "Hâ, hâ," she laughs, sans mirth. She looks again at the traffic far below. How small it seems. How small and virtually unimportant. How far away. Is it possible that she once actually *cared* for it?

Cortland, Colma's sister city, nestled at the foot of Mystery Mountain like a toy city in a Christmas display in a toy store in a great city which, covered with the first snows, seems like a photograph of a toy city, learns of the troubles in that fogbound burg. "Troubled tydinges, lyke spirites incorporeal, / Doe flye as shaftes from th' Amazon's marcial bowe." Ontology, yes, but true.

"I seem to remember that clever distich from *Cosmopolitan*," the rictal woman offers, picking herself up from the sidewalk. "I first read it in the Cotswolds, on our honeymoon. We lived, then, in a cunning little cottage, Cottage . . . Cottage . . . Cottage 33, yes! Cottage 33, which commanded and perhaps still commands a breathtaking view of the fields of scarlet-tipped sedge that ran down and perhaps still run down the gently rolling mounds, or knolls, to end in viscid crimson just at the point where the ancient emerald lawns of the Country Club began and perhaps still begin. I was, but doubt that I still am, Miss Cover Girl to him." She furtively wipes some dogshit off a Real-Mex Frozen Dinner. Unknown to her, Cox, here to buy the new issue of *Clothes Action,* regards her narrowly. His denim jacket, *finally,* is faded to a color which permits him to walk the streets looking like those who walk the streets.

"I would rather die," Cox says, "than dress like this hag. I would rather be boiled in liquid fire than appear so gauche, rather be beat like gold to ayery thinnesse than be seen with a copy of *Accidental Bodies.* My appearance? Elegant yet relaxed. Insouciantly rumpled. A falling drape of slender excitement. I have little time for long books yet feel the need for literature. E'en now, my nights, those nights o'er which grim Morpheus doth cast his tincted mantle, are partially given over to a satisfying moment or two with an amusing quarto, heavily annotated by a previous owner, that I picked up for a song at a dusty old bookshop, of a kind that is fast disappearing from the dynamic city."

"That wouldn't be my *Homo Ludens,* would it, champ?" Buddy Cioppetini queries.

"No, my hardworking dago friend," Cox answers. "It is a volume by Hart Crane, *White Bridges.* But thanks a million for your continuing interest. And, by the by, it is apparent that despite your polyester-cotton-blend shirt, whimsically buttoned to the neck yet tieless, you have deep, lasting roots in the community, love children, drink, but not to excess, adore noise of all kinds, and cannot be held responsible for the depredations of organized crime. In brief, thou'rt your swart Italiano. Got any clams?"

"Who is this fuckin' hardon?" Buddy says. Silence is his only answer, a rapt silence which seems to await his earthy laughter.

"What I miss is the pull of continuity. Or to put it more clearly: Although the continuity's pull is sometimes present, there is lacking a certain sympathy for the people involved. We don't, somehow, feel as if we are participating in *real* people's *real* lives. But do drop by for a cuppacawfee."

"Right. Without the pull of continuity, civilizations tend to crumble," Tadeusz Creon says. "For instance, the Cracow Incident, without that pull, cannot be fully understood." He puffs thoughtfully on his crusty aromatic. "Oh, you think it's *funny?*" Blows are exchanged and old friendships strained almost to the breaking point. A kielbasa panic. Painted Easter eggs are snapped up. Anti-Semitism is trotted out in new clothes. Yet who *knows* about this?

Crescent and Chattaway? Perhaps.

"Coffee?"

"Don't talk to me about Crescent and Chattaway," Grey Crimson says, his words angrily spurting out around the stem of his well-designed billiard meerschaum, a gift from his first wife and her "boyfriend," Dr. Trite. "They don't send out advance galleys, they have no clipping service, they take ads in *Gardening Fun,* they get a hundred returns for every book sold. I'm a well-known author for God's sake! And here I sit, smoking this piece of white rock or something from

Crete, flat broke, melting with ruth. I don't even have an interesting accent anymore."

Meerschaum is a fine white claylike material mined chiefly in Daly City. Adolf Hitler, the late German statesman, had a mania for pipes fashioned from this rare vignette.

"*I* still love his accent," Delilah Crosse says. She is stunning in an excitement of black silk falling ravishingly to the knee in a single crisp sweep of midnight magic. "As you can see, my taste in clothes is a manifestation of style, not fashion." She makes a small enchanting *moue*. "Some think that my love for things Continental and the fact that I ridicule everything Middle American with what amounts to precious condescension keep me youthful and vivacious. Perhaps," she says softly, with a hint of self-doubt, "my jugs could stand some improvement?"

"What did that woman say about jugs?" Lucy Brandon says.

"However," Delilah continues, crisply ravishing her excitement, "there are plans in the offing and not a few irons in the fire. Especially concerning my legs, which are at once my shame and my triumph." She proffers a lot of leg in silky sheer stockings to sustained applause.

"O.K. I'll give her the legs," Lucy says.

"With those legs I don't think she's a good Christian woman," Knute sighs, pausing in his search for rustic foodstuffs.

Tania Crosse has so much money that she believes that "Tania Crosse" is her real name. Her face, always beautiful, is cool and smooth, her makeup perfect, her hair a silvery blond. She's drinking Ricard and ginger ale, a famous affectation. She doesn't recall Delilah. She lights a Camel. She likes the still-pink scar tissue on her wrists. What to do? She sets out for her flagship store. Things are not quite as *à vau-l'eau* today as they have been recently. But they are *à vau-l'eau* enough, oh yes indeed.

Knowing a good thing when he sees one, the owner of the Crystals, another semi-pro baseball team, is also thinking of bringing suit against the sculptor. God only knows why. Proud contumely, vile disdain, imminent danger? All look O.K.

"Look," the sculptor says, "all I want to do is finish this goddamned book and get that foreigner with the neck thing away from my house. O.K.? Don't bother me with this asshole and his suit. O.K.?" In her pique, her humanity comes to the fore and it is, well, pretty darned *attractive*. But this is neither here nor there, for many are eager for news of the Cullinan family.

In the basement of their white frame house, not too far from things, Brian, a little slow for twenty-six, is forging his father's name to a check. He has his eye, a poor thing but his own, on a COMMANDO KNIFE, guaranteed to PUNCTURE, INCISE, LACERATE, SLICE, RIP, TEAR, AND HACK IN TWO!! anybody who wants to "Get Funny." INDISPENSABLE for camping trips, can be thrown with SPEED and POWER!! RUGGED SAW for barbed wire. 10-DAY FREE TRIAL. CHECK IT OUT!! Maureen is jacking off the ice-cream man inside the cab of his truck, and by now she is a whiz at it. May is on the phone with, of course, her sister, who is *still* in bed. Michael, in his "den" up in the attic, is filing away his newest ladies' underwear catalogue, *Frenchie Frillies*. But why are they all dressed in what they call their "best clothes"? It is that Mr. Cullinan the elder is dead at last and they are preparing to leave for the funeral home where he lies intestate in the largest room. Mrs. Cullinan, his widow, is already there, and many friends and relatives attend him. They speak in hushed voices, *de mortuis nil nisi bonum* their guiding precept, more or less.

A picture of health, he niver looked so good when he was aloive, Jayzus and ye'd think he's about to git up and go fer a pint the hard man, look at the roses in his dear owld cheeks, Christ and he's as pink as a baby, sure and I wished I looked half as good wit' the sinuses cloggin' me head wit' snot, he's a fookin' credit to the owld country, even stiff as a board he could lick a dozen men, look at the poor widow will ye now, I love the dear silver that shoines in her hair, I think the good woman has a few jars in her meself and who's to blame her, he'll be havin' a jar on the other soide about now that he will, he looks like a notorious saint he does, he made a foine act of contrition at the last they say, merciful Jayzus but he niver had much of a chin on him, 'tis a pity his poor owld tongue is stickin' out of his gob like a bloody snake's, ye'd think the pansy Orangeman of a funeral director would close his right eye for him for the love of God, by Christ ye'd niver think he had the walkin' glanders what me own da died of, and et cetera. Enter Brian, Maureen,

May, and Michael, in the splendor of their grief. Divers snots, tears, and wailings. Rudimentary ethnic artifacts of a celebratory nature are crudely passed about and shared, e.g., green cardboard derbies, clay pipes, lapel harps of plastic, etc., etc. All goes well, varied entertainments, some of a scandalous nature (see *Irish Wake Amusements* by Seán Ó Súilleabháin) proceed in good order.

"They are hardworking folk," Cox says, "like your dark-eyed ginzola."

Still, Michael, enchanted as he is by the wild Celtic jigs, reels, skreels, potheens, mashies, and kerries which command the floor, is troubled in his heart, for his new issue of *Cults and Coteries* is late. And this is the issue in which "Muffin" Cunningham, "Scummy" to her friends, is to model the entire "Cute Cop" line of *exciting fantasy-wear!*

"How is it, sir, that *I* have no intelligence of the 'Cute Cop' line?" Sir Bloom says from his chaise. "Am I losing touch with the still center of the turning world?"

Here let it be noted that we are interested in the Cullinane family, *Cullinane.*

John Greene Czcu buys a copy of *Buddy and His Boys on Mystery Mountain* for fifteen cents. The book is virtually unobtainable, yet this relaxed gentleman laughs only the harder. Certainly, nobody has any right to expect to find such a gem here in the fog belt, especially on grubby Rensselaer Street, which, at its best, looks like Avenue D on a magical summer weekend.

"It is so," Czcu says shrewdly, a hint of mockery in his voice. "Although I work hard, I play even harder, this dynamite city providing many opportunities for leisure fun, if one knows *where to look. Buddy,* for instance, one of the great tales of insouciant adventure in the considerable literature of rural capers and gambols, has bears, one-eyed gypsies, noble braves, simpering damsels, and chums galore. One might even say that in its rhetorical subversion of the 'chum as callow youth' theme, the privileged 'Ur-chum,' we witness a classic deconstructive technique."

"There is not one real stolid redskin in the whole book, motherfucker," Chief Blue Wind protests.

"Yet Buddy is delightfully attractive, don't you think, Chief?" Czcu says. "You're not, if I may say so, too hard on the eyes either, if you get my drift?" For a long moment, Blue Wind's humanity shines forth from *his* eyes.

There ensues that which is known to commerce as "brisk sales" of Louis Condy's *The Daddy and the Drake,* in the Black Ladder Book Shop. The beloved children's book, finally reissued after twenty-three years, has become the adored focus of an enthusiastic and pleasantly mindless cult, whose celebrants quack greetings to each other and wear T-shirts which display the book's most famous sentence, "The duck *talked,* Daddy!" Condy, his usually saturnine face wreathed in an uncharacteristic smile, sits behind a low table at the rear of the shop, autographing copies. Moved by the awed crowds, the author writes whatever is requested, e.g., "To Daisy, a swell gal and *some* character"; "For Dante, King of the Bores"; "Por María de la Concepción Dorotea Carolina Darío y Reyes, un abrazo y un beso."

Dark Victory is playing in a rerun house down the street, but such is the pull of the reclusive author's presence that the theatre is virtually empty, save for three or four avid masturbators whose sexual fantasies incline toward images of women who exhibit a lot of spunk despite the brain tumors which are the cause of their nagging vision problems. When the star of the film, Bette Davis, stumbles over a credenza and, bravely smiling, pitches forward into the buffet supper, a medley of unmistakably lewd groans is heard in the darkened orchestra.

"I thought she falls into the buffet supper in *Carom,*" a fan says. "Right after the scene in the cheerful, sunny kitchen, where she mistakes the jelly doughnuts, or donuts, for French crullers. Whenever I see that I bust out crying and invariably ask myself what *I* would do ensnared in such embarrassing instance."

A well-mannered group of older women from the Athene chapter of the Daughters of Durga International is massing in front of the Black Ladder to protest the fact that *The Daddy and the Drake* has but a single female character who is, early on in the adventure, eaten by a bear on a garbage-strewn nature trail. One of the women buttonholes a shifty-looking man heading for the theater, a grimy raincoat held, in the time-honored fashion of harmless perverts, in front of his pubes. The man, who identifies himself to the media only as D.D., stands impatiently, hoping that the jelly-doughnut scene has not yet been reached.

"While we mobilize, Mr. D., to protest the lack of an evenhanded *humanity* in Condy's insensitive work, you rush toward a rendezvous with the base fantasies excited by the Pink Sleeveless Dress Syndrome, a metonymy for female helplessness. Is it, then, strange that the Daughters adopted, long ago, fedora and overalls as counterweights to such male horseshit thought? As a way for us to deconstruct the very notion of the helpless woman?"

"Look, sister, I don't bother nobody," D.D. says. "All I wanna do is sit down, take it easy, and come in my old grimy raincoat here. I really *dig* chicks."

But now the women are forming into ranks and have no time to deal with this shuffling slave to the aberrant. Condy glances out the window and in his rampant egoism assumes that they are old fans, perhaps mothers who read his masterwork to their children long years ago, when things were as they are naturally supposed to be, and real men could nonchalantly curse, spit, piss, shit, and masturbate among themselves without fear of nosy women barging into the sanctum of club or swimming pool.

Dear Sir:

In your description of the Cullinan wake, the statements put into the mouths of the mourners are in execrable taste; indeed, they comprise a miniature encyclopedia of anti-Irish rodomontade presented as "realism." Sir, the Irish do not speak in this way, and despite the fond beliefs of the benighted, neither are they partial to green cardboard derbies, "jars" of intoxicating liquors, and the other claptrap noted in your callous and bigoted essay. May I suggest that you do some research before you again set pen to paper?

Sincerely,
A Concerned Irish-American

A piecework of heartburn, he niver looked so good when he was aloive, Jayzus and ye'd think he's about to git up and go fer a pinwheel the hard manakin, look at the rosins in his dear owld cheetahs, Christ and he's as pink as a bachelor's-button, sure and I wish I looked half so good wit' the sirs cloggin' me headgear wit' snowblink, he's a fookin' creep to the

owld coup, even stiff as a boast he could lick a dozen manakins, look at
the poor wigan will ye now, I love the dear silverweed that shoines in
her hairline, I think the good wonderland has a few jaseys in her meself
and who's to blame her, he'll be havin' a jasey on the other siderite
about now that he will, he looks like a notorious Sal that he does, he
made a foine actinomyces of contumely at the latchstring they say,
merciful Jayzus but he niver had much of a chink on him, 'tis a placard
his poor owld tonka bean is stickin' out of his gobo like a bloody snap-
back's, ye'd think the pantie Orangeman of a funk-dirk would close his
right eyehole for him for the lover of God, by Christ ye'd niver think he
had the walkin' glassman what me own dachshund died of.

Now *that's* Irish.

As the morning sun rose over the wooded slopes of Mystery Mountain,
sending its rays through the chinks in the walls of the rough-hewn cabin,
Dick Witherspoon laughed gaily and stretched, his eyes shining brightly
on Buddy, his lissomely strapping chum.

"I declare I slept like a log being a-sawed in two, Buddy," he
commented.

"So did I, Dick," Buddy admitted. "It is the pure air up here in the
mountains," he mused. "It cleans the cobwebs out of a fellow's brain."

"The cobwebs, Buddy?" Dick queried softly.

"It's a figure of speech, Dick, kind of like Mrs. Browning uses, a nice,
respectable one too. Like an ozone," Buddy said seriously.

"You're a strange lad, Buddy," Dick grinned. "But a right faluting
brick."

The two friends, having washed quickly and with many a boyish
whoop in the icy mountain stream that ran clear and cold behind
the rustic cabin, tramped back inside, shyly cozening each other about
the pangs of hunger that gnawed at them. For boys of their age need
a great deal of homely grub to ensure the rudest health! Buddy,
obviously exhilarated, decided not to tell Dick that he'd almost
injured his arm on the jagged pelisse which the furious rill had sent
crashing down on them.

"You 'most broke your arm on that dang'rous pelisse, Buddy," Dick
said admiringly. Buddy blushed and began energetically to lay the fire,
while Dick discreetly pretended to busy himself with his collection

of sturdy raiment. For all his love of hearty fun he was an estimable, gentlemanly boy.

"Say, Buddy," he soon called from the shadows that still lingered in the corners of the snug shelter, "it looks mighty like the other lads up and died during the night. I'll be piped!" he exclaimed in a voice of genuine concern. "They seemed tip-top and in the pink 'fore they turned in."

"Died?" Buddy echoed, his worried face framed by the firelight. "I suppose that we should have provided them with a supper more substantial than their fill of *crystal-clear spring water,* such as the mountain boasts." Both boys laughed merrily at Buddy's subtle levity, for it was well-known that even in time of the greatest danger, Buddy insisted on a genteel lightheartedness. Yet it was of no small concern to him that the untimely demise of the other lads was uncannily like an incident described in *Dead Beats,* a novel of mystery and danger that Buddy admired greatly.

"Well, let's get some chuck inter our bellies," Dick continued. "I'm so hungry that I could eat a very large horse, hooves and all!" Again the two youths' laughter joined in mutual clean fun. If Buddy had learned anything in his fifteen years on this mortal coil, it was that a sense of humor is no bar to advancement.

"Yes, let's quickly procure a meal," Buddy added. "For we've a long, hard day ahead of us if we expect to find that dago Blutwurst's hidden map before sundown."

"You don't have to implode me to agree with *that,*" Dick chuckled volubly. "In course, the dago's map sure ain't going anywhere. And neither is *he,*" he added jocularly.

"You should say '*of* course,' Billy," Buddy said quietly, "not '*in* course.' Incorrect grammar often proves a bar to advancement in the demanding world of business."

And with that, the boys began eating copiously of the smoked rashers that they'd found beneath the floorboards, and to which cache they'd been alerted just a week earlier by the Dean of Arts and Sciences, a coarse-looking man whose flushed face confessed that he was not unfamiliar with strong spirits. Buddy suddenly thought of the Dean's rubicund complexion, and, startled, helped himself to another generous portion of the nourishing fare.

It was mid-morning when the two companions, after lugging the bodies of their chums into the woods for the shy forest creatures to carry off, started along the north bank of the swift creek and headed for the distant crag, forever wreathed in forbidding swirls of mist, called "Misty Crag."

Literary Interlude

"Death to Emily Dickinson's Modesty"
(to the tune of "Moon River")

Death to Emily Dickinson's modesty!
Her reticent blushes? A malepig travesty!
They wish her to be but a brainless tootsy
Or one whose genius "just growed" like Topsy.
Death! To Emily Dickinson's modesty!

Let us strangle the nun of Amherst's modesty!
Photos reveal that Em wasn't too breasty,
Filthy pigmen think chaste means not chesty,
And consider poetic brilliance unzesty;
Let us strangle the nun of Amherst's modesty!

Let us drown in womanrage Emily's modesty!
We are sick and do puke at pigspeak that's "jesty,"
On how we are home-loving, docile, and nesty;
And if we speak out we are "broads" who are pesty.
Let us drown in womanrage Emily's modesty!

Let us drown in womanrage Emily's modesty!
Let us strangle the nun of Amherst's modesty!
Death to Emily Dickinson's modesty!
Death! Relentless death! See?

Father Donald Debris, S.J., long removed from his pastoral duties for teachings not only contrary to the Magisterium, but, some say, dangerously close to heresy (*vide* "The Effect of High Heels on the Cloistered Orders," *New Church Bearings,* XXII, 6, 1958), spends his days in a close study of the Décadence. This morning, he is startled to discover that his idiosyncratic and highly complex system of numerology—a system of numerological transference determined by an algorithmic permutational shift accomplished by a rigid adherence to the formula

$$a \div b = a \cdot (1/b) = a \cdot b^{-1}$$

—has afforded him positive proof that "Barbey d'Aurevilly" is an anagram of "Yvonne DeCarlo." Debris has long been fascinated by the film star because of her roles as temptress in *Blaze over Pago-Pago, The Hot Countess, Tongues at Midnight,* and *December,* the last arguably displaying her finest performance. Almost overcome by excitement, the priest reworks his formula and discovers that he has made an error in one step of the process. It is not "Yvonne DeCarlo" that is anagrammatic of the outrageous author's name, but "Barbra d'Eveuilley." Now Debris realizes that Miss DeCarlo had nothing to do with the roles, perhaps irresponsibly attributed to her by "loco" journalists, in the four films he so admires. Yet the priest can find no references to prove that Mlle d'Eveuilley appeared in the films either! Who, then, was the star? He rises from his desk, strolls to the window, and gazes at the traffic far below. Perhaps there is something "wrong" with his formula. Many otherwise intelligent people founder on the shoals of mathematics, or, in this case, arithmetic.

"Deejee," Father Debris mutters incomprehensibly to the blinds, or, perhaps, to the traffic. Then, "Thank goodness there will be mastiachis for supper. God bless, despite her ill-gotten wealth, Miss Crosse, our generous supplier."

Miss Crosse?

Madame Berthe Delamode ("Creations Tastefully Designed") packs up some old clothes, of which she is tired to death, to give to *somebody.* Truthfully, she's just going to leave them in a box out by the garbage cans. Really, they're slightly corroded. She spies something in the street. "Aha!" she laughs, yet realizes, now, that "it" is all so *unimportant.* For a moment, she looks blank, but then, in an untrained but pleasant alto, sings the first two choruses of "Time Will Tell":

> Time will tell
> I'll give you la de da
> Time will tell
> La da my heart

Dengised yllufetsat
Snoitaerc
Dengised
Yllufetsat

It is apparent that she is suffering from a female ailment clearly recognized in the 1783 monograph, *De l'influence des affections de l'âme dans les maladies nerveuses des femmes.* Among other well-known women whose careers were notably affected by this "maladie" are the actress Dolores Délire (see especially her performance in *Les Fureurs du péché*), and the author Viña Delmar (n.b., *Bad Girl*). Among the early symptoms of the disease is the overwhelming desire to tastefully design creations.

It's not so much a desire as it is an obsession! (Indicates "Confidential" file.)

There is a slender possibility that Benjamin DeMott may soon address the problem with, of course, an eye to its literary implications. For our time. Mr. Denim—Anthony Denim—supposedly wrote of the scourge in 1884 or thereabouts in his still-valuable *De praestigiis amoris,* or, *On Love's Deceptions.* In those days they called the disease "nervous prostration." Noble chicks got it a lot when their boyfriends like rode off with the hussars, shakos bulging in the slanting rays of the morning sun.

April Detective, in bed, is, despite the warmth of the day, cold beneath a sheet, two blankets, and a grimy raincoat, a bittersweet reminder of earlier, far happier days. Maybe not "far" happier. She gets out of bed to get another bottle of vodka, a favorite beverage, cheap, potent, and without any *frotteur* to interfere with the function of the alcohol. Her brain, steeped as it is in booze, is not working very well. "Such go the breaks of life," she says. "Tomorrow I'll get straight," she adds, proving once again, if proof is needed, that alcohol is no defense against the platitude. Abruptly, she falls down, and as abruptly, rises. She falls down again, abruptly, and rises again, slowly. She enters the bathroom, sits on the toilet, and pisses, aware too late of the fact that she has forgotten to lift her nightgown. "Not to worry," she says. "Tomorrow I'll lift my nightgown and relieve myself in more seemly fashion." She really hates this country house, if that's what it is. It looks like a country house, there is something warm and inviting and familiarly depressing about it, something bovine, something that reminds her of chickens and their manic clucks, something rich and smugly Protestant. She pulls off the sodden nightgown, dries herself with a glum country towel that gives off, as in all tales of squalor, a faint odor of urine. And so back to bed, naked, and colder than before. If it were night, she could lie awake, staring into the pitiless dark, wondering. As it is, she drinks some vodka. "Good booze," she says. "A crisp yet velvety sensation that speaks of the good life. Tomorrow I'll get straight." The phone rings. It's that goddamned May again. Yet again.

All the remarks here attributed to April are "translations" of what she actually said. Her exact words, here in her rustic bedroom, and bathroom, in order of utterance, are: "Much flow some grapes, dull wife"; "Moon, car, beau: wild sex-mate"; "Wazoo flurry!"; "Blues are woe, why sin I? I plow, stand, pee-pee, sigh; else grim corpse dreams, reams crank's cunt"; "Wouldst bruise?"; "Such pricks said, 'Well, well, we said dame grunts sad news—but her bush shines' "; "Moon, car, beau: wild sex-mate." It was the repetition of the last remark which led to the revelation of the true message which it concealed. After this, breaking the cipher was but a simple matter of adherence to the precept, "as it goes in, so does it come out."

The maddening itch and pain of Dick Detective's boils and pimples are driving him almost to despair. He takes his novel *Blackjack* from the shelf, and opens it at random. Who is he to fly in the face of convention? There is nothing more soothing to Dick than to read a page of the prose, the Ur-prose, which ushered in the enormously influential Parvanist (cf. L. *parvus,* L. *pavrus,* f. Gk. παῦρος) movement. Parvanism, a "style" celebrated for its smallness of mind and the meanness so representative of its era, was, as few now admit, foreshadowed in Dick's only book. He reads:

> . . . and I've heard a few things. Which is not to say that I'm smarter than the next joe. Like when I was in the army I learned plenty.
>
> We were sitting at the bar, Howie and me. Howie works in the Jack in the Box while he's trying to get himself straightened out. He's not all as funny as he used to be but he's still Howie. The gin's settled him down some. I lean to

a little Teacher's myself.

Anyway Howie and me we're doing a little damage to the stock at Stan's when this guy comes in, a little geeky-looking clown with a fedora under his shirt, one of those shirts that has a kind of shiny look, and over his left pocket it says "Fedora." Can you beat it?

"Stan," the guy says to Claude, the bartender, "I'll have a double ball of the best you got." Stan don't come in much anymore since Gladys left him two years ago to go to air-conditioner school up to Topeka. Stan said that he told her he was goddamned sick and tired of tuna casserole for supper and she lit out. He's a big guy, Stan, but he has one of those goiters. He takes it pretty well.

Howie looks at me and he's got "Oh, hell" written all over him and the same kind of sick look as when he ate the weeds behind the AA place.

It was just like when I was back in the army, I get this real itchy feeling all over. Alice always knew when that happened, because she'd set fire to the curtains every time. She used to be some looker before she got a little fat from the Hershey bars. Alice is my wife. We been thinking of buying a laundromat . . .

"Good God! What a genius I had!" Dick remarks, looking up from the page. "The way I informed the long look with all that was in my power!" To think that this man was once "Mr. Parvanism." It is enough to make Dick cry. It is enough to encourage, in fact, a touch of *saeva indignatio* in his carbuncular breast.

In Detroit, Michigan, founded as a fort and settlement in 1701, and called Ville d'etroit by the brilliant if emotionally bankrupt Antoine de la Mothe Cadillac, incidentally the original North American forebear of Berthe Delamode, there exists one of the 12,147 taverns named Dew Drop Inn. Dick, who is not to be confused with the author of *Blackjack,* nor with the Dick who is the brother of Dipers, the latter pair twin bastard sons of a powerful and ruthless nature magnate—although his identity is not important—Dick, *this* Dick, steps off a train at the suburban station of Agapa. He gazes in mild surprise at the heavily sweating people who run by him, their "clothes" drenched, their faces red and twisted into expressions which indicate agony, orgasm, or both.

"Have you heard about what happened at the Dew Drop Inn?" one says, a Mrs. Divan of the Condom League of West Agapa. She is jogging this fine morning in order to prepare her body for the inquiring hands that may, this afternoon, get a little fresh with her. The immaculate napery and the rich yet subdued place settings are almost always the provocation for somewhat forward advances on the part of a *few* of the ladies, as we suspected all along. Dick ignores the question and takes a long swallow from a pint bottle of Dixie Belle gin, the brand originally employed in the composition of the Gin Thrill, a fabulous mixed drink whose recipe is forever lost to us, like that for pizza. "Oh, fuck off!" Mrs. Divan says over her sweaty shoulder, and Dick turns to admire her delicious buttocks. "You don't see asses like *that* on the train," he says, and wonders why.

Chances are that the reason may be rooted in the fact that the trains which Dick takes are decidedly lacking in napery—immaculate or otherwise—as well as in place settings. In fact, the food served aboard such trains is fit only for someone like Oaky Doaks, who is currently reduced to playing clowns at shopping malls and fast-food restaurants. "A hell of a comedown in the world," Doaks admits from a shopping mall outside Agapa. "But I always let a smile be my umbrella, as the ruttish Zuleika Dobson might say. Or does she say, 'I'll think about it tomorrow'? Or is it 'Ball me, Ishmael!'? Or, perhaps, 'The diary, the diary'?"

"*Zuleika Dobson,* once an actual person, is Sir Max Beerbohm's only novel," Dr. Plot offers to a restive crowd. "Written while the master of authorial wit was still a student at Jesus Christ Almighty, its plot may briefly be summarized thus.... No, please! Don't go! Please...?"

ZULEIKA DOBSON

I

1. Cambridge Days ("Overture").
2. The "Rowdies' " Pre-Regatta Carousal; smutty stories of lecherous dons are recounted by the boys; puke contests; maudlin vows of friendship made.
3. Zuleika arrives to examine the famed "Water Willies" of Cambridge.
4. Buddy muses bitterly on his exclusion from the social whirl.
5. Dick Witherspoon chides Buddy; Dick's allegorical tale of the "yellowed newspaper."

6. Zuleika, depressed by the sad fountains, hikes into nearby Scone Canyon.
7. Buddy searches for and finds the old Dodge hidden in Scone Canyon; digression on the Dodge's traditional role during "Regatta Month."
8. Buddy and Zuleika meet; share cheese and bread despite class differences; "Buddy's story" recounted.
9. Zuleika tells a horrified Buddy "the Girdle Story."

II

10. The "Rowdies" overhear Knute's plan to pollute the river with glög; they continue to carouse heedlessly.
11. Strange deaths of the Dolly Sisters; history of the "good-time trio" recounted in a letter found by Dick.
12. Zuleika meets the mysterious Lutheran, Knute, and falls in love.
13. Buddy throws himself into river and disappears; digression on the dangers of the river; its victims' fates recalled; disquisition on the water's potability, piscine inhabitants; enumeration of submarine autoerotic acts from the reign of Alfred the Swollen to the present, etc., etc.
14. Dick discovers pollution plan; troubled, he weeps; hurries to Buddy's rooms.
15. Old Dodge decays; "yellowed newspaper" clipping blows into nearby furze.
16. Dick searches frantically for Buddy; finds Zuleika packing her trousseau while whistling "I Love a Big-boned Viking."
17. Zuleika ignores Dick's pleas; refuses to tell him "the Girdle Story"; dubs him "nosy shithead."
18. The "Rowdies" find "yellowed newspaper" clipping; tell Dick of Knute's true identity therein revealed.
19. Dick swears vengeance; whittles furiously; he and the "Rowdies" recall Knute's older brother, Lars "the besmirched."

III

20. Zuleika marries Knute; finds his diary on honeymoon; pales at secret, depraved ideas expressed therein.
21. After a night of unpleasant surprises, Zuleika drowns herself; is found wearing seven layers of clothing and makeshift chastity belt fashioned from old copies of *Kirkus Reviews*.
22. Dick finds Knute's unposted letter to Lars; suspects the ugly truth.
23. Knute is confronted by Dick; denies all heatedly; surrenders moleskins.
24. Buddy attends Zuleika's funeral; accidentally spies the guilt-stricken Knute in "Chevrolet owner's" disguise.

25. Buddy and Dick turn the craven Knute over to the Constable; the University grudgingly cancels the Regatta.
26. Buddy tells the story of his drowning ruse to admiring coeds in shorts.
27. Buddy leaves for Mystery Mountain and the sad peace of solitude.
28. The "Rowdies," sober at last, marvel at Knute's infamy and Zuleika's bold fashion statement.
29. The mystery explained; Knute's diary made public; strong men sicken; women vow eternal chastity.
30. Cambridge Nights ("Coda").

Corrections of Earlier Errors

Item: Dolores, who took part in at least two orgies, or "wild parties," as she now calls them, the particulars of which are not pertinent, is not the same Dolores who was one of April's friends. The latter Dolores may still be one of April's friends, but since, as we know, April spends most of her time in bed, the chances are excellent that they don't see each other anymore. Or perhaps they do. It is difficult for us to keep track of so many people. Very few of them keep in touch.

Item: Donatien Alphonse François, the "Divine" Marquis, later Comte, is not to be credited with the authorship of the novel *Le Bousingot,* definitely by Théophile Dondey, contrary to the somewhat persuasive arguments of Jean-Claude Rififi, Curzio Toffenetti, and Gil Roulure.

Item: Don Juan, by George Gordon, Lord Byron, is *correctly* pronounced, despite the "confirmation" of years of usage, and the agreement—one might say the collusion—of scholars, as its author pronounced it, Dawn Jee-WAYN, and not Don JOO-un.

Item: The "Jimmy Dorsey" heretofore mentioned in passing is not the famous bandleader (brother of Tommy), whose best recording is probably "Long John Silver." Selected lyrics follow:

> John Silver,
> Long John Silver;
> John Silver,
> Long John Silver.

The "Jimmy Dorsey" who plays a small role in this place and on this day is the grocery-bagger at the A & P, the one who "looks blank."

"Grocery-bagging" is often considered a menial, dead-end job, but the incidence of job fatalities in this position for 1985, the last year for which such records are available, was one in 11,002,593. It may therefore be argued that "Jimmy Dorsey" has a better chance at a long life than did Long John Silver, who had, as the phrase goes, 'is bleedin' neck stretched.

An epiphany from *Treasure Island:*
"Har, har, Jim! Har, har, har!" Long John Silver croaked, vigorously bashing his peg leg against the mizzen-poop gunwales. "Belay me if I'm not sorrprised as a barkenteen caught in a sudden yar! The apple barrel, ye say? Har, har, har!"

"In *Doubles Cross,* by April and Richard Detective, with additional material by Karen Cornfield, Keats is mentioned more than once in what seem to be meaningless and even self-indulgent digressions." The lewd Flo Dowell is speaking, reclined voluptuously on a tiger skin. She is trying, yet again, to teach her current lover something of the fascination of literary theory and research. He is unresponsive, and wondering why she is called "lewd," since you can't prove it by him. "These digressions, however, are the key, or, if you will, the keys to the entire work, much as the descriptions of weather in Cornwall hold the true meaning of *Dracula*—I speak, of course, of Bram Stoker's famous novel, not the short story by Theodore Dreiser. But of course you know this." The lover, still unresponsive, waits for a few tried-and-true sentences to arrive and get him out of this. Suggestions:
1. He doesn't want this forced intimacy, despite Flo's good intentions.
2. He knows that she means well, and feels a sudden rush of sympathy for her.
3. He rises and walks toward the door.
4. He opens the door, and as the light floods over his wasted face, he hears Flo's voice falter, then cease.
5. He suddenly feels old, yet realizes that he feels old as if for the first time.

All the original members of the old band Dress Rite die within the

space of an hour. This is truly amazing. It's almost well-nigh unbelievable. Who ever said that truth is stranger than fiction? Or was it
"stronger"?

That was some shitty band, by the way.

Diane Drought, known to her neighbors as "Hickey," for disputed
reasons, is waiting for her daughter to drop her grandchild off for the
day. Diane doesn't know that this grandchild is not the daughter of her
daughter's legal husband, but that of a lover who, at this moment, is
dying. And no wonder, since he is the ex-bassist of the long-defunct
band, Dress Rite. Diane's daughter, in her turn, doesn't know that she is
not the daughter of the late Mr. Drought, but is the illegitimate offspring
of a certain Bob Doran, whose name is the same as that of a character in
Dubliners. Life seems to become ever stranger, even though one buys
riding clothes and waits patiently in hospitals for what seems *forever*.

Bob Doran also appears in *Ulysses,* if you're interested.

Fine.

The doorbell rings! In they come! They have a little conversation,
e.g., "— —— ———— —, ————." "——. ———, ————— ————?" "———,
———, — ————." "——— ———— — —— — ———. . . ." Etc., etc. Things are
going along, going along. But why does Diane's daughter wear knotted
about her neck a pair of ice-blue panties? Odd things tend to happen on
Rensselaer Street.

While Miss Dubuque, humming to herself in her cheery kitchen, puts
up enough mastiachi peppers to last through the long winter, since her
"boyfriend" is a stickler, a small tragedy is unfolding at Rudy's
Superette. Rudy, tired and irritated because of an argument with his
artistically minded brother, is preventing the young Duey, one of
Blast's "pals," from examining the labels on the varied yogurts carried
by the market.

"Look, kid," Rudy bellows, "this market fairly bustles! Out! *Out!*"

On her way to Coney Island in a car of what is no longer the Sea Beach
Express, but is now revoltingly called the "N" line, a decidedly familiar-
looking woman of about fifty opens her bag and takes out a letter,
creased and worn soft from dozens of readings. She is not dressed for

Coney Island but wears a black suit which, though flattering, is somewhat too tight and decidedly unfashionable. She opens the letter, which
proves to be from an anonymous correspondent who is, the woman is
virtually certain, a high-school career advisor, Margaret McNamara
Duffy, now deceased. It is an erotic, not to say obscene letter, offensive
to all but the most degraded community standards. It is included here
for the sake of what is usually considered the "record," but can easily
be skipped or crossed out by those who fear for the purity of their souls.

Dear Velvet Pie,
    You don't know me, my slickertwaddy, but I feel I know you from things that
people have told me about you, and things that I've read. We also met at a
party once, but I can't tell you when or where. I know that you are gorgeous!
    I wish I had a picture of you naked with your beautiful nummo completely
exposed. I would kiss it and lick it and play with my bim-bim until I fainted
dead away with maddened pleasure.
    I'd love to have you here right now with me so I could put my tongue into
your crunge and bite your gozos, and then I'd beg you to get on your hands and
knees and I'd wamble you from behind, then huche your swickie and your shy
little waz too! God I'm wet! And my coonze is itching, is yours?
    I know that you like men, but I know that if I had the chance to fondle and
mouth your piz, I'm certain that you'd consider "changing your luck," as they
say. I wish I could tell you my name but in the town I live I'd be hounded to
death by the Methodists and Lutherans who run things, especially considering
the sensitive job I have on the Purity Vigilance Committee.
    In the meantime, I only hope and pray that this "mash" note makes you at
least once in a blue moon fondle and stroke and finger your scump with your
intoxicating thones spread wide open, and think about this letter and the
"unknown adorer" while you're *doing* it.
    Oh, I have to go and miche myself, I'm just *drenched.*
                                    A Secret, Burning Admirer

"Buzz" Duncan, whose intimates lovingly call him "Buns," no longer
content to be a mere humorist, yet not quite fully realized in his new
profession of saying important things, is brought up short as he sees a
delightfully attractive man, his face a study in concentrated frustration,
leaning awkwardly against a frozen-food case. Although his body is
uncomfortably twisted into an unnatural position, the man cannot conceal the scandalous bulge which distends the crotch area of his trousers.

Several women regard him with intense interest as they pass, and one, thoroughly fascinated, drops a stack of Durango TexMex Frozen Chimichangas on the head of a young fellow who, crouching, appears to be examining a shelfful of canned soup. "Buzz" takes a playful step toward the distraught man, who now gazes up at the ceiling imploringly. The thud of two bodies colliding on the street is heard throughout the market. It is almost as if Durga, the Destroyer, the Serene, the Ineffable, the Thunderbolt, is exerting this day her malevolent will against all who strike her as unworthy. This may indeed be the case, for, as we know, one of her many manifestations is as the Albanian Lard Goddess, in whose form she is called Crusher of Cities, Scourge of Suburbs. And now, perhaps too late, we realize that she is also the young woman who appears, ecstatic, in the photograph which sullies the cover of *Anal Fancies.*

"I don't care what they say," Dwight grumbles. "I'm *going* with Allen and Chet to Connecticut! Just because I spit little bits of licorice on people when I laugh doesn't give them the right to exclude me."

Another waiter listens sympathetically, his thumb partially immersed in a plate of the *soup du jour.* He doesn't particularly want this forced intimacy.

"Everybody has faults," Dwight says, gazing distrustfully at the vat of succotash on the gas range. "I saw a documentary on TV about Thomas Edison—Edison!—and it said he used to whack off whenever one of his perplexing experiments failed. *Edison.* Those stories about the apple pie and milk are a lot of crap."

The other waiter knows that Dwight means well, and he nods appreciatively.

"They told me to go see the Eiffel Tower. I don't want to go see the Eiffel Tower. No damn reason in the world why *I* can't enjoy the way the sun lightly touches the gorse leaves with gold and ruddies up the timothy. Is there?"

The other waiter thoughtfully licks his soupy thumb, thinking of happier times, especially that one particular happier time, and sticks it back into the soup. It looks as if this shift is going to pack a riveting wallop.

Eligor, the Lustful, Eligor, the Concupiscent, Eligor, the Seductive. It
is he who exerts his uncanny powers upon certain events of this otherwise quite ordinary day, turning and twisting them to suit his caprice, so
that all seems somewhat out of kilter, so that what is clear is muddled,
so that candor becomes a synonym for desuetude. The works of T.S.
Eliot are silently removed from the trusted anthologies used in literature courses, and the renowned poet scandalously presented to all as a
femme entretenue. Elmhurst is mocked, badgered, and finally brutalized
into submission. Chalmers Endicott-Braxton, affectionately dubbed
"Paleface" or "Polefast," is made to crawl, half naked, at the feet of
"Queen" Endiva, who exposes herself to him while she reads aloud
from pamphlets on holistic medicine, the meaning of rock and roll, the
benefits of whole-grain aerobics, and the delightful climate of California. An Englishman of no small repute in the savage yet compelling
world of textile factoring leaps upon an Englishwoman, the mother of
two fine sons at good schools, and, despite her obvious pique, ruthlessly
violates her tweeds. They do, however, share an English Oval after-
ward, when he gallantly suggests that men will be men. *Envelopes*
closes immediately, the actors able neither to remember their lines nor
to recognize each other. *Environments,* the new magazine devoted to,
among other interests, the whys and wherefores of composting privies
as viable alternatives to death, disappears from the newsstands, and
Eppie, locked in the cellar of the Crown SuperMart, where he has
hidden in order to try on his "Cute Cop" outfit, is abandoned by Eros,
and instantly develops a rash from the synthetic material used to make
the costume's gunbelt. Other things are also done by Eligor, many of
which may be recorded in their proper places. For now, suffice it to say
that our quest for truth, our search for understanding, and our quest for
truth, as well as our quest for truth, may be seriously compromised.
May have *already* been seriously compromised.

   You mean, for instance, all that business about Banana Amaze may
be . . . ?

   Precisely. The hand of Eligor. And other things. The problem being,
of course, that we don't know *which* things. For instance, we know that
an Eskimo Pie is a frozen confection, although there is doubt that it
currently exists in its true form. It has probably gone the way of Moxie,
Frank's Orange Nectar, and Dixie Shake.

But isn't Dick, at this very moment, more or less, about to fall down in the streets of Agapa because of the rapid ingestion of the latter?

That's Dixie Belle, a cheap gin. Dixie Shake is—or was—an imitation-chocolate drink which turned the toper's mouth an arresting beige. But now that Dick has been brought up, something as unimportant and essentially gratuitous as his bout with Dixie Belle *also* shows Eligor's interference. Dixie Belle, too, is doubtless no more. Further, although we can vouch for the "whatness" of Eskimo Pie, we can have no idea who *Miss* Eskimo Pie is. Is she Karen Cornfield? Is she a *femme entretenue*, like T.S. Eliot? Or his first wife? Is she the desired subject of a Buddy Clark ballad? It would also be of value to know a little about Vince Esposito, or "Vinnie," or "Eppie," an early, unsatisfactory lover of April's, and a man forever stigmatized by Eligor as He-Who-Comes-in-His-Handkerchief.

"I am *not* Frieda Canula, mother!" Diane Drought's daughter is troubled and bewildered, and at the limits of her patience. Diane smiles sweetly at this strange Albanian.

"Some of the difficulties faced by all concerned on this too-hot day are, strangely enough, adumbrated in a brief and rather superficial exchange I recently had with my wife, Zenobia," Ethan Frome says. "You may recall her saying to me,

" 'Ethan, I get so that I think I'll go crazy with you reading all the time about Europe in those fancy books Mattie brought. As far as I can see, them Evangelists was right when they said she is a sinner with a soul black as pitch 'neath that purty face. Mercy me!'

"And my reply, 'Zeena, it's not Europe I'm reading up on, but the Everglades, the Everglades and their pure, white snowfalls.'

"So, you see, the clashes I have with Zenobia, par'lyzed as I am an' at her mercy, are much like those that you are . . . that you seem to be . . . that it may be that you think that . . . seems I lost my train o' thought."

Tabitha Bramble and Lucy Brandon, their quarrel temporarily postponed, exit from the Electra. They have just seen *Every Girl's Dream* and *If You Could Only Cook,* a pallid double feature. The Electra is an art house, owned by Baby Brownie, who opened it to do something to repay the community that gave him his chance. Right.

"George Brent has got one hell of a schlong on him," Tabitha ventures.

"And how!" Lucy agrees enthusiastically. "I'd haul his ashes for him any time."

"He's dead, I think," Tabitha notes. Lucy, chastened by this news, walks in silence by the side of her old friend. She knows that Tabitha, although sometimes abrupt, means well, and this evening, if all goes as it should, perhaps they will together gaze out their window and see a large bird, or the lights of Rudy's Superette. The large bird may even fly directly toward the lights of the bustling market. *That* would be something to record in her diary! Or, under "symbol," in her notebook!

Fagapa, a small volcanic island which is part of the Solomons group, is often confused by Karen Fairgrounds with Fanapa, the native word for a large and, to some, embarrassingly detailed herm on Mt. Cyllene; and with Fantoine, the fabulous "devil fish" of Assyrian mythology. Karen suffers from an aphasic disturbance which manifests itself in random verbal substitutions, yet this distressing malady doesn't prevent her from doing her job. In *Farfetched,* a popular study of certain types of aphasia, by William Faulkner (not his real name), a representative specimen of Miss Fairgrounds's speech is presented in a lengthy footnote to chapter 33, "Aphasic Disturbances of the Substitution Order." The specimen follows:

> "Hi! I'm Karen! I bend over so that bodies get hard when I engage sweaty parties of men. But when I'm on a streaming ogler's back, I apprise that special man of the existentialism of Abbagnano's Clouds—between the details of divorces and the spirited debates with my certain values. They're getting a 'ground' soon, and then it's quiet bye-bye to those times forever!"

Mr. Faulkner observes, "The veteran flight attendant's case is especially beguiling and puzzling in that her rare type of aphasia seems to be held in check, and indeed, for all practical purposes, *disappears completely* during the month of February. Each year, during this month, Miss Fairgrounds is lucidly communicative when she speaks of the details of her professional and personal life. Nor, most surprisingly, does she have any memory of ever having spoken otherwise."

In an apartment of the Felo-de-Se Towers, Fems, the fraternal twin brother of Blammo, the cold-cereal devotee, is attempting to seduce, by means of a display of color slides depicting the erotic sculptures of Ferozepore, the Punjab, Mrs. Feuer, who is, as the cruel phrase goes, old enough to be his mother. Fems is attempting this seduction because of persistent rumors that Mrs. Feuer is currently bestowing her considerable favors on Whitney fFrench-Newport, a brilliant if undisciplined bibliographer, and the notorious bisexual, May Fielding, "the lustful hiker." *Filter Blue,* in its current issue, provides photographic evidence of what the editor purports to be clandestine meetings between Mrs. Feuer and Mr. fFrench-Newport, and Mrs. Feuer and Miss Fielding. Photographs can be misleading, of course, and *Filter Blue*'s editor, in a note accompanying the somewhat risqué portfolio, states that he invited John Crowe Ransom, the impeccably qualified scholar, to comment on the veridicality of the pictorial evidence. The editor, in an unusually courageous display of candor, admits that his request was gently but firmly refused by Professor Ransom, whose gracious reply is given: "I would prefer to leave the documentation to those who are better qualified." But Fems believes the persistent rumors and has absolute faith in the magazine's sensational feature, and so he continues feverishly to project his slides, lingering for some moments over those which depict the frieze known as the "Rajnapur Flesh Triangle" and the astonishingly detailed bas-relief called the "Punjabi Thigh-Grasp." He fantasizes Mrs. Feuer's sudden surrender to passions which the slides have enflamed, and of, as the author of *Finnegans Wake* puts it, "making her love with his stuffstuff in the languish of flowers and feeling to find was she mushymushy." Let's wish him luck.

"Allen, I'm going to Fire Island right *now,*" Chet says, "so that bore, Dwight, won't be able to find me. Or find *us,* if you want to come."

"Sounds wonderful," Allen says. "It's funny you should think of Fire Island, I'm just reading a poem in the *New Yorker* by Mamie Morsett, listen":

> I saw the clam, alone upon the Saltaire beach,
> And thought of the wind-splashed October day
> That you and I, our hands cold-smooth as its secret hut—

"What's a 'secret hut'?" Chet asks.

"The clam's house, I guess," Allen replies. "I don't know. Where clams live, in nests or something?"

"Let's get packed," Chet says. He's had enough of this clam.

"Filthy" Yvonne Firmin is also packing, if you want to call it packing. Into her old leather suitcase she throws four pairs of shoes, not one of which can be called "serviceable" or "sensible," four Merry Widows, black, white, red, flesh, and a chocolate bunny. The mountains, lately, have been visible in her dreams. She is probably packing for the mountains, for her "gear"—save for the ever-present chocolate bunny!—is the sort recommended in the August issue of *Mountain Action* for such deserved and carefree respite from everyday concerns. The chocolate bunny has to do with a deep psychological need of Yvonne's, with something dark and vaguely menacing, rooted in her childhood, surprisingly enough. We are unaware of what it is and so Yvonne must, we fear, remain but a two-dimensional character, not one who is so convincingly etched that we feel as though we've participated in her life. So go the breaks.

It is, by the way, not at all surprising to learn, as many have, that the A & P doesn't carry *Mountain Action.* There is little call for such a publication here amid cosmopolitan environs and their attendant bric-a-brac, most of it *raffinée.*

"I prefer *Mountain Action* to almost any other magazine," Knute remarks. "It was what saved my sanity in the penitentiary."

On the other hand, the A & P does carry *Fist!,* although there is no readership for this journal either. Its features and articles have to do with what the editors are pleased to call "the main chance." For instance, in the current issue, there is a long photo-essay on the "after-hours" haircuts favored by the patrons of the newest art club, the Five of Clubs; an interview with Lorna Flambeaux, this year's winner of the Leonora Speyer Prize, conducted by her half-sister, Roberte Flambeaux, who, although not as celebrated as her famous sibling, is a poet in her own right, and does the weekly column "Trochee Trix," for *American Poets' World,* the indispensable consumer journal; and the fascinating story behind Annie Flammard's dazzling portrayal of Marcella Butler in the legendary twenty-year-old underground film soon to be released under its new title, *Days with Marcie*. "That broad is utterly devoid of a whim of grit" has, of course, become the film's most famous line, and has passed into the language, although no one is quite sure which one.

The sculptor, who is luxuriating in her unexpected false incarnation as the Lard Goddess, ventures, "I used to go into town once a month to pick up *Flikk* in the A & P—the only thing worth buying there. Then the magazine changed." She rushes about on her lawn, suddenly peevish, eyeing the Adirondack chair. "Do I need stories about ascots? Old Dodges? Starlets' knockers? Come *on!*"

"My husband reads magazines for the ads for big knockers on the girls in the back pages," the rictal woman says. "They made one of them into a movie or something with Red Butler or somebody?"

"Shop at Rudy's Superette!" Rudy pleads. "Look, I undersell those thieves at the A & P and you can rest assured I keep my arty brother in the cellar so you don't have to worry about talk about Don Byron and that kinda shit. Who needs magazines?"

"Yes, but make sure you *squat over* the toilet seats, ladies," Blast warns, "and do not *sit on* them." He displays a terrifying "before and after" photograph of Sol Blanc and Saul Blanche. "These guys once had the world in an oyster and now look at them. But shadowoi of their former selves."

Then too: Flint, "City of Promise," to Bake Three-Ton Jelly Donut; Florence Once Part of Florida, Geologist Maintains; Tamara Flynn Wins National Book Critics Circle "Great Legs" Award; *Fly of Metal Star*, Rex Focalor, Will Direct *Drowner of Men*.

After examining, however briefly and superficially, the current issue of *Fist!,* it might be well to turn to some richer fare, and take a look at a page of the scholarly essay "Food Imagery and the English Mystical Tradition: The Role of Bacoun and Eys in Medieval 'Convent Tales.' " Chancing upon the epigraph, a bit of doggerel from Chaucer's "Nun's Priest's Tale," we are made immediately aware of the interesting textual risks, such as they are. Yet of even greater interest is the curious relevance the essay proper has to "things as they might have been," all things, that is, being equal, as is, unfortunately, rarely the case. For example:

The medieval "convent tale," the labile cornerstone of the mystical tradition in English literature, or at any rate that tradition which has valorized the hypotactic strategies of the classical canon, displays, as one of its early and persistent tropes, that one called, somewhat inaccurately, the *ekphrasis*. Although this trope is still occasionally found in modern literature, most usually as a pallid and somewhat tenuous positing of the *mise en abyme*, it is to be discovered in its purest state in the currently popular board game, The Fool's Paradise. In this paper, I propose to show how the "convent tale" may, surprisingly, be elucidated by a deconstructive approach to its use of recurrent *topoi* by, so to speak, "working backward"; i.e., from the board game to the medieval genre. "Bacoun and eys," a prescriptive *topos* which occurs in virtually all the "convent tales," and which is a figure plucked almost rudely from the axis of selection in order to validate the extraordinary combinatory power of the metonymic, is the key, or primary *topos*, in the pattern of recursively enumerable recurrences. In The Fool's Paradise, the problematically designated "Penalty Cards" include one which depicts two fried eggs and three slices of bacon, and is called *Sunny Side Up;* the imagery, however unsophisticated, is remarkably clear in its bold attempt at a grammatization of a pictorial rhetoric sim— [article breaks off]

Deo gratias.

"Hi! I'm Karen Forage! When I'm sailing through the peaceful aether, however you pronounce it, my always interesting job is to attend vivaciously to eager travelers by optimistically pressing small comforts on them and pointing out fascinating topographical oddities, like, for instance, sediment-filled structural depressions between crystalline highlands. But when I'm on the rich old soil again, it's nothing, thank you, but running, sensible exercise, all-natural foods, avoidance of caffeine, and thrilling—in those special, personal ways—the young sharp-eyed exec who's just, well, *outstanding*. Hi!"

Two more demons are pressed into service in order to carry news of the general debacle to the Lightbearer, the Prince of Darkness, the Great King, He of Hollow Laughter, the Cankered Beast, the Scourge of Ministries—in short, the Boss. They are Foras, Great President of Strength, and Forneus, the Evil from the Sea. Foras has assumed the shape of Jane Parker, and his companion, whose usual manifestation is ominous enough to frighten Brooklyn rats, looks exactly like Preston Foster in his salad days.

"Lan' sakes," Foras says, toying with an eggbeater, "if you don't agree that sinkin' your teeth into one o' my scrumptious baked goods ain't better 'n makin' a Pentecostal beat his pumpkin, I'll heave you into a lake o' flamin' snot." She hasn't quite got the hang of homely lingo, yet how *tidy* Jane looks! She's wearing an Agfa apron over her pert gingham dress, or frock, and is a vision of domestic chic. Forneus says nothing, but quietly seethes. Within, of course. He feels that if he can't be a sea monster, what's the point? And just what does "news of the general debacle" mean? "Fotch," his bent, grizzled head encircled by wreaths of pipe smoke, knows who these two infernal pretenders are, but he is, unfortunately, on his merry way! He also feels that, since no one ever does anything for him, he has no obligation to apprise his fellow citizens of the possible danger that they face. Celerity is all, or so he thinks, but he has the wrong word.

The "newest art club" mentioned earlier is not the Five of Clubs, but the Four of Clubs. We wish to thank Miner X. Beely for calling this matter to our attention. Mr. Beely, taking a moment or two out from his relentless and exhausting labors, writes that he caught the mistake because of his professional interest in "Fourth of July-like symbolic pyrotechnics" and "great shale bluffs." Thanks again, Miner X. Beely, a million.

At the bar of the Foxhead Inn, Chief Blue Wind is bitterly complaining that the firewater is not only diluted but that it costs heap much wampum. The other patrons barely notice his grumblings, since they are horseplayers, and most of them have just dropped a package on Fox's U-Bet, a quick little three-year-old chestnut that should have run away from the field at a tidy 7–5, but who, as turf parlance has it, is still running. The winner of the race, the seventh at Bowie, is none other than a hitherto undistinguished nag who usually fades badly in the stretch, Banana Amaze.

"The son of a bitch paid 133.40!"

General weeping and fearsome maledictions. Threats against the well-being of both horses. Howls. God is given the figs.

"I at least shoulda put a pound on him to show!" And so on.

"I did not notice one fucking Appaloosa, Pinto, Paiute, Reno, Paint, Cayuse, or Ziti in the race," Blue Wind says. "Nothing but your pale-face horses, not an American among them." But it is as if the Chief is not there. He'd probably be better off at Fragonard, a dark, quiet "lounge" in which the patrons discuss the subtler ramifications of applied skewbald. In, of course, the light of recent French developments.

"What the goddam hell is this glass beads for change?" Blue Wind asks.

In François of Fargo's, a small soup-and-salad restaurant made famous by its mention in the socko-wallop *Accidental Bodies,* the Frankenstein girls, two minxes who, though no longer abloom, are as scandalous as they used to be when they made jabbering idiots of leaders of industry, powerful political figures, religious pundits, and other depraved solons, are enjoying a light brunch of croutons and beansprouts with Fred, a doddering, retired reinsurance clerk, who is being led on by their subtle hints of frenzied and degrading lubriciousness to come. Little if any decency is being shown, and no wonder! For the girls have, over the years, but *added* to their collection of curious implements. Fred, on his part, is oblivious to memories of his seasoned rubber stamps, his collection of maxims, e.g., "Crime is the hole of the world"; "To the sewer, all things are sewers"; "Wisdom comes to no one in pants," etc., and his treasured letter of December 27, 1963. All that Fred, in his rapidly increasing pullulation, can think about are the *les femmes* on either side of him and the pressure of their warm *les cuisses* against his.

"I understand that you're interested in enlightened and serious fiction in foreign languages," one of the girls says, letting her tongue loll out of her mouth on the first syllable of the last word.

"Yes," Fred gasps. "And in my retirement I'm pursuing a study of the shadowy Baylor Freeq. That is, who is he? Or, who was he, and is he still? I'm afraid I'm not making myself clear." The other Frankenstein girl lets her hand fall, as if accidentally, on his *ramazza.*

"Isn't he a French-Canadian?" she asks, widening her eyes expertly. Fred is silent, all his energies directed toward the act of breathing.

"No," the other girl whispers. "He married a Frenchwoman, somebody who took photographs, I think. Would you like to take some photographs—of *us*—Mister Clerk?"

"Mister Fred," Fred croaks. "Call me Mister Fred. What kind of photographs?"

The girls' crystalline laughter is informed by a delightful sweetness. Fred is acutely aware that his shako is bulging.

Cox, *White Bridges* safely under his oxter, moves down the street in restless search of clams, but is tempted by yet another dynamic old bookshop. On a bargain table he spies *Fretwork,* a forgotten volume of poems. Forgotten, even though a statement by a respected critic, now dead, graces the jacket: "Not only is *Fretwork* a remarkable display of the gritty poetry which one actively awaits in these sad times, it is a collection of intensely personal rhythms." Cox opens the book to check the truth of this statement:

> Great explorer of the dark and dread of mind,
> Humbled in kinship with drear lunacy,
> O Freud! When Phoebus' cart each Friday disappears
> And Moses' Sabbath winds you in strict nostalgia,
> Do you then think of—

He stops. Even Cox has his limits. He neglects to look at the author's name, since it isn't his business. We've been led to believe that certain interested parties know who the author is, but there may be many books entitled *Fretwork.* This is possible since book titles are not, being insufficiently creative, copyrightable. More troubles!

The denizens of "the City" coincidentally feel that "Frisco" is not sufficiently creative as a short version of or nickname for their beloved urbs. Many think that it is uncomfortably close to "Crisco," which, wags argue, is what "the City" often looks like in sunlight, as it lies whitely gleaming against the blue of the Pacific.

One had thought it looked more like "a bunch of cupcakes."

An interesting description, and one decidedly removed from "Crisco." Or "Frisco." We definitely need a less cumbersome name than that with which it is freighted. Something clear and simple, yet redolent of the free and easy nature of the place. Like "Pork and Beans," for instance.

General agreement. Shouts of "Down with Rupert Brooke!" and "Hand me my old autoharp!" Rustlings. Hard falls. Vigils for things in general. Someone begins "The Girdle Story," eyes frantically signaling the collision with prose like a house on fire. What a town!

In *From Natchez to Mobile,* Dolores Délire has pertinent things to say to the actor—someone who was once called "the right answer to George Brent"—who plays the hoary poet Robert Frost. The scene takes place with the principals over steaming earthenware bowls of bavette de boeuf sauce chasseur, and in it, la Délire, playing the racy Parisienne, Mlle Froufrou, opens her *la chemise de nuit,* exposes her generous and shapely *sequins,* and peremptorily enacts a *tableau vivant* rooted in a detail from the faux-Fauve painting *Fruits and Dross.* It is widely agreed that this scene is a landmark in postwar cinema. Frost, his white "mane" streaming in the "wind," returns to his garret, kills his hired man, and in an orgy of sublimation, composes "Birch My Apples!" The film is now rarely screened, since Fugazy's owns all rights and the directors of the comestibles giant are loath to display foods which, so company attorneys say, are "inimical to our client's traditional menu." Such piddling legalisms and censorious pettifoggery are worthy of the ordinary machinations of Xavier Furcas, a cruel old man, and Whitney Furfur, a much-married earl. Indeed, this pair may well be involved in the wretched enterprise Artistic Suppression. It is in such instances, too, that one almost automatically looks for the hand of Gaap, He Who Makes Insensible, He Who Digs Chicks. It's a good bet that he is entranced by Dolores Délire, even more desirable now that she has the stamp of experience upon her.

"With a quart of Gallo Burgundy in me, do I care if she's fifty-nine?" Gaap smirks. "Though Dolores is but a two-dimensional celluloid icon of postadolescent masculine dreams of domination, penetration, and illicit adventure, this symbol of sexual dread and the ambiguity it confers upon the 'copulative gavotte' is preferable to a sharp stick up your nose."

Gaap delivers this last phrase with a perfectly straight "face." So it may be seen to what lengths Gaap will go in order to carry out his program.

What program?

Something about a general debacle.

Despite having been trapped in Gallup for many years, where he felt constrained to instruct the rustics in the lore of the Cult of Gamygyn, to wit, "post few bills," Dexter Gapoine finds, upon his return home, that things in the little village of Misty Crag are about the same as they were during his formative years there, when he larked about with lynx and tambourine, hey nonny-nonny-no! The short-skirted waitresses, "slaves to fashion," as they are called in Stan's Tavern by the out-of-work, almost-but-not-quite-defeated customers, still gambol on the outdoor terrace of the venison hangout, The Garden of Earthly Delights, and the gossip, as always, is about the little town's favorite son, Craig Garf, who went to the big dazzling city and wrote a play, or so it seems. Craig still lives amid the ceaseless pistonings of the thunderous dynamo wherein restless lives beat ever faster, or so runs the good-natured chitchat. "Well, that's art for you," Albert "Hap" Garrett remarks to Dexter, as they gaze past a vista of redundant brambles to the hulking mountains brooding in the east. Or south, depending on the direction in which "the buddies" face. "Hap" is a lighthearted bozo, and because of his uncanny resemblance to the town's demented lighthouse keeper, now retired, who harmlessly if obscenely signals to the café's notorious waitresses, is called, on those festive occasions when spirits soar with the mill's afternoon whistle, "Paco" or, sometimes, "Allie." "Hap," not surprisingly, has a continuing interest in the arts, as witness his carefully selected comment. Yet Berta Garrett, his once-beauteous wife, a glowing spitfire of a peppery woman, neither hears him nor notices the leer with which he appraises the stunning blond who just now stumbles on high heels toward the trio of old friends lounging at the edge of town. Berta is struggling nowadays with an encroaching quiescence not unlike embarrassing jock itch.

"Hi!" the stunning blond says. "I'm Karen Gash! Although I no longer cut the fine figure I once did when ambling down the aisles of mighty jetliners in which I earned an honest salary amid the cumulus, now I'm back on the confused streets of divers favorite metropolitan centers, and I cut a rather remarkable figure when I *thereon* amble. That's why I seem, despite steady losses, to élan so nicely!"

Brambles approach her outstanding legs hesitantly, then fall back into their characteristic stupor before flattening themselves against the far horizon. The three friends are not aware that Karen knows that Barry Gatto is Baylor Freeq's real name, and that he still tunes pianos. Annie Flammard knows, of course. And she has the photographs to prove it! So it is clear that Fred, insofar as his research is concerned, would be better off here than in François of Fargo's, where he is, even now, saying to the Frankenstein girls, "I fear that I tend to ridicule everything with what amounts, I suppose, to precious condescension. Can you forgive me?" The girls think that he is, as they might put it, a scream. "Open your fly, you old geezer," they giggle in unison bold. They have attractive smiles and are, on closer inspection, seen to be quite tidy. Meanwhile, the four pastoral figures stand glumly transfixed before the thought of the café's menu. For it is August, the deer-bloat season.

Looking up at last, after hours of dazed reading, from the worn and foxed copy of *Géométrie descriptive* on his desk, George, who for years made a decent if precarious living as an orgy photographer, realizes that nothing, absolutely nothing of the classic text has been absorbed by his reluctant brain. We should here note that Arthur Rimbaud, disgusted with Jack Armstrong's venture into letters, a short story which takes place in a bowling alley, is now wandering about, not exactly sure of where he is. The poet quickly realizes that George is reading a book dear to his heart, and a tear comes to his *l'oeil* as he remembers the letter to his family in which he wrote, "Envoyez-moi *Les Constructions métalliques,*" a companion volume by the same author. Filled with disdain at George's obviously desultory studies, he says aloud, "Ce peuple est inspiré par la fièvre et le cancer." George looks up but sees nothing, of course. Then he looks out the window at the abandoned Chevrolet which makes this ugly street into a "bulwark of perfection." He hears Georgene's key in the door and turns back to his book, a practiced look of expectant curiosity and unabated delight on his face.

"Whoosh!" Georgene exclaims, putting a bag of groceries down somewhere, perhaps on a table, chair, or counter. Or a credenza. "I'll tell you one thing, Georgie, it's too damn hot to wear this old fuchsia suit! And it's out of style and too *tight.* I got a lot of clearly insulting looks over at Rudy's, as well as some compassionate glances."

"Well, *I* like how your attractive gozos are thrown into—how shall I say?—*relief* by that suit," George smiles. "Shit on the people at Rudy's, they don't pay the bills, dear."

"With all due respect, darling," Georgene says, throwing herself into a chair in an unladylike manner, the better to gaze distractedly at the Chevrolet, "neither do you. My mother is beginning to refer to you as George the Polack III, after the blind cripple who used to sing for loose change in the good old days of her lamentable youth."

"Ha! Ha!" George laughs, slapping the rude wooden table with his calloused palm. "That's darned good!" Yet there is a fleeting but perceptible imago of resentment beneath the bonhomie on his ruined mask of a face. "Your mother always reminds me of my old partner, Georgette. Do you remember her?"

"The one who did the original watercolors for that children's book. I *knew* you'd bring her up. You never miss an opportunity to annoy me, do you? First it's the old suits so that everybody can see my *jayumbos,* now it's that bitch!"

"No!" George laughs again, and rather heartily. "Not *that* Georgette, the *other* Georgette."

"What 'other' Georgette?" Georgene asks. Her face is a mask of barely repressed insouciance gone wild.

"Oh, bosh!" George replies. "I'm really not up to this conversation *again,* sweetheart." He smiles, his teeth falsely lambent in the sudden gloom.

A strained silence fills the little apartment, broken only by the soft ticking of the clock, which has, yet again, appeared. A few far-off shouts in the street, also, are heard. Georgene wonders if she should tell George about Getting the Most out of Your Leotard, a really great course that she's begun at the Y. But with his fixed ideas on fuchsia, lavender, pink, and dusty rose so recently in the troubled foreground of their marriage, she decides to put it off until a better time.

"How's the book?" she says at last, flagrantly kicking off her "things." "Compelling? Or merely fashionably obscurantist?"

"I know, darling, that you really *mean* well," George says, "and I do feel a certain sympathy for you. But despite your good intentions, I don't want this kind of forced intimacy."

"Have it your way," Georgene says, rising so as to give George a tantalizing look at her nummo. At the door, she pauses and turns, in time-honored fashion. "By the way, I ran into *Gig* today. He said to give you his *best regards.*"

Her silvery laughter grows, as it must, progressively fainter as she proceeds down the hallway, since she does not raise the volume of her laughter the farther she gets from the door. We speak, of course, of her laughter in regard to George's position, which, for the duration of her departure, remains fixed. His face a rigid domino of ill-concealed ire, George begins to tear the pages from *Géométrie descriptive.* "Frogs and math—what a combination," he mutters. Then, unable to control his rage any longer, he rushes to the bathroom, where Georgene is, perhaps, freshening up.

"So you saw Gig!" George shouts through the door. "So? What did he say? What *does* he think of my schlong?" He listens to the sound of, probably, water running into the tub, and then, her voice heavy with recrimination, Georgene says, "He said he thinks it can be amusing and even funny in a waggish way."

George reacts as if, as they say, struck. As if in the face. He is as if rooted to the spot. So much for this afternoon's trip to Gimbels. And the guys in Dress Rite are all dead!

Gin City, a sculpture which is now usually attributed to Annie Flammard, has a history of ownership the details of which have to do with the curse of glossolalia. At present, Annie is smoking the last of a pack of Gitanes, a morale-booster designed to strengthen her for her look into the envelope where she keeps her cash. There is no cash, and Annie knows this. She seems rather distracted and a little dowdy, the result, perhaps, of life, coupled with the unwanted biweekly visits of a clubfooted man whose wheezing outside her door is always followed by his demand—never acceded to—that she tell him the secret of the "yellowed newspaper." Annie unfailingly sits in silence, and waits for him to go away. She knows nothing of Maureen Cullinan's "athletic tricks," either, another of her visitor's subjects of inquiry. After a time, the clump and swish of the desperate man's unspeakable foot moves away down the hall, and she relaxes, but awaits his inevitable parting sally: "A sense of humor, for Christ's sake, is no bar to advancement, you unfriendly bitch!" On this particular morning, the gimp is almost banjaxed in the street by the rushing figure of Glasyalabolas, the Murderer, summoned by the Lard Goddess to punish the woman who currently impersonates her. Glasyalabolas, who has no sense of direction, soon finds himself not in Agapa, but in a neighboring town, Gnatville. He promptly joins a barbecue-in-progress.

". . . badly burned *chicken* for God's sake . . . Stekel and *whose* boots? . . . and only vegetables you say . . . charming old jalopy . . . could eat you in that white dress . . . needs refueling . . . perverted rock stars' what? . . . in the *fucking* chicken coop yes . . . then the refurbished pillow . . . Oaky Doaks? . . . a *frisson* of icy terror . . ."

Glasyalabolas soon determines that the counterfeit Lard Goddess is not located in this burg, but decides to linger. A young woman, who introduces herself as what his demonic ears take to be "Saybuddy," is wearing a short, tight, crocheted dress which, as Viña Delmar might say, leaves little to the imagination. The striking young woman is going on about a wonderful club, really hip, really fun, called the Gold Coast Bar and Grill. "Kind of a boîte," she says, getting very close to the infernal visitor, who can't help but wonder what she'd do if she were to see him as the winged dog whose form he usually favors. "What do you say we go tonight?" she smiles, coquettishly waving an incredibly charred chicken leg at him. Well, as coquettishly as possible, considering. Glasyalabolas, who is slightly deficient in the art of small talk, and ignorant of flirtation, replies, "I teach all arts and sciences simultaneously, incite to bloodshed, am the leader of all homicides, discern past and future, and make men invisible." He beams, more or less, at her, and she is a little surprised at the size of his canine teeth. "You are really a cute guy," she titters while mincing. Then she lowers her eyes, raises them, and licks her lips. Glasyalabolas, unable to interpret these signs in a civilized manner, frees a monstrous red phallus from the constraint of his seersucker trousers, and at the same time reaches a hand, on which the wiry hairs are crackling with blue fire, toward the young woman. So much for this jovial gathering.

The Gold Coast Bar and Grill is a joint on the Brooklyn waterfront. Once frequented by stevedores, longshoremen, and merchant sailors, it is now a chic watering place for people with little time and too much money, a murderous combination. They delight in the atmosphere, rigorously preserved, and the nightly entertainment, always of minimal talent. The patrons think of this entertainment as camp, and are thus ennobled in their lives. It doesn't take much. The current entertainment comprises two acts: the Gold Dust Twins, who bear an uncanny resemblance to Barry Gatto and Annie Flammard; and their "opener," a skinny, middle-aged woman, her face leathery from the sun, in a fifties-style puce cocktail dress. The Gold Dust Twins specialize in dramatic readings from little-known plays, and at present are offering scenes from *'Tis Ruth the Whore's Dead,* by Thomas Ballantyne. To give you an idea:

CAZZO (*discovered alone*):

> Now dread varlets hold the welkin dear,
> Wherein doth, marry, phials incarnadine
> Fume so that a king may felter'd be;
> Yet all the glories of that drear assemblage
> Lack physick and the puling of a maid
> Whose mincing mows pricketh th' ebon Saracen!
> Meet that, an't be a shining poniard
> Pluck'd from the massy comet that dread Jupiter,
> Blanch'd ere he wrapp'd his corse in finest lawn,
> Shall grin the bony skull whence fled the fiend.
> But soft! Keep venoms sealed up tight,
> 'Twas ne'er a lady pecked at asp so bright.

PUTTANA (*entering*):

> Yet methinks sweet Cazzo in his license
> Vents our news of most strange things, that, seconded,
> 'Twill be brutish to th' extreme of unguento.
> Still, his ducket and this blizzardy wet look
> Belike unto an apeish picture out o' wax
> Do crown the common bawds and ruffianos.
>   (*To* CAZZO):
> How now, my lord? Doth blood run pure as babes
> In the painted honours of dissembling coins?
> Or doth my breast, blue as the spicy carbuncle
> That prov'd a pomegranate of worse favour
> Drop, as it must, thou know'st, unto chill sooth?

My soul, as the curious lizard of far jousts,
Blinds my womanish nature like the frighted whelp,
And speeds me to a doom of mummery.
   (*Dies.*)

Miss Golden Delicious, the aforementioned opener, warms up the customers by showing slides of the Golden Gate Bridge, Construction of; Repairs to; Renovations undertaken of; Calculations concerning; Romance of; Legends about; Suicides off; Moods of; etc., etc. These arresting photographs, many *in full color,* are accompanied by Miss Delicious's enthusiastic, if unlearned commentary. Nevertheless, in the last few months, surprise raids on the boîte have been carried out by the more radical members of the Golden Rose Fellowship, the action wing of the Immaculata Syndicate, a group dedicated to the eradication of public and private restrooms. The organization feels, as its literature indicates, that the restroom is an "area in which men and women" alike "loosen, open, and dishevel" their various "garments" and in the process "expose" themselves, this "activity leading to sin or thoughts of sin." The "Goldie" chant, chilling to many, is well-known throughout the city, and illustrated copies of its verses are currently on view at the Gom Gallery in its controversial "Corners of the City" exhibition. One chorus, especially, has caught the public's fancy:

> *Chorus:*   Oh Jesus sweet and fine,
> Oh Jesus strong and pure,
> Oh Jesus so sublime,
> Oh Jesus will you cure
>   These sinners who should burn in hell?
>
> *Response:* Sure!

It may be obvious that the city is no longer the one that Zuleika Dobson tells us of in *The Goiter Story,* lines 116-72, despite its electric atmosphere, vital people, and numerous interesting activities, many free of charge. Still, no one, as thousands regularly point out (indicates gesturing crowds), can "know its heart."

Lincoln Gom, whose hair has turned to silver, yet they love him just the same, admires his pictures as he does whenever he has a moment. He can almost hear them appreciating before his eyes, or ears, and both organs, though not as gosh-darn attractive as they once were, are still sharp. He is especially delighted with himself today because a piece in the newspaper on the "downtown art scene," which you've all read before, has a flattering reference to him as a "shrewd connoisseur" in the "ecology of the thriving new art world." Odd how ecology, in all of its vainglorious manifestations, has always been a big part of Lincoln's life. He's elegantly dressed today, for "lounging." He takes another survey of his pictures, which he calls "holdings," among the more valuable of which are *Connecticut Condo, Silver Mercedes, A Cool Million, Vintage Port, Fake Diner, I Want It All, Trump, Studio Apt. $3000, More Skyscrapers,* and his favorite, *Koch's Paradise.* He sighs, and makes a mental note to read more poetry like the one about killing men rather than hawks. Hawks! He used to read a good deal of poetry until, well. There's something wonderful about how it makes order out of chaos, kind of like real-estate deals, and he needs a little order in his frenetic life of gathering. He cannot "lounge" for *too* long, not with all the sharks in the water. Sharks!

"Babs" Gonzales, who occasionally travels under the name "Boobs" Consundays, tired of reading Mrs. Browning, who can be tiresome indeed in her amazed mode, "marches" into The Good Company to return her "Cute Cop" outfit, piqued because "Muffin" is currently featured as the model for this costume in the latest issue of *Cults and Coteries.* Of all people, "Muffin"! She must be forty-five if she's a day, the bitch, and she's running to Anglo wrinkles.

So much for sisterhood.

"I don't much like these holester," she says to the man behind the counter. He is a *bored salesclerk.*

A little verisimilitude to truly depict life in our time so that it's as if we're living it ourselves instead of other people pretending to live it for us but in such a way that it is not quite believable.

Check.

"In what way don't you like these holester?" the *bored salesclerk* says mockingly.

"It is bumping me in the wrong personal intimate place, coño," "Babs" says. "Makes the bruises."

"I'm afraid, Madam," he says, *yawning elaborately,* "that we can neither take in exchange nor accept for refund any costume that has been, uh, worn. Your best alternative would be to go to a Good Will and donate it for a tax deduction."

"Can I change these holester maybe, only? For a peg leg?"

"I'm afraid not, Madam," the clerk says, *studying his fingernails.* "That peg leg is part of our new Long John Silver ensemble and cannot be sold separately."

"Babs" walks out, cursing Michael Cullinan under her breath. He's the one who really objects to the holester! She doesn't really give a damn about it. "Muffin" makes the costume odious, anyway. What she needs is a double Gordon's gin, no ice, and so she enters a dim saloon, the Gotham, and puts her shopping bag on the bar.

An epiphany from *Treasure Island:*

"Har, har, Jim!" Long John Silver laughed, his salty earring trembling as if schooner-rigged. "Keelhaul me if I don't be struck blind as Pew! H'isted in a wicker basket, ye say? Har, har!"

The boys, exhausted by their courageous climb, sat across from each other in the rear of the little country inn, its rough-hewn pine walls sending forth a rich, spicy aroma of aging splinters that soothed their spirits. The day had brought its share of agonizing worries to the hearty chums. Taking a long swallow of his refreshing beverage, Dick Witherspoon vigorously banged his glass down on the crude wooden table, and laughed joyously.

"Well, old man," he said to Buddy, "I 'spect we won't be reaching Misty Crag *this* evening," he opined. "Might's well batten down here for the night."

"I'm afraid you're correct, Dick, as is sometimes the case," Buddy confessed, his cheeks peculiarly flushed. "And yet that priest, Father Graham, seemed a regular sort, despite his suspicious complexion, ruined compass, and odious religious beliefs." Buddy set his jaw with perplexed vim.

" 'Pears he took us for a brace of yokels, Buddy," Dick nodded. "I thought for certain that we'd be hallooing on the dangerous crags long 'fore now. Maybe even scaring up some chuck food and c'lecting dead wood for the fire. I pondered something was mighty odd when the Romish galoot told us to foller that bear trail." Dick raised his schooner to his smiling lips.

"Had I but paid heed to my father's woodland tips," Buddy said softly, his eyes bright with the memory of old Mr. Buddy's plaid mackinaw, "now gathered, at last, under the title *A Grain of Salt*—and how good it is that we now have them all together—we would certainly have directed ourselves toward the sought-for crag. By means of moss-growth. And other such lore."

"Well, my friend," Dick replied, retying his colorful habanera with a flourish, "there's no use to spoiling the milk now. Let's wrestle some hot grub and bed down."

At that moment, a young lady, her dark eyes glowing with health, walked into the inn and sat, her nether limbs modestly crossed, at the long bar. Buddy and Dick, with an exhibition of youthful pluck, leaped onto their chairs and stood respectfully thereon, watching her drink a large tumbler of gin, neat.

"She must be dusty of throat," Dick remarked, "like the little pals we left behind."

"Indeed," Buddy whispered admiringly, "although she does seem too much disposed toward strong spirits, yet there is something refined about her carriage, something naturally superior in her bearing. I would not be at all surprised to learn that she occupies a position of some importance and responsibility in the business community."

"There sure isn't nothing of the dago about her," Dick commented, and then, jumping lightly to the floor, he continued. "Say, Buddy, do you remember the strapping feller who used to join us on those occasions when we held our feral clambakes?"

"Indeed I do!" Buddy replied clippedly. "Dick Grande was the lad's name, I believe. A tall boy, slightly but not unpleasantly hirsute." He quickly joined Dick on the floor, and stood, a slight smile of nostalgia on his sculptured lips. "But why do you inquire?" Buddy continued, an expression of hesitant longing rippling across his chiseled features.

"Well," Dick said, biting his lips together one at a time, "do you remember his sister?"

If Buddy remembered anything of his fifteen years on this terrestrial globe, it was the beautiful coquette, Jeannette Grande. She had, on more than one occasion, made him doubt the advice on personal hygiene given in his weathered *Handbook for Lutherans.* Beaming jovially, he bounded again onto his chair so as to gaze at the young woman at the bar.

"Well?" Dick cried anxiously. "Is she . . . ?"

But Buddy, with a cry of pure brawn, had fallen heavily from his chair into his comrade's arms, his eyes rolling nervously about. The young woman had gone, and at the place where she had been lately sitting, there lay a bulky shopping bag, and, pinned to it, a letter on daintily scalloped, lilac-hued stationery. There would be, Dick Witherspoon guessed, as he smoothly laid Buddy's insipid head on a nearby dado, no meatball sandwiches for them tonight!

Although the wind seems about to blow up, and the trees on their quiet street threaten to sough at any moment, a lady of unchaste proclivities, Edith Granger, stern in the cruel, iron-ribbed foundation garment that is "doing its job" beneath her purposeful tweeds, and her newfound friend, Lady Granjon, are putting the finishing touches on their amusing ad. Not to reveal the verbatim copy of what the ladies consider an "appeal," it may be noted that the message contains promises of mutually enlightening cross-dressing, mirror larks, Greek interludes, *tableaux vivants,* discipline *à la* the Greengage School, and stimulating episodes featuring cooking oil and Green Goddess salad dressing. "It has to be good for *something!*" Lady Granjon quietly jokes of the last. There is also a reference to a Greenwich Village masque, depending, and quite properly so, on the weather. So they continue to polish their verbiage as carefully as Mamie Morsett polishes her clam poems; perhaps more carefully, since so much more is at stake.

Then too: Richard Gross, Bart., Will Return to Prison, D.A. Says; Author Claims *Growing Dark* Basis for *Dark Victory* Screenplay; Swiss Tourist Board Admits Gstaad Does Not Exist; "The Guards" to Take Acting Classes; John Crowe Ransom "Secret Structuralist," Eloise Stephanie Gump Reveals; Russell Gunge, Inventor of Insolent Pompadour, Dead at 87; *Guns in Action* May Hire Michelle Caccatanto as Cultural Editor.

Gusion, the Duke of Those Who Discern, is sent to rescue Glasyalabolas from the barbecue, which the ingenuous sprite, as one might have guessed, has reduced to a shambles, the exact nature of which will be discreetly passed over in silence.

"Are you crazy?" Gusion says, mucking through broken glass and Christ knows what else. "You're *supposed* to be looking for the counterfeit Lard Goddess, so that we may send storms of flies and lice, fire, and poisonous winds against her. You are *not* supposed to be wreaking havoc on these professional persons here (indicates clusters of abandoned barbecuers) strewn about. I'm going to have to put this *faux pas* in my report."

"What does 'cute' mean?" Glasyalabolas asks.

"You haven't heard one word, have you? Let us go and find Agapa," Gusion says, levitating slightly.

"All right. Say, how come you don't look like some big fido-head today?"

"*Here?*" Gusion shakes his head at such a display of naïveté.

The two slowly fly off, scattering bits of garbage and carrion, and marveling at the bodies writhing in various pleasant combinations on the emerald lawn below. Slabs and gobbets of dead animals send up thin plumes of smoke.

Eddy Beshary definitely decides to buy the lissome yet muscular Berthe a drawing by Philip Guston, if the charming maid promises to stop walloping the unfortunate tourists who sometimes surprise him amid the flowering shrubs.

"Who?" Berthe asks suspiciously.

"Never mind on it," Beshary says, hanging up rudely on a mogul. "Suffice it to proclaim that it is of a pulchritude to emboggle the mind's eye. It also promises seriously to attain monetary values sufficient to enable you the ability to purchase plethorous ruffly aprons and bewitching caps when old age shall reft your earning powers from off of you."

"So you say," Berthe replies. "I'll ask 'Guts,' the savvy bartender, about this guy before I promise to play the coward or the regular guy 'mid the blowing foliage, you'll pardon the expression."

"As you wish, my enchantress of a fellow," Beshary smiles. "Now, if you will permit me to create an excuse, I must open a deal on the telephone which waits obiediently on this cheap wicker table."

Berthe pushes wisps of silken hair under his bewitching cap. What he doesn't know is that "Guts" is about to throw up his job at the hotel bar, for he is in possession, by means of a delicate ruse, of a rare bibliophilic item, *Gusty Ghetto Tales.* This famous anthology, on which all others of its genre are modeled, is actually entitled *Gutsy Ghetto Tales.* The misprinted item, which contains the error on its spine, half-title page, part-title page, full-title page, and in the running heads throughout, is but one of a rumored seventeen in existence. In his delight, "Guts," in defiance of hotel rules, mixes himself a celebratory Banana Amaze, "the drink that made Bermuda laugh." The heretofore secret recipe follows:

Banana Amaze

1½ ozs. Gypsy Rose wine
1 oz. banana absinthe
½ oz. mastiachi pepper extract
   Shake well with cracked ice and strain into a frosted cocktail glass. Decorate with two thin rounds of ripe banana and a sprig of pink brilliantine.

"Guts" takes a sip, rolls his eyes, and grins. To the bar at large, he proclaims, "*Habits and Wimples* has nothing on this, despite its clear and complete index and exemplary notes."
   Habits and Wimples?
   The, ah, reference is obscure. But that's just like "Guts."

The Bluebird Inn, a small roadhouse specializing in fox-trot contests, lies just outside Hackettstown on the road to Budd Lake. It may well be the "little country inn" in which Dick and Buddy are playing yet another scene in the mundane drama of their prescribed, yet fully eustachian lives. Did they only know it, Misty Crag is but a two-hour walk from the inn. But they are confused, and Buddy is still only semiconscious. The possibility that they may not reach the somber heights today is very real. Their predicament is made even more complex by their map of the area, for it shows Hackettstown as Haddam Neck. This transmutation may be the work of Hagenti, Maker of Gold, sometimes, because of his penchant for pranks, called "the Halloween Kid," and his vicious thug of a comrade, Halpas, Burner of Cities, who likes to go by the name of "Hans," a kind of acknowledgment made to his old Nazi pals. But why they should decide to toy with the map used by Buddy and Dick is an unanswerable question. It may not even be a proper question, and, besides, Halpas does not take kindly to interrogation.

Eleanor Harding, whom the years have made no less depraved, puts her signature to a letter written to a certain Harlan, a man who is invariably described as "a train passenger." He is, coincidentally, on a train at this moment, passing through the environs of the real Haddam Neck, hoping against hope, as they say, to catch a glimpse of a startlingly attractive young woman who occasionally used to be found sitting on a flat rock in the open field which abuts the tracks. Eleanor's letter has to do with her special program of "good reading, intelligent discussion, judicious exercise, and the employment of a time-honored and infallible love philtre obtainable, at great cost, from a pepper that grows in the gardens of Greenpoint." You won't be far off the mark if you guess that Eleanor, in her middle age, is reduced to varied confidence games, and that Harlan is her latest mark. Harlan believes that some one of Eleanor's programs can bring him into friendly intercourse with the girl in the field, even though she exists only in his imagination. This Harlan, by the by, is nothing to Joanne Jeanne Judith "Bunny," since the latter's maiden name is *not* Harlan. This is old information to veteran investigators, yet it never hurts to insist on the facts. Neither does he have anything to do with Lady Harlan and Lord Harlan, the former a mysterious Frenchwoman implicated in the international scandal known as "the girdle story," and the latter an ineffectual, but sweet, bumbler. And he would be shocked, and rightly so, to be associated, even peripherally, with the Mr. Harlan who has an unspeakable affliction, which, in tandem with a mind-numbing suit, he exploits so as to be able to raise the dead, create typhoons, catch the falling stars, and make the oceans boil, and who intimidates all those with whom he comes into contact. This sinister cripple, or as he prefers to be described nowadays, this walking-impaired gentleman, is not, in fact, "Mr." Harlan at all, Harlan being his given name. As Harlan looks out the window of the train in fruitless search for the nonexistent girl, "Mr." Harlan is heard to shout ". . . advancement, you unfriendly bitch!" The train clatters past the field and Harlan returns to his book, but the back of the head belonging to the man in the seat just in front of him stops him cold. There's something about it that gives him a strange chill.

"I call this automatic writing," Florence Claire says smugly. As we know, Florence is pretty dumb. "Right!" say experts.

Anton Harley cannot believe that his ex-wife's phone is still busy, but there's the manic buzzing! He hangs up and dials again, for the seventeenth time. She's taken the phone off the hook, that's for sure, and all he wants is to arrange to pick up some things of his that he knows are in her goddamned kitchen drawer. He's entitled to them. They have certain, ah, certain *redemptive* qualities. Is this too much to ask? What else does he have after all these years of marriage and separation? A bleeding ulcer, gout, emphysema, colitis, ormolu, and pyorrhea. He calls again, no use, and then he sits to look over the list—a short list, for Christ's sake!—of the items he wants, the items he *needs:* six corkopeners, a beer-can coaster, an amazing banana, a photograph of a novelty garter, a picture of three young girls in pale blue ruffled satin, the recipe for wickless candles, a list of recent immediate classics, a chart showing the narrative line and plot development of *A Clubfooted Man,* some red glass stirring rods, and Viña Bad's *Delmar Collection Girl.* He calls again and yells incoherently into the busy signal. Antonia Harley is indeed there, and, as Anton guesses, the phone is off the hook. She doesn't feel too good today, the faded scars from her numerous pig bites are troublesome in the oppressive humidity. But she is busy! What else should she be doing but throwing away those things which she knows that Anton wants, the old bastard! Into a paper bag she puts a spool, a novelty basketball made so as to be confusing, corkscrew tape, three self-indulgent novels about sheiks, and a masking condom. It is obvious that the Harleys have, even now, no understanding of each other.

"Is fonny thing in draw she keeps," Frieda Canula says.

There seems to be no way to stop Frieda from roaming. Lucky for her!

By the way, one question: Is Lady Harley identical with Lady Harlan, the mysterious Frenchwoman?

Glad you asked. No, Lady Harlan is often called Lady Harley by people of malicious intent, the purpose of this misnomer being to ally, in what we like to call "the popular mind," Lady Harlan with a woman, well, with Antonia, who is whispered of as the "Pig Lady." Lady Harlan is, of course, above all this pettiness.

A correction: Harris tweed is not manufactured in Hartford, Connecticut, as noted on page 37, but in Hazie, Scotland, a small town in the Outer Hebrides, covered to a depth of some thirty-one feet throughout the brief, dazzling autumns of those parts with great mounds of purple gorse and rainbow heather. "The Heart Is Lo-onely," a haunting folk song popular some forty years ago, is, perhaps, the most famous of all the many panegyrics to Hazie's unearthly fall beauty. The chorus in which this seasonal enchantment is memorialized runs:

> Hazie, wi' your parple garse,
> Hazie, wi' your rannboo hitherr,
> It is the baywitchin' fall
> Tha' carts the bonny witherr
> So lak the braw bricht Harris tweed
> Tha' stands so tall.

Florence Claire, exhausted from her critical labors, dips into *Heavy Machinery,* a recently reissued novel, one highly recommended by her friend, Buddy Cioppetini, who is just about to run amok, like an eye rolling wildly in its frantic socket. But *Heavy Machinery* bores her with its bullying tone and obdurate blankness. She jots "obdurate blankness" down in her notebook, a neat little item in mottled shenango. The novel is unintelligible to her, so much so that it might as well be written in Hebrew. "In Hebrew," she writes, or jots. Well, there's time enough to wonder at Buddy's enthusiasm for the obdurately Hebrew blankness of the work, but for now, Florence needs a few pages of John Crowe Ransom to soothe her raging chancre, picked up, doubtlessly, from the toilet seat in Rudy's Superette, whence all dread diseases flow.

"You bet," Heff, a barber, comments. "Rudy's—witness my pal Blast's indictment earlier today—is, indeed, a pigpen." His voice falters, cracks, then ceases at last!

"I agree with my brother, Heff," Hefty, a barber, chuckles. "Rudy, even in this era of enlightened health habits and nourishing foods, seems to place little credence in the idea that craftsmanship is more important than speed or handsome profits."

"Here, here! And hear, hear! as well," Heff enthuses.

Our problem with these brothers is that we know for a fact that they are being paid what Thomas Holly Chivers once called "a tidy sum" by the Bleecker Street store of Village Victuals to denigrate Rudy's and Crown SuperMart. The owner of the Village Victuals chain is the irrepressible tycoon Baby Brownie, "the Mayonnaise King" of the food world. The story of Baby and his adopted son Balte's mania, gives this sobriquet a savage yet enthralling piquancy, an aura of what Hegel terms *das geistige Thierreich.* Yet Hegel, as always, is not the sort who desires a *forced* intimacy. For instance, everyone knows the story that he purportedly told Heidegger during one of their innumerable chats on the greensward. He mentioned Keats, Chapman, and rock and roll with what all biographers term a "dazzling insouciance." Perhaps most indicative of his relaxed attitude toward the camaraderie of philosophy is discoverable in the fact that the end of the story, "a lolling Stone slathers no boss," was delivered in flawless, unaccented English. To his credit, Heidegger, rather than exhibiting the rage one might expect at being victimized by Hegel's "lust for punning," smiled sweetly, and said, "This story, Georg, is proof of your affection for me and my ideas, strange as they may be. It is, in fact, what our good friend, Heine, somewhere calls 'a garter of thy love.' " So the two thinkers laughed and talked into the small hours, swatting mosquitoes, their meerschaums fuming without surcease.

"Hi! I'm Karen Heineken! When I'm zooming through the atmosphere I wear pale beige pantyhose, with just a *wisp* of control, under my flattering yet dignified uniform, but later, lounging in tastefully appointed apartments from which the lights of swell cities can be observed to flash, and some glitter, I favor suggestive black net hosiery held up by pale blue garters of ruffled satin to please my highly intelligent electronic-realty wizard of a fella. Hi!"

Helen and Troy's café, close nestled under the looming cragginess of Mystery Mountain, is the scene this day of tension and heartbreak.

Helen and her husband, Troy, for whom the café is named—although they originally planned to call the place Harry and Mary's for its chic— have been distressed of late to learn that their only daughter, Helene, is the subject of an alarmingly frank lesbian poem, "To Helene in Hell," a work which deconstructs the very notion of the normal American-café ethic. After weeks of tears, threats, and recriminations, this afternoon finds Helene, after a long search, sobbing quietly in her chintz-covered bedroom as she packs her bags. With hope and fear combined, she is leaving home! Outside, the soft summer wind blows the yellow crenellate into a sea of nervously sparkling gold. In the silence, broken only by her sobs and an occasional hawking-up of phlegm, Helene can hear the hum of traffic on the distant highway. "So it's always been," she thinks, "and so it will thus be, for always." She lays her cherished videocassette of *Hellions in Hosiery* atop a small pile of patched yet immaculate lingerie. The hum of traffic grows louder. "But why?" she thinks. Outside, by the crude wooden table beneath the ancient elm, Troy is mechanically pitching horseshoes, his face a mask of grief and rage, a bottle of Jax beer held in his mouth at a jaunty, yet somehow pitiable angle. Helen is in the kitchen, cleaning crimps for supper. All is normal, all is as it is every day, and yet. . . . Helene, who has realized—with a clarity so intense as to be well-nigh incommunicable to her bewildered parents—that her sexuality, her gender, her very nummo is a political act, something like the Tennis Court Oath, is leaving, despite all! Now the hum of traffic seems to be just outside her door of innocent chenille, and she raises her head, knowing in her heart's deepest recesses that the hum is a message: She is a *woman.* Troy, sensing the pain of defeat, defeat and loss, brains a passing Guernsey with a horseshoe and decides to call it a day. His voice thick with repressed sorrow, he shouts an oath at the stunned cow, who reels, with almost unbearable irony, into Helene's own little patch of bitter vetch. Helene suddenly appears on the porch, her bags in hand, and as she smiles wanly at her father, he throws his forearm across his streaming eyes. Then the cow falls down.

Jimmy Blackhead is directing the hanging of the painting, popularly known for many years now as *Hell Mouth,* on the rear wall of the Black Basement's dining room. Jimmy doesn't know nor would he be pleased to discover that this painting is a flawlessly rendered copy of the original. Hem, the foreman, takes orders from Jimmy and passes them on to two workmen who are struggling with the large canvas. There's something strangely unsettling about it. "This is the finishing touch!" Jimmy says. It is possible that like the painting and the Black Basement itself, Jimmy is a replica of the original owner of the original club, but there is no evidence to support this conjecture. Which is often the case, as Heidegger knows. In any event, this Jimmy Blackhead looks like the Jimmy Blackhead that we *do* know, even though he's changed his name from Caponegro. Hem is Hem, absolutely. Look at that fedora! Look at those overalls! Look at that cold cigar clamped between his teeth! We've seen *him* before, plenty. Now the painting is successfully hung, and with the vast space of the white wall behind it and the perfect lighting evoking its every nuance, *Hell Mouth* looks even better than *Hell Mouth.* This will be one sweetheart of an opening night. "Nice work, guys," Jimmy says, in Jimmy's voice. Oh, this surely must be Jimmy. Look at that tie! There's something strangely unsettling about its odd, almost eerie shade of blue.

Lou Henry, having arisen late, is now searching carelessly and un-methodically for his mascara, his tea, his hat, his eye shadow, and his knife. It looks as if his smile is just *beaming,* but close observation reveals that this smile is but an involuntary rictus. This must be something recent, some currently entertained and quirky manifestation of his middle-aged loneliness, of his aimlessness. There is no football, of course, so that's out. Besides, the fucking hole of a room has a TV set that gets only one PBS channel. He comes across a photograph of a woman standing by his old car, and holds it up to the light. In her shift dress, which is probably white, she seems familiar. And here's another photograph, of a man looking directly at the camera with a demandingly inquisitive expression on his face. Lou feels uncomfortable, and begins to sing, off-key. Where is the knife? Where is the mascara? Where is anything? And anybody? He sits in a sprung armchair and looks out the window at the window across the airshaft, but the young woman who sometimes comes to the window in her peach slip to wave at him isn't there. He slept too late. "Where's my tea?" he asks the airshaft. The picture of the woman next to the car intrigues him and he gets up to look at it again. Maybe it's someone he met once, he used to own a car, of course. But he wants his tea, he wants his knife. He wants his mascara so that he can paint a moustache on his face and think about possibly leaving the room. But he needs his hat, if he paints the moustache on and has no hat to wear, that's no good. He needs his moustache, his hat, dark circles under his eyes, and in his pocket, his knife. Then he can think about possibly going out, the A & P is open pretty late. What kind of dress does the woman have on? It is an old picture. He sits again, and smiles, not a real smile, since close observation, etc., etc., but it will have to do. If he has his moustache, his hat, and so on, and goes out to the store when almost everybody else is gone, no one will really see him, or not many, not too many. And even if they are still out, still shopping, he can take his car! He still needs, surely, his hat, his moustache, and so on, but the car seems to have solved his basic problem of being in the streets. He begins to sing again, off-key. It's a nice dress, modest yet provocative. It's very familiar. Nice car. He did have a car?

Sheila Henry sits on the Coney Island beach near Sea Gate, a curiosity to the crowds in her unfashionable black suit, pearl choker, matching earrings. She adjusts a little close-fitting white hat, decorated with a spray of tiny pearls, slips off a pair of black pumps, and places them side by side on the sand next to her. She likes these shoes, particularly the thin strips of white leather that run around their vamps. How *very* nice, but perhaps too young for her. The heels are a little too high. Her stockings are a misty flesh, a bride's stockings, her legs are beautiful, still. She looks out at the sea, straining to find where the azure of the sky meets that of the water, but there is haze far out where the horizon line should be. She is oblivious to the crowds around her, the noise, smells, heat. Why is she here? Fully dressed? Her clothes are out of fashion, and are somewhat too tight for her, but they are in near-perfect condition. Why? As she sits, her mind begins to tell her things, disquietingly. Oddly. Sheila simply allows this telling to happen, it seems to consist of skewed answers, obliquely given, to unasked questions. Unknown questions. Forgotten questions. The illusion is intense, and she stares fixedly at the sea and listens.

The first name, not so much literary as operatic. While walking on a beach during her unhappy honeymoon, August 14, 1966, she was a stranger to the art of whistling. She liked its name. Films had initiated this action because of their well-known power of suggestion, she did not. She is being confused with someone else, or so it seems, since she never wore these items on any occasion that can be called happy. It gave her a glimpse at the life of the successful adulteress. There is a question as to whether she "always" wore white underwear, the kind that makes men bump into trees and lampposts. Because of the kinship of water and snow, during one of her solitary jaunts through the garish lights and mechanical hilarity of Coney Island. And because she wanted to be thought of as tough and worldly. There is extant a bill of sale for its legitimate purchase. No, she enjoyed pornography of all kinds, Christian or otherwise. No, this observation is to be found in an obscure novel by an author whose name is best forgotten, most certainly! This was too good to be true. It suggested to her that life, though tragic, is also, and more importantly, glamorous. Such a description lacks both acumen and breadth. Only when she ate one, because the first time she ate them was with Yankee pot roast. She knew that academics pretended a lack of interest in television and she wanted to fit in, to get even with Sir Thomas Wyatt for "My galley charged with forgetfulness," a poem which improbably gave her nightmares. She did, when she was faced, for perhaps the hundredth time, with an order of pot stickers. She did, especially when she played the "egg game" with her lovers. It did not. Because of the delicious contrast between the modesty of the dress and the voluptuousness of her figure, she didn't want anybody to know that she had no favorite color. Perhaps a passing mention in the "Books Received" listings of various little magazines. She was not dead, not yet.

Not so much embarrassed or chagrined as irritated at my own naïveté. Between twenty and twenty-five times, because Lou thinks that this book contains the secret of happiness. It is an imagined place, absolutely, yes, and sometimes my annoyance is overt. The lines, "for / you, dark / celluloid fury / of forgot / -ten imagery": I've never been able to figure this out. No, I'm really filled with pity, not always, but almost always. Because that's where Lou first fucked me, it's none of his business. Because it's better than anything he ever wrote. It is not boredom, anxiety, and disgust, in that order. Because the chances are good that we'll get lost, no, since it is an imagined place. No, since that scabrous tale was written by Regina Fury, he does, and, or so I hear, with much embarrassed bluster. The Orchid Boat, Jade Mountain, Yung's Oriental Gardens, and The Three Mandarins, invariably. That he is lost in some strange neighborhood whenever he reads my prose. Very unlikely! When I forget something, he remembers. Mutual masturbation while standing up, often. If you've read her poems you know why I say, "Oh, please!" I have no idea. For the same reasons that lead me to dislike the way he sips his tea. On rare occasions, yes, yes, and he also reminds me of this whenever he eats doughnuts as well. *Buddy and His Boys on Mystery Mountain* is my favorite book, at present. We *are.*

Because I've always liked the name, I don't remember anymore, I can't tell you what goes on in his mind. The name sounds familiar. By telling him that I'm going to spend a weekend with *Finnegans Wake,* I will indeed! Because he'll doubtless be handsome, because she'll sign her name. I don't remember; it's possible; but not probable—all three. Because pale blue flatters my figure, complexion, hair, and eyes, making me more desirable. Malice and a touch of recklessness. To audition for a role as a street-wise rock poet, I'll think, for instance, of "A Hundred Collars." Not only believable, but probable; all the others are locked away. Lost near Mystery Mountain, I'll find my way to the Bluebird, be attracted to that rube because of his resemblance to my image of Buddy, and enter the contest to get away from the bartender, a depraved-looking man with a clubfoot, yes. "Justified" is much too weak a word—pure *malice.* Hysterical laughter. Hands down, "Clarinet Polka" awakens tender memories of a very private nature. That bitch of a whore doesn't know anything *about* me. I will not! It will not exactly be "stealing"; it will happen because of $5,000. I have no idea. Saul Blanche is always *becoming* something; he has no patio garden, which the floor plans of his apartment will show clearly. He will figure that I told them I'd be there, because the book is very much like a mulligan. I won't care and I don't know. Or care.

Then Sheila's mind stops suddenly. She is still staring at the sea. Still. Still as death.

Venetia Herbert, whose "vocational nymphomania" (cf. Radner, *Workplace Oddities*) occasions periods of delirium during which she believes herself to be the great-granddaughter of the beloved composer

Victor Herbert, has a funny feeling. In fact, she is reeling from the shock of having just read Mrs. Banjiejicz's recipe for Poires en Crème, for the directions *do indeed* contain the key words of the lyrics to one of the choruses of her imagined great-grandfather's self-suppressed and long-missing "He's a Voyeur." (See "Aspects of the Ziegfeld Follies" by Elisa Hess; *Greasepaint,* XXII, 11, 1942.) Louis "Slim" "Che" "Luigi" Hess, the saturnine roué and ex-husband of the gorgeous Elisa, sits in an armchair and observes the shock of this intelligence register itself on the obsession-creased face of Venetia, then turns again to a vulgar contemplation of her generous "melons."

"Rings the old bell, don't it, baby?" he says in his untrained yet pleasant alto.

"Good God!" Venetia exclaims. "No longer content to be a mere humorist, now Mrs. Banjiejicz thinks to attack the soft underbelly of my uncontrollable mania! This (indicates recipe held in trembling hand) is too sinister to be mere coincidence."

Poires en Crème

4 Ripe (MAMMOTH-size) pEARS
½ pint heavy CREAM
2 tablesPOONs (or 4 LUMPs) sugar

1 cup minceMEAT
2 tablespoons xochiCUN Tlapec sweet chili powder
2 leaveS TARES à Provence
1 or 2 cinnamon sticks, or to taste

1½ ozs. cognac

The pears should be FIRM and without BUMPS or bruises. Avoid tHOSE with soft spots or blemishes. Cut them in half the long way, REAM out cores and seeds, and PRICK all over. Place in a glASS baking dish, arranging the halves in a circle. To the cream, add sugar, chili powder, and tares. WHIP UNTIL STIFF. Add cognac and cinnamon to the mincemeat and leT IT Simmer over a low flame until HOT thROUGH. Place a tablespoonful of the mincemeat mixture on each pear half, then cover with the whipped cream. Bake in hoT (400-450 degrees or "HIGH" setting) oven for 7-8 minutes. Serve when dish COOLs to room temperature.

Did Mrs. Banjiejicz create the recipe and consciously encode the key words of Victor Herbert's lost song? Did the "food writer extraordinary" unconsciously and unknowingly stumble on the words, reviving them, so to speak, in the writing of the recipe? Does Mrs. B. know more than she is telling about Mr. Herbert's past? Are the words, only guessed at by Dr. Hess, much more than mere "ritualized expressions of a crude American erotics"? Was Therese Herbert-Föster, Victor's strapping diva of a wife, the, as it were, object of his song's affection? Venetia knows nothing, but Louis's bold capitalizations of certain elements of the recipe's text (q.v.) are enough to plunge her, much to Louis's lascivious delight, into a brazen enactment of the vocation she embraces. It is possible, of course, that the recipe is bogus, created by Louis himself with an eye to the ends being realized by him and his unhinged companion, who is now thoroughly enmeshed in the toils of her dementia. Without the chorus itself, nothing can satisfactorily be determined, and the chorus may be but the rumor of vaguely crazed scholars. Not even the indefatigable Dr. Hess, her grizzled head encircled by wreaths of pipe smoke, has turned up a line of it.

"Venetia!" Louis says, his voice muffled, "I am deeply enchanted when you completely lose control of yourself and act in such an unseemly yet thrilling manner. Oh, my darling embouchure!"

"Louis darling! Rears! Mammoth cream! Poon lump! Ream stiff!" Venetia yelps.

Although the couple may not be precisely noble, their very humanity is attractive and thus will be favored by our discretion.

But the world, as always, staggers along. If it's not one damn elision it's another. For instance, the curtain is about to rise on a matinee performance of *Black Ladder,* an experimental theatre piece of some twenty years ago. It wasn't received very warmly then, even though the cast rambled through the theatre in a "liberating flesh involvement" with the audience. Questions on the order of "Where's your head at, man?" and "Is that cunt your wife?" were directed at hapless theatre-goers, and so on. The audience reaction, which ran the gamut from rage and confusion to ennui, contempt, and hilarity, was, of course, proof of the "work's unsettling eagerness to confront bourgeois values." Fine. This current production will be played in the round, and the cast will wear identical costumes—"Cute Cop" to be exact—and skull masks, in order to, as the playbill has it, "relate more meaningfully to a new, more cynical generation's needs." Fine. Adelaide Hester, who is remembered for her prickly Mona in *Girls Are O.K.,* will play the lead, and on this occasion, her "guy," John Hicks, is in the audience. Adelaide is a little long in the tooth for this role, but then Hicks is a bit hoary to be anybody's "guy," so it all works like a house afire, as Buddy once said to Dick anent a nocturnal varmint who speedily made off with their pajamas. John Hicks once had something to do with the Buildings Department, and found himself in a "passel" of trouble (indicates rustic word in copy of *A Grain of Salt*) concerning what the press insisted on calling "collapsing condos." A canard if John ever heard one, and a moot, kike-inspired canard at that! In any event, he awaits the performance with interest, since he suspects that it may present him with some peripheral data needed for a study of modern caterwaul-niece-bonding systems, a line of "research" he is pursuing in his current interest in anthropology. His most recent theories have to do with the *hieros gamos,* or marriage fete, as practiced in certain ritual-prone societies inhabiting tropical crystalline highlands. He theorizes that the wedded couples celebrate their "state of rejuvenation" or "joyous swelling" by whacking each other's buttocks, turn and turn about, with wooden paddles which uncannily resemble Hi-Lo bats, an idea that has made the college-educated, middle-class sadomasochistic community proud once more, and hence much less likely to run amok in school-yards and choir lofts. The mass weddings and frenzied paddlings take place in large, semi-enclosed sylvan temples not unlike Hilton hotels, and these temples are invariably named "Spank-Good Place" or "Big Space to Do [Make] Nice Pain." Hicks believes that these descriptions are but vague approximations of virtually untranslatable syntagmatic structures, but that they have their linguistic roots in the honorific given the ceremonial priest, or *vinnie,* He-Who-Comes-in-His-Handkerchief. "Of course," Hicks writes, "they don't actually have *hankies,* but this quibble in no way detracts from the overall theory, or, as I like to call it, 'picture.' " Indeed not! colleagues spiritedly confess.

So he awaits the curtain, looking around every so often for Michael Cullinan, an acquaintance who often provides him with interesting materials from his vast, if highly specialized, catalogue collection. For reasons unknown to Hicks, Michael, who has for months planned on attending this performance, is nowhere to be seen. Comprising the rest of the audience is a man who looks disturbingly like Himmler, a Nazi of recent notoriety; a Hindu, afflicted with what Shakespeare termed "a raging tooth"; Hips, a laconic dairy-products worker at the A & P; and the theatre editor of *Hip Vox,* who is in a bad mood, having just seen a puppet-theatre production of *Histoire de l'oeil.* It is not too much to say that she wants to crucify *Black Ladder,* on general principles, and at the moment she is composing the lead of a coolly malicious review in her head. She hates these idiotic actors anyway, nattering on with other people's words, and always *wearing* things! Pushed by the demands of what many innocents think a glamorous job from her living room and *The Real Ho Chi Minh, My Lover,* she is ruefully thinking that she never dreamed that a drama critic would have to unearth facts about early street theatre at Hofstra, the reasons behind the denial to Billie Holiday of the role of Scarlet O'Hara, and Vittorio Holo's theft of the intricate plot of *All My Sons.* "The usual dago machinations" was her explanation of the last, surely an unfair if not bigoted remark. But now the curtain rises and her heart sinks. On an otherwise bare stage is a large stuffed pig, listed in the *dramatis personae* as HOMER, *a hog.* The Himmler look-alike chuckles. "Schwein!" he rasps coldly.

Hong Kong is drenched by yet another simoom, and so the Chinese production of *Black Ladder* is postponed again. How strangely the threads of experience meet, touch, intertwine, and become entangled, Father Debris thinks. It's almost a phenomenon! Excitedly, he wonders if these ceaseless permutations can be plotted by means of Fibonacci's series, but he knows that he must resist this idea's temptation, at least until he gets a grip on another problem, called to his attention by an anonymous correspondent, who suggests that a curious "lost" fan letter from Herbert Hoover to one Hoppy, a cowboy star, is in code. After breaking the letter down into its varied morphemic, phonemic, and graphemic groupings, the priest realizes that the code, if there is one, might possibly be solved according to the Cartesian-Eulerian formula for polyhedra ($V-E + F = 2$), and he is now "transliterating" the linguistic elements of the letter into terms of vertices, edges, and faces. He feels that he is on the edge of a breakthrough of historical significance. Settling himself at his desk, he reads the letter for "the thousandth time."

Dear Mr. Hoppy,

I recently saw you in *Range Riders of Yellow Canyon* and was thrilled, in a manly way, by your shooting, riding, roping, and pugilistic skills. Many of the "varmints" to whom you dispensed your special brand of range justice had the look of anarchists and communists about them, and some seemed downright swarthy. Not a self-starter in the bunch! Punching and even shooting are too good for such types as these.

The way you leap into the saddle, tip back your head with a broad grin, and then sit your horse, remind me of something pretty darned wonderful, but I have no words right now to tell you exactly what it is.

Your ardent admirer,

Herbert Hoover

Father Debris considers that Mr. Hoover's letter may conceal a proclivity for refined amours, much like those of the poet Horace, of whom Suetonius writes that "it is reported that in a room lined with mirrors he had harlots so arranged that whichever way he looked, he saw a reflection of venery." Such a life, the priest knows, leads but to grief and heartache, and this opinion is bolstered by his recollection of a magazine article read many years ago, "The Horror of My Forced Abortion." Father Debris cannot remember the title of the magazine in which he read this compelling mea culpa, but is certain that it couldn't have been in the only publication to which he subscribes, *Hot Action,* which usually publishes pieces (indicates latest issue) like "How to Order Wine—for HOT ACTION"; "Want HOT ACTION? Swimming the Hudson at Midnight!"; "A Car for Those Who Crave HOT ACTION —The Classic Terraplane Is Back!"; "A Hungarian Freedom Fighter Tells of HOT ACTION in Her Hollywood Designer Kitchen," and so on. But Debris realizes that he is allowing his mind to wander, and so returns to the ex-President's fan letter, slightly troubled by the comic presence of invalidating non-Eulerian polyhedral "monsters," whose lurking reality might call into question any solution to the letter's code at which he may arrive. Perhaps he'd be better off working with the "threads of experience" and the always reliable Fibonacci, or even returning to his contemplation of the authors of the Décadence.

Eugenia Hunter, as handsome as ever, and, with her hair now shot through with silver, perhaps even more handsome, sits at her desk to write the letter to *Flikk* that she's been putting off for more than a month. It's not an important letter, yet is certainly one that she feels must be written in order to set the famous "record" straight.

To the Editor:
    In a recent issue of your magazine, the "Town-Crier Tidbits" page states that my first husband was Tab Hunter, the noted movie star. This is quite incorrect. My first husband was William Hunter, affectionately called, by those who had a truly caring relationship with him, "LuLu," "Rosita," and "Sweetums," depending on occasion and milieu. He was a gentle, even somewhat effeminate man, and was, indeed, a sometime author, as you correctly state. However, the title of his much-praised story is not, as you claim, "Like a Dream Am I," but "I Can Dream, Can't I?"
    This story was included in the well-received but long out-of-print anthology of "new voices from the creative-writing workshops," *An Idiot's Pleasure,* edited by Katharine A. and Michael K. Ignatz. The collection, incidentally, was given a very favorable mention in the syndicated newspaper column "I Got Mine," where, among other words of praise, it was spoken of as "a shaft of moral sunlight amid the darkness of the ethical muck of puling 'experiment.' "
    But this is neither here nor there. I merely wished to write and correct the trifling errors in your otherwise admirable "Tidbits" feature.
                    Most sincerely,
                    Eugenia Hunter

    Eugenia is not aware, fortunately for her peace of mind, that "I Can Dream, Can't I?" is currently being filmed as a low-budget horror movie, *I'll Eat Your Eyeballs.* The shooting is being done entirely on location in the beer garden of Imbriale's Clam House, where, at this writing, the director is on lunch break, his feet on a table and his full attention directed toward—of all things—Sheila Henry's senior English paper, "Impotence in Silver Age Poets."
    "Yes," the director says, looking up with sudden warm alacrity, "one might think it strange that a worker in the cinema has an interest in such scholarly arcana, but I find that such reading refreshes my visual sense, makes me more aware than ever before of the truth that a word is a word and an image is an image. Along with the poets of the Silver Age, Cowper and the like, Afro Benny, artists to whom words were always and forever words, yes, but then, so much more, words that were— song! Song and beauty, and factual experience as well. Yes. Along with them, as I said, I'm also attracted to writings on Heinrich Himmler, the Impressionists and their fascination with the cravat, the heartbreaking saga of the construction of the IND line, and the romance of the meer- schaum pipe."

Is such refreshment merely an escape from cinematic discipline, or does it assist you in your work?

"Definitely. Assists. A bewitching essay on Manet's love of locomotives which I came across in *Hip Vox* some years ago was the direct cause of my making *Indelible Experiences,* starring, if you'll recall, Dolores Délire as the India Ink Murderess. The film was not only a *succès d'estime,* it packed real box-office wallop!"

Very interesting.

"Thank you. . . . Say, what's that Indian doing over there? Hey, greaseball!"

"I've been watching the filming of this movie for three hours, white-eyes fuckhead," Chief Blue Wind says, "and although I see ethnic types of virtually every persuasion in the crowd scenes, nowhere do I detect a redskin! If redskin not on set (indicates Imbriale's beer garden) by time Indian corn (indicates strangely familiar Indian-corn door spray) falls to floor (indicates clam-bespattered flagstones), all die!"

"Give the fucking greaseball a little part in the Indo-China scene, O.K.?" the director calls to his assistant. "Jesus Christ, if it's not one kinda greaseball it's another. But where were we?"

Then too: Current Poetry Scene Prompts Jean Ingelow to Return from Dead; Edward Beshary Names Ralph Ingeman Inspector of Buildings in Lightning Maid-Swap; "Mr. Insight" of Radio Fame Denies Charge of Carnal Insensitivity; Iowa Lawmaker Claims Iowa Writers' Workshop Makes State Laughing Stock; Bones of Ipos, the "Angelic Lion of Stuttgart," Found in Block of Meerschaum; Scholar Contends *Paradise Lost* Authored by Anonymous Irishman; *Isolate Flecks* Now Viewed as Attack on Smiling Italian.

Buddy, his head clear and his eye bright once again, set his jaw squarely, and gestured toward the forbidding heights, in whose swirling miasma there could dimly be descried the beetling scarp of Misty Crag.

"I think it best if we make a snug camp here for the night, Dick," he laughed sincerely. "There's an abundance of fresh, cool water from the many capital rills hereabouts, and I allow that we're fortunate in that the immediate environs are rich in the spangs that have but lately plunged to their deaths from the dense trees."

"Say! That's a crackerjack idea, Buddy," the indefatigable Dick opined. "I recollect them Meskin bandelitos in 'Jacks or Better' made a reg'lar feast on them, lightly sautéed and topped with *cacahuate* sauce." His eyes fair shone with primitive glee.

"I'd almost forgotten that neglected example of the storyteller's art," Buddy mused distractedly, the cold wind pummeling his slender body and bending the tares à Provence, amid which he stood, almost to the ground. "But," and he smiled wanly at his dear chum, "you should say *those* Meskin bandelitos. Even here in the wilderness, precise, business-like speech can't hurt a fellow's chances."

"Sorry, Buddy," Dick muttered. "I sure do try, but somehow my words come out all mixed up, like as if it 'pears I've been listening to Mick Jagger."

"There's no need to trouble yourself about it, stout Dick," Buddy assured the crestfallen lad. "There's many a man who speaks as clearly as Count Janos, the Hungarian blzcky, yet has a heart as black as stone."

"As black as stone, Buddy?" Dick queried, straightening up curiously with his arms full of dry tares for their campfire.

"Perhaps black as pitch or cold as stone is the better expression, Dick," Buddy chuckled, an expression of hesitant infarction on his face. "But here, let me help you gather up these tares, and then we'll select the largest and tenderest of these bashed spangs for our evening meal. Although," and Buddy's smile beamed like a demented light-house, "I fear that we'll have to make do without the *cacahuate* sauce!"

The infected laughter of the two boys echoed off the shadowy peaks which surrounded them and was, indeed, hearty enough to be heard in bustling Chinatown, far below. Soon the fire of tares and dead planks was burning brightly, with the not inconsiderable assistance of the pages, used as kindling, torn from a copy of *Absalom! Absalom!* that Dick had found in a small, concealed cave. The boys ate their fill of flame-broiled spangs, and toasted each other, with many a goodhearted jest, in the cold waters of the ever-plashing rills.

"I've been meaning to inquire, Buddy," Dick said, leaning back and heaving a sigh of contentment, "s'posing we *do* find Blutwurst's map, what in the Sam Hill are we going to do with it?"

Buddy, his face grown pale with anguish, stared long into the dancing flames before answering, "Well, Dick, it all depends extraordinarily on what the dago's map *shows*."

Dick looked quickly at Buddy's face, but it was hidden in shadows, and before he could further inquire about the map, Buddy whooped, "But, drat it! Let's not permit the ruffian to intrude upon our evening. How about a poem?"

"You know I have a powerfully enlightened interest in the art, Buddy," Dick shouted rather alarmingly, "even though I'm not as deep read as I'd gosh-all like. By all means, a poem!"

Buddy, heartened by his friend's enthusiasm, laughed quietly, and fetched a copy of Jean Ingelow's poems from his frayed puccoon. "Since you seem so partial to Mrs. Browning, Dick, I expect that you'll also warmly respond to yet another lady of perfect taste. In fact, Mrs. Browning and Miss Ingelow make, in effect, two opposite faces of the same Janus coin." He stopped, slightly bewildered. "Or, I should say, the same Janus faces of two opposite coins." The lad's flustered puzzlement seemed to increase. "I seem, Dick, unable to get my meaning straight. It is as if I, too, have been listening to Mack Jigger."

"Mick, Buddy," Dick lightly mumbled. "Mick Jagger."

"Mick, of course," Buddy flared inconsequentially. "In any case, permit me to read at random from this good lady's works, so that you'll be able to discover a verse that is sympathetic and compassionate, though tempered by the poet's observant, cold, yet not pitiless eye." With that, Buddy opened the well-fingered volume, and read:

> What next?—we started like to girls, for lo!
> The creaking voice, more harsh than rusty crane,
> Of one who stooped behind us, cried aloud
> "Good lack! how sweet the gentleman does sing—
> So loud and sweet, 'tis like to split his throat. . . ."

But abruptly, Buddy stopped, and glanced piercingly into the crepuscular fastnesses of the thick foliage just beyond Dick's reclining back.

"Wh-what is it, good friend?" Dick inquired. "Please continue! This brief snatch of verse already promises to expand into a subtle bas-relief of a grey world of which the more fortunate among us cannot even imagine of." But Buddy had let the book slip from his inert hands, and now he stood, staring into the woods. Dick turned, just in time to see a tall young man, in mackinaw and worn moleskins, stride into the circle of firelight.

"Can we be of help to you, stranger?" Buddy inquired politely. "It's not usual to get nighttime visitors here on Mystery Mountain," he continued easily, but Dick noticed that his hand rested casually on the butt of the Majolica-steel knife in his belt.

The stranger stepped closer to the fire, spat, and then said gruffly, "My name is Kurt, though it's no concern of yours. I'm looking for an old diary, a book I've sworn to possess once again!" His face was terrible in the shifting light, and his moleskins gave off an overpowering odor of menace. "You fellers ain't seen it, have you? It's got a kind of crude map of sorts drawn on the cover, but the map ain't a map of noplace, or . . . *so they claim!*" he rasped, his voice more harsh than rusty crane.

Buddy, his eyes aglow with belated recognition, held Knute in their manly gaze, and said, "Aren't you the younger brother of the besmirched criminal, Lars?" With a cry of rage and surprise, the depraved Swede turned and fled heavily through the underbrush.

At this point, problems may arise, and become, through a lack of attention and a possibly misplaced trust on the part of the reader, "well-nigh insuperable." Therefore, to take a "leaf" from Eugenia Hunter's "book," let the record be set straight, to wit:

a.) Jeannette is but a character in the novel *La Bouche métallique.* She is not what is usually referred to as *a real person.*

b.) Jeannette is but a character in the English translation of *La Bouche métallique.* She is not what is usually referred to as *a real person* either.

c.) Madame Jeannette is but a character in the English translation of *La Bouche métallique.* Ditto on the *real person* note.

d.) Sister Jeannette is but a character in the English translation of *La Bouche métallique.* Ditto again on the *real person* note.

e.) Madame Jeannette and Sister Jeannette do not exist in the original of *La Bouche métallique.* They are not what is usually referred to as either *real persons* or *characters.*

f.) These *unreal persons* may be the same *unreal person,* known variously as Jeannette, Madame Jeannette, and Sister Jeannette.

g.) This Jeannette's last name, or these Jeannettes' last names, may be Grande, the woman on whose account Buddy recently plunged headlong from a chair. If this is the case, then she may be what is usually referred to as *a real person*, unless Buddy himself is what is usually referred to as *an unreal person*.

"Buddy is, it 'pears, stoutly realer as you are or I!"

Thank you, Dick.

"You're welcome. And now I have to hie to Mystery Mountain, where the fields of gorse bend to the relentless winds, afore Buddy finds me gone." With a proud laugh, he turns on his heel and strides into a fog not unlike that which envelops Colma.

Jeff, callow to the core, is still aroused by the "breast quarrel" between Tabitha Bramble and Lucy Brandon, which it was his unhappy fate to overhear. So aroused, in fact, that an early (ca. 1940) edition of the *Handbook for Boys* sternly prescribes a cold hip bath or a brisk run around the block as remedies for the alleviation of this state, or "fix." Jeff, despite his affliction, caused not so much by the subject of the quarrel as by the very fact that *women* speak in this candid way of their glorious bodies, knows that if he doesn't start restocking the frozen foods, that will be *it* for him at Crown SuperMart. He relies, therefore, on his tried-and-true, absolute, and powerful anaphrodisiac, the poems of Robinson Jeffers, especially his favorite, the one he privately calls his "shooter" (see "Marbles in City Streets," *Urban Games Annual*, LXIV, 3, 1942). As he cuts open a carton of fish sticks, he murmurs, "I'd rather, except the penalties, kill a man than a hake," and, as always, his distended prunella begins a return to its normal state.

A film of grimy sweat covering her body, Lee Jefferson is rummaging through the back-issue files of *Hip Vox* for articles, essays, reviews, feuilletons, and short fiction to be considered for inclusion in an anthology, *Twenty-Five Years of the Hip: The Best of "Hip Vox."* (A prospectus detailing the "editorial philosophy" behind the anthology's contents is currently available, but will be omitted in order to spare the reader needless agony.) Lee is surprised to discover the concerns addressed by the magazine over the years, and wonders if the planned anthology might be too *refined,* too *specialized* for an audience not attuned to *Hip Vox's* intellectual bent. So far, she has come across "*Wuthering Heights:* Is Lockwood a Chump?"; "The Pyramids Were a Mistake! Deconstructing Egypt"; "I Put on High Heels and Finally *Lived*"; "Jazz: Finally Dead?"; "Can Sexists Eat Pussy—And Live?"; "Banana Kings of Greenwich Village"; "Milton, the Running Dog"; "Lost Poems of Lydia E. Pinkham"; "Pizza—Cold at Last?"; "*Wuthering Heights:* Is Lockwood a Pussy?"; "Sexists Eat Pizza at Last"; "Pizza, Chump?"; "The 'Pyramids' of Greenwich Village"; "Banana Kings and Running Dogs"; "Milton Deconstructs Egypt"; "Put on High Heels—And Jazz!"; "Finally Dead: Lydia E. Pinkham"; "Lost Poems That Lived"; "*Wuthering Heights:* Is Lockwood a Running Dog?"; "Banana Kings That Lived"; "Lost 'Pussy' Poems"; "Sexists, Pizza, and Egypt"; "Milton Deconstructs Jazz"; "High Heels at Last!"; "Pizza and Pyramids"; "The Greenwich Village of Lydia E. Pinkham"; "Finally Dead, Chump?"; "*Wuthering Heights:* Is Lockwood Milton?"; "Milton Deconstructs the Dead"; "Finally, Jazz for Chumps"; "Bananas, Kings, and High Heels"; "At Last, Pizza!"; "Pyramids That Lived"; "Lost Pussy in Egypt"; "Sexists and Lydia E. Pinkham"; "Greenwich Village and Pizza." She continues her search, trying to remember just *who* Lockwood is.

Although Allen, the waiter, is on record as preferring the Alps, where "the poppy and the pansy blow," to Akron, some prefer Jersey City, a sediment-filled structural depression on a crystalline peninsula. Onny swokkee molly ponce, to fetch a pail of water.

It may as well be noted here that "The Horror of My Forced Abortion," a not unimportant item in Father Debris's painstaking construction of his "philosophy of live and love," as he so nicely puts it, was originally published in *Jesus!,* a magazine out of print for some years now. This publication, much praised by those who would conserve our heritage of humanist ideals and really *good* clothes, published other articles as compelling and thought-provoking as the one which caught—and still catches!—Father Debris's fancy; for example: "Should Jews Be Allowed to Vote?"; "I Listened to 'Good Golly, Miss Molly!' and Saw Lucifer Naked"; and "Karl Marx and Devil Worship."

"That was one hell of a magazine," Jiggs says, careening down the pet-foods aisle. "Blammo? Say, Blammo, do you remember *Jesus!*, that magazine that had the fairly amusing rebus on the inside back cover every issue?" But Blammo is torn between checking the pervasiveness of additives intended to insure freshness in various cold cereals, and looking up the skirt of the cherry-cheese-dip woman.

"He cares not for your queries, Jiggs," Jimmy says. Jimmy is usually referred to as "somebody" or "Jiggs's friend" or "man in super-market." He doesn't look at all like Jiggs's friend, but then nobody in the entire world looks like Jiggs's friend.

"Deo gratias," Father Debris says, trying, once again, to arrive at an analytical solution to the Jordan Curve Theorem, an exercise, to quote Jordan himself, akin to "pissing up a rope."

Joanie, on the other hand, may simply be yet another case of mistaken identity. No pictures, no records, no letters exist anent her life. In order to place her so as to obviate the horrible possibility that she may simply "float around" on this scorcher of a day, we might say that she was the "girl at the orgy," and let it go at that. For a clue to the orgy referred to, see earlier comments on *Houses, adobe; Floors, oiled; Vigas, original.*

Joanne's White perfectly images the balanced horizontal and vertical conceptions of space in the process of political collapse. It is a "tone row" of propositions that are at once finite and yet open to the possi-bilities of an imperialist-induced compromise. Although a static and seemingly vapid statement of a decorative refusal to assert that which might fairly be called an extra-artistic kinesis, the contrapuntals and polyrhythms of the painting's color range claim for themselves the right to subvert the canonical conception of phallic mass and the thrust of density. Not, surely, as chastely or as puritanically inept as the "vaginal metamorphoses" of recent reductionist art, *Joanne's White* is nonethe-less a remarkably prescient example of the skewed painterly syntax which informs such contemporary works as the straight-facedly bitter deconstruction of Melissa Queynte's *Jog Your Way to Orgasm*, in which the banal words unmask the almost luscious impasto of rich pastels upon which their message is paradoxically set. Seen in this historical perspective, *Joanne's White* begins to look less and less like the "bourgeois excrement" it was condemned as by Consuelo Van Shunt. Perhaps, it seems to say, unapologetic strategies of form and color, worked out on a rigorously adhered to picture plane, can serve as unmasking techniques as well as or better than more overtly registered statements of an intransigent, and perhaps too naïve suspicion of the status quo.

Pamela Ann Johanssen, who writes as Pamela Clairwil, tired for many years now of pandering to base male fantasies of the lesbian way of life, is thoughtfully brushing her crewcut, admiring the way the light brings out the silvery highlights of her fine hair. Should she call Florence Claire, whom she has heard is reviewing her book for *Virginia's Beat*? She's heard that Florence, although pretty dumb, has a soft spot for automatic writing, as do most of the reviewers for this important organ of enlightened literary opinion, yet to call seems gauche if not crude. Perhaps she might call just to tell her that the photographs, which accompany her text, are as automatic as the writing. She hears that Florence really, well, *likes* young women, although, God knows, Pamela is no longer young. Not really. Was she ever young? Was she ever what they call a "chick"? What precisely *is* a "chick"? When does a woman stop being a "chick"? Is there such a thing as an old "chick"? What's the difference between a "chick" and a "broad"? One sees the sort of thing that vexes Pamela's days. Hell, she screams inside, if Johnny were still around, he'd know what to do. (For *Johnny,* see *Joanie.*)

Joizy Cidy, Jersey City's "sister town," has little to recommend it other than that it is a crystalline structural depression on a sediment-filled peninsula. It is from this crystalline material that domestic meerschaum is extracted for connoisseurs of pipes and "pipe lore." They seem to be legion. For an amusing and instructive sidelight on meerschaum, Heinrich Himmler likes to point to some exercises in a textbook for which he acted as cultural consultant, *Learn German Immediately!* The genial ex-poultry farmer, bored with the play, is on the street right now. And pointing! "I vill translate zo ass you may get der flafor uff der text," he barks, and commences.

Willi vishes to go to der department store undt puy der meerschaum pipe. Der meerschaum iss goot. Der Fuehrer luffs der meerschaum.

Willi's vater goess mit him to der department store. Hiss vater's name iss Rudi. Rudi iss goot. Rudi luffs der Fuehrer undt der Party. Der Fuehrer luffs der meerschaum a goot deal.

How fine Willi undt Rudi look in dare prown zhirts. Willi undt Rudi luff der Fuehrer, ezpezially hiss mouztazhe. It iss prown from der tobacco in hiss meerschaum pipes, prown like Willi undt Rudi's zhirts.

In der department store, Willi undt Rudi infesstigate der meerschaum pipes. Rudi tellss Willi zat der Choos hate der meerschaum undt zmoke zigarettes like a bunch of sissy pervert animals. Vater undt zon zen plaze some Choos unter arrest.

Willi decides on a pipe. It iss a meerschaum pipe. Willi iss choyous to see zat der powl iss a zkull. Der saleslady pleases Rudi ven she asks Willi for his paperss. She says, "Your paperss, pleeze!" She iss a goot Cherman girl. Alzo, she hass a nize mouztazhe, prown like der Fuehrer's.

Rudi undt Willi look out der vindow at a train. Der train iss taking many Choos to der meerschaum mines in Poland.

Willi undt Rudi haff a good laugh. Dare are no meerschaum mines in Poland! Vot a choke on der Choo perverts! No more zigarettes for zem!

"Dose vere der dayss!" Himmler says, stopping the fleeing theatre editor of *Hip Vox* to check her papers. She looks suspiciously effeminate to his discerning eye.

"I possess that which addicts of controlled substances were wont to call, in the good old days when schmeckers were schmeckers and not forever whining about this program and that program, a 'Jones.' " José leans back in his colorful raffia chair and takes a lazy, a long and lazy look at last Christmas's gay piñata. "Except that my Jones is for sexual activity. How well I remember Chester, 'the baron of the baths,' and how can I forget Harlan, 'the man on the train'? Not to mention Fatso Willy, 'the guy who could not break his parents' hearts.' I think of the four of us in interesting dalliance, and my Jones becomes well-nigh insupportable, emotionally speaking-wise." José sighs. "I might say these cogitations still amaze the troubled midnight and the noon's repose—and even the untroubled midnight." He rises, tears the gay piñata from its suspending ribbon, and, troubled, hurls it from the window. "Feliz Navidad!" he shouts at the—oh no!—*traffic far below*.

The man whom some call, rather uncharitably, Mr. Joy, and others call fink, weasel, stoolie, rat, nark, snitch, and liar, misses being interrogated, as he has missed it for many years now, most acutely in August, the month of his initial "performance." He is aware of the names that he is called, but it is certainly not his fault if his testimony contradicted that of others. He soothes his aching nostalgia for his brief moment of splendor by reading the letters sent by James Joyce to his wife, Nora Joyce. The latter has been dear to Mr. Joy ever since he read a remark she made to her husband on his work: "Why don't you write sensible books that people can understand?" That Mr. Joy is aware that his testimony forms a large part of a book which he himself cannot understand makes Nora's remark one that affects him deeply. When he occasionally browses through the book of which his testimony forms a third, it seems to him that his remarks have been twisted, falsified, taken out of context, and even invented! Yet, and yet, he'd like to answer the questions again, or answer *any* questions again, no matter his answers' final disposition. As he gets up to leave the apartment and stroll over to the A & P for a cold sixpack, something resembling a gay piñata sails past his window. A gay piñata? In August?

"I hate those books you can't understand," Knute remarks, picking burrs from his dreary mackinaw. "They're all written by kikes if you ask me, kikes who like to have their way with modest Christian girls. Here's"—and Knute pulls a well-thumbed paperback from his rucksack—"one revealing wallop of a read I *never* tire of!"

It is, of course, *Joys of the Square Knot,* red-blooded stories of bondage and domination for the American outdoorsman. Perhaps this is the sort of thing that Sheila Henry objected to as "Christian pornography."

"It was! It was!" Donna Julia calls from the shallow end of the pool on the roof of her building, where she is "teaching" the recently divorced Eleanor Julienne—her beloved "Taterhead"—to "swim." She has her right hand on Eleanor's *mons pubis* and her left hand on Eleanor's right breast. In July, her right hand was on Eleanor's belly and her left hand between her breasts. In June, her right hand was on Eleanor's knees and her left hand on her chest. So things, for Donna, who must exert every ounce of charm and guile in order to "score," are clipping right along at a fairly good pace, considering. After all, as Jung said, feeling is more likely to be dominant in the woman, and Donna has always been quite good at feeling.

A recent note from Jung's attorneys protests the use of the word "feeling," claiming that it is, as used, a "distortion" of Jung's ideas. Whatever *they* are.

Munching her tofuburger, Karen Aileron opens *Jungle Action* to the first story, "Sex-Crazed Gorillas Ripped Off Her Jodhpurs—And Fought for Her Love!" Pretty slim pickings, but it's too hot to smile brightly. To whirl gaily through the quiet streets. To play badminton. To lounge on an emerald lawn. To skydive. To spelunk. To tramp through the woods. To poke through enchanting, out-of-the-way antique shops. The tofuburger is making her sick, but soon her real life may start. A bird lands on the windowsill, and what does Karen say to this bird, his head cocked in time-honored fashion? "Hi!" she says.

The perils of Justine, the unfortunate heroine of *Justine, ou les Malheurs de la Vertu,* are, once again, being followed avidly by Bart Kahane. He sits under a palm tree, reading this work for perhaps the eighth or ninth time since emerging from his long coma. It may not be his favorite book, but his identification with Justine is so strong that it can, in truth, be called his bulwark against adversity, of which he feels he has had more than his share. Especially now, today! Edward Beshary has not only torn up his best lace cap and broken the heels off his black pumps, but, just this morning, *again* began to call him by the nicknames that Bart despises—"Nando" and "BeeBee"—and to refer to him as "the twisted" Bart. "Berthe! Call me Berthe!" Bart sobbed. "I'm fairly cute for my age, I've got good legs still, and, God knows, I'm learned, but not, I hope, annoyingly so!" But Beshary only laughed at him, then gloatingly informed him that the Guston drawing is but a clever fake, done by Annie Flammard years before, in payment for Beshary keeping his mouth shut about an indiscreet interlude involving a physics professor, two nuns, a Weimaraner, and a quart of mayonnaise.

Bart looks up from the ceaseless degradation of Justine, her endless surprise at the cruelty of men, her impossible innocence, and begins to weep into his ruffled apron. His tycoon is preparing for another board meeting somewhere, and "Guts," his confidant, is, even now, happily packing his bags. Out of his tear-filled eyes, Bart spies three tourists entering a copse of exotic shrubs and gorgeous blooms. Yet he sits, immobile, the idea of walloping them senseless because of their impertinent glances as they passed him, not even half-formed in his mind. He thinks of his twenty-year coma as a blessing, then despairingly returns to Justine's fruitless pleas for mercy. From the copse he hears the gross laughter of the gross world.

Somehow, the lovely Conchita Kahane has lost five or six hours of her life. Perhaps it's been five or six years. This is not our business. She's also acquired a box of daintily scalloped, lilac-hued stationery. She has a cloudy image of quarreling about something with what seemed to be a bald mail clerk. She pulls her panty girdle off, wondering when and why it was that she started to wear such a garment, and discovers a bruise over her pelvic bone. Somebody or something packing a crushing wallop put it there, that seems certain. And who is María de la Concepción Dorotea Carolina Darío y Reyes, to whom the copy of *The Daddy and the Drake,* lying on the coffee table next to the stationery, is dedicated with "un abrazo y un beso"? What is an "abrazo"? What is a "beso"? Why does she keep thinking of police officers? Why does the word "boobs" keep recurring to her? Why is her hair almost completely grey? Is she a "chick"? What is a "chick"? She sits at the kitchen table, trying to recall the faces of the two young men who stood, unaccountably, on chairs to gaze at her. What she needs is three or four fingers of gin, and as she rises to get it, the phone rings. The caller, who identifies himself as Stan Boils, wants to speak to "Babs" Gonzales. Conchita shocks herself as she listens to her voice reply, "Jou 'ave the wrong nomber, pendejo." She hangs up, and, dazed, turns to the window just in time to see an attractive vegetarian couple stroll by, hand in hand. And what remarkably slender, vigorous hands! Almost like fylfots intertwined.

She still seems to have as much trouble as always with words, so Lolita Kahane dog-ears page 92 of *The Girdle Story,* and puts it on top of the refrigerator. She seemed to be following the narrative, more or less, until she came across a reference to Kansas City, at which point she thought of a toy airplane or a perverse Continental gentleman, then, as always, Karen came to mind, but which Karen? Certainly one who had something to do with a chic but practical uniform or the too-cold room. Lolita realizes that almost any Karen knows more than enough about sailing through azure skies, not to mention creamy clouds. But does this knowledge help her? It seems not. *The Girdle Story,* like most books, is filled with words, the trouble, necessarily, with all of them. The invitation to the barbecue at Katydid Glade is still on her kitchen table, but it's much too late to go. The "problem" recurred almost instantly upon her opening the invitation, for Katydid Glade immediately gestured toward the girdle story or magazines scattered about. She mutters, "Oh, Jesus, Gnatville or the open window," and begins, once again, trying to climb into the cupboard above the sink, knowing, as she does so, that the cupboard is sure to be full of dishes, Bart's "frillies" or memories of dark highways. Still, "Something, something or something," she says, getting up on the sink.

Maybe it's not too late to mention that Katydid Glade and Gnatville are the same place, the former name that of the town before its incorporation. In one sylvan precinct of this burg, the barbecue guests are tidying up after their extemporaneous orgy. Although they are sophisticated people (indicates sushi restaurants, a plethora of natural fabrics, local-talent poetry readings), as they search for their clothing, much of it in sad disrepair, they turn embarrassedly away from each other, and no wonder; for as Bataille says with his usual frigid clarity, the orgy, by its very nature, "is necessarily disappointing." And this *despite* its clear and complete index and exemplary notes.

Elmhurst, mocked, badgered, and brutalized into submission by fashionable journalists who find its mores wholly lacking in an awareness of the sexual politics apparent in the commercial cinema, can no longer, it is clear to Anne Kaufman, support her little religious-supplies store. It is almost time to leave, or, as Anne puts it, "give up the post [*sic*]," and as she completes her inventory, she fights the scream that rises in her throat, the latter a little flabby. It doesn't help that Father Frank has gone off to wage his lonely battle against gonorrhea and indulge his profane taste for gossip. No, it doesn't! She is alone in the store, stunned by the oppressive heat, and wondering why she still has fifty-four copies of *How to Think Like Jesus.* The bell over the front door jingles, and a man enters, smiling benignly. Anne smiles back, suddenly conscious of the fit of her skirt. They stand, appraising each other, the stillness in the store broken only by the soft ticking of the clock which has, yet again, appeared. It is a sound which one can often count on, even though things, for the most part, are silent. Will this potential customer have the effrontery to introduce himself as the reprehensible cad he is, Miner X. Beely? "Good afternoon, ma'm," he says. "I'm Jeff Chandler." Beely chuckles lightly, his gaze resting on a richly embroidered quadroon prominently displayed above the counter. "Not *Jeff Chandler,* of course," he laughs. He has plans.

Ellen Kaufman bustles around in her small kitchen, preparing dinner for two, for soon the shades of night, et cetera. A lovely and discerning gentleman, Mr. Chandler, will be coming at about seven, and Ellen wants to make certain that her meal will possess the indefinable perfection which lies at the heart of all great dining experiences. She is vaguely hopeful that a postprandial event of an intimate nature may occur, which is probably why she is in her old turquoise cocktail dress, a garment to which a few happy memories still precariously cling. Mr. Chandler displays rapt attention whenever Ellen speaks of her past travails and victories, e.g., her aberrant ex-husband, the decline and subsequent demise of her father's candy store, her delight in "bleu" cheese, her broken wig, the fedora which nobly speaks to her of liberation, and so on. Rapt attention, understanding nods, bloated vocabulary. So this will be one heck of a meal! Cold tomato soup with dill-and-paprika marshmallows, kohlrabi *en brochette* with clam sauce, anchovies *à gratin,* roast range-chicken with okra and yogurt dressing, crabgrass salad with dandelion oil and "bleu" cheese—gobs of it!— Banana Amaze, and herbal coffee. Ellen isn't aware that Mr. Chandler is Miner X. Beely, at this instant getting off the subway at 90th Street-Elmhurst Avenue. If his plans work out, and what plans!, he may not be coming to dinner at all. There is little reason to expect that Ellen's new overalls will be enough to rescue her from misery if Mr. Chandler breaks the dinner date. But at the moment, all is well, Ellen is smashing the kohlrabi with a kitchen utensil meant for the rote task, and singing, listen:

> . . . consider poetic brilliance unzesty,
> Let us strangle the nun of Amherst's modesty!

It is from "Death to Emily Dickinson's Modesty," of course, the lyrics of which were written by Ellen herself some seventeen years ago. The song now serves as the "rally chant" of the Daughters of Durga International, which organization holds the copyright. How Ellen was cozened out of this "property" makes for a long and ugly story, and this is not the place for it. Sufficient unto the day is the evil thereof. Wham! That takes care of the kohlrabi, now on to the tomatoes! Still singing, Ellen rummages in a drawer for her favorite secant.

Isolate Flecks seems, to Leo Kaufman's amazed eye, much too good to have been written by him, yet there's his name on the stained, ripped jacket. There's his biographical note appended to the flap copy. The apartment in which he sits, drunk on Old Mr. Boston Mint-Flavored Vodka, a beverage long considered by experts in the distilled-spirits field to be a symbol of despair, is cluttered and filthy. "I like it homey," Leo insists to the rare guest inveigled into entering. "Good God! What a genius I had," he says to the vodka label, which appears to him to be merrily dancing, like a *cabola.* On Leo's scarred and battered portable phonograph, a badly scratched record presents *Civil War Songs of the Northern Armies,* many of whose titles create grave doubts as to their authenticity, viz., "They Go Wild Simply Wild Over Me," "Can't Help Lovin' Dat Man," "Babalu," etc., etc. "Oh, Anne!" he cries. "Oh, Ellen!" he cries. He takes another drink. "Fish gotta swim!" he yells. There is no need to describe Leo, although fans may be interested to know that his once-luxuriant bush of undisciplined hair is now rather becomingly thin, and his beard is missing, revealing a face pitted with the acne scars which testify to an unhappy young manhood. Generally speaking, he looks a little like a totally collapsed Buster Keaton. He smashes a roach, groggy and adventurous from some spilled vodka, hence a little slow on his *tarsi,* with the spine of *Isolate Flecks,* then flicks the crushed body off the table to watch it land on a stained fedora perched atop a pile of pornographic magazines beneath the window, through whose grime each day appears reassuringly grey. "I gotta love one man till I die," he sings along with the virile chorus, hazily aware that he is hanging his misery on, we might say, the wrong song.

"And not *only* Getting the Most out of Your Leotard," Georgene says through the bathroom door, "not only that, but also I'm considering the Keep Fit course, which is going to be taught by Chet Kendrick."

"Chet Kendrick?" George says. "Chet Kendrick, the hambone actor? The muck of the boards?"

"Look," Georgene says, "dear. I know you really mean well, but despite your good intentions, will you please do me a favor and stick it up?"

"Chet Kendrick," George says quietly, inundated by jealousy.

Is she still taking a shower?

"Are you still taking a shower?" he asks.

She's taking a bath, George.

"I'm taking a bath, George," Georgene says. "If it's *your* business." Chet *Kendrick,* of course, knows that she's taking a bath. Chet *Kendrick,* despite the motherfucking, cocksucking, popeyed, sag-mouthed, rotten-toothed bastard's splayfooted walk, high-water pants, and tiny book of derivative poems on his marvelously varied sex life, oh yes, *he* knows that she's taking a bath, and every inch of her pussy as well. Doesn't he, George?

"May he be doomed to a life of bureaucracy forever!" George mutters. "May his wife prefer a cucumber to his crude attentions! May he never learn how to tie a tie!"

Some submit that jealousy runs, a violent and irresistible thread, through all societies. Certainly, evidence of it can be found among certain tribes in Kenya, those afflicted by the depredations of the passion giving themselves over to the relief to be found in ruthlessly bothering ants. (Gilberte Brie mentions this custom in "Spanning the Azure.") When people, especially the French, unexpectedly blurt out such words as *la veste* and *la corde,* they are obviously in the ineluctable passion's toils. State Trooper Kimberley Butz was regularly stalked because of it. Betty Barker maintains that she invented Key Lime pie when tortured by its ceaseless agonies: "At Barnard I knew a lot of girls," she writes in a crabbed hand, "and that did it." Information soon to be released by Scotland Yard reveals that the unfortunate Cambridge don, seized with a huge cache of stolen baseball cards and strapless bras, was goaded into his sociopathic transgressions by, right-o, jealousy. And Henri Kink's famous poem, which appeared many years ago in the long-defunct magazine *Blue Filter,* treats this universal weakness in, as a critic wrote, "a terse monologue developed amid a welter of illocutionary symbols," although he probably meant "symbols."

So George is not alone, then, in his torture?

George is not alone.

"And what about me?" Knute howls, "me and Zuleika? With a choking cry, he makes a lumbering dash toward the abandoned Chevrolet. The heather shines in the sunlight. Shines and glitters. Shines and glitters and . . . sings!

A man known only as Kirk, whose disturbingly penetrant cologne years ago attracted the amorous attentions of Sheila, edges nervously into François of Fargo's to use the restroom, but his shabby suit and scuffed shoes draw the glance of a resentful waiter—well, not *actually* a *waiter* —and Kirk strides, or, better, shambles to the stand-up counter and orders a small cup of okra-orange peel soup. "Just to take a piss," he grumbles. The healthful concoction arrives in a small bowl (a "cup") decorated with two blackletter F's intertwined in a design reminiscent of one of the Ferozepore sculptures—the "Lingam Twist"—and accompanying the robust liquid is a small slice of fresh asparagus bread. Oh-oh. Kirk takes a sip, nods dramatically to indicate that the soup is "up to" his culinary expectations, and makes for the Gents'. The waiter smooths his blond hair, smiles mockingly at this crude *gonif,* and thinks on subjects theatrical. Let's say Chekhov and his attendant plays. Can it be possible that the waiter is an *actor?* Well, not *actually* an *actor.*

As the door closes behind Kirk and his aching bladder, the Frankenstein girls are helping a trembling Fred from the table. His smile is vacuous, and touched with longing and expectation. The girls have been whispering naughty things to him, and his acute excitement has precluded his touching the remarkable bowl of oak-leaf salad with lo mein, huckleberry vinegar, and cod-liver oil, wittily dubbed the "White Man's Burden" by the salad chef.

Fred pays the cashier, his hands querulous as he carelessly pulls bills from his wallet. The girls, on either side of him, are amusing themselves by thrusting their hands deep into his trouser pockets. "Ooohhh," they say, a number of times. "I think Fred would like a good fleer," one says to the other, who replies, "A long drawn-out, *double* fleer," and they laugh. "A Saint George fleer!" they scream in unison. The light here, near the window, points quite objectively to the fact that the Frankenstein girls should, perhaps, be called the Frankenstein women, or, more brusquely but humanely, the Frankenstein broads. Fred, a broad in his own right, according to some, seems their perfect companion, and, as we can see, is. The three leave François's, arm in arm, and Fred, his brain a cauldron of unholy images, asks hoarsely, "Is a fleer painful?"

Kirk returns to the counter, takes another sip of the ominous soup, gags, and shambles, with renewed *esprit,* toward the cashier. Just outside the door, he comes upon a sheet of paper folded over and over into a small rectangle. He picks it up, and, chewing on a granola *digestif,* reads:

December 27, 1963

Dear Fred,

I'm writing because I'm embarrassed to speak to you. Actually, I'm also embarrassed to write.

I won't be able to see you. I'll explain. Due to my "clear-eyedness" and not to my clear thinking, I've hurt someone very much. Next, you were going to be hurt.

Last night, my future husband made visible his jealousy and disproportionate dislike of you. I was unable to assure him of the innocence of our future meeting. Prehaps I wasn't convinced myself. You see, I find it difficult to understand why anyone would accept "one-time only" circumstances without having some "designs." The more I tried to explain, last night, the weaker, I felt, my convictions were becomming. No, I don't understand at all.

I think you'll not be too angry with me, though. You may or may not know what it is to love someone and be hurt because you've hurt them.

Sheila

Underneath this message, in a different hand, Kirk reads, "and a happy new year to *you,* you little cunt." Kirk shakes his head. Sheila? Impossible. Not *Sheila* Sheila. He feels a slight manifestation of sexual desire as he remembers divers enchanting postures which Mrs. Henry liked to call her "own." And of course there was also her fleering ability.

Then too: Kirkwood, Missouri, Named "Sink of Depravity" by Noted Educators; *Klactoveedsedstene* Called Authentic Franz Kline by Art Experts; French Publisher Claims Pierre Klossowski Victim of "Character Theft" by Obscure American Author; Knights of Columbus Deny Bishop's Charge of "Kodak Worship"; "Ko-Ko," Bebop Classic, Termed "Gross Misrepresentation" by Black Authors Group; Crescent and Chattaway to Publish Janos Kooba's Novel.

Krazy stands before the meat counter, oblivious to the quarrel going on between a flushed, perspiring young man with an obviously "put on" accent, and a group of older men, each of whom wears, in his lapel, a metal device in the form of a crimson heart crowned with silver thorns. Krazy likes to stare at the packaged ground beef, which, to his weak eyes, looks like a display of red bricks. As the argument rages, the hallucinatory figure of a heart, not unlike those mentioned, rises from Krazy's head and hovers in the air. The quarrel ceases for a split second, then is resumed. The word "mufti" is heard again and again. There is something warm and inviting and familiarly depressing about the moment.

Tania Crosse changes her mind and decides to return to her apartment. She takes off her suit, blouse, and slip, puts on a burnt-orange robe of heavy silk, then mixes herself a Ricard and ginger ale. At her first taste, she puts the drink down, walks into the kitchen, and takes some pirogi, which she made a few weeks ago, from the freezer, then removes a container of sour cream from the refrigerator.
    "Krelewicz?" she says. "No, Krulewicz." Her eyes are shining, the scar tissue on her wrists glowing pink. "Krulicewicz!" she says, triumphantly. "Thelma Krulicewicz!" She leans against a huge butcher's block, bought from a wholesale butcher just off Little West 12th Street, astonished, feeling her thighs, her hips, her breasts, her shoulders, her face, her shoulders, her breasts, her hips, her thighs, her face.
    "Why am I wearing this demented robe?" she says to the utterly silent pirogi. "And where is my dear, my darling Rose?"

His stuffstuff is pandy and her grout is mushymushy. The educational value of visual aids cannot be underestimated. This looks like the "Calcutta Finger Spin."

"We can thank our lucky stars, Dick," Buddy said rather evenly, as the light from the Indian "star" fire he had carefully laid threw his powerfully etched face into virile relief, "that we happened on this crackerjack cave just as the fierce storm, that even now, as we may discern, howls outside, struck with primordial fury." He settled his Impetigo pack more comfortably between his broad back and a rough outcropping of porous oast.

"It 'pears I 'low tarnation bully well inter *that*, Buddy," Dick Witherspoon said seriously, thrusting a charred newt back into the glowing coals.

"What?" Buddy asked quizzically, his eyebrows meeting in stern disregard for appearances.

"Nothing, not a durn thing," Dick replied, looking up quickly from a grisly ember. " 'Nother morsel of critter, Buddy? This un's done to a right bully turn of crackling goodness."

"No, I think not," Buddy mused, looking at his friend with something approaching plangency. "I've just about eaten my fill of those tasty Magma lizards. It's time, anyway, for us to search this cave with a fine-tooth comb, if one remembers what the debauched Norsk seemed to suggest."

"What in the land of Goshen *did* the Scandihoovian say?" Dick asked pleasantly, his eyes filled with strange, thick smoke. "I'm blameder'n a coot if I can recollec' anything 'cepting his pizen glance." And with this he shuddered like a trembling aspic.

"He suggested that—but here, let's see if we can unearth the map that he mentioned, again and again, as he fled, heavily as I may recall, through the cruel fire-brambles."

"I surely do wish to blessed heaven that we find the durn thing, Buddy," Dick weakly enthused, "else it 'pears we might be here in till Labor Day!"

The chums, hastily casting their dining utensils into a shadowy corner, fell to their knees and began crawling toward the dark and forbidding recesses of the temporary shelter, their onerous way lighted only by the uneven, dancing flames of Buddy's expertly "wrapped" crutchberry torch.

"Whoosh! Oww-ww! Heck!" Dick ejaculated manfully. "My knees are being scraped right raw, even through my heavy canvas trousers that wear like iron yet get softer with each wash."

"Steady, old brick," Buddy urged, "and thank the good Lord in His wisdom and omnipotence that we are not women all a-scramble in such wise, else our sheer nylons would be torn into shreds by these infernal boulders."

"What are 'nylons,' friend?" Dick asked, his mouth quickly filling with shards from the many splintered stalactites lying about.

"Although," Buddy grinned happily, halting his progress for a moment, and leaning wearily against a wild hummock, "such a question is remarkably out of place, and should be answered with the strained silence it so richly begs, I'll deign to reply that 'nylons' are a species of feminine hosiery discovered some years ago by restless Science in its quest for marketable coal tar."

"Thanks, Buddy," Dick wheedled. "Can a feller find his way by means of such things?"

"What?" Buddy blustered, his eyes bulging in consternation.

"Nothing, not a solitary durn thing, Buddy," Dick replied, crawling forward again at a smart pace. "Say, Buddy," he soon called from a looming penumbra, "it 'pears to me there's a sort of cardboard . . . objeck . . . back here. Come and take a gander at oncet!"

Buddy scuttled quickly into a position that permitted the guttering torchlight to fall upon his comrade's exciting find.

"That is a cardboard box, Dick," Buddy laughed, "not an objeck. I am of the opinion that we may discover the shifty greaseball's map before too many more moments have fled into that mysterious area where les neiges d'antan ever hasten."

"Lay nage, Buddy?" Dick intoned good-naturedly, gazing wearily at a damp spot staining the granite fastness in which the lads were enclosed.

"But a literary allusion, simple pal," Buddy sneered. "Now! Let's to work!"

The bruised boys tore at the cardboard box enthusiastically, their facial expressions tense with hope, until at last, after long minutes of labor, made somewhat lighter by a spirited discussion anent the myriad differences between an "objeck" and many other things, the hefty container lay open before them. There glittered a cache of interesting items! Wordlessly, the boys glanced at each other, secure in the knowledge that their long friendship and its many larks and adventures had rarely yielded so astonishingly rich an oblate.

"I shall call out to you the names of these interesting finds," Buddy said, rather superciliously, to Dick. "And you may place them in the taxonomic groupings which seem to you rational or attractive. Is that clearly understood?" he masterfully concluded.

"Certainly, close pal," Dick said too quickly through gently clenched teeth. "Let's commence, then," he added, his two large hands theatrically raised toward a cloud of curious bats.

"Indeed!" Buddy agreed, adjusting the sputtering fasces attached inventively to his head by a handy thong neatly knotted with a double spinney, a knot known to all woodsmen as "our delight." "One copy of *Labors of Love,* apparently a novel based upon the screenplay for *Carom.* One can of La Basurita Aztec Food Products mastiachi peppers in tequila, hmm, I wonder if a fellow might make a passable *cacahuate* sauce from this delicacy? One copy of a slim booklet entitled *Lace Me Tighter!,* containing black-and-white photographs of a pair of corrupt female chums in various lewd postures and states of undress, with what appears to be an accompanying risqué text. One copy of *Lack of Evidence,* possibly, from a quick survey of its lamentable prose, an academic study of some sort. One copy of a short *récit, Chattering Fools,* which seems to be about two French sissies. Are you segregating neatly, dear fellow?" Buddy inquired with quick asperity. "And avoiding the steamy photos in that bestial publication? Such trash is the first step toward moral shipwreck and utter ruin, as you possibly may have heard."

"Deuced right," Dick replied, sprawling in maddened torpor against a knobby juke of plinth granite. For the first time since the friends had set out on their trek, Dick's voice had taken on an edge of unmistakable peevishness. "Dang!" he whispered, as if for the first time.

"One photograph of the ruins of a dwelling of some sort, with, on the reverse side, the words 'La Coste,' written in what is probably a No. 2 pencil. One empty envelope addressed to a Mme LaCrosse, said envelope of heavy rag stock in a delicate lilac hue. Getting all this, meathead?" Buddy hissed playfully.

"You bet, *chief,*" Dick chuckled sarcastically. "You mmphh . . . gndhnnghn."

"What?" Buddy demanded, whipping his brightly burning head around with the celerity of a mongoose.

"Nothing, not a durn thing, Buddy," Dick whined familiarly, absently pawing at his nether equipage.

"One rusted steel blouse. One pair of iron high-heeled shoes, likewise rusted. Another rusted steel blouse with Peter Pan collar. Two, no, three brass skirts, rather becomingly covered with verdigris. An iron-mesh, ah, an, uh, slip," the boy whispered blushingly, "tangled in which are some dried furze petals. And, finally, the collected stories of Campo Dawes, *We Don't Please Easy.* That seems to be the long and short of it, Dick," Buddy sighed, briskly rubbing his hands together with the dry sound that many had often admired.

"But," Dick began, a note of hysteria in his voice, "but wh-where's the dago's map?"

"There is no map, my simplehearted friend," Buddy replied, controlling his emotions as carefully as a lighthouse keeper runs amok so as to resist encroaching dementia. "We've been, I fear, the dupes of an intrigue methodically constructed to keep us roaming futilely about on these beetling scarps and great shale bluffs."

"Thunderation!" Dick cried, getting to his feet. "And . . . and all *this?*" he asked, flinging his calloused yet shapely arms about in the general direction of the neat piles he had made of the interesting items.

"It is the end result of bestial, useless labor," Buddy sobbed, an expression of half-sardonic melancholy on his pale lips. "We are not, it is clear, dealing with the regular-fellow forces daily encountered in the business world." He shuddered obtrusively, and, as he fell supine to the floor, the torch's flames reached his thick, lively hair and set it ablaze.

"Unconscious again?" Dick muttered in the silence of the grim cave.

Although she is still a stranger to the art of whistling, Sylvie Lacruseille has had her fill of men. She is settling herself comfortably on the old couch given her, in a spasm of uncharacteristic generosity, by Annie Flammard, although it must be said that Annie displayed this sudden penchant for gift-giving at a time when she thought Sylvie to be Luba Checks. Let it be stated unequivocally: there is a good deal of evidence to prove that Sylvie is not Luba. For one thing, we cannot find a single article on the crisis in Israeli morality anywhere in the apartment; for another, Sylvie despises mayonnaise, Hellmann's or otherwise; and finally, she neither wears nor owns contact lenses or reading glasses. Now she is settled, and prepares to give herself over to one of the many healthful exercises detailed in *Plaisirs Singuliers,* her eyes vacantly fixed on the trees just outside the living-room window. They are threatening to sough at any minute. On the phonograph, a rare, pirated recording of Lady Day performing "Southern Scandal" is softly playing. Sylvie is quite efficiently deshabille for her purposes. On the roof of the building across the street, a shifty-looking man, a grimy raincoat held rather nonchalantly before his lower torso, discovers that he can see directly into Sylvie's apartment, and that she is, quite unconsciously, displaying most, if not all, of her carnal charms to him. He says a silent and doubtlessly sacrilegious prayer that at some point this "toothsome" (he favors this word) woman will rise and stumble over the credenza standing against the wall. But why should she rise? And, if risen, why should she stumble? And over the credenza? Sylvie is most certainly not *blind,* more's the pity. Still, the watcher prays on, hoping against hope, although he can see that despite the presence of the credenza, there is ascertainable no evidence of a buffet supper. Maledizione!

To digress from the narrative, which thuds on, or, in any event, seems to thud on when we're not looking: Doctor Plot asserts that Raymond Chandler's *The Lady in the Lake* is indisputably the model for *Ladders at Last,* a work of fiction which "redefines, for all time, the much-abused 'historical' novel," and that the latter's protagonist, Lafayette—Brant Lafayette—is a more sophisticated version of Philip Marlowe. This literary nugget is to be found in "A Laff a Minute!," Plot's art-and-letters column published in the *Laguna Colony News.* The Good Doctor, as he prefers to call himself, is the paramour of the lecherous Nancy Lammeter, the wealth of whose cupcake empire has permitted her to buy up any number of weekly rags. Strangely enough, the *Laguna Colony News* is edited and published in Brooklyn, in a small loft building at the foot of Baltic Street, the same Baltic Street from which, even now, if we listen carefully, we may hear an inadequate imitation of the sound of popping champagne corks. If it hasn't occurred to you, let us suggest that coincidence is omnipresent, or, as we have a fondness for saying—at, some declare, the drop of a hat—"small world."

Item: We have been asked by the Lamoille County Sheriff's Department for any information we may have concerning an unpaid parking summons, issued to Henri Kink, who is carried in their files as "Deceased." One can almost see the troopers' bent, grizzled heads encircled by wreaths of pipe smoke as they bend to their necessary tasks. Such is the power of the objective correlative, in life as in art. Literary art. Certain literary art, some of it unacceptable.

Surrounded by the three or four thousand intractable typescript pages of the novel on which he has been sporadically at work for some sixteen years, Antony Lamont surrenders, finally, to the suspicion, long held in abeyance, that he has no idea what he is doing. For instance, he doesn't remember what his novel is "about"—is it "about" anything at all? He picks up a handful of sheets and riffles through them, stopping now and again to stare at a totally unfamiliar name. God! He doesn't even remember the names of his characters! Maybe he should keep a list? Will that help? What goes on in the chapter he calls "Jelly Doughnuts"? Or this one—"Time Will Tell"? Or "Gozos"? What about "Burnt-Match Moustache"? Jesus Christ! He looks at his published books, lined up chronologically on a shelf above his desk, in order to affirm his, well, reality. As always, he remembers, immediately, the vicious review, "Lamont's Ink Not Permanent," by that corrupted bastard John Hicks—he'll never forget *that* name. Where did he read or hear that the little prick is running some pop anthropology scam? The son of a bitch is dashing around now confessing to his past "cultural misogyny" in any newspaper that will print him. Lamont arranges his typescript in three ragged piles on his desk, vowing to read it through soon. Really. Very soon. To see if there's anything in it that can be saved. That makes some sense. That has maybe a paragraph or two which won't make him howl in disgust. Then he slits open the envelope, lying on his desk since yesterday, from the erstwhile publisher of his first novel, *Baltimore Chop.* It's a review—a review?—from *Virginia's Beat.* What the hell? It must be twenty, twenty-two years since. . . . Written in a cramped hand across the top of the yellowed clipping is "just found this in the files, thought you'd like to see." The review, one of the important journal's SHORT TAKES, reads in its entirety:

> "He felt as if he were about to float off on some cloud or other, somewhere into the blue . . . he felt as if he wanted to bite the rim of the glass." The reader will feel the same way as he plods through this dismal first novel, a supposed detective story without plot, tension, or characters we can care about. There is a lot of kinky sex, tough-guy talk, and tabloid sentimentality, all set down in a thick, unwieldy prose that has the clarity of axle grease. Keep your hands clean.

Lamont lays the review down and begins to laugh. The motherfuckers come right out of the grave to get you! He takes *Baltimore Chop* down from the shelf. Christ, what a lousy dust jacket! "What a lousy dust jacket!" he says. They have always been, as he tells anyone who will listen, his burden and his cross.

Excitedly, Father Debris suddenly "sees" intuitively into the heart of Lange's famous treatise on "les vapeurs," discovering therein what may well be termed subtle predictions anent the Décadence, the life and career of Yvonne DeCarlo, and the "lost" films of Barbra d'Eveuilley. Disregarding his older formula, which he grudgingly concedes has been leading him, of late, into hopelessly opaque solutions to the problems it is supposed to unlock with ease (*vide* the anagrammatic confusion in re: "Barbey d'Aurevilly"), he decides upon a new formula, that of Girolamo Cardano,

$$\chi = \left(\tfrac{n}{2} + \sqrt{(n/2)^2 + (m/3)^3}\,\right)^{\frac{1}{3}} - \left(-\tfrac{n}{2} + \sqrt{(n/2)^2 + (m/3)^3}\,\right)^{\frac{1}{3}}$$

which he then applies to Lange's text, so as to confirm his "flash" (or *perruque*) of insight. That section of Lange's text most receptive to the transforming powers of Cardano's formula reads: "Myrrh and aloes preserve corpses," which discovery inexorably leads to the noted physician's deduction that these elixirs are also beneficial against the vapors. Working swiftly, Father Debris sees that the Décadence, Yvonne DeCarlo, la d'Eveuilley, etc., etc., are specimens of "maladies nerveuses," curable by applications of *metaphorical* "myrrh and aloes." From here, it is but a short step for the good priest to—but let's allow him to work in peace.

Speaking of the vapors, it is the "dirty" (surely a slanderous descriptive!) Lydia Languish's vaporous plight to strip naked, accidentally, at every picnic or other outdoor social gathering to which she is invited, embarrassing the women and inflaming the men. Most of them. Well, many of them. Something, as they say, *seizes* her, and she is thus helpless. A glimpse of hardboiled eggs, or, as they are called on the *al fresco* circuit, "oeufs of a long boil," or a glance at a platter of potato salad— or even macaroni salad or cole slaw!—and Lydia is tearing at her garments. "Helpless!" she often cries out at such moments of humiliation. Today's picnic, at the bosky Scone Canyon Recreation Park, is no different from the others. There's Lydia, just beginning to pull off her sundress amid the smoke of rapidly charring hamburgers, steaks, and chicken. Question: If myrrh and aloes are effective against the vapors, is L'Ardent perfume? Do any of the women have a phial? If so, will it be employed? Lydia has her sundress off now, and neglected beans are turning black in neglected pots. Does *anybody* have a little L'Ardent? Lydia is in white underwear, the kind that makes men bump into trees and lampposts, put charcoal into the gin, and gnaw on their casual shoes. But there is no such thing as the vapors! Then what *does* Lydia have? In addition to her body, which we, because of our responsibility, have sworn not to notice? Now Lydia is . . . Lydia, please, Lydia. Lydia? Lydia!

Nota: "L'Ardent perfume is manufactured somewhere in Latin America," the comely, vivacious Miss Laughter says from her cool, elegantly appointed apartment overlooking the *marvelously* frenzied crowds sweating on the avenue below. "It contains neither myrrh nor aloes, but employs as essential ingredients two roots native to the region— *cagajón* and *pucha*. Isn't this a breathtaking view? And by the way," she turns, suddenly smiling, "what do you think of my jugs, you pig?"

Léonie Aubois looks up from the floor. "*I* used to be Miss Laughter, you can ask anybody. For Christ's sake. That was about the time I was nominated—*me,* not Sheila!—for the Ralph Lauren Medal for Literature, argent with two mounted Labrador retrievers sable in orle." She pulls herself to her knees, looking for the vodka, sees that the bottle is empty. "The fucking bottle of fucking vodka is fucking empty," Léonie says. A scene of rage and heartbreak, made more powerful by the tension of the setting, follows. But *we* don't have to observe it!

Few people consider Lawton, Oklahoma, to be a hotbed of interesting artistic activity, fertile ground for avant-garde experimentation, and, aesthetically speaking, a burgeoning regime of irrepressible new ideas in many exciting areas. Yet it is. Not many would expect to discover the attractive, well-built, and engagingly bemused middle-aged author of the prize-winning *Leaves of Yearning,* Lorna Flambeaux, living right here in the center of town. (Indicates "center" of town.) There are also occasional heavy rains in the area, and Lefty, as Miss Flambeaux is known here, is usually to be found, soaked to the skin, in Lena's Rest, a popular tavern. According to the blue-neon message in the window, Lena's has the BEST BUGGERS IN TOWN. One *heck* of a claim, and yet many can testify to its truth. More or less. Lena, and there really *is* a Lena (indicates shapeless figure in filthy apron), offers, as well as her famous "buggers," a wonderful selection of jelly donuts (indicates grease-oozing pastries) and color photographs of all sorts, with a special emphasis on open wounds. A little slimy, yes, but Lawtonians seem to adore them. This *is* the heartland. People hereabouts are quite anxious to chat with Lefty about her new work, *Lengthy and Serious Talks,* but opinion decrees that she has "passed out" again, despite the presence of the whole darned crew from *Lens and Shutter.* Few expected *this!* The gang, by the way, is a crack outfit, no expense spared, no detail too small, yet always with some time for a racist joke and a good laugh, etc., etc. They're certainly unlike the last bunch, inept misfits characterized by the town rabble as "right dumb schlongs." (Indicates anatomical photograph.) Lorna doesn't seem to be moving, although she's been known to go into orgasmic trances in the past. Well, let's hope for the best!

Lento's Bar and Grille, in Brooklyn, is always quiet in the afternoon, and today is no exception. To that general rule. If it may be so designated. As such. It is not, hell, *actually* a *rule.* The real Anne Leo sits at the bar, chatting with Henny, one of the more spectacularly drunken bartenders in this part of the world. "What's my name, Henny?" Anne asks. "Ha, ha," Henny answers, and falls to his knees on the duckboards. "What?"

Anne asks, "what is it?" "Ha, ha, ha," Henny answers again, undecided whether he should remain kneeling or just briskly fall over. "That's *right,*" Anne says, "and I don't need no goddam Jew bitch with eclectic experiences and life skills taking my name, you hear me?" Henny may hear her, but it seems as if he has no wish to reply. Looking at this rather seedy bar, the lone customer, the semiparalyzed bartender, it is very difficult to believe that Evelyn Leonard, First Lieutenant Evelyn Leonard, once sojourned herein. Yet photographs occasionally tell the truth. Look. You see? Is that Evelyn Leonard or is that Evelyn Leonard? It was from this bar, Lento's, that she shyly edged into the high-powered urban milieu, starring at last in *Black Silk Stockings,* an acknowledged early classic of the sticky-floor school. Evelyn may have begun her long and somber journey to fleeting fame and lasting moral degradation on the sad evening, now happily obscured by time's opaque raiment, when she agreed to enter a "motor inn" with a female acquaintance who pretended an interest in the young officer's descriptions of close-order drill and cold-cock suppers. Leo Kaufman, in his last poem, "Leo's Last Poem," hints at the motor inn goings-on in the lines

> Like a lost clam, so
> the sweet scent
> of your breath amid
> the rust-
> ed Chevys.

"Drunk as I am now and may yet get later drunker even," Leo protests, "I never wrote this poem, never wrote 'Leo's Last Poem,' and believe me I know about the back-stabbing bastards who call *Isolate Flecks,* my always interesting and occasionally brilliant novel of city life, *Leo's Lunge.*" He sits back. "Should I look into the bathroom mirror to see, with a start of shocked surprise, my sad, defeated face? Or what? Shall I look so that I may . . . *hate myself?* Huh?" Nothing except the animal grunts and groans of Fred and the Frankenstein girls can be heard in reply. We had no idea that the vivacious sisters lived in Leo's building. Neither did Leo.

Lerajie, Creator of Strife, Great Marquis of Lacerations, complains quietly to a waitress in Les Lobsters that his shrimp cocktail is far from chilled, and that his lemon wedge appears to be, well, *used.* He is dressed in a crisp, khaki-colored, tropical worsted suit, rather than in his usual macabre green. It is not what we would call "good news" to find him here. As the waitress cocks her head to stare in rude wonder at this astonishing creature who has *complained* while scores of cuisine devotees wait patiently to be seated in this, the "best and most authentic" of seafood restaurants, we, as they say, do but cringe at her ignorance. The waitress, "Chickie" "Hips" Levine, the putative mother of Andy, the canned-soup admirer, laughs unpleasantly, and casually notes that if the patron doesn't *care* for the appetizer, she not only has no idea what she might *do* about the situation, but she is really, uh, not very *interested.* Y' know? Lerajie, distressed by this inhospitable information, gazes pleasantly at "Chickie," whereupon large, suppurating lesions appear "as if by magic" upon her arms, legs, face, and probably those areas of her body not readily visible because of her fetching uniform. Lerajie smiles engagingly, fingering the knot in his pale-yellow tie. "I certainly, oh yes indeed, *would* be pleased if you'd bring me another shrimp cocktail! How very kind!" he says brightly. "And you might ask the maitre d' to come over here too. When he has a minute, of course." There seems to be a question as to whether "Chickie" hears Lerajie, since her screams are ear-splitting. A thin, yet decisively blunt odor of putrefaction settles over the restaurant's patrons, and many disquieting, we might even say disgusting things begin to occur. Lerajie, however, considers them to be among the indefinable perfections which lie at the heart of all great dining experiences. Including the notably attentive swarms of flies.

Guy Lewis is sitting on his fifth-floor fire escape in a pair of boxer shorts and an "athletic" undershirt, now, we understand, Back in Style Again! Can this be a fact? Athletic undershirts?

Now they call them "tank tops" or "top tricks" or "truck stops" or something. They're cut different, Come in colors and such.

Thanks. Guy, as you may have surmised, is deeply concerned about fashion, so much concerned, in fact, that he refuses to be seen on the streets of his teeming and electrically-charged polyglot neighborhood while wearing said "athletic" undershirt, or, to be precise, while wearing

one or another of the two "athletic" undershirts he owns. Not for Guy
the current "truck stop" or something. He is sweating in the vicious
sunlight and working on his third large drink of blended whiskey—Four
Roses today!—and ice, which he sips from a large Hellmann's Mayonnaise jar. The recipe for this summer cooler is a simple one, simple, yes,
and like so many simple things, elegantly understated: Place plenty of
ice in a large, clean jar, then fill to the top with a good blended whiskey.
Four Roses is excellent, good body and fine nose; Schenley's Silver
Label has a slightly bolder aroma and a persistent coppery aftertaste;
Paul Jones has a brusque nose and will make the eyes start forth from
the head in horror; and etc., etc. The most important thing to remember,
Guy would be delighted to tell you, could he but form more or less
reasonably intact sentences, is to have plenty of ice. Guy doesn't want
much from life, but when he sits back to enjoy a well-earned rest with a
reassuring drink by his side, or in his hand, or for that matter anyplace,
he insists on plenty of ice. Right to the brim is not too much! Ice cubes?
Fine! Cracked, shaved, any kind of ice will do. But wait! Guy is grinning
his boyish grin through the bars of the fire escape, and it seems as if . . .
yes, yes! He's going to tell us himself just what it is that makes a merely
pleasant afternoon into an extraordinary leisure experience. Guy?

"Plenty ice. Y' need plenty of ice. Plenty of ice and plenty of whiskey
and that's it. Wow! Wow!"

As we have just heard, it is ice and plenty of ice that spells the difference between humdrum occasions and memorable fetes. Guy stands
up and holds onto the fire-escape railing. He puts one leg over, then the
other. He jumps into the street. One "Wow!" too many.

Joanne ("Bunny" to all who have followed the twists and turns of these
twists and turns) Lewis wheels her father out into the sunshine, adjusts
a light cotton blanket around his legs, and settles his ludicrous green
visor on his head. Mr. Lewis doesn't really need this visor, but there has
been, we understand, an overwhelmingly emotional vote for it. "Do
you want anything else, Poppa?" she asks. "Orange juice? The paper?"
Her father makes no sign, but settles his gaze on the chicken coop,
which, as Bunny knows, he thinks of as the site of his victory over the
onslaughts of Eros. She wonders again what became of Mrs. Feuer,
who is certainly, God knows, getting on in years. Yet on the day, not too

long ago, that the lady left Gnatville for good, or so it turned out, she wore a grotesque mask of white makeup, black fishnet stockings, and red patent leather four-inch heels. Bunny looks at her father, whose hands, in the great tradition of afflictions, are "trembling uncontrollably" in his lap. She suddenly feels disgusted, as she uncannily thinks "stuffstuff," "mushymushy." Ugh! "The languish of flowers." *Disgusting!* She is just about to go back into the house, out of the impossible sun, away from thoughts, if that's what they are, of Mrs. Feuer, when she sees an odd-looking woman, a strange, blue, filthy *something* knotted around her neck, standing in the middle of the street, looking at a pall of smoke which hangs in grey oppression over the northern part of town. Now Bunny sees it, and then smells it, a curiously repellent odor, a fetid mixture of charred meat, smoldering garbage, sweat, urine, feces, and sulfur. "Something—excuse me?—something seems to be . . .burning?" she says to the woman in the street.

"Bees burning? *Bees* burning, ah," Frieda smiles wisely, and gestures toward the smoke. "Is barbecue foods? Cooking bees?" She smiles again, and sniffs the air. Bunny stares at her. Can this be Mrs. Feuer, come to take her father away from her? "Have you come far?" Bunny asks. "I mean, are you visiting, here in town?"

"I like much jelly donuts," Frieda says. "From corns, donuts?" Then, standing with her back straight and her arms rigid at her sides, she closes her eyes and recites, "Up from meadow rich with corns! Who arms hair on a grey head, dies! Like a dogs, march on! And so, he said." Frieda winks at Bunny, and says, "American poem good like donuts, yes?" and then takes a step toward the porch.

"Go away!" Bunny cries. "My father is very sick! The chicken coop is, is, it's broken! We don't have any more Indian corn! And this is an old dress, you see this dress, this is an old dress that I hate!" She is pulling desperately at her old and familiar white crocheted dress, pulling at it with both hands as if to tear it off her body. Her father stares at the chicken coop, drooling onto the napkin knotted around his neck. Frieda stares at Bunny, astonished by this new American custom, then begins to tear at her own clothes. Bunny feels as if the mouth of Hell has opened for her.

Corrections of Earlier Errors

Item: The ugly Henry Lewison, known in his fizzling youth as "Hank," "Chico," and "Hen," does not actually fall *dead* when surprised with certain judiciously selected poems of John Crowe Ransom. His vacant stare, on such occasions, can, in good conscience, be called a "trance." According to John Greene Czcu, a well-appointed and nicely turned-out psychic researcher, this stare is akin to an Interzonal Receptivity Modal, or what Czcu describes, with perhaps a hint of good-natured mockery in his voice, as that place "where all art begins—art, that is, for chemists with some spare time."

Item: Plain Lucía Lewison, at one time Henry's wife, was not locked out of the Kodak Motor Inn, "allegedly nude," by John Greene Czcu; she was ejected from the Lido, a hotel which Czcu, with perhaps an edge of weary bravado in his voice, terms a "fleabag."

Item: Lincoln Center is assuredly not a "fleabag," as Josh Cabernet rather surprisingly claims in his tawdry and sensationalist book *Cameras Work.* Our deepest apologies go to the directors of the renowned arts complex, their relatives, loved ones, friends, and not least of all, to the dedicated cohort that "keeps it all going" year after triumphant year, the incomparable gang familiarly known as *"les embouchures."*

Item: Although the Lincoln Inn and the Lincstone are most certainly not the four-star hotels they once aspired to, neither are they "flea-bags," in which one can "get his or her ashes hauled" at any time of the day or night, as alleged by Doctor Plot in the *Laguna Colony News.* Doctor Plot is, in the words of a little-known *tummler,* no better than a fleabag himself.

Lincoln Gom finishes reading another really terrific and interesting article on composting latrines that pay for themselves in *Green Sunshine,* the ecology magazine to which he is a Patron. To think that human excrement—not attractive in itself—the ever-busy *prunellae* bacterium, and assorted tits and nuthatches can make the garden literally *explode* in riotous color! But at present, his hair silverly gleaming, or is it shining softly with what might be called silvery highlights?, it's time for Linc to grapple with sober business thoughts! Lincstone

Productions, for some years now the perplexed victim of a disturbing and wholly inexplicable surge of "good taste"—well, not precisely "good"—on the part of its audience for cultural programming, is on its way up again! Lincoln beams through the aromatic smoke from his mellow meerschaum, and settles more deeply into his robe of Maraschino silk. Picking up Elizabeth Barrett Browning's secret journals, *My Secret Journals,* in his all-leather study, he comes across more than one virtually intoxicated reference to Charles Paul de Kock in her pages. She is mad for *Georgette,* passionate about *Gustave ou le mauvais sujet,* almost delirious in her praise of *Mon voisin Raymond,* and virtually inarticulate concerning the ardor she feels for *L'Amant et la lune.* This is good enough for Lincoln, for if there is one writer he trusts above all others, it is Mrs. Browning. There's something febrile about her best work. In any event, Lincstone Productions is about to begin shooting on a film based on *Mon voisin Raymond.* Good God! Lincoln exclaims, laughing sternly into his rich arras at the sheer coincidence of, well, *things.* The story needs some changes, of course, so as to make the visual images this and that, and to make sure that the book's introspective qualities are that and this, and so on. The cinema is, after all, the cinema, and pictures are, after all, pictures. Words, too, yes, words are, after all, words. The film will be released as either *Raymond and Desire* or *Lace Me Tighter!*

"Hi! I'm Linda, once in a while, most 'specially when I'm spanning the azure empyrean, raptly bent on those womanly tasks that only women excel at, or is it bent over? I can't quite read this. Whatever, when I'm on my square-jawed industrial engineer's arm, casually strolling toward his high-performance car for a moonlight spin down country byways, I'm just another American Karen. Hi!"

"Hi yourself," Lips says, flashing his most delightfully engaging grin, the sort of grin that Lips knows Lips excels at. We feel constrained, however, to admit that this sunny greeting and benevolent grin are intended to mask the fact that Lips may be about to steal the copy of *Absalom! Absalom!* abandoned atop the Granny Smith apples. He may also steal an apple or two. All depends on whether or not the attractive vegetarian couple browsing among the slabs of tofu will stop

looking at him. Every fucking minute for Christ's sake! Don't they have anything better to do? Wash their running "togs"? Invest some capital?
"Is someone talking to us, dearest?"
"I think it's this walnut-grape leaf tofu, darling."

Then too: Author of *Little Cabals,* in Speech, Claims Pollution Will Kill Only Rich; Twelve-Million-Year-Old Woman with "Liz" Ankle Bracelet Discovered in Bronx; Study Finds Harold Lloyd May Have Written *Revelations*; *Lobster Lays* to Be Sex Show for Kids on Cable; Lochinvar's Spirit Said to Molest Locust Valley Matrons; Loire River "Mostly Urine," Expert Reveals.

LoLo smiles uncertainly into the camera and nods rather pleasantly as she is introduced by Emil Krasch, your Dynamo! reporter, as Bam's twin sister. They both, as the reporter points out, share a delight in plaids, the charming pair adhering to a ludicrous belief—which has absolutely no basis in fact—that they are Scottish. The program, if that's what this is, ends with Emil's noting, in a tone of mild alarm, that LoLo is attracted to handymen, superintendents, deconstructionists, fisherfolk, in short, men who wear tool belts, preferably filled. "A well-filled tool belt," Emil says, his face so sincere that it could make Himmler weep—
"Vot?" Himmler shouts. "Vot iss dot Choo saying?"
—his eyes, steady and cold, yet somehow, shifty and warm. "Yes. Tool belts. Something to think about. This is Emil Krasch for Dynamo! News, in London."
He's not in London.
"Ve could haff plown London off der map! Shtinking English fairies!"
"Am I the star or am I the *star?*" Emil says. "Besides, I didn't say *London,* I said *Jack* London, open your ears for God's sake!"
Jack London?
"Yes, Jack London, Jack London. Right. Jack London!"
As if at a given command, these stars of the electronic news media and their charming flunkies disappear into *really* marvelously comfortable dressing rooms, the appointments and accoutrements of each clearly contracted for. Are they stars or are they *stars?*
"All said contracts legally signed by all said proper parties in all said proper places," an attractive flunky smiles.

Thank you. Is she (indicates attractive flunky by filing cabinet) an attractive flunky or is she an *attractive flunky?*

Nice jugs.

"Both 'jugs' are legally contracted for," the attractive flunky sighs. "It's utterly remarkable how far we've come in the rough-and-tumble world of the workplace. Makes you kind of think."

LoLo, however, is *still here.* "I really don't like plaid all that much, and I don't think Bam does either, and I don't think, also, that Bam is my twin brother or any kind of brother at all."

From the recesses of a nearby supermarket we hear "POP! POP!" What a day.

It is mere coincidence that so many things are happening on Long Island today. The Lard Goddess, *soi disant,* falls heavily into a pastel sandbox; an inscrutable message issues forth from Hicksville, i.e., *krik-kk, krik-kk;* an idiotic adolescent, Looy, who looks exactly like Jiggs, is subjected to the "Moussogorsky *Pictures* torture" after reporting the sighting of two rather indolent airborne dogs (he calls them "doggies"); the Glen Cove Public Library discovers an unknown manuscript by D.H. Lawrence, whom all of Glen Cove likes to think of as "Lorenzo" because of the miniseries *Lord Chatterley's Plume*—the item is found in a copy of Viña Delmar's *Kept Woman;* a hastily called emergency session of the remaining members of the Gnatville City Council results in a fistfight over the proposition: Shall the City of Gnatville be burned to the ground and the ashes sown with rock salt? Certain other things have happened as well, but we feel that the gross laughter of the gross world may greet their telling. Suffice it to say that whichever way we look we see a reflection of venery.

"That's the way it is in small towns," the big guy in green work clothes says. "They tend to take it pretty well, but they get those goiters, you know? Like when I was dry that time up to Missoula for a spell? Alice knew. Hell, that's when we had the motel with a swimming pool, those nice little chairs around, umbrellas and all. Really nice, but then the leaves just came right down and it was fall again somehow. Then the concrete sort of cracked, I don't know. I used to be some looker then, before Claude, you know, put me in the way of the Teacher's and those damn Hershey bars. Might's well have lit out for Topeka but the Chevy threw a rod. I'm getting straightened out now though. Want to hear about it? Or about any other instances of gritty reality told just as honest as I know how to tell it? Or them? Things that'll just make you nod your head in recognition?"

We feel as if we really don't. But thanks. Anyway.

Bored for some years now with the golden sands and endless golden sunshine of distant golden and exotic lands, Annette Lorpailleur now lives in the city, and is still a little "odd." Many recall the issue of *Lorzu* which ran an article on her voice, "The Performative Function of the Ventriloquial Utterance." There were ugly recriminations, but the essay had its effect. Now she is looking at her copy of *Kept Woman,* which Annette has had translated into French as *Femme entretenue,* with her name given as author. The translator, Henri Kink, is never seen anymore, and gossip, as usual, careens about. Somebody by that name has something to do with something on television or something, but he's only twenty and thinks that Stan Getz invented jazz or whatever! That can't be Henri. Can it? There are lots of people who think that Stan Getz invented jazz, but academics don't count. Annette looks up and smiles her stop-action smile, and a smell of molten copper and smoldering hair hangs sour and metallic in the apartment. The walls are shifting with deep shadows and bright slivers of what may be light, although it hasn't the qualities of light but seems a kind of impossible incandescent blackness. Annette lays the book down and walks away, the terrible illumination glittering off the skintight metal sheath which covers her body, while her thighs, brushing lightly against each other in their humid darkness, create a faint chiming. The apartment is swelteringly frigid. It may as well be added that Annette looks about thirty.

She stops and turns to stare. As they say, *look out.*

Lee Jefferson unexpectedly comes across a color advertisement for Lorzu Fashions, and is "borne back in memory" to her brief and ultimately unsatisfying partnership in the little boutique that was before its time—or was it after its time? Perhaps it was just right for its time, to no avail. No matter. Still, it was a shame to have had the place torched. She looks at the ad and for some private reason thinks of a certain Louie, whose animated descriptions of the "indiscretions" of notable

leaders at the parties given by Lincstone Productions were responsible
for getting her through many a night. For instance, the story of the
Senator, the pantyhose, and the pint of vanilla ice cream, and the one
concerning the CEO, the blowgun, and the tubful of mustard were real
"life savers." Louie, *dear* Louie! Lee smiles her best editorial smile,
which antic grimace she can no longer control, and thinks, astonishingly enough, of Lourdes. Lourdes? She begins to tremble. Lourdes?
Maybe because the word is so close in shape to Louie. Lourdes, Louie.
Of course, that's it! Is it? She leans back on her elbows amid the files
scattered about on the floor, her eyes amazed, her brow glazed with
sweat, her jaw clenched. Much of the rest of her body is also sweaty, but
that is not our business, although she does have a spot of trouble with
underarm "moisture," truth to tell. Perfectly natural, as far as we're
concerned, although we must confess that there is a good deal of cruel
laughter to be heard from certain areas, especially those located on the
great shale bluffs which overlook Chinatown. Chinatown! Little, if any,
decency is shown.

She keels over onto the sand and we can see now, dare we have the
temerity to invade her grief-stricken privacy, that the object she
clutches to her ample bosom is her most beloved doll, Lu-Lu. It is
shabby and tattered by the years' sad, long and sad passage, yet is as
dear, still, as sweet, as wonderful as ever it was in the bloom of its
novelty. The uncaring rabble, in their ignorance, gambol rudely, as best
they know how, poor souls, about the still figure. Yet up Above, and
gazing kindly Down, whenever, that is, Chance and a Busy Schedule
permit, that most cherished Helpmeet of the Creator's, the Doll Queen,
knows the heartache of the quiet Shape on the Strand. Smile, oh Doll
Queen, smile in Joy on your best Servant and her dear, her beloved and
faithful Lu-Lu, who seems about to break into an aria of surpassing
Beauty. Probably in German.

Lyons, world-renowned for its humble potato dish, and, among the
cognoscenti, for the Macedero Club, where the immaculate napery
hides many a furtive adventure of *amour à doigts,* is losing its pre-
eminence in the world of latenight entertainment.
    "But of course, darling!" Lady Bustier says, sparing a moment from

her roses, and what beauties they are! "The frightfully boring evening when they banned me because of my 'Madame Doctor' costume was *really* too tiresome. The beginning of the end, really. I mean, it's not as if I wore the frightfully revealing things that one sees in films like, oh, *Madame Delbène,* for instance. The city once had a great deal of charm, but now, I fear that it's *so much* like Madrid, I mean with all those frightfully tawdry statues of saints and things and all sorts of bells ringing and Catholics just *everywhere* and goodness knows what else. But do let me get back to this new hybrid, The Magician they call this one. It's the most delightfully *red* red."

"As far as I'm concerned, the 'Madame Doctor' costume *is* pretty damn revealing, thank God," Sir Bloom remarks to Lord Bury, who is gazing abstractedly—a kind of gazing which, or so it's been discovered, is much in favor with the reserved nobleman—at a young man breaking into an apartment on the ground floor of the building across the court-yard. "I say, Bloomie old darling, there's a young chap across the way who looks *awfully* like Billy Magrino."

"Who on earth is Billy Magrino?" Sir Bloom says, irritably. He is still fuming because of his belated discovery of the existence of the "Cute Cop" line. "And why on earth should I care?"

"Magrino was your original apron purveyor, old boy. Good heavens, have you become so *frightfully* jaded?"

"Of course he was," Sir Bloom says. "Of course. And an absolutely topping boy, too, as I recall. Had a remarkable way with starch."

Billy may still be wonderful with starch, but he is not prepared to discover, in the room to which he gains entry, absolutely nothing but two irregular heptagons of an indeterminate material propped against the dark wainscoting. One is blank, and the other whispers—at least to Billy—the word "ciel." "Oh Jesus!" Billy mutters, backing toward the window, "I'm in le palais des rideaux." Then other things begin to happen, among them the preposterous onset of a wracking *jouissance* which not even Billy's considerable literary intelligence may detain. So we leave him, as smart as ever, writhing against first the walls and then the floors, clutching at his well-made trousers with, apparently, no discernible plan in mind. Thus comes to pass the occasional betrayal by the flesh when it finds that it's been taken into strange rooms.

To return to our wealth of anecdotal material on René Magritte: Magritte is still, after all these years, fondly remembered in Curtin's Palace, a diner specializing in seafood, most especially Crab Mah-Jongg. This dish was the delicacy much favored by the controversial, yet well-dressed French surrealist during his American sojourn, or, as Magritte liked to call it, his "visit to America." Quite an *homme!* Ed Curtin, the owner, who was but a teenaged boy when the celebrated avant-gardist "dropped in," as Ed's father, Cliff, often put it, is happy to recount Magritte's remarks for inquisitive guests, as he is just about to do.

"Mr. Magritte would always say, 'Ah lav zees creb deesh.' And then, later, he'd say, ' 'Ow modge ees zees?' He'd always say that, always ask the price. Then, sometimes he'd say, like as not, ' 'Ow far ees Maine?' When he'd ask how far it was to Maine, well by thunder you could hear a pin drop."

"What does 'cute' mean?" a rather hairy stranger barks from the rear of the small crowd. Before Ed can answer, the stranger's friend, clearly exasperated, hurries him out of the diner.

We understand, by the way, that Curtin's Palace has the best burgers in town.

Thought that was Lena's Rest.

That's the best *buggers.*

What?

April Detective, sitting irresolutely in bed, drunk and naked, as in so many tales of squalor and defeat (indicates photograph of "library of filth and degradation"), ignores the ringing phone. It's her sister, May, of course, calling yet again with the usual unbearable tales about her disappearing underclothes. This week it's slips. April, squalid to a fault, takes a long swallow of vodka and scratches her pubic hair, which has just a little distinguished grey in it—young men no longer suddenly catch their breath when she is passing. The vodka is, as you may have guessed, Majorska, made (or better, created) from the water of pure mountain streams that plunge from their sources in the immaculate snows of beetling scarps inviolate; a vodka that is then filtered, not once, but *thirty-eight times* through expensive imported charcoal, a charcoal that is the product of the rare hardwoods of Corsica, hardwoods that have

long been the source of the world-famous meerschaum which is lovingly carved into one-of-a-kind pipes by colorful old men who speak
no English. They use only the "heart of the bole," and so do the folks
at Majorska, tending the slow fires for weeks until the meerschaum
turns into silken black charcoal. This, then, is April's drink, so much so,
in fact, that she is known to some as Miss Majorska, a monicker first
playfully hung on her by a clubfooted acquaintance of interesting carnal
appetites. He's often seen about town, trying to locate potential partners
for a business-tips scheme. Unfortunately, his affliction, which is at
times referred to as "unspeakable" (as in, "Great Scott! When he takes
his socks off it's *unspeakable!*"), serves to make him the object of pity,
fear, and disgust. The Earl of Bodoni and his inseparable companion,
Mr. Stanley Boils, insist, amid gales of sadistic laughter, that the
walking-impaired gentleman was literally *driven through the air* in
Malibu by the strangely powerful Tony Malinger, who instantly took
offense at his clothing—something about a "weird suit" which frightened starlets and looked "shoddy" against the genteel backdrop of
pastel Rolls-Royces. Rumors still persist that Malinger's pet crow is
actually Malpas, Friend of Fake Artificers. He of the Hoarse Voice.
He Who Answers Questions Incorrectly. He Who Sends Muffie on
Her Demented Shopping Orgies. He Who Makes Delilah Crosse Im-
modestly Expose Her Legs.

Only the most dedicated researchers among students of the cinematic
arts know that the celebrated café scene in *From Natchez to Mobile,* in
which Dolores Délire, as Madame Froufrou, her gown "trackt to the
daintie thies" so that we may almost, but not quite glimpse her *cache-
buisson,* hands Baylor Freeq, who plays Robert Frost, a jar of apple
sauce, was filmed in Mama Gatto's restaurant, right here in old
Manahatta.
   "Are you *sure?*" Mandie asks, rather belligerently. She's a kind of
girl about town, *loves* fashion, cooking, campy movies, hip novels
about, like, real people, really tough political satire, and cultural
nationalism as a solution to the problems blacks face. She also has a pet
theory that Elvis Presley invented rock and roll. For Mandie, it's best
that he did. "And what's this like Manahatta?" she says. "I mean it's
Manhattan, right? Like, a borough and a kind of a drink for old lushes,

like a cocktail or something, right?"

Any point in going into anything at all with Mandie? Or does she seem, despite her intrinsic worth as a human being, essentially a bust?

According to a tall and rather pale young man, not too pale, but with a complexion not unlike that of Natty Bumppo's, or Gunnery Sergeant Caleb Magrane's, there is no point to it. This young man, a possible victim of hyperbolic neurasthenia (indicates staring eyes and "nervous" testes), identifies himself as Mandie's brother, and one who is "best nameless, or, if not nameless, then best forgotten!" The young man goes on, "If she's caused me one moment of tension and heartbreak, she's caused me a dozen. Ever since we moved here from Misty Crag and its huddled environs of encroaching tares, things have gone wrong. Whichever way we look we see reflections of venery, the trees are constantly threatening to sough, and *wildly* sough!, and little if any decency is shown by anyone. Mandie has become a devotee of the radical Olga Begone's hate-filled poetry, and I, once an innocent stranger to the art of whistling, now find myself removing my underwear every evening, despite my rigorous Baptist upbringing."

"That was a *nice* introduction from that nameless wet dream," Olga says contemptuously. Her upcoming and highly publicized aluminum diet has made her the momentary center of media attention. "Can it!" Olga invariably snaps brusquely, "and keep your compliments for some dumb broad who thinks good things about stiff wee-wees, O.K.? As far as I'm concerned, all the stiff wee-wees in the world aren't worth my Mandie's smallest, sweet, swell, subtle smile." Olga sits at a table piled rather terrifyingly high with black spring binders, and asks if anyone remembers the title poem from *Man-Kill.* Mandie's brother, eyes straining, bolts in horror from the poet's vicinity. He may very well know something that no one else does, something about Begone's conviction that the artist has the duty to subvert the canonical conception of phallic mass.

"Man-Kill"

Crowds of man-shit drunk on whiskey,
Crowds of macho snots, all hot,
Crowds of scum-tongues, fingers frisky,
Filthy scab-cocks pushed at twats.

A semen sky! A world of schmucks!
Greasy balls on rapist goons!
Sisters! Let us kill these fucks!
Cut the balls off all the goons!

Slit the testes in sweet fury!
Burn the stiff prongs with our flames!
We need no "just" and "sober" jury
To slaughter beasts! Come, let's to games!

Coincidentally, a much-belated review of *Man-Kill* is appearing today in what is usually referred to as an important literary journal. Mannix Lambert, known to his adoring students and bitterly jealous colleagues as "Mans," is the reviewer, as is only just and right. Who else knows as much, or for that matter, understands as much about contemporary radical lesbian leftist feminist non-penetrant academic poetry as good-old-hip-deeply-caring-hell-of-a-guy "Mans"? This is a rhetorical question, of course. Marpas, the Transformer, who usually appears as a mighty lion but quickly assumes comely human shape when confronted with chocolate or photos of naughty citizens "in," as they say, "action," Marpas himself was once so astonished by Professor Lambert's acumen and sympathy, perception and compassion, and so on, that one dark night he changed him into a woman. For a few hours. Just to see what he'd look like. One of the things that makes Marpas Marpas is his endless and ever-fresh curiosity. The professor doesn't know of this change, lucky for him, given the events of that night, but there are many things that people, especially professors, don't know. As Thomas Ballantyne writes in *'Tis the Thief Is Prejudicial,* "Belike unto an apeish picture out o' wax / Oft men are stumbo'd in drear ignorance." But we digress. Let us see what "Mans" has to say about Ms. Begone's collection.

Hm. Odd.

It seems that the important literary journal has somehow disappeared. It can't be found at the moment, at any rate, but we'll be bringing you the report, the *gist* of the report, just as soon as possible. Or maybe it's the grist. Hot off the wire, so to speak. Or fire. Out of the fire?

"Goddamned slime! Syphilitic hulks!" Olga yells in the general direction of that area in which the important literary journal is *supposed to be.* There, all is warm, inviting, and familiarly depressing. "Macho slime won't even do the dishes!" Olga shouts. It looks like a clear case of *les vapeurs.*

"Right! Right!" Olga shouts again. "Turn righteous fury into female emotional illness, you disgusting cock!" She squats and pisses on a photo of Hugh Hefner.

The news that inquiries are being received from interested females concerning the "looks" of Treadcliffe Marche can no longer be suppressed. There have been more inquiries than is absolutely necessary, and the suspicion is that many girls and women have inquired more than once— an old trick! It is also suspected that the subject's name itself awakens great interest, a phenomenon which Krafft-Ebing has termed *nomen-erotism.* To accommodate this flood of morbid queries, the following description of Marche is being furnished to the public:

> Treadcliffe Marche is a young giant, carrying his huge shock of blond hair six feet three inches from the ground, moving his immense limbs, heavy with ropes of muscle, ponderously. His hands are enormous, red, and covered with a fell of stiff yellow hair; they are hard as wooden mallets, strong as vises. His head is square-cut, angular; the jaw salient, like that of a carnivore.

Some Reactions to the Description

"Good heavens!" "Utterly rambunctious!" "Stiff yellow *what?*" "Whoo-ee!" "I can't even *imagine* his picciumiduno!" "I'm all *for* ropy muscles!" "What does he do with those *enchanting* hands!" "I think that really I might swoon!" "What does 'salient' sort of *mean!*" "My entire body is simply on fucking *fire!*" "Sweet Jesus, Mary, and Joseph, give me strength!" And there are other reactions, too many to list here, but available, perhaps, on request. Maybe. We'll see. All are equally admiring, adoring, lustful. So great is the hubbub raised by the crowds of fevered women that Marchosias, the Wolf, of great power in the Order of Dominations, strong in battle, from whose mouth issue gouts of fire, makes a special trip to see Treadcliffe for himself; for beauty, of whatever kind, resident in whatever sex, fills Marchosias with a lively sense of the salacious. To put it more plainly, if Marge "Somebody" is not available, "Mark" (not his real name) will do very nicely. For Marchosias, everything is a sexual object, and friendship often rapidly metamorphoses into that situation which may best be adumbrated in the words of the ancient poet (here left in his own tongue so as not to disturb the sensibilities of the delicate):

> deprendi modo pupulum puellae
> crusantem: hunc ego, si placet Dionae,
> pro telo rigida mea cecidi.

It goes without saying, of course, that Treadcliffe Marche is, to Marchosias's eye, a perfectly wonderful "Mark," one he'd delight in teaching a few amusing tricks to brighten the close of a long day of fruitless literary study.

"Woof!" says Marchosias. "You bet your life, kid! I'd also, to use a phrase I gleaned from the guys at the VFW hall between games of really bush-league straight pool, not kick Marlene out of bed, either, whoever or whatever *he* may be."

No intelligence concerning any Marlene has crossed "the desk," although not much of anything is crossing "the desk" today. It's much too *hot.* Still, professionalism decrees that the persistent rumors which connect a Marlene with a mysterious clubfooted man be made public. So be it.

A late-breaking story from Glen Cove on Lawrence's manuscript reveals that the literary find of the century—some are already calling it "the literary find of the century"—is a collection, or, a "sheaf" of detailed notes for a Laurentian essay on the sexual role played by sugar in the dark, secret blood. The title of the lengthy essay, or so the notes indicate, was to be *Marmalade Eros, Shadowy Imaginations of the Libido,* or *Lace Me Tighter!* More later on this story of the literary find of the century.

Ellen turns the flame under the clam sauce very low and runs to get the phone. The rustlings of her taffeta cocktail dress!

"Ellen Marowitz?" "Well . . . Ellen . . . yes. I'm Ellen Kaufman now, I mean not now. I mean I was Ellen Maro—" "I understand. Ellen Kaufman?" "Yes." "You don't know me, Miss Kaufman, but I'm a friend of Jeff Chandler's, Miner X. Beely?" "Yes, Mr. Beely?" "Uh, well, Jeff asked me to call and tell you that he had to leave suddenly for the, uh, mountains. His brother, little Buddy, is sick, and needs blood, and a lot of other things." "His brother, Buddy? I didn't know about any . . . the mountains? . . . I've got a chicken." "Thanks for being so understanding, I'm sure Jeff will be in touch after little Buddy walks again, or breathes, or whatever he has to do to live, grow, and make the most of his opportunities. Thanks again, Miss Kaufman, you're a brick." "A what? Hello? A *what?* Hello?"

How may we, at this late date, understand the seamy tragedy of Ellen Kaufman Marowitz's life, a life which at this moment discovers her slaving in the kitchen for a man who is even now making smutty overtures to the first wife of her ex-husband? That this is a day for coincidences would seem to be an understatement, indeed. There is no sure method whereby we may see with clarity the incidents which have brought Ellen to this pass, her eyes filled with bewildered pain, her brow beaded with finials of perspiration from the overpowering heat of the kitchen, her cocktail dress grown suddenly and hatefully gauche, her gourmet meal even more uselessly elaborate than it seemed but a moment since —and it was pretty uselessly elaborate even then! However, a brief survey of her immediate family might furnish, as Coleridge may well have written, "clues," or "clews." He was an odd duck, often laboring under the influence of narcotic substances found amid the drenched lichens.

Jacob "Jack" Marowitz, Ellen's elder brother. Large head. Heavy "city" accent. Weakness for white-on-white shirts. Pathological delight in what he has hidden away as his "collections."

Jack "Jacob" Marowitz, Ellen's father. Grey face. Not quite four feet, six inches tall. The butt of many bawdy jokes because of his petite size, these fortunately lost on him, since his only English was a whiningly enunciated "gumballs?"

Sandra Marowitz, Ellen's elder sister. Disappeared near Lebanon while, in the words of a communiqué, "hustling cheap cosmetics kibbutz-to-kibbutz already."

Sheila Marowitz, Ellen's younger sister. At the moment, pitched forward onto the hot sands of Coney Island. A comely woman, changed by the loathsome Lou Henry into a "flesh beast."

Tessie Marowitz, Ellen's mother. Dead from the neck up, as Jack said, of mambos, blue hair, Mah-Jongg, and rum cokes.

So. That Ellen should make a shambles of her life, that she should, at fifty-one, be pathetically enthralled by a slime like Miner X. Beely, that she should—

"Hold it! Hold it just a second, O.K.?"

Who's this?

"I've been listening to this crap and just want to say there are plenty of us who just won't stand still any more for this stuff. This glib 'survey' of yours is filled with racial, ethnic, religious, and sexual stereotypes, slanders, bigotry, the disgusting leer of naked prejudice. No, this won't be tolerated!"

Who *is* this?

"Buddy Cioppetini, if you want to know so bad. I been trying to keep from losing my grip on myself and running amok like your garden-variety lighthouse keeper is wont to do as I search for a missing book I just happen to love. I passed by and heard your, ah, callous bigotry, and had to come and defend my people against this sort of thing."

What people? This is the Marowitz family. More or less.

"The Marowitzes? Lived over the candy store? Oh. I thought you were talking about *Italians.* I'm in, so to speak, the wrong place? As it were?"

As it were, Buddy. There's no missing book here either.

"Sorry, I didn't know you were talking about Polacks. I got it wrong, O.K.? Made a mistake, anybody can make a mistake. I love kielbasa, by the way! Stuffed cabbage with mastiachi peppers? Hey! You gotta hand it to them the way they take advantage."

Right. Say, isn't somebody calling you?

Item: The suggestion, implication, or declaration that Sheila Henry may have been born Sheila Marowitz flies in the face of every scrap of verifiable information presently in hand. Inquiries will be made, however. The identity of the woman who lies on the sands of Coney Island will also be checked, although there is no reason to doubt that she is, indeed, Sheila Henry, whatever her maiden name. But time will tell.

Item: The charming and remarkably attractive receptionist—the sort of woman who makes men bump into trees and lampposts—of Marquis Meetings, Inc. ("Blue-blood Bimbos Do Your Bidding"), calls to remark that the "description" of Treadcliffe Marche, whose name, she confesses with a spicily heuristic chuckle, intrigues her, is uncommonly similar to that of the protagonist of a novel with the unlikely title of *Blix*. Thanks for the literary tip, lovely lady! And thanks also to the others who called in with the same observation: Betty Barker; that awfully attractive vegetarian couple; a Frieda Canool or something like that; a don calling all the way from Cambridge, England, who also asks for your prayers to release him from his unhealthy obsession; and finally, the truly delightful lady—who said that she's happy to be known now simply as the "Queen of Marrakech"—the Empress of the Trembling Golden Gown.

"What makes you think I'm Anne Marshall?" Anne Kaufman says to Miner X. Beely. "A man who would come out with a remark like that to a woman who manages a small religious supplies store, well, strikes one as a man who . . . has plans." Anne is alarmed by Beely, who looks like the sort who might abandon a Chevrolet.

"Why, of course you're Anne Marshall—I mean you *were* Anne Marshall," Beely says, taking a step toward her. "I heard all about you from the fellows over at the Guinness place."

"The what?" Anne says, certain that this unwanted visitor is a psychopath who, without warning, may become unmanageably disheveled. She picks up an enameled-steel spoon rest cunningly cast in the form of the New Testament.

"*The Guinness Book,* you know?" Beely says, "I'm not really Jeff Chandler, I mean *any* Jeff Chandler. My name is Miner X. Beely, Beat-Off Beely? Well, that was a while ago and now, I mean to say that, well, now I really dig chicks."

Anne brains him with the spoon rest and pulls his corpse behind the counter, where she covers it as best she can with the embroidered quadroon. A scream rises in her throat, but she bravely swallows it, a trick she learned while married to Leo. And then it strikes her: This slender madman must have learned about her *from* Leo! She stands straight, flushed with anger, her eyes clear with the knowledge of what she must do. Then she is womanfully striding toward the door, busily smoothing her skirt and adjusting her bonbons, while her jaw performs its wonted and age-old clenching procedures.

Jack Marshall and Tessie Blankenship Marshall look up from the Mah-Jongg game they are "playing" and Jack turns the volume down on their favorite recording of "Mi Amor Pendeja, Chíngame." They "know" that something is amiss with Anne, even though nothing like this has ever happened to them before. Like what? "Egg cream, Pa?" Tessie asks, her eyes, rheumy at best, clouded over with stunned bewilderment. Jack, his face greyer than ever, pretends that he understands what Tessie has said, as he has so pretended for fifty years. Fifty years! Jack smiles, for some reason. He shrugs noncommittally, as he has so shrugged for fifty years. Fifty years! Jack smiles again, and shrugs even more noncommittally. "Perhaps we must go to her!" Tessie cries. "Must we?" She makes a tentative move, as if to rise from her chair, but it is really more like a *rustling*. What is? Jack turns the volume up, and smiles again. "Mambos are excellent," he notes. "Right, dear?" Tessie idly clicks some tiles in her dignified, gnarled fingers, and looks sweetly at him. "My little grey shrimp," she says tenderly, as she has so said for fifty years. Fifty years! Tessie smiles, a smile that—

Is there some kind of a mistake? Who *are* these people?

Let's leave it be, it'll probably sort itself out. Too hot to worry.

Then too: Ex-Hotel Bartender Believes Vodka Martini Cause of Homosexuality; Marvelous Magazine Management Corp. Will Drop Controversial *Professors in Action;* Survey Finds "Mary" Favorite Moslem Name; Minister Decries Mary Janes as "Sin Shoes"; Sister Mary Magdalene, 114, Envisions Protestant Heaven as "Condo Complex"; Mason Jars Occasionally Useful in Sex Therapy, Says Dr. Massa; Massachusetts Evangelist Claims World Created in 1815; Mast Grogan, TV Host, to Change Name to Henri Matisse; Marcus Matz, Expert on Frank Norris, Disappears in California.

A woman signing herself "Maureen, an old pal of April's," writes to suggest that Olga Begone's "Man-Kill" is highly derivative of the early verse of Jean Ingelow, especially the poem, "Divided," in *Poems* (1863). Miss Ingelow, from her thatch-roofed, cuckoo-rife cottage in Kensington, has kindly released the following statement:

Although Maureen, who was once a girl, the very embodiment of Fancy, is now a woman, who is Imagination brooding over what she brings forth, she would do well to remember that the domains of Poetry and of History are represented by two purple peaks. In brief, I am not pleased to have my name linked with that of Olga Begone. As my beloved half-brother, Max, is fond of saying, "Better to starve in England than to be a moiety of the *Mayflower* rout and rabble." I don't know what dear Max means, but there, as they say, it is.

Lips slides *Absalom! Absalom!* into his pocket, despite the stare of a middle-aged woman in a too-short skirt, too-tight blouse, lace-patterned black stockings, and spike heels. She is a bit ridiculous in these things, "desperate" might be the cruelly proper word to use. However, Lips is no less ridiculous than she, and his T-shirt, which bears the message LOVE MAZATLÁN? GET YOUR M.B.A., is no less crass than the woman's ill-fitting clothing. Lips is afraid that she might make a scene, or inform the manager, or otherwise disrupt his plans. He is therefore pleasantly surprised by the sudden intrusion of an outsider into the game of watcher and watched that he and the woman are playing.

"Hello! I'm Thom McAn! I mean the *actual* Thom McAn, the, if you'll pardon the expression, McCoy. Although Marcie Butler, over there by the green beans—it *is* Marcie Butler?—is got up in a devastatingly stunning costume the likes of which is perfect for larking about with lynx and tambourine, pipes and timbers, and oaten reed and thorax, it is not *exactly* what the well-dressed woman wears while shopping! Take it from me, the world-famous designer, manufacturer, and purveyor of affordable ladies' foot stylings for God knows how many years!"

Marcella—for it is she—finishes picking up a few forgotten items and sidles toward a checkout counter as best she can, considering her heels and skirt. Perhaps she doesn't sidle so much as career. Lips pretends to be examining the green peppers. A somewhat embarrassed priest, his physical state the focus of a group of admirers of both sexes, tries, to no avail, to interest his fans in McAn.

"Yes, Marcie," McAn goes on, "I've sold shoes, although flogged is more in keeping with what I did with them, yes, to no less demanding a personage as Charlotte McCoyne, not McCoy, but McCoyne, the true, natural mother of Anne Kaufman, who, at the moment, I feel, is in grave danger, although why I should feel this is a mystery to me. Jayzus McGlade, whom some of you older shoppers (indicates two grey-haired folks who dodder convincingly) may recall as an Irish youth of manly vim and *élan vital,* loved the snappy little ankle-strap number in six fashion shades for fall. By God, they never hurt *his* football playing! And they were no small factor in his all-around locker-room popularity either, take it from his cheerfully brutal pals. Helga McGrath, loving grandmother to a maturely bewitching hearing-seeing-speaking-walking-impaired study in courage with an enlightened interest in painting—don't ask!—was very big on the kind of footwear designed to laugh off the filth and rough going of rural byways. So, when I have an opinion about women's clothing. . . ."

McAn rambles on, while Marcie makes good her escape, and Lips, partially hidden behind a Perrier display, slips *Absalom! Absalom!* out of his pocket to find that it is called *L'Amant et la lune* by Paul de Kock. It also seems to be written in a foreign language, and since Lips knows no language but his own, he can say, with Casca, that it is Greek to him, and be absolutely correct. Lips doesn't say this. Rather, facing the ice-cream freezer, he makes a mincing mow in order to, in his own disturbed words, "pricketh th' ebon Saracen!"

Literary Interlude

"... though I am not enthralled
To be here in Old Méjico," Melanie said, "land
Of the homely *taco,* eaten in these parts
For bread, and the *mastiachi* peppers
Of great heat, or as the natives say, *calor."*
She sat then nervously upon a window seat,
Like a haunted skylark, and took up again
Her wretched tatting. Melissa, dark temptress
And the wife of Baron Darke, felt pain as sharp
As the sting of the *ñorga* bug for the dear girl!
Such a golden child, lisping of "fireworkth"
And "picnicth" and indeed, "hot dogth," too!

"I'm sorry, Melanie, my dearest child,"
The older woman crooned, sweeping in her

Silken gown like a perfumed typhoon,
Majestically, to sit in ladylike perfection.
"But did I know why the Baron colors crimson
And faints dead away, like a high-school girl,
When e'er you fix him with your eyes as blue
As my forgotten irises beyond the kale,
Perhaps, perhaps I, I might. . . ."

Here the noble beauty paled impeccably,
Then clutched her breasts with trembling hands,
And said, "Perhaps, perhaps I'd know just why
He sent his couriers as swift as Death, toot sweet!
To rainy Nottingham from Eagle House
That fateful and, I understand, ironic afternoon!"

"Oh! How I fondly wish you *did* know, kind Melissa,"
The young maiden whispered softly as a balmy
English breeze upon an English moor. The while
Her gnarled and knotted tatting fluttered weakly
On the brooding, soot-encrusted andirons!

"Just because I am possibly," and here
The girl shuddered like a mast before
A mad simoom, "the unborn child, the baby
Grown to blushing womanhood—dare I ask how?
—The dream-wight of the weird Detectives,
Well! That cuts no ice, whatever that may mean,
Insofar as the dreadful summons in the heat
Of Nottingham's bleak, blazing noon goes!"
Silence fell upon the pair at once.

"Dearest Melanie," Melissa breathed, "as one
Warm, full-blooded woman to another, to a
Puzzled woman, a puzzled virgin given o'er
To primping prettily and blushing, puzzled,
Like the citizens of Thebes, by unanswered
Queries, cunning riddles, and sly tricks
To 'crack the brains like nuts,' as Hesiod said,
I must speak openly and with a heavy heart,
A heart as heavy as the pine log in the hearth."

At this moment, the elder dame was not
The proud and stiffly distant Baroness of
Eagle House! No! But suddenly disclosed
Her steaming, vulnerable soul!

"Dearest Melanie," she said again,
Catching up with her bejeweled hands
The wild folds of richly ornamented
Tulle which ached, or so it seemed,
To detonate themselves in beauty free
So as to make the gloomy welkin sound!
Like, then, was a goddess she.

Settling the massy stuff about her, Melissa
Sighed, "That you may be the unborn child
Of the lugubrious Detectives serves you
No purpose here or there! We welcome you!
As sister, daughter, cousin, niece, or aunt,
As any sprig or twig of femininity, we
Welcome you into the dancing light
Of each night's blazing, merry *fuego!*
And I pray," and here the Baroness heaved
Her splendid bosom toward the heavens,
"That my lord, the Baron, proud scion of
These ancient piles, and plain Bert to me,
His yielding wife, will reveal his chilling
Secret to us twain. And soon," she cried.

At these words, Baron Darke, his doublet
All undone, his hose askew, his boots
All encrusted with the dreadful mud of
El Durango, his blazing eyes wild-staring
In his head like two mad lighthouse keepers
Run amok, entered the great hall of the *hacienda*
And in a voice as sharp and threatening
As a schizophrenic crazy man, he thundered,

"Woman! Or, women! As the case may be!
Good God and blast! I reck not, nor do I wot!
Where is the latest issue of *Men's Action*?
I had begun a hypnotizing tale

Of a comely female anthropologist,
As game as she is desirable in her
Close-fitting khakis, pursued by rabid
Crocodiles, controlled by Moscow! So,
My handsome brace of quails, o-ho! Speak
Quick and bright as popping flashbulbs
And you may avoid my petulance and dump," he spoke.

In the great room, one could hear the soughing
Of the wild *atascaderos,* and the fall
Of a distant pin to the red tile floor,
Tiles red as *hombre's* gore!

"And while I await your female answer,
Which will be, I'll wager my brood Appaloosa,
Soft and sweet as chocolate pudding still a
Little warm, tell me, Melissa," the Baron smiled,
"My bosomy, long-leggèd spouse, dear girl
Who graces lawful bed with flesh so firm the very
Roast beef of the dinner table seems to shrink
In consternation, aye! Tell me, I say, or
I *was* saying, tell me, wife, I will say again,
Why did you, in contradiction of my wishes,
Made *crystal clear* in a hurried, yes, but
Legible and cogent memorandum, invite, and
For *supper,* this next bleak and damnèd Friday night,
The dismal, dastardly, the homely, and the
Hopelessly idiotic Mervishes? Whom all folk swear
To shun?"

Suddenly, a mad gust of desert-hot *viento*
Carried a large cactus in, and past them,
On its blast! Which broke the sullen tension
In the moody room. But not for long.

"I've brought you something to read, Ethan," the slatternly and sullen Zenobia says, shaking the broken gimp dozing in the homemade wheel-chair by the fire. "Here." And with that, she furtively jettisons a copy of *The Metal Dress* onto her husband's partially collapsed "chest."

"Thank you, Zeena," the man says courteously, horrible pains shooting through what was once a recognizable face, but which now resembles a twisted mask of agony. "But, you know, that since my, er, *foe paz,* I've been attracted exclusively to works of non-fiction—such as this marvelous new study of the Everglades and its zesty and informative secrets, entitled *Secrets of the Everglades.* A nice little item."

"Well then," Zenobia snaps cruelly, "if you don't like racy, suggestive fiction now that you're but *half a man,* I reckon that reading up on eyetalian swamps is just about up *your* alley!" She grins dully through dingy, broken teeth, the usual oral equipment of a slattern, at her husband's obvious psychic discomfiture. "There's also—I 'forgot' to tell you—a hamburger, there, on your wizened 'chest.' Best burger in town, or so they claim, danged fools! So go on and *eat up,* while I go and *wake up* Mattie," the harridan concludes, pulling a six-inch hatpin from the shrewish effluvium of her wispy coif.

"Eat?" Ethan furiously croaks. "Eat!? You cruel slatternly virago!" he cries weakly. "How can I eat when you know full well that I am *par'lyzed?*"

Zenobia, happily tucking a brick under her arm, leaves the room, humming. Ethan, shrugging what remains of his once-broad, tanned shoulders, manages to cast both hamburger and "pop" book to the floor, and then, by means of a cleverly designed pulley system imported from the Amazon Basin, turns once again to read in *Metallic Constructions.* This tome, which fascinates and oft bears him away on flights of healthy, manly fantasy, contains a favorite chapter, to which he now directs, once again, his full, if not precisely rapt attention. It is, of course, "How to Build a Strong Sled Out of Scrap Iron," and, reading it, for perhaps the dozenth time, he tries, as best he can, to blot out the vicious oaths and wrenching cries of pain from the coal bin, by placing his wrists deep into the "things" where once his shapely ears had been.

"I will not read *The Metallic Fly* to you again, Zeena!" Mattie's girlish voice quavers. "It's a bad-foul, bad-mean, devil-bad book, and I don't like the strange things you try out when I read it, either! Oh God! If I weren't *par'lyzed,* I'd gather Ethan up in my yearning arms and be gone from this living hell in a moment!"

The sickening crack of brick against shriveled flesh rings clear in the silent household. Ethan, tears coursing from gaunt sockets down his "face," reads on, pitifully. There seems no point anymore in admiring the rude chairs and rough-hewn wooden table placed neatly about.

The quarrel is fast approaching that point at which the closest and most understanding of friendships can be strained almost to the breaking point, even though we may feel, probably mistakenly, as if we have shared, in the best sense, their travails, and followed avidly their "ups and downs"—and how wonderful it is that we have them all together at last!—with a well-nigh hawklike attention to detail. Yet at such moments, little if any decency is shown, and the crystalline highlands often echo with weeping.

"For the last time, Lucy," Tabitha Bramble says, her lips white with anger and her heavy, melonlike breasts straining to burst from her revealing gown, "the Métro is not located in Mexico, thus cannot serve the population of Mexico City. It is, on the contrary, the famous mass-transit system of Miami and Miami Beach. I don't care *what* that vile sexist stud, Mickey, who so enthralls you with his large bologna—how I hate that word!—has to say."

"Mickey's bologna, I trust, is not going to be dragged into this discussion," Lucy Brandon replies, with some asperity, her enormous, girlish bosom heaving with unleashed fury. "Mickey labors under the burden of being a man of the Midwest, a simple man of potatoes and edible roots, an earthy churl of joss and mandrake, a feral galoot, yes, innocently proud of his *machismo,* which he boyishly conflates with baseball caps and cans filled with 'beer.' Yet it is this flaw, if flaw it be, which paradoxically permits Mickey to speak with authority on the Métro. So, in your nose, you painted slut!"

A hollow, ringing silence descends on the room, much like the silence which usually reigns in the Frome household, a silence broken only by the soft ticking of the clock which has, yet again, appeared, and the hoarse panting, or pantings, of Tabitha and Lucy. Their eyes, spiritedly flashing and snapping with full womanly abandon, meet, their hearts race, and without thinking of such trivialities as "Métro" and "bologna," they are suddenly in each other's arms, weeping in joy, relief, and, naturally, excitement. They are not aware—and were they, would they care?—that their surrender to sapphic sensuality and sensational sex, stuffed with superb and socko surprises, will, as usual, pander to the basest of male fantasies.

"Sure. 'Mike in the Morning,' the title story in Mikky Way's runaway success of a collection of superb fictions is just *like* that—really base," Jack Armstrong remarks from deep within the recesses of his comfortable leather-and-tobacco armchair in which he is wont to reflect. "Packs a hell of a sensuous wallop, and though the sex is utterly gratuitous, it's attractively steamy, in a paradigmatic way." He puffs thoughtfully on his richly encrusted meerschaum, his eyes resting for a moment on the papers, most of them of a decidedly cultural nature, scattered on his warmly cluttered desk, with cat. "While some have called 'Mike' a sophomoric display of cynical attitudes toward women, others, despite wide learning and a shithouse full of degrees, have developed respectable erections which have stood them in good stead at social functions and made them decided 'hits' at home. There are," he concludes excitedly, "two schools of thought on, like, broads in bed together. Right? One is about what they're up to and the other focuses on how many of them there are!" Armstrong sinks ever deeper into his chair, pleased that his literary views are finally under consideration. Or whatever it is they're under.

A curse, more than likely.

"Have I ever told you of my trip to Milan?" he says. "Wonderful! Something *about* the Continent. Italy. We'd been, of course, to *Italy.* But the North! So refreshingly non-American, so friendly. Nothing like an Italian! I mean, of course, Italians in Italy! Well, have I? Told you? About? Perhaps next summer we'll. If you've heard this, just, please, just say so, and I'll tell you about my meerschaum. (Indicates smoldering pipe while are heard the panicky sounds of a number of citizens in full flight.)

The Milky Way candy bar is manufactured, as label-readers know, in Hackettstown. Those of you with long memories may recall that just outside this town, on the road to Budd Lake, lies the Bluebird Inn. It has been suggested, and with some vigor, that this is, indeed, a day for coincidence. Had things turned out otherwise, Ellen Kaufman, called, in her youth, Miss Milky Way (!) by those who were put off by her overpowering sweetness, would today have *been* in Hackettstown. Instead, blinded by love, she is, as we know, "bustling about." She is going to get, as the hoary phrase crudely has it, "the shaft," as we may surmise, but that is neither here nor there. In Hackettstown, just about to leave his house and drive to the Bluebird for a few beers and an invigorating, blues-chasing spate of fox-trot delight, is a certain Mr. Mille, a collector, if it can be believed, of 50's trivia, memorabilia, and artifacts, including, most especially, the cocktail dress!

In other words, Ellen had an appointment with this Mille to. . . ?

Precisely. But love, in the grotesque guise of Miner X. Beely, is keeping her at home today. Had she journeyed to Hackettstown, her arms laden with the exotically hued garments coveted by Mille, her life might well have changed utterly.

"If truth be told, I might have waylaid her for some Christian badinage on that little stretch of lonely road what's just beyond the hideously gnarled apple tree," Knute remarks sociably from his hiding place in a dense copse of thornbushes, which are, incidentally, rending his flesh and turning his clothing into tatters, *à la* King Sweeny.

"Rags, actually," Knute says apologetically. " 'Tatters' sounds to me like a fairy word, and as the whole world knows, there are no fairies in the thornbushes!"

How about at the bottom of the garden?

"Well, sure. *There,*" Knute agrees.

Mr. Mille is dancing. In a half-hour or so, besotted by breaks and dips, he will have forgotten all about Ellen's letter, or, as he thinks of it, Miss Milky Way's letter.

"Hi! I'm Karen Millpond! When I'm popping open cans of *really* cold soft drinks, as modern technology, fantastic engineering know-how, and personal savvy whisk us through the heavens, I'm the consumptate professional! But when Milt, my taciturn creative consultant, roars up in his new BM, my nipples get just as stiff as the next girl's. Hi!"

This "Milt" cannot be the same "Milt" who was Sheila's first lover?

"Hi! I'm Karen Minet! An actual professor I met while pouring hot, stimulating coffee and rubbing a few of my female charms up against his tweedy shoulder just *miles* above Denver, told me that 'minet' is French for 'pussy.' When I'm dancing in one of those *hot* new clubs with my sleek fella, cute as can be in my *bitch* of a haircut, I really *feel* like a sexy kitty, or a depraved character in *Misterioso,* the new Broadway hit. Hi!"

"Actually," the actual professor says, interrupting his casual disquisition on his LATEST TRIP TO EUROPE, "the coffee was *not* stimulating, since it was caffeine-free. That's the only kind I drink, else I might die too young to make all the TRIPS TO EUROPE which, I feel, are a scholarly necessity. If you follow me?"
Thanks, Professor, and so long. (Indicates door.)

Léonie Aubois still possesses the three curious fan letters sent from Herbert Hoover to Tom Mix. She has kept them with her for many years, resisting the sharp temptation to sell them time and time again. Indeed (music heard softly in distance), these letters serve, perhaps, as Miss Aubois's anchor to reality (music stronger now, bright with gouts of whipped cream spurting in a major key), perhaps, even, as testaments to *hope.* (The sound is upon us, happily merciless, thick with pseudo-wonderful, Jesus as a regular guy, and death as, sort of, like a better job.) Perhaps we should discover for ourselves the fascination of these letters, sent, no doubt, in remarkable humility and heartfelt egalitarianism, from a Great Statesman, "the Man who whipped Inflation," to an International Western Star. Let's take a look. Léonie surely won't mind, particularly since she's going into seizures as the horrors descend upon her (lush chords softly crash).

Dear Mr. Mix:
I saw you in *Rifles on the Pecos* recently and was quite bowled over by your manly skills, and your American spirit of rugged individualism. Many of the desperadoes who felt the sting of your brand of range justice looked very much like dago anarchists, moustaches and all. "Hanging is too good for them," as you say in the last scene. Well, this is the pass that modernistic nonsense has brought us to, with its kike ideas and sissy foreign pictures. I like a statue you can understand, a manly statue!
I have a lot on my mind right now with the nagging unemployment problem we have, which is caused, as these darn fools around here don't seem to know, by there being so many people out of work. They are *unwilling* to work. But I'd like to tell you that the way you sit on your horse fills me with a manly pride and

also reminds me of something.

Yours in prosperity,
Herbert Hoover

Dear Tom Mix:

Thanks for your gracious reply from the ranch and your busy life. I personally don't have a great deal to do right now, what with people crying to me all day long with their hard-luck stories about unemployment and hunger and gosh-all knows what else. If they had any gumption and Christian backbone, they could get a job almost anywhere. Fellows like you and me, self-made men, don't lack for work, but that's because we weren't raised to be mollycoddles expecting everything to be given to us on a silver platter. When I was a boy I walked 22 miles each way to school, usually through six-foot snowdrifts, with only a raw potato for lunch. But it made me into a manly boy and a manly man, if a little thin.

I *thought* that maybe that's what it reminded me of but I didn't really know whether I should think so or not. It seems darn manly to me, in a special, private sort of way, I agree. But you're right that not everyone understands.

Yours in the coming prosperity,
Herbert Hoover

Dear Tom:

Well! Last night was simply the crackerjack event of the year for me. I saw a special screening of *Guns of the Colorado* and never have you acquitted yourself so nobly or bravely along the lines of shooting, fistfighting, strangling, clubbing, and so forth. When you strapped your Colts on in the dry-goods store, I could feel the weight of those "shooting irons" around my own waist. Whew!

As you may have read, I haven't been re-elected. The cabal of communists, socialists, anarchists, and the Eastern kikes and dagos has put me out of office just as I was about to present a plan based on self-reliance, grit, and pluck. There's plenty of money to go around, but people are hoarding it!

Yes, I do have that famous photo of you with your guitar, singing under the live oak with Jackie "Pinto" Moline. But, you bet, I'd sure *love* to see the other one you mention. Believe me, I'd treasure it.

Yours in real Western values,
Herbert Hoover

Many epistolary specialists, political scientists, Depression "buffs," and historians of the cinema feel that these letters, along with the one to

Hoppy, are apocryphal, if not maliciously spurious. The conservative scholar, M. Plaid Soup, writes that his inspection of the letters leads him to believe that they were forged by "a swarthy man, probably Jewish or Italian."

"Hi! I'm Mom! Any Mom at all! Do me a favor, darling, and don't call so often, all right? Keep in touch, sure, nice, but you don't have to be a fanatic about it. Today, for instance, it's so hot that I'm trying to stay as cool as possible by sitting nice and still. I don't, you know? need to be running to answer the phone! Tell your troubles to Jesus for a change, all right, darling?"

Calls have been coming in inquiring whether this day, this ordinary day, is a Monday. It is not, but we are not yet authorized to tell you what day it *is*. Those of you with old calendars or the gifts of an idiot savant know already, of course. That is, if it matters to you.

Gaspard Monge, discovered alone, in the kitchen of a three-room apartment in Bensonhurst: This cannot possibly be *the* Gaspard Monge, the latter having died in 1818. On the other hand, Monge, a Mongol No. 2 pencil in his hand, is excitedly putting the finishing touches on a method which will permit geometrical problems in three dimensions to be solved in the plane. He smiles, puts his pencil down, stretches, yawns, and says, "Voilà! It sims zat I 'ave invent ze descriptive géometrie! Now to calling up a lay-dee frien', Gail Patrick or Deanna Durbin or Freddie Bartholomew, even maybe Marilyn Monroe, to 'elp me zelebrett. Zom wan of zees honey bunches!"

General perplexity. Some *hard questions* must be asked, or so it seems to a clear majority of the Board.

We welcome all interrogations and cannot wait to be persecuted. Names, after all, must be cleared, reputations repaired. Oh, it's easy to *accuse*, yet we ask only that our answers may be given in writing and that we have an undisclosed period of time in which to prepare them. Done?

Done.

1. Does Deanna Durbin buy her tasteful frocks at Namm's of Brooklyn or at Tarnation Emporium of Montana?

2. Is there any truth to the rumor that Gail Patrick and Marilyn Monroe gambled recklessly and also committed several vile acts with persons unknown in Monte Carlo, "sewer of Europe"?

"Eez no wan going to pay a mind to may deezcovérie?"

Quiet, Monge, please!

3. Why has George built a small fire of the pages torn from *Géometrie descriptive*?

4. Is it proper, given the sensitivities of the dizzyingly raised consciousness of our truly enlightened time, to call Freddie Bartholomew a "lay-dee frien'," and to refer to him as a "honey bunch"?

a.) Are *some* men "honey bunches"? Or perhaps "cinnamon buns"? Are they "yentas," "shtarkers," or "gonifs"? Are they, essentially, "obsolete"?

b.) How, then, fare the adventurous, twisted denizens of the quiet suburbs?

5. When Bobby Breen, in the rollicking musical comedy-drama *A New Dimension* (never released), cries, at the climax of the rubber game of Moo Goo Gai Pan he is playing with Gloria Jean (no relation), "Bamboo shoots, four, twelve; bean curd, eight-slam doubled!" what does Miss Jean do? In what key?

"Oo are zees pipple?" Monge asks, understandably. "Bobby Brin? Gloria Jin? Ah weel invite zem too, non?"

Quiet, Monge, please!

6. Anybody? Six? Six, anybody? That's it, then? O.K. The *hard questions* have been asked. We expect full compliance with the agreement?

Absolutely.

The Board stands adjourned.

"Ees Bobby Brin ze fellow wiz ze curlee 'air which makes you cray-zee wiz ennui as he sings a song?"

No one answers Monge, who seems to be more and more representative of the neglected genius. To crown his so-far hopelessly unsatisfying day, his calls to Patrick, Durbin, Bartholomew, and Monroe cannot be completed. However, this cannot be *the* Gaspard Monge, as earlier noted.

"Il n'etait jamais Gaspard Monge," Gil Roulure says. "Il est Théophile Dondey." So he says, but Gil is liable to say anything. We know Gil!

Morax the Bull, a great President and Earl, who knows the virtues of all herbs and precious stones, who imparts skill in astronomy and the liberal sciences, and in all the geometries, especially hermetic, speaks: "It's hot and I won't keep you long. Please forgive me, and accept my apologies. I'm afraid that I must take full responsibility for the sudden and crass appearance of the man who passes himself off as either Gaspard Monge or Théophile Dondey, both of whom, as you know, are dead. *This* man, who has lately embarrassed himself and his unfortunate fellows with his fake French accent and his unfounded gutter allusions to famed film stars of the past, is really a friend of Page Moses, often called, in justifiable denigration and mockery, Doctor Plot. I thought to embarrass Moses by putting *his* "Monge" into a situation too difficult and complicated to be weaseled out of by means of various threadbare devices, e.g., fires and explosions, sudden love or death, trips to strange places, long waits in hospital corridors, boring causes for dull effects, or the bleak knowledge that people are beautiful, after all, even though the air-conditioner is broken and Dad has the shakes. But "Monge," too stupid to realize his danger, embarrassed neither Moses nor himself; rather, he has humiliated me, my staff, and my fellow demons yet again, and I apologize. As a token of my gratitude for your kind attention, here is the solution, on the blackboard behind me, of Fermet's last theorem." (Indicates solution.)

Page Moses, sweltering in the heat like everyone else, and disappointed that the small audience for his impeccably presented summary of *Zuleika Dobson* has drifted silently away, is entertaining himself by working on the plot for a book he means to write. This is a bona fide, absorbing time-passer for the good Doctor, but boring for us, since all that *we* may see of the vaunted "creative process" is Page's face. Luckily, Morax, to make up for his recent gaffe, peers into Plot's head and relays to us the skeletal framework of the planned novel, or so he says.

MOTHER LOVE

Story to be told in the first person by a grizzled Chevrolet dealer and part-time woodsman, Knute, who puts together the pieces of the dark tale of the inhabitants of a grim, hardscrabble farm in the gorse forests which loom. Mother

Church, known throughout the bleak hills as "Ma," drives her hardworking husband, "Pa," almost to despair with her whining complaints about her smoky stove and the crooning scarecrow, despite her knowledge that Pa has all he can manage to put a few, frozen, half-rotted ears of corn on the rude wooden table. Ma's young cousin, Mother Machree, who has been stigmatized since childhood, and is known in the bleak fens as "Sherri," is left penniless, and comes to live with the Churches. Within a month, Pa and Sherri have formed a deep friendship, arousing Ma's bitter jealousy. One day, at Ma's request, Mother Theresa, an old school friend, whom all her previous employers know as "Muffin," appears at the farmhouse door, ostensibly to act both as Ma's amanuensis and Sherri's helper in the bleak and smoky kitchen. In a month or so, however, Muffin and Sherri are locked in furious daily quarrels over the value of Robert Motherwell's "Summer Light" series, with Ma coming down on Muffin's side, and Pa defending Sherri's opinion. Goaded into an uncharacteristic fury by Muffin's and Ma's sneering references to him as "Mister Mouth," and "the world's greatest unknown art critic," Pa cuttingly refers to Muffin's heavy ankles. In the weeks that follow, an uneasy truce is often broken by Ma's vicious attacks on Sherri's current reading—*Mouth of Steel* by Henri Kink—as "pervert trash," and Muffin's almost frantic insults anent the music and sexual tastes of W. A. Mozart, a well-known composer whom Pa and Sherri hold in high esteem. A curious tome entitled *Mrs. Dalloway* also comes in for some alertly savage slander. After a particularly bitter exchange, during which Pa's and Sherri's pleasure in enlightened and serious fiction in a foreign language, and their innocent love for fried nougat are subjected to venomous raillery, Ma insists that Sherri leave. On their way to the bus depot, Pa and Sherri realize that they are in love, and decide to die together rather than part. They zoom down a steep hill on Pa's sled and crash into a brooding bay tree, whose stark, bare branches look like the twisted arms of several maddened lighthouse keepers. However, they are not killed, but are found and carried back to the bleak farmhouse by Mud and Mugg Waldbaum, local cow folk. The drunken village physician, Dr. Johnson Mulloon, is sent for, and, polluted as usual, his surgical attentions leave both Pa and Sherri *par'lyzed* for life, under the cold and cruel eyes of Ma Church and Muffin Theresa, who have become an item amid the bleak hills.

Annette removes the tattered and stained manuscript, entitled "Mademoiselle Mummy," from the book in which it is kept. She unfolds it, and smiles a brilliant, icy smile as she recollects the fate of the man who wrote and then threatened her with it, as if she cares, as if she *could* care!

But the temerity, the vulgarity, the crude *actuality* of the threat! Intolerable, of course. She recalls the expression of awe and terror on his face when he first heard the whispering rustle of the flying rats' wings, an odd, high-pitched sound. Poor man! Now she looks over the manuscript again, for the first time in almost twenty years, and its prose is, indeed, as she remembers it—the dull, sincere, determined mono- tone of a man with something to expose, something to *say*. How much more delightful the silly excesses of the book in which she keeps the manuscript—*La Dame aux trois corsets*. Annette smiles again, the subtle ochre lighting gleaming dully off her silvery teeth, as she remem- bers de Kock's delighted laughter when she suggested, with the levity of youth, that he should, by right, call the work *La Dame aux corsets d'acier*. Those were, indeed, the days. Sudden lightning.

Charles "Chuck" Murphy, an Irish-American, who, in his wily manner, often gives his name as "Carlos" or "Chaz" Murphy—the grass doesn't grow under *his* feet—takes his wife, Constanza, grey-haired and with crow's-feet around her eyes, yet still almost as lissome as a young bride (lover, mistress, girlfriend), to the Museum of Modern Art. They've had an amusingly gauche but interesting brunch of canned pork and beans, Jane Parker jelly donuts, mu-shu pork, and Banana Amaze—the dessert which seems to be sweeping the neighborhood, a quiet one in a small suburb, populated, for the most part, by attractive vegetarian couples. Despite their intense if not overtly active dislike for art in all of its unlikely manifestations, the Murphys have heard and read for weeks now about the Modern's exhibition of erotic drawings made for the original, limited, subscription edition of the famous pastoral novel *La Musique et les mauvaises herbes,* known to cognoscenti as "Chords and Swards." Not only has the Modern managed to locate *all* of the original drawings and their numerous preliminary studies as well as a score of unused drawings, but the curator for the exhibition, Mus Musculus, the brash Danish expert on the *fin de siècle,* makes a strong case, in his catalogue essay, for the theory that the hitherto unknown artist can probably be identified as the irrepressible social satirist and society "wit at large," the arrogant dandy known only as Mutt, pro- nounced "mōōt." Charles and Constanza find themselves to be the only people in the wing, and, given this unexpected privacy, the heat of the day, the aphrodisiac effects of the Banana Amaze, Constanza's lissome qualities (already mentioned), and the decidedly arousing drawings to serve as amorous examples, one thing leads to another and then, of course, to another. Ten minutes later, Mr. Mytilene, a Greek shipping magnate with a special interest in cafeteria growth stocks, comes upon the couple, happily engaged in frantically oblivious coupling. Mr. Mytilene stares, and then, perhaps remembering his Catullus, walks quietly toward the writhing Murphys, delightedly muttering, "Ανθρωπος φύσει ζῶον." The cock of cocks, Naberius, who, invisible, has been enjoying the drawings by, it is said, "one who well served the Goëtic Art," instantly comprehends the situation, and, in his hoarse voice, urges Mr. Mytilene on. The Museum of Modern Art often packs a surprising wallop.

Then too: Women Named "Nancy" Liable to Explode, Experts Say; Studies Reveal Nash Favorite Car of Overweight Rabbis; Historian Contends Natchitoches Once Part of Albania; Nathan's Famous Settles Phallic Symbol Suit; The *Nation* May Display "Boss" Tweed's Magic Violin; National Guard to Host Combat Weenie Roast; Directors of National Multiple Orgasm Fund Charged in Office Orgies; Naughtie Nightie Boutique to Market Polyester Lingerie Despite Christian Bowlers' Protests.

Sir Bloom and Lord Bury, idly chatting of things ephemeral, cannot see into the "palais des rideaux," where young Billy Magrino is still twitching and trembling, albeit more rhythmically, on the floor. More importantly for them, they cannot see into the small basement laboratory *cum* sewing room where the prototype of the "Naughty Nurse" costume is getting its final nips and tucks, ruches and gathers. This is not surprising, since the workshop is in a small Nebraska town, Nemo (pop. 49), huddled at the foot of Scotts Bluff, the latter named after Robert Falcon Scott's famed poker hand, 2D3H5C8S10S, which won him monies sufficient to buy the supplies he needed for yet another crackpot jaunt.

"Such ignorance of history surpasseth human understanding," Chet Kendrick says, momentarily setting aside a new collection of essays by his favorite Neo-neo-Humanist, the brilliant if depraved Countess

Nettie, whose extraordinary good fortune in the Nevada casinos is matched only by her breathtaking beauty, a beauty paradoxically enhanced by the raucous bimbos who attend her.

"Actually, the young women so unjustly maligned are not 'raucous bimbos' but a *spirited entourage,*" Chet says. "Two have had *small but important* roles in Academic Playhouse of the Air presentations, three more have served with distinction—*à la* the lady friends of Quintus Horatius Flaccus—at the remodeled New Ecstasy Motor Inn, one was Miss New England Shore Dinner, and another Miss New Jersey Wetlands. Still others have *distinguished themselves* in public service, such as which can be easily checked out with ease and the utmost alacrity. I submit to all fair-minded people the notion that such ladies are *precious adornments* on the body politic, and not 'bimbos,' raucous or otherwise." Just then the phone rings. Or is it the clock that ticks? No, it's the phone. It's Georgene, calling from her bathtub, or so she stoutly maintains. Let's leave her and Chet to their conversation.

"On a day like this a bath is a pretty good idea."

Who said that?

"I did. Me, George."

George seems still to be locked out of the bathroom in which his wife relaxes. He is, too, in the words of the old song, waiting in the lobby of her heart.

It should be said here, and not in a spirit of malice, that most, if not all of the young women who make up the Countess Nettie's "spirited entourage" worked, for a time, at Ofelia's Chateau Joi, where they often found themselves entertaining clients in what Ofelia calls the Newlywed Room. On occasion, they were found by others, usually the police. They are, that is, a bit more, ah, worldly than either the Countess or dear Chet makes them out to be. The Newlywed Room, patterned after a less elaborate model constructed by a gladhanding, clubfooted man in New Mexico, not only imitates, parodies, satirizes, and elaborates upon the fantasies, pleasures, surprises, and disappointments of the usual honeymoon, it most tellingly *invents* specific possibilities of which the honeymoon is most often incapable. The room is equipped with such dazzling appurtenances as a thermostatically controlled blusher- and sweat-machine, a graduated series of rampant pintles, a complete selection, in all sizes, of smooth-bore rustic spheres, a two-way purple-crystal mirror harness, leather pediment straps and velvet-padded snood chains, a perfumed-steam collard vaporizer, a tremble-inducer, and interchangeable mollyprongs of fuchsia, cerise, lavender, chartreuse, strawberry, and lobster plastic, to list but a few. This information is given, as suggested, so that these young women may be fairly judged. It may well be that they *are* "raucous bimbos."

Her father finally asleep, or at least supine in the darkened room, Bunny peers cautiously out of the kitchen window at the woman who still stands in the street, her dress in oafish disarray. Bunny shudders, for the woman unaccountably reminds her of the vicious Nora Avenel, who insulted her *New Mexico Blooze* in art class, then, later, tried to melt her pastels. Bunny wonders where her old painting is, but idly, idly. It *was* a terrible painting, callow, pretentious, arty. That man said, "admirable talents, small but fine," but when she wouldn't. . . . Oh yes, *then* it was, what was it?

He said that it had all the aesthetic excitement of the *New World Dictionary.*

She can't remember what he said. She looks out the window again to see the strange woman heading down the street in the general direction of New York, where most of Bunny's friends no longer live. They've moved away, disappeared, died. Those who are left seem exhilaratingly indistinguishable from each other, especially when they insist on their unique particularity. They like to say things like, "Look, I'm an indi-vidul, see?"

"I think I'll burn down the chicken coop," Bunny says. "That's a start." Chances are that nobody will notice the smoke, not today.

"Damn!" Ted Buckie-Moeller blurts, "as I look up from my clut-tered desk. If I knew how to get to Joanne's parents' place, and felt like it, and still had my really good Nikon, and *Black Silk Stockings* wasn't coming on in a few minutes, I'd dash out there in the hope that I might add some really fine studies to my 'Conflagrations' series. Hell, I mean it! No, really, I *mean* it." There is *something,* something warm, warm and inviting and familiarly depressing about Ted's false enthusiasm, and his toupee doesn't help much in adding sincerity to his remarks. At least he doesn't say "Wow!"

Nina, whom you may remember, last saw her old friend April propped up, half-comatose, in bed, her peach slip damp with urine. She's thinking, at this moment, of how lucky she is that she isn't April. Here she is, almost fifty, sitting in 99, one of the 687 "best downtown restaurants," sipping a Banana Amaze, and waiting for Josh Cabernet. Josh! Josh! Josh is not quite thirty, a successful lawyer, casual, relaxed, well-dressed, an excellent if hopelessly sane lover, and a man whose "star" is, well, *on the rise!* Look! There it is, right there with those which know the heart and boldly tell of the dynamic pulse and rawness of the ceaseless electricity and dynamics of the harsh urban glamour! You bet. When a mover and shaker like Michelle Caccatanto suggests that a young writer's grit-packed first book may well be the prelude to an eventual Nobel Prize—well! Am I lucky, or am I lucky? Nina thinks, or asks, checking her makeup in her compact mirror. Nina doesn't know that Josh, who is sympathetic and compassionate, yet blessed with an observant, cold, yet not pitiless eye, will not be meeting her today at 99, or anywhere else. A young woman with the cinematic name of Noël is presently tarrying with the dynamic author. As he looks down at her glossy newscaster's hair and her busy junior executive's mouth, he remarks how wonderful it is to be the young and newly famous recipient of a "blow" job in an elegant and expensive hotel room in dynamic, electrically gritty New York. New York! Wow! He adds, thoughtfully, that this is "living." Noël takes a short break—she thinks of it as a "lunette"—from her amorous labors and looks up adoringly at Josh, adoringly and, yes, perhaps saucily, pertly, and impudently. "I love Noo Yawk!" she breathes, and returns to "blow" job tasks. Josh thinks of Nina, and immediately begins humming "No Regrets." But just then a powerful and unexpected *jouissance* that not even *his* notable literary intelligence may detain racks his harshly ceaseless body and puts Noël on her youthful mettle. We are pleased to report that she seems to be acquitting herself as well as or better than the standard, run-of-the-mill, blue-blood whore of the sleepless city. Did we mention that Noël is intelligent, capable, has her Master's in forage-crop communications pathology, is currently working on a novel, two operas, "small ones, really," loves the beach, prefers to kill raccoons with her bare hands, is almost unbearably gorgeous, likes to repair subway cars, and is about to open her own restaurant-supply boutique? We did. Fine. Did we mention that Josh's response to her venereal ministrations is a series of grunts, yelps, pantings, and screams, interspersed with comments which those of a religious bent would term blasphemies? We didn't? Well, so it is.

"I can't, stout Dick, thank you enough for extinguishing the petty inferno which could well have done away with *all* my hair, and, I fear, my skull into the bargain," Buddy said, his deep voice trembling with wonted sincerity, and his knees knocking in the chilly mists that enveloped the sickening mountainside.

"Jiminy, Buddy!" Dick blushed becomingly, " 'twarn't nothing but what you'd or any feller'd do yourself, or himself, or, shucks, even *themselves,* or something of that nature. Fellers just got to stick together and beat out the flames they 'pear to notice on each other's heads—or any darn place *else,* I'd venture, otherwise they'll hang separately! 'Sides, you were prostrated 'count of sick grief and shock."

The boys' relieved and manic laughter quickly echoed from hill to wild ravine, from tarn to smiling cataract, as they stood, sooty, impugned, and weary from their recent adventure, in the small clearing into which the mountain twilight was wildly clambering. Luckily, the fire blazed high and their lorelike meal of boiled junco beans and Dick's by-now legendary big-rock "slagger" simmered tastily in the old black iron pot which Buddy's mother had made for him during one of her numerous tear-stained vigils. Suddenly, a young fellow strode into the circle of firelight, and gratefully stretched his thorn-studded hands toward the blessed warmth.

"I am Manly Normal," the young man said with pleasing candor, "and I feel as if I know Mystery Mountain better than any fellow living. Hurrah!" Then, seating himself, after consigning his attractive Saskatoon to a nearby stand of autumn milkmouth, he looked at the two boys as if seeing them for the first time. "Looks to me," he said to Buddy, "that you almost had your head scorched right off while looking for a *non-existent map.*" His eyes blazed strangely as he carefully enunciated this last phrase.

Buddy and Dick almost fell to their respective knees before the incomprehensible stranger, but quickly recovered their dignity, and then sat, relaxed but alert, in the manner prescribed by Cliff Coiffure in

Campfire Manners. "Well, Manly," Buddy ventured finally, "it's without a doubt crackerjack impressive that you should know of our fruitless map search, as fellows call it. Hmm, I'd have to agree that you know the mountain better than any fellow that *I'm* acquainted with!" With this frank admission, the three lads relaxed, and deftly filled their plates with the rejuvenating victuals. They chatted merrily throughout the simple repast, their whoops of comradely laughter sending, for some reason, a rather large avalanche hurtling down upon the University of Chicago and the teeming streets of Chinatown!

"Let me make a long story as short as possible, new friends," Manly sighed contentedly, as he pushed himself away from the fire. The other boys were sprawled insensitively about the leaping flames, and all three had fallen into a digestive reverie, aided by the pungent fluid of the rusk shoots which grew in abundance amid the surrounding faucet-sedge. Manly then quietly continued, his features gleaming in the dancing firelight, a dancing firelight which Buddy, understandably, shied away from jerkily, his usually virile eyes unattractively bloated, and his coat, shirt, shopping bag, and gallus clips cunningly piled upon and wrapped around his sere and shredded "hair."

"I'm what men call," Manly began, "a regular sort of footloose bindlestick, the kind of fellow who tramps about a good bit and sees to it that things, well, that things happen in a certain order of occurrence, more or less."

"Somewhat like the artistic or businesslike sort of experience?" Buddy queried from beneath his protective ziggurat. "In that one seeks a hierarchy of order that one long ago gave up hope of one ever discovering in one's diurnal experience? Or would that be one's occurrence?"

"Gosh all hammock!" Dick marveled frantically, "you are right informed, Buddy, 'bout *ever'thing*. I guess you up and know 'most all the things worth knowing *on!*" As the doughty Witherspoon spoke, he cast more than one surreptitious glance at the shadowy form of the Saskatoon still lying quietly in the weeds.

"You are correct, Buddy!" Manly roared happily, his large face shining moonlike in the mincing firelight. "Presently, for instance, I'm working deuced hard for a strange sort of foreigner named Norman, who owns a genuine oil painting concerning death and perdition and other singularly unhappy ideas, a painting of which he is . . . *inordinately fond,* if you follow my leering innuendo? He hired me pronto, outfitted me with all the abject coolies, rotgut whiskey, and ogives a fellow could ever hope for, and sent me to California's North Bay, supposedly to investigate the role which salad and opera play in cuteness of local thought, word, and deed. From there, I hurriedly departed for Northeast Boise A & M, where the library's collection of primitive treasure maps rivals that of the notorious Ned Blutwurst, the dago, and from th— wh-what's the matter, Buddy? You look as if you've seen a ghost!"

Indeed, Buddy's rib cage was in the distended state usual in such situations of unavoidably horrific manifestation, and he had leaped to his feet to perform a curious "dance" from which even the coarsest forest creatures turned away in embarrassment.

"Is the name 'Ned Blutwurst' somehow responsible for this display of pseudoerotic shenanigans?" Manly whispered to the inured yet plucky Dick, who stood ready to snare, if necessary, his comrade by whatever protuberance presented itself to his grasp.

" 'Pears it's tarnation sure that that's the way it seems likely on being," Dick smiled candidly, for there was little or no guile in his plain-as-aprons American character. "The dago's driv poor Buddy plumb crazy with his pert and saucy tricks, just as he drivved Buddy's father, Old Buddy, plumb crazy. On the old feller he used some mighty pert and saucy tricks, including," he reflected wanly, "throwing him from a beetling crag hereabouts."

"But what does all this have to do with Norman, my foreign employer?" Manly cried. His Midwestern politeness, honed to a keen edge by countless lanolin biscuits and hot, noisy kitchens, barely triumphed over the sudden dislike he felt for the blank, placid "face" which looked upon him, its—the "face's"—lips shining with "slagger" and the fugitive halvah shards which had been Manly's tactless but sporting contribution to the rough repast, a repast which was now, he thought bitterly, concluded!

But all—feigned politeness, smoldering dislike, shaky grammar, and the shenanigans which had brought the usually modest Buddy into scandalous contact with a flowering *bozito*—and a remarkably large one!—*all* was reduced to insignificance as the Northern Lights lit up the icy sky! The three boys stood in silent awe, as the spectacular display of what is often called "Nature's fireworks" spread its attractive colors across the looming vault of heaven.

"Great Scott!" Manly expostulated warmly. "They look like the skyline of North Miami! Or even of Miami Beach, home, as you surely know, of the famous mass-transit system! They are, indeed, spectacular. Hmm, I'd go so far as to call them, let me see . . . 'Nature's fireworks!' Yes, I like that enormously, 'Nature's fireworks.' And so *shall* they be called from this time forth."

Buddy, pleasantly shocked out of his uncharacteristic "manifestation frenzy," nodded in agreement. "An excellent descriptive, Manly, and a metaphor of which, I venture, even Miss Ingelow would be proud," he gaped. "Oddly enough, they remind *me* of the North Shore of Long Island, perhaps because it was there that I first became truly keen on pastel-hued art objects. Somehow, the colors of these noble lights cajole me into a kind of happiness, despite the alarmingly bad luck which Dick and I have been so far fated to endure in this dratted boondock!"

"Goldangit, Buddy!" Dick called softly from the crepuscular weeds, where his dim shape could just barely be made out as it furtively scuttled about on the ground, "you know that things're liable to change for the better. It's a long road that has no silver mining, or something like," he gamely concluded.

"I understand, Normal old man," Buddy said, wisely ignoring the erratic behavior of his somewhat silly friend, "that the Northern Lights are Norwegian in origin. Have you heard or read anything of interest touching on this theory?"

"Indeed I have, friend," Manly nodded queerly, pouring himself and Buddy a generous draught of a hot, nearby beverage. "They appear in the skies only on those occasions when our distant Norwegian friends pay homage to St. Olaf, five days and nights of swinish celebration. The womenfolk cook without surcease, and the fumes of the lūtefiské, língonbèrries, drammenbëer, koñgsvingér, øddaglög, slágénsláw, and other barbaric delicacies, are said to mix in the atmosphere—just below the notoriously transparent Van Allen belt—with high-speed electrons, photons, protons, neutrons, ions, bions, quarkons, nougats, buicks, and irrefragable gases; this rich mixture instantly producing the breathtaking, luminous extravaganza which I have always called 'Nature's fireworks.' "

"Astonishing!" Buddy inveighed, quickly reddening. "You may find it diverting that in a book recommended to me by my old Dean of Arts and Sciences—a crapulous yet withal droll gentleman—*Nouveau traité des vapeurs,* published in 1770, the Lights are claimed to exert a malign influence on the fair sex, and to cause in them the nervous affliction known as 'the vapors.' Amusingly bully, is it not?" Buddy grinned toothily, glancing toward the thrashing in the weeds which lay beyond the now-forgotten hot-beverage source.

"Amusing? Ha, ha, ha! Why, my young friend, it's more than amusing!" Manly enthused, staring askance at the contents of his cup. "But tell me, precisely what is meant by 'the fair sex'?" He looked up quickly, his expression that of a tired but undefeated Zouave.

"Ha! Ha!" Buddy rejoined, smartly slapping his festoons. Yet his laughter died quickly as, in a trice, he saw Manly flush as deeply scarlet as the Dean of Arts and Sciences, one of the most egregiously flushed men that Buddy, and many others, had ever seen. "I-I-I-I'm sorry, Manly, please forgive my rude laughter. With that phrase I refer, as do most others, to *women,* women and *girls.* I intended you no picayune mental anguish, of that you may be assured. I know only too well how the fellows that one passes on the way up the ladder are the same fellows one passes on the way down the ladder, lest they have passed one on the way up the ladder, or one has not descended the ladder, or certain fellows have jumped or fallen off the ladder, or whatever. Surely, you get my drift."

"Women, eh?" Manly said quietly. "Girls and women? What a crackerjack notion! Hurrah! Is Gloria Jean, for instance, a fair sex?"

"Indeed she is!" Buddy cried delightedly, for he had always thought highly and in the purest way about Miss Jean and her wonderful anklets.

"And then," Manly pursued, "does it mean that Gloria Jean has the vapors? Or did she *have* the vapors, as, for instance, the cult poet Olga Begone did? Or so we read," he added apologetically.

"It's hard to know, Manly," Buddy said in all sincerity, as he poked the fire with a dried bandeaux. "In Hollywood, it is sound business practice for the large studios to guard the privacy of their major stars. For instance, it is rare, indeed, for a star to have his or her advancement barred because of reports concerning said star's incorrect or slipshod speech. The studio moguls simply will not permit such speech to be made public. If, for instance, Gloria Jean or Deanna Durbin or Dolores Délire, in an unguarded moment of excitement or pique, should say, 'It don't make no difference to me, Mac, I ain't eatin' the lousy grub,' the moguls would not countenance the broadcasting of such extemporaneous crudeness."

"This is utterly fascinating," Manly smiled, seating himself next to Buddy on the massive humidoro log which served as a rude banquette. "And what about a girl like Peggy Ann Garner, would it be the same? Would she, too, refuse the lousy grub?"

"Precisely the same," Buddy said, wondering how this conversation had begun. "Speaking of Gloria Jean, I've always had the notion that in the rollicking musical-comedy-drama *A New Dimension* both she and Bobby Breen, her crabbed putz of a co-star, displayed unmistakable and serious signs of the vapors in the climactic game-scene. I strongly suspect that this is why the film was never released. *Much* too powerful and revealing, most pointedly anent the fate of Breen's odiously curled and lacquered hair."

"Hmmm," Manly mused brusquely. "So then, the refusal to release would be an example of the studios' expert business savvy? Much like their expert actions concerning demotic references to dining refusal?"

"Exactly," Buddy said in quiet alarm, his eyes casually fixed on the unbuttoned figure of Dick Witherspoon as he lurched into the firelight, an athletic smile on his sweaty face.

"By the way," Manly urged, "is *A New Dimension* based on *Une Nouvelle dimension* by the great hydrocephalic geometer Gaspard Monge? His only novel, so far as I know, although some putative experts insist that it was written by Théophile Dondey. How incessantly droll! Ha! Ha!"

"I think I've read that it is," Buddy rejoined with cheerful vigor. "Perhaps in *Screen Action,* at one time my favorite periodical. But that was before I began this compulsive, obsessive, and fruitless quest for the blasted, phantom map!" he shouted at last.

"Ah, hello, Witherspoon," Manly said, making room for the weary Dick. "I had an inkling that you were somewhat curious about my retiring Saskatoon. A remarkable example of the *fair sex,* is she not?" he winked at Buddy. Dick smiled, then keeled over to lie prostrate before the fire.

"I've seen Dick once or twice like this in the past," Buddy confessed. "I fear that he occasionally surrenders to the baser passions. Unfortunately, such carnal weakness has proven to be a substantial bar to his advancement in the demanding world of business. Although, in all honesty, I must admit that his divers problems with grammar, syntax, vocabulary, as well as his delight in abrasive slang, have also been a factor. Surely you've noticed?"

"In all candor, I have indeed," Manly quickly agreed, nonchalantly placing his urbane feet on Dick's sated body. "And although my Saskatoon *is* eye-catching, I am always surprised when a young fellow of Dick's caliber is drawn to her. I mean to say, drat it all!, the wench is no Gloria Jean!"

"As long as we're being candid," Buddy sobbed, "I must confess that Dick has always been embarrassingly crass in his manly tastes. It may well be because his father"—and here his voice fell to a whisper—"was a Millinery of the November League."

Manly Normal visibly paled, and for a moment it seemed as if his generous mouth would open wide as prelude to a bout of unrestricted vomiting. But he controlled himself, and spoke earnestly to his new friend.

"Then . . . then the search for the map and for the dago, even the map itself—the entire quest—is but a subterfuge on your part to make rudely healthy in mind, body, and spirit, *if humanly possible,* this pathetic slave to the flesh?"

"You've guessed the bitter truth, comrade," Buddy smiled tightly. "But now, let's turn in, or bed down, for tomorrow may well be a day of impending crisis."

"Good night, Buddy," Manly said throatily, his large eyes clear at last. "I'll see how my young Saskatoon is surviving the night chill—if you don't require my presence?" But Buddy humorously made a crude but universally understood gesture with his fingers, pulled his hale benny around his shoulders, and put another persimmon on the hot coals. The whippoorwills, wise beyond speech, screeched horribly, then all was silent. Nearby, the tree line seemed to lurk nervously.

"There's been some subtle and some not-so-subtle denigration of late of the poet Olga Begone," Michelle Caccatanto says, for some reason, probably literary. "To wit, vulgar remarks about her going on what is ludicrously called an 'acclaimed aluminum diet,' lubricious suggestions concerning her physical attributes and maddening lusts, sneering references to her taste in couture, and excerpts from her works maliciously arranged to depict her as a wild-eyed, radical man-hater with a closetful of ugly shoes and a fear of bananas. Yet how many of these unreconstructed mockers know the delicate poem of nostalgia, lost love, and ineffable longing, 'Still Life with Scotch and Agony,' unaccountably deleted from Ms. Begone's last collection, *Nutless!*? It is, thank heaven, still available to those lucky enough to get their hands on the first and only issue of *Nuts and Bolts,* a journal dedicated to the preservation of true cultural values in a time of decay and specious 'stardom' in the arts. Permit me to read the opening stanzas of the poem, which is cast in the formal structure called a phantom":

> Though parting with a kiss, a smile—
> I had a funeral in my crotch!
> Her quick touch, her blush, the while
> We slowly sipped our favorite Scotch.

> I had a funeral; in my crotch
> There was no love for friends or jobs.
> We slowly sipped our favorite Scotch
> And let our wild tears flow, like slobs.

> There was no love! For friends or—

Thank you, thanks, Michelle! Thanks a million. We'll most definitely remember both you and Olga when next we bump into Halpas, Burner of Cities. Now there's a guy who appreciates a phantom!

Eligor still roams about, the increasing heat of the day seemingly exacerbating his desire to intrude upon those things which strike his fancy as open to playful meddling. The inflammatory contents of the latest issue of *Nylon Pussies* are transmuted into photographs of "the friendly cockatoo" and "wonders of the desert," as well as feature articles on "Building Your Own Soup Can Art," "Sleeping under Glass," and "Cherry-Cheese Dip—Boon or Bane?" Clive Oak, abandoning a compliant snake of his acquaintance, is suddenly convinced that he is someone named "Octave," and is then compelled to ask everyone he meets persistent questions about a dinner party of which none of them have ever heard. Anthony Octavio, a translator of precise if meager gifts, in contact with the spirit world, insists that a young woman named "Muffie" served as the model for the character of Ethan Frome in an unreadable coterie novel, *Odd Number* or *Odd Numerals* or *Old Bumbler.* The spirits—known to the "channeling community" as the Official Mouths—cannot be sure of this because of malignant static somewhere over Gnatville. Eligor is immediately interested in Muffie, a young, svelte shopper, and her relationship with what seems to be a *tugboat.* He goes in search of her, halting, at least temporarily, his ludic pastimes. It is a good bet that he—being a demon—is sexually aroused by what are often called "degrading images and depictions." Demons have little interest in social and cultural acceptability, none at all in anybody's dignity, living or dead, and they shit on all flags.

"Hi! I'm Karen O'Grady! When I'm cavorting 'tween cirrus and cumulus, a vicious minority dubs me a French whore, *n'est-ce pas?* But when I've got these spike heels planted on the *la terre,* I know that I'm the hardworking daughter of a hardworking mom, as well as being the hardworking sister of hardworking sisters. Some of *them* are French whores, but heck, we can be whatever we put our minds to being, to be, what we want to be! That's what my guy, an important hotel *hotelier,* says, and he tells me never to forget it. Hi!"

"Hello. Sure an' oi'm the ghost o' Rosie O'Grady, sure an' oi'm be-jayzus sick an' toired, sure an' may all the mavourneens an' cruiskeens be me witness, sick an' toired an' thoroughly banjaxed in me poor owld dead moind, o' hearin' me daughter Karen's name linked wi' that o' Karen O'Grady, the notorious French harlot. Sure, an' me daughter's knees were niver chained togither, but sure, that's a good bit different, bejayzus, than playin' at heathen things loike 'Jello-me-crock' an' 'the egg game,' jist to tink o' which'll send yer sowl to a Protestant hell. Hello." Her voice falters, then ceases.

We are grateful to more people than we can here name for calling to our attention the important information that the "vegetarian couple" who are here, there, and everywhere, are none other than the vivacious Benita O'Hearn, even more delightful with her newly pert breasts and ravishingly inviting lipo-sucked buttocks, and her husband, the pious Charles "Chick" O'Hearn, known to his closest friends as "Momo" and "Cheech," depending on score and inning. "Chick" seems to have had parts of his well-known ears placed to either side of his carefree "nose." Thanks again, heads-up friends!

"The word 'Ohio' is not a palindrome," Oiwin states belligerently, filling his hand with his ever-reliant capstan. He's taken it into his head to guard the cherry-cheese dip woman from possible insult by the outrageous "priest" whom nothing, seemingly, can assuage, save the unthinkable. "Chet and Allen have fled to Fire Island and its vagrant clams, Dwight may, if they're unlucky, join them, others are celebrating in suburb, wood, glade, copse, brake, fen, and atop shale bluff and beetling scarp! Someone, then, must stay on guard!" The cherry-cheese dip woman smiles at him, then looks brightly at Andy, who is writing down certain items of information from suspicious soup-can labels. "Anyway," Oiwin says again, "the word 'Ohio' is *not* a palindrome. To be such an item of linguistic interest as that there, it would have to be 'Oho' or 'Oio.' Get it? You got any questions, just line up in an orderly fashion and as far as this lady's concerned, look don't touch. Right, kid?" She smiles companionably and opens another noncarcinogenic plastic tube of genuine dip.

It's not generally known that Miss Caccatanto—soon to be the wife of Page Moses, the gifted person who is hard at work on a new novel which will, we understand, "blow" the lid "off" New York's glitterati—is interested in the preservation, cataloguing, and study of old films, many of which have not been screened in decades, as well as of more recent cinematic "cult" items. But let's let her speak for herself: "Thanks. It's a pleasure to be here, as you know, and thank God it's air-conditioned. I think you could probably fry an egg on the sidewalk! Really! Anyway, yes, I'm really interested in the old cinema, which I find to be impressively intuitive in its grasp of human affairs, as you know. For instance,

I've just had the good fortune to see *The Old Confederate Dead Man,* a grittily sophisticated look at gays in the Civil War, their travails and triumphs, their crude and fumbling humanity. Incidentally, the film has little to do with the sympathetically gritty poem from which, as you know, it takes its title. Then there's *Old Hoboken,* filmed in Hollywood about 1902, a saga based on *Blix,* a novel of cold despairs and pitiless triumphs, as you know. *Old Hoboken,* by the by, served as the inspiration for the Tin Pan Alley smash, 'I Got the Old Joe in Old Hoboken (and I Don't Want Your Oysters Anymore),' a song that still stands as an amusingly compassionate depiction of early slum life—somewhat like the later 'Old Shep,' with its compassionately amusing refrain, 'Old Shep he daid, / Old Shep he daid, / Old Shep, de maid / Done be afraid.' Of course you remember it! As for contemporary films, I'm extremely interested in rescuing the only extant print of *Lace Me Tighter!,* which uses non-professional actors in all its roles and thereby achieves a kind of impressively grey grittiness, as you know. It was filmed, I believe, in a motel room outside Missoula—speaking of *grit!* Although the characters are not fully realized, their very *humanity* is attractive. Well, it's been marvelous, but I really have to run out to Old Weskit, Page's family's house on the Island, as you know. I foolishly left the proofs of *Too Soon the Loon* there and I *have* to review it this week. It's by *the* Count Olivetti, as you know, and from what I hear around town, it's going to simply blow the lid off the international glitterati—tells absolutely *all.* They say that *some* people won't even be able to hide in Omaha! Well, as Rory the gambler says in *Old Hoboken,* 'the wages of sin is time and a half.' Listen, really, it *has* been marvelous, as you know."

Countess O'Mara is watching, in a kind of senile splendor, *Aini, the Destroyer!* on television. She's already seen it twice this week, and now waits impatiently for her favorite scene, the one in which a middle-aged ex-stewardess prepares lunch for herself in a small efficiency kitchen. The Countess is fascinated because the actress looks, allowing for the passage of time, exactly like a stewardess who was once introduced to her by Lady Bustier at somebody's garden party, long ago. She had been a delightful girl, at once complaisant and demanding, without either false modesty or a penchant for larceny. Countess O'Mara waits patiently, pleased that this ridiculous movie has awakened such a poignant memory. The same sort of possible mistaken identity as the cause of bittersweet pleasure is thoroughly explored in *Le Bousingot* by Théophile Dondey, writing as the anagrammatic Philothée O'Neddy.

Didn't Dondey-O'Neddy also write *Karen, Ma Cherie?*

He did. Now there's a book that *nobody* reads anymore.

The O'Neills, Ed and Kate, are playing gin rummy and drinking iced tea. Ed has lost most of his hair and suffers from mild emphysema, and Kate, although her face still retains traces of a wild Irish beauty, has put on a good deal of weight and has high blood pressure. They are grandparents three times over, and their children think of them as affectionate and loving, though a little too concerned with the petty details of everyday life. Ed and Kate still seek out sex orgies once or twice a month, at which they are vital, inventive, and highly experienced participants. They worry a little about dread diseases, but not enough to keep them at home. They are nominal Catholics, and occasionally go to mass, for sentiment's sake, although neither, understandably, has received the Eucharist in years. All this seems rather strange, almost unbelievable, since this couple— "Pardonnez-moi," Rimbaud interrupts. "Le maître, Monsieur Baudelaire, dit, 'la volupté unique et suprême de l'amour git dans la certitude de faire le mal.' "

Merci, Monsieur Rimbaud.

We have just received word that the woman known as "Onette" is *not* actually Annette Lorpailleur; neither is she Corrie Corriendo or Berthe Delamode, whom you will recall as "colleagues" of Mme. Lorpailleur's. It is, then, clear, that the suggestion to the contrary contained in the Ornamental Sheet-Metal Workers' Union newspaper, *On Their Metal,* is *only* a suggestion. Much more to the point is the revelation that Onette's full name is Onette Oogotz Op, that she is allergic to metal clothing and hosiery, and that she was never taken by surprise in the John Keats Lodge with three dwarfs, a short-order cook, a rope ladder, five gallons of apple sauce, and a home-economics teacher who would not stop singing "Orange-Colored Sky."

"Thank you," Corrie says quietly. "Since I've been looking at the traffic far below, I've realized how small it all seems! Small and virtually *unimportant!"*

"I've got little or nothing to say," Berthe adds, "em nopu era sropav eht ecnis."

Annette turns to stare. Oh oh.

The Orange Dress, at once product and cause of heartache, despair, misery, bankruptcy, dyspepsia, flabby thighs, high cholesterol, asthma, premature ejaculation, and the horror of secondary cigarette smoke, will soon be published, pundits surmise, in a new edition and sporting the new title of *Orange Steel.* Convinced that the quirky novel by Sheila Henry will find its audience this time around, the publisher, Oriental Food Products, is bringing its high-powered marketing strategies, rarely witnessed in the gentlemanly profession of publishing, into play. "We feel that we can sell the book the way one sells cranberries or imbroglios or bean sprouts," Louis Hess, OFP advertising chief, remarks in a recent story published in *Laguna Colony News.* "The whole idea behind modern, or should I say postmodern marketing is to make people lose control of themselves and act in an unseemly yet thrilling manner. We know a little about *that,* don't we?" he smiles at his energetic yet ruthless assistant, the veteran adwoman, "Tits" O'Rourke, known to the "boys on the Avenue" as "Big Tits," an insulting sobriquet which Miss O'Rourke unaccountably cherishes. She looks up brightly from her richly cluttered desk and puffs thoughtfully on her delicate meerschaum. Her figure, after all these years, is still trim, although she takes care to wear severe suits in order to conceal her body from the frankly lecherous stares of the lustful beasts in the office, who—

All this is in the *Laguna Colony News* story?

Well. Not exactly. Not *all* of it, exactly.

So stick to the facts, all right?

"Of course," Hess continues, "we're relying on the usual literary prepublication horseshit quotes for use in ads, on the jacket, in store displays, and so on, the works, whatever that means. I flatter myself that I've put together a group of real beauties, by really big book-names, current celebrities, well-known nobodies, the works! The works? Anyway, who said life was fair? Ha! Ha! Anyway, we should definitely sell some big-number *units,* amigo!," he concludes spiritedly, jumping up to pat "Tits" on her bottom, which she has done her level best to conceal, and to make an obscene suggestion concerning egg rolls. "I love this guy!" Miss O'Rourke says, quickly slipping out of her clothes and pressing her voluptuous body—

Come on!

. . . he concludes spiritedly, and jumps up to look frantically out the window, searching for that indefinable something that makes success in a high-powered urban environment worth that thing which it can be worth only if all else is sacrificed to its demands! He thinks, for a moment, of the demands made upon the modern career woman, the insults, the patronization, the humiliation suffered by, for instance, someone like Miss O'Rourke, and chokes back a guilty sob. For he knows, in his heart, that *he,* yes, *he* has been unfair to this beautifully built, irrepressible career woman! He stares unseeingly at the traffic far below. How would I feel if *I* had "big tits"? he agonizes. Then he turns—

All right. Let's see the goddamned quotes!

Here they are, straight from the office, and O.K.'d by the bright young people who are hip and who also know hip when they *see* hip.

"Looks like an Oscar or a Perry bid to this jaded listener."

—Reginald Ose, author of
Turn Your Delusions into Cash

"O'Callaghan and his famous suit of brown paper was never half so much good, clean fun."

—James Joyce

"I like an Oriental girl—and that's what this read delivers!"

—Kate O'Sighle, TV guest

" Ἐν ἀρχῇ ἦν ὁ λόγος, καὶ *The Orange Dress* ἦ ὁ λογος."

—St. John

"I couldn't put this searing wallop of a page-turner down and finished it on the squash court."

—Rory Blentz, squash devotee

"I'd sure like to meet Sheila Henry or even just look in her window! My goodness, what daring filth!"

—D.D., film buff

"Har! Har! Cutlass me lanyards if it 'twarn't like a-sittin' in a hogshead o' warm apple sauce. Har, har, har!"

—Long John Silver

" 'Tis like a Golden Spiritual Lamp which casts pure Beams that make a House a Home away from Home."

—Ella Weller Wheeler Willis, author of
Crush Rainbows to My Bosom, Please!

Karen Ostrom, tired from the heat and the wet, grimy wind that is beginning to blow up, rings Sylvie Lacruseille's bell. She knows that Sylvie hates to be disturbed, but she has news, or so she believes, of Sheila Henry, or someone who seems to fit Sheila's description. It is not good news. Karen is carrying it to Sylvie because so many of the other people whom she once knew are simply unavailable—disappeared, moved, hiding, insane, living under aliases, or dead: "Our Gang" is no longer even a small group. She rings again, and is about to turn away when she hears a long, high-pitched moan through the door, a sound composed equally of ecstasy, pain, guilt, and loneliness. She stands transfixed, for she recognizes a sound almost exactly like the one she herself occasionally produces. Inside, Sylvie, on her old couch, is lost in the kind of unbearable orgasm that plunders the soul and that she can usually bring about only by playing the "egg game." She feels another orgasm crowding against the one which is slowly subsiding, and begins to sob raggedly in anticipation. The shifty-looking man on the roof of the building across the street has dropped his raincoat, and stares at Sylvie in a kind of religious awe, actually frightened by the holiness of the pleasure he is watching. The movies never prepared him for this! The experience, delicately balanced between the sacred and the profane, may change the course of his shabby, seedy, sexual life. Or not. The time may, indeed, be ripe for such changes, since it is common knowledge that supposed visitations by Our Lady to two local churches —Our Lady of the Bleeding Eyes and Our Lady of Crushing Sorrows— have been testified to by numerous people, none of whom are especially given to religious visions. The shifty-looking man begins to shiver and weep uncontrollably as he watches Sylvie's body being swept by another manic climax. Karen leans against the wall in the hallway and lights a cigarette. She, too, has tears in her eyes.

"Yeah," the big guy in green work clothes says, beginning to sweat, "that's the way it goes. You do what you can and if it comes up a chicken-leg flush, you're all right, hell, halfway home, as they say. The Chevy just burned out its engine getting Alice up to Topeka, or was it Missoula? Anyway, she wanted more than anything to join up with Gladys there, she was convinced Gladys was living the high life. She didn't say anything but I know Alice and the funny way she looks at her housedresses. Gladys would send these picture postcards of the shopping mall and the new glass insurance building downtown and write messages like 'Here's the big story,' and 'I've got it now, honey,' and 'The X marks my window.' Well, after a while, what with the dead grasshoppers in the freezer, and her denims that wouldn't fade, and the way the snow would sort of drift over the pile of empty beer cans in the barbecue pit, and the damn fool baker and his stories, she just took off one night while I was lubeing Jack's pickup for the bear hunt down to the town dump. Yeah, took the Chevy and the Donald Duck insulated ice chest too, and about sixty dollars in cash I'd been saving up for a pool umbrella, because that was kind of our dream. I got a card from her showing the Hotel Pachuco with these two little clouds floating right over the roof, real white they were. They give me a funny feeling, sort of the feeling that you get when you all of a sudden look right into somebody's face in the parking lot. She wrote that she'd be home soon and to lay off the Hershey bars. I always had to hand it to Alice, she had a hell of a sense of humor. Made a nice beef stew too, when she put her mind to it and stayed away from the muscatel. And she fried things from the creek up real tasty too."

It is interesting to listen to these stories of the heartland and its people, who, although inarticulate in their longings and duped by the unheralded courage with which they struggle to evade their humble obligations, are yet the kind of folks who, when they get theirs, keep it, and into whose eyes one longs to stare while the wind blows straight across the gulch, crevasse, or ravine. Many of these stories are collected in the noted pathbreaking anthology *A Pack of Lies,* sometimes characterized as "the Bible of the new, unfrightened American realism," "a Packard to metafiction's ridiculous Edsel," "a gallery of people we can care about in their courageous nullity." Most notably, and coincidentally, one of the stories—"The Paddy in the Brake"—by Bronco Dungaree, inexplicably contains a purported fragment of the purported screenplay for *Lace Me Tighter!* Although there is nothing intrinsically interesting about a piece of shoddy soft-core pornography (and, in our opinion, a spurious piece), a little-known essay on the comparable merits of the film and Dungaree's "germ" story, by Mary Jane Alice Oaktag, points out that the amateur cast was headed by a Gladys and an Alice (!), and was, furthermore, shot entirely in and around a Hotel Pachuco (!) in Missoula (!). Such coincidence leaves us no alternative but to include the suspect fragment. It's right here in the files. (Indicates color-coordinated file cabinets.)

Lace Me Tighter! (Scene 14)

The boodwoire of a very rich French lady, Mme Vermouth. Mme Vermouth enters with her French maid, Fifi. Mme Vermouth slowly lets fall her luxorious penoire which she drops on the bed to reveal her voluptuose body in a cruel whalebone corset. Fifi is also scantily clad in a little short skirt and not much more but a pair of sheer silk hose and high heels. Mme Vermouth gazes sadly at a picture of two poor old tired horses in a meadow, their heads partially hid in thick gorse bushes, then she looks at Fifi.

MME VERMOUTH: It is very warm this evening, eh? (*She glowers strangely.*) Oh God! My bewitching Fifi! Lace me up!

FIFI (*sweating profusely*): It is, to be sure. You bet I will, my lady. How's . . . *this?*

MME VERMOUTH: Oh, my stars! Lace me—tighter!

FIFI: How then is this, my lady? (*Pulling vengefully on the corset strings.*) Is *this* tight enough, Madame?

MME VERMOUTH: No! No! (*In a towering rage:*) I wish greatly to have some trouble with my breathing!

FIFI: Ooff! Phew! That is about as tight as I can lace you up, without splitting you into two pieces, my beloved mistress! Ha! Ha!

MME VERMOUTH: I don't care a thing, my innocent girl! How little you know of the unhealthy sexual desires and practices of the corrupted wealthy class! Tighter! Tighter, I say! *Make* two sections of my trunk . . . if you dare!

FIFI: Sacré blue, Madame! You are laced so tight now that you are panting and pop-eyed, like some sort of wild feral-type animal!

MME VERMOUTH: Pant! Pant! Even . . . tighter . . . than . . . THIS! I feel almost demented, as if I am some kind of a fruit cake!

FIFI: This is quite a formidable performance of womanly pluck!

MME VERMOUTH: It is sweet agony! My well-cared-for body trembles with sharp aches! Now . . . just a little TIGHTER!

FIFI: Puff! Puff! Here we go, Madame! (*Apologetically:*) My arms have not the strength of old since I have damaged them puttering golf balls with the old Earl.

MME VERMOUTH: Yes! Yes! That's it! Oh Fifi! Torture me like a savage redskin of the North American plains and woods! Let me swoon myself to heights of pleasure and fall prostrate on my luxorious couch! (*Falls, sobbing in ecstasy, and almost bent double at the waist.*)

FIFI: Phew! Watch where you are falling in your swoon of passion, Madame! (*She looks at her dazed mistress.*) Hm. Madame has fainted, as usual. All her wealth and power cannot help her to achieve a happy sex life such as is enjoyed by rough miners, neat office clerks, and dedicated schoolteachers much of the time. I am disgusted with her depraved bourjoise lusts—and yet, I feel that she labors under a strange family curse.

Manuscript breaks off.

The Frankenstein girls haven't really given Fred a moment in which to speak to them of his favorite theory concerning the identity of the elusive Baylor Freeq, i.e., that he is actually the bath-and-boudoir-accessories tycoon, Biff Page, currently on his way to an *al fresco* buffet and cock-tail party somewhere near Gnatville—but not the buffet and cocktail party in, at present, a jagged shambles. It might, however, give Biff pause to know that the mighty Paimon, obedient to Him who was Drowned in the Depths of His Knowledge, has decided, in demonic irritability, to "annoy and abrade" Gnatville and its environs because of faulty information that this locale is playing delighted host to the false Albanian Lard Goddess.

"Did I ever tell you of my Freeq-Page theory?" Fred asks from beneath an ironing board.

"Did you ever see anything as cute?" one of the girls says, slathering her body with cold cream. "It's something about the way his eyes look when the board falls on those naughty distichs of his," the other giggles, filling her notorious *purge à souffler* with warm chocolate pudding.

"Girls? Just a minute, all right? Girls?" Fred says, scrambling—too late!—to his feet. "Can't we just talk for a minute? Can't we have a little intelligent modernistical conversation like in an interview with Paul West? Where in heck are my pants?"

"Just as cute as a button!" one of the girls screams. "His *pants!*"

It may be helpful to include at this point the information that Dr. Miriam Paimon (no relation to Fred), a Freudian analyst of the "uncanny" school, maintains, in a recent paper, "Hungarian Tendencies in Pseudo-Adolescent Erotic-Games Tableaux in Marin County" (*Erotomagnalephon,* XI, 2, 1982), that such manifestations of anti-societal behavior as may be observed in "the acting-out of prelibidinous Athenic fixations, such as those produced by the clitorally subsumed superego (inversion) in its predictable clashes with masculine id-icons, e.g., the herm, the hot dog, the ironing board, etc., are, rather surprisingly, controlled by the look, feel, odor, and taste of Pall Mall cigarettes."

"And the opposite is also the case," Dr. Paimon says, "despite ill-tempered assaults on the proposal by the few Adlerian nitwits who still have the gall to admit their allegiance to that pompous shrimp. And, of course, there's always the health thing," she muses.

"No, no, no!" one of the girls whoops. "*Bend* the nozzle, silly, *bend* it! Fred, you are *priceless!*"

Corrections of earlier errors:

Item: Manly Normal erred when comparing the Northern Lights to the skylines of North Miami and/or Miami Beach. The correct comparison is to the skylines of Palm Beach and/or Palm Springs. Normal's error sprang, according to John Crowe Ransom, from an imperfect understanding of the geographical function of the axis of selection.

Item: Panama is not *only* a country; it is also, as Rupert Brooke suggests in the line, "and things are done you'd not believe," a musical composition.

Item: A Panama hat—despite fashion dictates from Paris—is never to be equipped with a string which attaches to the wearer's lapel, even though worn in the *craziest* season.

Item: The Parisian: Dossiers of Longing, by Jean-Claude Rififi, was not employed as the "anchor" by means of which Zuleika Dobson kept herself submerged beneath the cold waters of the fateful flood.

Item: Although Jack Spicer's remark, "None of you bastards / Knows how Charlie Parker died" was once accurate, it is no longer. Time marches right along.

Cox has definitely given up hope of finding any clams on this street of dynamic old bookshops. Yet in one of them he comes across a first paperback edition of *Parts of the Gangs,* a novel by Rajneesh Coney, and a work variously described as "a devastating look at the pleasures and agonies of health worship," "something like a very large, fascinating fish," and "a delightful exercise in today's spurious entelechy." Quite the companion volume to *White Bridges*! Cox thinks. He is not aware that *Parts* is under continuing option to a Major Motion-Picture Studio, and that it may soon start production as *The Party.* This latter is not to be confused with the abortive attempt to film a version of an obscure French novel whose original title we cannot, unfortunately, ascertain. That film was also to be called *The Party,* although we have it on reasonable authority that *The Party* was not the title of the French novel, or, more precisely, the translated title, of course. There is, however, a film still available in videocassette called *The Party,* but it is amateur pornography filmed in and around the bowling alley adjacent to the Naughty Nightie boutique, and has nothing to do with the aborted *The Party,* the potential *The Party,* the French novel, or *Parts of the Gangs.* Or so we have been led to believe. There is, too, the one-act play *The Party,* by Craig Garf, but this is an utterly obscure item.

"It's a *wonderful* play even though nobody will produce it," Craig whines. "I still feel, however, that craftsmanship is more important than speed or handsome profits. Yet I'll be forever grateful, for it was the writing of *The Party* which permitted me to flee Misty Crag and settle amid the ceaseless pistonings of the thunderous dynamo of the dazzling but heartless metropolis. And there is no business which can compare with the theatre business, or, heck! let me be all-embracing, with *show* business. But is it fair to call show business a business? Is it not closer, in every way, in all its manifestations, both large and small, to the—"

Thank you! Thank you, Craig! Wonderful. Absolutely wonderful! Even compelling. Certainly heartfelt.

To recapitulate: The potential *The Party* has nothing to do with the aborted *The Party,* neither of which has anything to do with the pornographic *The Party,* and none of these three has anything in common with Garf's one-act play (indicates coffee-stained, dog-eared, heavily annotated typescript), *The Party.* However, for our own purposes, which are manifold if obscure, all of the papers, correspondence, notes, memoranda, contracts, photographs, promotional materials, etc., etc., which have to do with or are germane to any or all of the above-named projects, shall be placed, before this day is over, in a group of sturdy cardboard cartons, each of which shall be sealed, and then clearly marked, in dark, permanent ink, with the words, "The Party."

"There's more fuss about all this crap than there is about Passover," Cox says, waxing semi-religious. "I wish to Christ I never bought this stunning companion volume to *White Bridges.* Bibliophilia leads one to strange places. Wouldn't you say so, friend?" he asks Craig Garf. "I didn't do anything!" Craig whimpers. "Get away! Get away! That only *looks* like me in that snapshot! Go on—get away!"

We won't trouble ourselves to discover what has upset the unsuccessful playwright, but allow him to disappear into the maw of the forever-pistoning dynamo, a dynamo which bears ultimate responsibility for *The Party.*

Which one?

Shh.

"Hi! I'm Karen Peachy! Well, I'm not *actually* Karen Peachy, she's out just now, but I'm sort of the next best thing, like, I'm Karen Complexion! You might remember me because of my beautiful grooming and competent grammar. I also know how to handle the tell-tale hair that can do so much to ruin the sheer *fun* of wearing a mini-bikini! That's I! And I know that Karen—the other Karen—is *just* as carefully depilated in the No-No Zone. Oh, hi!"

Albert Pearson definitely does not like what he's just heard from one of his spies concerning Berthe's treatment in flower-glutted Bermuda. Beshary has clearly become—although Pearson has discounted such rumors for years—a ruthless mogul and a heartless tycoon, although some have thought him closer to a ruthless tycoon with a heart of stone. Seating himself at an antique writing table of zither-inlaid mahogany teak, Pearson settles his gold rimless glasses on his face and writes:

Dear old friend and partner,

I know that you mean well, but if the reports I've received today are correct, I feel that you're treating Berthe terribly. He is a very nice man, and I know that you agree with me and Janos that we three are somehow responsible for his "galoot fever" and his penchant for patent leather—often, yes, to the exclusion of really nourishing foods! Be that as it may. I don't understand what pleasure a downright wealthy tycoon, like you, can possibly take in tearing up the poor man's best lace cap, breaking the heels off his black pumps, and taunting him with false stories about fake art works. And stealing his last alimentary strap! Really, Edward, this is beneath even a heartless mogul. In any event, please send Berthe to me as soon as possible! Perhaps a new fall wardrobe from Peck and Peck will brighten his tear-filled eyes. Or some other tasteful store. Whatever, I'm the man to buy such things, as you, to your regret, well know. I'll also replace the collection—Berthe always called it his "pack" —of ceramic Pekes which I know you shattered in a pineapple-induced frenzy some weeks ago. After a time, when the dear man has recovered from your cruelties, I'll introduce him to Pepe—you remember Antonia's Pepe, don't you?—and watch anxiously to see his craggy face light up as Pepe begins to display his flimsy but irresistible repertoire. I *am* disappointed in you, Edward. I will not tell Janos of these things, even though, as you've probably heard, *The Curse* will finally be published and our old friend and colleague is impenetrably euphoric. I will, of course, reimburse you for Berthe's fare. And for goodness' sake, let him take whatever makeup and undies he still has!

Your troubled partner,
Albert

"Hi! I'm Karen Pepsi! Isn't it just *great* how Karen Complexion filled it in, or however you say it, for Karen Peachy, and winged through turbulence and the stray gout of vomit with the best of 'em? Karen Peachy is at a demonstration right now, demanding that nobody call us 'stewardesses' or 'flight attendants' *ever* again! I don't understand it real well, but I do know that I'm all for our demands, which is that we should be called 'stars' or 'bosses' or something like that. Politics isn't my teacup but when I'm amid the snowy billows I smile a whole heck of a bunch! My guy, a weathered, greying exec, thinks they should call us 'honeys.' He's so fun! Hi!"

Diane Drought's daughter, unable to convince her raving mother that she is, indeed, her daughter and not "some Albanian bitch," walks purposefully into Anne Kaufman's shop, just as Anne is striding womanfully out. They meet, bumping into each other softly, yet with an insouciance fit for the virgin bush and its attendant marmosets. Anne steps back, entranced by the pair of ice-blue panties knotted carelessly about her young visitor's alabaster neck. No telling *what* direction fashion will take among the restless young. She smiles carefully, whatever that may suggest!

"May I help you?" Anne asks professionally. "I was just closing, but if there's anything you might need. . . ? A Day-Glo crucifix? Plastic biretta? Mickey Mouse pyx with matching paten. . . ?"

"Aren't you Anne Kaufman, the author of *Perfumes of Arabia*?" the forward minx demands.

"Why yes, I am, but . . ."

"My mother—never mind her identity!—told me about it, and even though you used the pen name 'Anne Leo,' you're a dead ringer for the real tough broad you are, or so it seems, in actuality. The body of Beely, the Whack-Off King, still behind the counter? Or have you, ah, disposed of him?" (Indicates vat of boiling lye.)

"Actually," Anne replies foolishly, "there is a *real* Anne Leo, a well-known barfly. Some maintain that she bears a strange resemblance to the abused heroine of *The Perils of Pauline*. But that was before your time, Miss. . . ?"

"So *this* is Beely," the visitor whispers gutturally, looking down in awe at the grotesque, manly shell of cold fleshly mortality. "He looks like one of the endpaper drawings in the first edition of *Permanent Guests*. By the way," she snaps in the manner of a wily martinet, "why is it that the narrative structure of *Guests*, and its anal-retentive architecture, is so much like that of *your* novel?"

"That's Dr. Perrie's argument precisely!" Anne yelps happily. "That wonderfully warm and famous old geezer! However," and here she smiles and leans quixotically against a fake relic, "the problem is that my book is not a novel but a memoir."

"What have *you* got to remember?" the girl mutters savagely, kicking sharply at Beely's corpse. Suddenly, though, she snaps out of "it." "Wh-what am I doing here?" she complains girlishly. "And wh-who are you? Wh-what and wh-who? I recognize this slumbering figure as Miner X. Beely, sex therapist to the big stars and annual Guinness luminary, b-but h-how are you? I mean wh-who are you?"

"My dear child," Anne gushes profligately, "you are as simple and ingenuous as a corporal in the Peruvian army. As innocent as Dick and April's unborn child, Peter. As chaste as Sister Philomena Veronica, who, in the piss-redolent classrooms of O.L.B.E. Parochial School, taught me the Palmer method and the reasons that Methodists look funny and thus have little chance at heaven."

"So . . . you're Anne Kaufman, my mother's cherished friend!"

"Perhaps I am. But don't interrupt me as I conjure up the past, else you may join the defunct pervert at my still-attractive feet. Yes, Sister Philomena Veronica! So enthralled was I by the sexual mysteries of a chaste sisterhood and the vague, waxy odor of the epicene cloister, by the torturous lusts held in tight control by *women without men,* indeed, so fascinated and psychologically disturbed was I by these carnal puzzles, that just a few years back I played the role of the 'good nun' in a, ah, candid film—whose title I cannot now recall. But I've said too much already. May I make you a nice cup of tea, Miss Drought?"

"But you know my name! How wonderful! But how?" the girl laughs immediately, startling a blasé passerby.

"Who else would disguise herself as the Albanian lady, who, today of all days, haunts the sterile suburbs? And only someone with a knowledge of the summer lard festivals who know of the significance of underwear as outerwear!"

And the two women, one old and marvelous, the other wonderfully vivacious in her obvious bloom, laugh and laugh, forgetting, for a blessed moment, the tell-tale cadaver stiffening, as he so often did in life, beneath a heap of fallen scapulars.

Is that a chapter from *Buddy and His Boys*?

From what?

Buddy and His Boys. You know, Buddy, Dick, the mountain?

A *chapter*?

A chapter, a chapter, yes, a *chapter!* What are you looking at me like that for?

Hard as it is to believe, Phoenix, who Lispeth as a Child, who Appear-eth as the Bird of His Own Name, singing in dulcet Tones, Phoenix, the excellent Poet of the Seventh Thrones, flies swiftly toward François of Fargo's, in order to avail himself of that establishment's asparagus bread, a bakery product ignored, if not rejected, but a few moments ago by Kirk, known chiefly for his overwhelmingly cheap cologne. How-ever, a recent note states that Kirk has not yet ignored or rejected the asparagus bread, but soon will. It appears that certain things are achronological, insofar as Kirk is concerned. This *is* August 29, 1982. Léonie's calendar is correct, even if *she* is what might be called "wrong." More news: It seems that a number of things may be achronological. Oh well.

"I mean well," Léonie says.

Then too: Scholars Dispute de Kock Influence on Late Picasso Ceramics; Mr. Pimples, Adult Film Star, Claims Sugarless Gum Caused Sudden Sex Change; Biochemists Suggest Some Pistachio-Oval Ice Cream May Be Alive; Pittsburgh to Enter Bid for Leisure Moustache Owned by Pope Pius XII; Murray Baddle Billows, "the Platinum Priestess," Says Most Men Prefer Whores Who Look Like Her Mom; Researchers Fear Famed Plaza May Be Covered with Microscopic Layer of Excrement; Norwegian Methodist Woodsman to Bring Libel Suit against Dr. Plot on Grounds of "Shameless Idiocy"; Donald Plot Charges Joggers Act as "Hosts" to *E. coli* Organism; Studies Reveal Plymouth Favorite Car of "Regular-Guy" Priests; *PMLA* Mulls "Egghead" Comic-Strip Feature; Heart-Shaped Bath-tub Cache Found in Poconos.

"The critic who spoke of Henri Kink's 'Poem' as 'a terse monologue developed amid a welter of illocutionary symbols' clearly based his sincere if specious characterization of the poem on the text as it appears in *Blue Filter,*" Professor Raoul Blinque sniffs. "However, the poem is much more than a simple monologue, and it is not in any way *developed* amid *symbols* of any kind! Among Kink's papers I've discovered a final stanza of 'Poem' which must change the way we think about it—and perhaps about the rest of Kink's oeuvre as well. Kink, for whatever reasons, suppressed the stanza, although it is superior to the conclusion as we now have it, a conclusion, by the way, which has always troubled me because of the essential *nescience* of the *faux-naïf* locution, 'pieces of sky faded blacker.' In any event, here is the 'lost' stanza":

> Oh! How my case is wrapped
> with the soft basses in the phonograph,
> suddenly, my mommy makes fudge
> from some pieces of pie, and from lacquer!

Would you say, Professor, that the, let us say, macroparatactic strategies of the stanza function as a kind of microcosmic reflection of the larger charnel house motifs found in, for instance, Defoe's fiction?

"Indeed I would!" Professor Blinque says, sitting up straight and joyously whacking his crusty brier against a nearby stand of ivy. "Indeed! Indeed I *would!* Wonderful observation! Yes! Daniel Defoe! Indeed, yes, remarkable, *wonderful!* Acute and perceptive! *Indeed!* Would you care to come over this evening for drinks and little slabs of cheese?"

It might be interesting to note that "Poem" won the annual *Blue Filter* prize, which was, as far as we can recall, a "novelty" Polaroid camera, blessed by the Pope.

Wasn't the camera green, a kind of disgusting green, with some comic-strip character involved? Something . . . I just can't quite remember.

Right! Right! Loathsome green with a ferocious little Popeye figure on the side. Some kind of promotional deal, a tie-in with frozen spinach. Something.

Henri gave it to Benita and "Chick" O'Hearn, I think. Right?

Maybe, yes. People who were against caffeine, ate hay and seaweed?

"Mr. Congeniality" drags his unspeakably deformed foot over to a sweating member of the group from the Confraternity, and asks him if there really is *nothing* that can be done about the depraved priest who is "knocking" morality into a cocked "shoe."

"And who are you, wiseass?" the weary Catholic says.

"I'm the man who called in to complain," the walking-disabled person replies briskly.

"A Mr. Popeye called us—that's you?"

"Not Popeye, Poppy. Mr. *Poppy*. I called to complain because this display really put the finishing touches on my mood. I'm feeling pretty low, what with the broken toaster and the rust on the motel pool, and how the leaves have been falling on the bears who are up to something funny with Stella, that's my wife, used to be some looker before she started in with the potato chips up to the pool hall in Bozeman."

"What? You got I.D., Buddy?"

"Sorry," Mr. Poppy says. "I got a little—I guess I'm a little confused," he laughs. He turns away and quickly clumps and swishes into an inviting aisle.

"Bears? Stella? Pool?" the bewildered Confraternity brother mutters. "All this because some dumb fake priest bumped into the wrong magazine," he says to the magazine display. And what a display! Have we mentioned it?

Isn't it about time we told the real story about the priest's behavior? No.

Leo, almost paralyzed by now with Old Mr. Boston, sets the needle on the record to play, for the eighteenth time, "My Heart Is Melting (For My Ice-Cream Gal Said No)," by the Ohio Brassy Wamble Aggregate Marching Band. There seems to be a tear, or there seem to be tears, in his eye, or eyes, since he's thinking of one or another of his ex-wives. It must be, aha! Anne, for he sobs, "Oh, Anne! Anne! My sweet Miss Popsicle!" However, it is Ellen who was once called "Miss Popsicle," and not by Leo, but by Anne. So does bittersweet nostalgia falsify the past and make yo-yos of us all, or, in this instance, does it make a yo-yo of Leo.

Dexter Gapoine refuses to be intimidated by the café menu, and, turning to his three companions silhouetted dramatically against the looming pinkish morphemes, he suggests seafood for a welcome change. "I have my Porsche parked on the crumbling hummock of a nearby corduroy. Heck, we can all squeeze in!" he laughs, looking suggestively at Miss Gashe's legs.

"Seafood? Around Misty Crag?" "Hap" Garrett marvels. "But where? Real seafood?"

"Some people know where to get things, 'Hap,'" Berta sneers.

"Am I right, Dexter?" she adds trillingly, directing a powerful simper toward her trim addressee.

"Certainly," Dexter agrees politely, moving as close as he dares to Karen's delightful protuberances, thankful that he is not, after all, what his rather heavyset dad calls "queer." "I'm thinking of a little place that serves the greatest fried clams—oh, not the kind that you can 'tie in to' on the Cape or in Portsmouth, but say! They've got four legs like every other darn clam in the world!"

And with that, the four, with a collective halloo!, begin running wildly toward Dexter's vintage Porsche, their faces registering nothing but contempt for the vetch and thorny snapperweeds which clutch horribly at them.

Edmund Posherde, who, as a respected and rather stuffy insurance executive, no longer remembers that he was, some decades ago, called "Blinky," and, occasionally, "Bunky," by his beautiful mistress, Constanza Murphy, hears some unexpected yet wholly familiar sounds from one of the museum's less-accessible wings. Entering, he discovers a woman and two men, all grey-haired and prosperous-looking, much like himself!—in, surprisingly, various states of undress, and, even more surprisingly, comprising a tableau reminiscent of Catullus's fifty-sixth poem. As he steps back against the wall, he experiences the greatest surprise of all as he catches a glimpse of the woman's rapturous face.

Wasn't Constanza Murphy once known as "Honey" or "Hummy" Potts, or sometimes Pazzo?

No, you're thinking of Berta Garrett.

The Berta Garrett on her way to eat clams?

Yes. Right. That Berta Garrett.

But didn't Mrs. Murphy have *some* sort of alias years ago?

Well, now that you mention it, there have been stories that she was mixed up in some sort of smuggling racket as a "Queenie" Antilles, although some argue that "Queenie" was a wholly different woman and that Mrs. Murphy's alias was "Cunty" Uncles. But nobody knows for sure about any of it.

"Whatever or whoever she is or was," Mr. Mytilene interjects in his Greek-restaurateur accent, "with those legs I don't think she's a good

Christian woman, thanks be to God!" Suddenly, Mr. Posherde makes his considerable presence known to the sweating trio.

"Although I've definitely cast my rather impressive lot with the contemporary," Jack Armstrong says to a group of fawning admirers, "you might be somewhat startled to realize that I sometimes amuse myself by writing in the manner of the minor Elizabethans. For instance, here is a snatch—ha, ha—from the plea of a lovesick swain":

> Dainty darling kinde and free
> fairest maide I ever see,
> deare vouchsafe to look on me,
> listen when I sing to thee,
>> O do not dwelle
>> with that Prell
>> sing fare well to Prelle.
>
> Prettie, wittie, sit mee by,
> feare no cast of anie eye,
> we will plaie so priuilie
> none shall see but you and I,
>> O do not dwelle
>> with that Prell
>> sing fare well to Prelle.

Jack, as is his wont, has neglected to mention a couple of things, the most important being that the greater part of these verses are—how can this be discreetly put?—not his own. Those lines which are his, and which serve as a refrain, a kind of repeated *tornada,* were invented because Jack feels that the inclusion of brand names in a literary work gives said work sensitive wallop. "For instance," Jack likes to say, "take Plumtree's Potted Meat." Everyone smiles, pretending to understand. But who can argue with success?

"Well, it might be good Armstrong, but it's not worth a God damn like real poems like 'The Prelude,' " Leo mumbles, deep in his drunken yo-yo phase, as recently noted. He crawls across the room and pulls a book out of a pile of ghastly "things," then leans against the wall. "Listen you want? Real poetry?"

A cottager leaned whispering by the hives,
   Telling the bees some news, as they lit down,
   And entered one by one their waxen town.
   Larks passioning hung o'er their brooding wives . . .

"See what I mean? This is the fucking President compared to Jack, who
is an Assemblyman. This is the stuff!" Leo smiles, bends over the book,
and throws up on its yellowed pages. Then he passes out. Just as well,
or else we might have been constrained by honesty to tell him that this
fragment is not from "The Prelude," but from "The Female Vagrant,"
a poem much loved by Francis Cardinal Spellman, who always took a
copy of it into battle, where, they say, he always fell—and *hard.*

An elucidation: While it is true that Lange's famous treatise on "les
vapeurs" is currently creating some excitement, or "stir," in its relation
to Father Debris's continuing research into the true meaning of the
Décadence, the good priest has asked us to make clear to his admirers
that the fortuitous and inspired application of Cardano's formula to
Lange's text was made possible only because of his, Debris's, ex-
haustive study, some years ago, of the curious mathematical patterning
of thought in Jean-Baptiste Pressavin's *Nouveau traité des vapeurs,* a
book much revered by Buddy and some of his older and more sophisticated Boys. But let's allow Father Debris to tell the story.

"God bless all of you," the wily Jesuit smiles. "I have an old copy of
a Spanish primer, *Primer curso de español,* and I'm really pleased that
I can tell my story and bring in this bit of fascinating irrelevance. This is
a book like where if you hold it and flip the pages very quickly, like you
riffle them sort of under your thumb, from the back to the front, holding
it right-side up, the pictures go by very fast and they, they sort of, connect. The pictures which are drawings about, say, the present indicative
or the subject and object pronouns or the cardinal numbers, sort of tell a
story. Not actually a story, but more like a slice of life, an insightful
look—yet another one!—into the heartaches and hopes and fears and
nobility and all of the people in the drawings and their grappling with,
for instance, the subjunctive, which is tricky in Spanish. If you thumb,
or riffle, enough times, the little people who go flying by, really *fast,*
kind of begin to take on meaning. I don't know how to explain this but

they make you feel as if you want to tell your own story, about the little
people *you've* known, getting into cars and all, drinking whiskey and
playing bingo and talking on Princess telephones, sometimes pink ones
or yellow with push-buttons, shampooing with Prell, eating odd treats
like Mandy's Mustard Macs and all. Regular people. Anyway, it's
called *Primer curso de español,* which means, from what I can gather,
well, I really don't know what it means. Prime curse or something. It
has these black-and-white drawings. The women's hair looks very
glossy."

Thanks, Father, really, thanks a lot. Thanks a million. This way,
that's right, no, not that way, just right out that door, watch your step,
why don't you lie down for a while when you get home?

Elkins E. Pritchard, whom many claim to be the true author of *Blackjack,* as well as being the founder and prime defender and theorist of
Parvanism, a foolish idea, so others claim, of no merit, is waiting in
what he *insists* is his "blissfully air-conditioned" apartment for Anne
Kaufman, with whom he has arranged an afternoon of carnal dalliance,
which he *insists* be called "hijinks." (Indicates apartment and hijinks
area therein.) Anne, as we certainly suspect, will probably not be
coming because of the adventures of her day, q.v., but Pritchard knows
nothing of these. He is doing the crossword puzzle in an old issue of
Genuine Morocco, or, as it's known to its readers, "the Sin of Creams,"
perhaps. There are a few blanks left.

  – Procel the Geometer's antique ice-cream bingler. (11 letters)
  – Sheila and Lou ——— - ——— think of Prospect Park with horror.
(17 letters)
  – Protestants wear these under their embroidered postulants on
Brooklyn Day. (7 letters)
  – Mel Proud and His Melodics made this nauseating song famous.
(21 letters)
  – "In Provincetown, the sun cracks deuce and warranty, for ———.":
Lamont, *Baltimore Chop.* (6 letters)

From Guy Lewis's window, someone looks down at his broken body on
the street below. There may even be some traffic. Then, in a spirit of
contempt, defiance, hatred, and scorn, this person hurls Guy's rolled-up

Provincetown Alba out the same window, although this seems to be a much larger, less delicately brushed version than the first. The canvas is followed by a copy of *Psychopathology of Everyday Life.* Although there is no known reason for her to be anywhere near Guy, it is indisputably the case that the hurler is Charlotte Pugh, reputedly the owner, still, of the notorious Naughty Nightie boutique in depraved Kirkwood, Missouri, dubbed by wags "the lucky town that mimes forgot."

"Didn't she get the Pulitzer Prize for that?" Tabitha remarks to Lucy. The two young women are strolling down Renselaree Street, their cocktail dresses, or "frocks," grown suddenly and hatefully gauche, at least to certain passersby. It may, however, be the glare of the sun!

"Who? For what?" Lucy snaps clumsily, wondering if she's going to be quizzed, once again, on the power of the objective correlative. How tired she is of these sudden examinations! She thanks her lucky stars that her cantaloupes are larger than Tabitha's.

"Why, Charlotte Pugh, of course, for *Psychopathology of Everyday Life,*" Tabitha laughs melodically. How she tosses her head and her proud mane of auburn hair!

"Oh, Tabitha! You are my burden and my cross!" Lucy seethes.

"Crosse? Well, she's not much on looks, and she knows less than you do about literary matters, but Delilah has the most *gorgeous* legs," Tabitha admits. "However, I got bigger knockers than she possesses."

"Once again, I must take issue with your feckless knockers boast," Lucy replies reasonably. "Meerschaums put, let's face it, your jugs to shame."

"It's not enough for them two broads to disgrace themselves indoors, no," Rudy says. "Now they're talking that stuff right out on the public streets! Legs, knockers, psychophilogy, Jesus Christ. Soon they'll be writing poems about themselves like my useless fucking brother!"

Harlan Pungoe can hear the faint chiming from Annette Lorpailleur's apartment, even though he is some half-mile away. He is in an electric-blue suit, single-breasted, and quite possibly older than Pungoe. In the August sunlight the bilious brilliance of the fabric has already blinded a horse, two dogs, a sweaty jogger, a militant activist, and a hearty child-molester. If this is indeed Pungoe, how is it that he seems to be in more than one place at the same time? Or times? He *seems* to be Pungoe, and, if so, the years have barely touched him. His pielike face, so malleable in its expressive possibilities and powers that it has driven several men and women mad, is much in evidence. Ditto his rustic twang, store of rural tales, all of which point a homely moral, his camera, twisted tie from wardrobe, and attendant equipment. Sketchy reports are about of children fleeing in dumb terror, of eviscerated cats and strangled dogs, mostly terriers. He is the man with his hand in his pocket! Who takes pictures! Of preadolescent girls! Preferably in their shorts! He's the man who made the phone call at the A & P! And just a little while ago, he was banging on somebody's door! And cursing! Wispy white hair to give him the look of a besotted ham actor playing a besotted ham actor. The clubfoot? Well, of course, there it is, as ugly as, more ugly, we should say, than ever, in a "shoe" of the same blue color as his suit. Good God! He hears the faint, sexual chiming more clearly and his lurching roach-crawl gets faster, something spilling now, something fine spilling from his trouser cuffs, it is sand. Sand from Coney Island. Coney Island? Faster, faster he dips and scuttles, it is Purson, of Bears, Purson, of Glittering Trumpets, who urges him forward. The children run wildly away, and women cover their ears so as to block out his murmured tales of pastoral tragedy, all of which feature stupid homosexuals bashing their heads against trees. The chiming, the chiming, he can see in his boiling mind her spread thighs. Chiming.

Eugenia Hunter, capping her pen, suddenly has an eerie vision of Pungoe and is made to remember her days of shameful debasement as his sexual slave, when she was constrained to answer to the name "Big Mama" Pussie or "Big Mama" Fussy. This servitude quickly effected the destruction of what little self-respect "Sweetums," her first husband, still possessed after his misadventure with the large cardboard object mysteriously "forgotten" at his office door. Soon after, Eugenia began wearing *those* things, and "Sweetums" slowly started thinking of himself as Paul de Kock, even though he didn't know more than three thousand four hundred and twenty-six words of French. From this dementia to his ultimate disappearance in the mists and fogs of Mystery Mountain was but a matter of weeks. Or, let us say, a few short weeks.

Eugenia shakes her head to drive Pungoe's leeringly affable face from her thoughts. Well, her whole story, all of it, everything, will go into her autobiographical memoir, *Qualifications.* In the meantime, Pungoe scrapes and shuffles closer to Madame Lorpailleur, the sweat soaking through the back of his jacket turning it into a mirrorlike surface. Into which no sane creature dare glance.

The Frankenstein girls decide to bid farewell to Fred on this luxurious summer afternoon with a virtuoso ritual which they learned in the crystalline highlands of Cambodia from a priestess of Cetriuolo, "Lord of Carrots." The girls call the ritual "Queen of Sheba," for reasons unknown. Prepared, executed, and concluded properly, "Queen of Sheba" most often leaves its masculine participants unconscious, comatose, psychotic, or dead. Although everything concerning the ritual proper is "veiled in secrecy," to use one of the girls' favorite phrases, we do know some of the materials necessary to its successful execution. They are: a can of Franco-American spaghetti; a spiral-bound 3 x 5 assignment pad; two white candles which have been left overnight in an imported-cheeses store; an aerial photograph of the *Guns of the Colorado* shooting location; a bottle of Dixie Shake; two tablespoons of Frank's Orange Nectar; a copy of Ernest Poole's *His Family;* a bawdy lipogram of at least three hundred words; any page of Faulkner on which Quentin appears; a two-foot length of white silk rope; five white sneakers of different sizes; a small can of *cacahuate* sauce; a pair of badly run white nylon stockings; any fifty words of any poem to an inanimate object, clearly typed, and stained with dried vomit; a pink latex dildo on which is clearly lettered "Live Free or Cheap"; a couple of jiggers of moonlight; a small star. Fred lies naked on the king-sized bed, watching the girls' preparations with what is often called "mounting horror." And yet, his shako is unmistakably bulging.

Guy Lewis's *The Raid* catches, as best it can, the harsh sunlight coming through the window of Ralph's den. Ralph stares at it, pleased that it has been so thoroughly neglected over the years that its crimson and Prussian blue both are now the same greasy, excremental brown. How Ralph, who still despises Guy and Joanne, has come to possess this small painting is a mystery, and why he wishes to display it, more mysterious still. Some of his acquaintances from "the old neighborhood" suspect that his wife, the former Margaret Ramsay, has something to do with it, but since her salacious nature goes hand in glove with "the vapors" as defined by Raulin, and since she, as helpless victim of Ralph's phallocratic beliefs, indeed suffers from that malady, how she could have anything to do with concerns touching on *The Raid* is inexplicable. So far as can be determined, Ralph and Margaret are, as always, at odds. He despises her for her enviably promiscuous past and she him because he compares her, unfavorably, to Joanne. Perhaps. There are certain problems with our received intelligence, given the paucity and quality of questions asked and the contradictory nature of answers received. In any event, Ralph stares at *The Raid* and seems oddly comforted, complacent, almost happy, although he cannot yet know of Guy Lewis's death. Can he?

Isn't that Raum, of the Order of the Thrones, flying, as a crow, from Ralph's neighborhood? Raum, who discerns past, present, and future? Raum, the croaking gossip?

It could be, or it could be, just, you know, a crow. Why?

Well, couldn't he have told Ralph about Guy's death?

Oh, I see. That could well be. That might explain Ralph's—you'll pardon the expression—shit-eating grin.

Item: The recently deceased Sheila Henry's maiden name was neither Ravish nor Ravitch, despite biographical asseverations, public records, and the sworn testimony of a bizarrely accoutered couple representing themselves as her mother and father. Her maiden name was Mulloon, the same as that of the disgraced physician. So she may well have married, in ignorance, her own brother, had Lou's name, that is, been Mulloon, which, fortunately, it was not, and is not now, or so we have been assured.

Item: Antony Lamont's *Rayon Violet* is to be published in Great Britain as *Reams and Reams,* by Dickie St. John-Mouse, a celebrated publisher-raconteur and purchaser of truly fine vintage automobiles. Bertie Crotchlip will star in the thriller as the traditional, implicated thug with pederastic leanings.

At fifty-six, Ann Taylor Redding is one of our loveliest scholars, although "loveliest" may seem a strange word to use in reference to a woman whose masses of shining hair occasionally riot. Although the years have added a few pounds to her generous professorial figure, her straight legs, with their swelling calves and slender ankles, are still beautiful. Dr. Redding's penchant for stack-heeled shoes with small metal buckles, leafy burgs, shady volumes, large fruit pies, and phony Englishmen is, as always, very much in evidence. She also admits, with a blush, that she still has a weakness for "lady soldiers," as she insists on calling the female members of the military, despite feminist frowns. When Evelyn Leonard (who, as Tiffany Cartier in *Black Silk Stockings,* set new standards for the erotic cinema) is mentioned, Dr. Redding speaks, rather too quickly, of lapidary prose, larking about with sphinx and bombazine, and her sister Phyllis, who is, as she assures her listener, often lionized by the little people she identifies only as the "others." No snob Phyllis! Ann crosses her legs, modestly arranges her skirt over her knees, and coolly studies her fingernails, glistening with the shade of polish marketed as Red Moon.

"Red Moon is the favorite of hardworking airline pilots!" a woman who resembles Evelyn Leonard/Tiffany Cartier says. "It doesn't chip or fade, has the color of a California sunset seen through a haze of fresh fruit, and is *all natural!* Good news for you guys—and gals—who bite your nails or suck your thumbs! If you like to pull large combs through your hair with noticeable abandon—it's Red Moon. For the nights of your life, and the life of your lights, uh, nights, life nights, life of night life. Red Moons." She is promptly dropped into a vat of creative directors.

A number of publishing rebels are standing at the bar in Caliph's Walk, speaking of their lives, loves, hopes and fears, those they hate, their careers, and other relevant and revelatory congeries of delimited psychology. For instance: "used to be Chinese . . . chink's Red Silk . . . Red Swan you mean . . . syrinx and flutes and frillies . . . the Red Ink . . . Elizabeth Reese's orgasm . . . O'Nolan . . . in the garden with the fairies . . . Reeve in chains . . . red Chinks at swim . . . swans lutes and pyrex . . . an orgasm of ink . . . Nolan's old bird garden . . . Reeve O'Reese . . . Elizabeth's red frillies . . . *whose* red chink . . . two swans like silk . . ." Someone mentions a book and silence descends like a luff.

"It's interesting to listen to *young* book people speak of things pertinent to their vocation," Sol Blanc wheezes to Saul Blanche, who totters in time to his partner's ragged breaths. "Just from the few snatches of whose conversation we were privileged to hear, it's clear that the pub biz is alive and well, flourishing as never before, energetically killing the weeds of the mast obliquity we like to consider the incriminating speeder who will not accept pap by any beans, but yes! insists, as I have song doted, on being CHALLENGED by the BEST and most COURAGEOUS how shall I say? WORDS!"

"And yet," Saul utters feistily, full of pep and vig despite his corrupt body, while Sol just sort of, well, sits down, "while much space and attention are given rockbuster wallops like *Nouveau traité des vapeurs,* and rightly so, our saloon clientele (indicates youthful rebels), if actually representative of the hip rebels who are *making it all happen,* oddly never mention *Réflexions sur les affections vaporeuses,* the seminal work on the illness which afflicts those who work harder and play harder in sweaty shirts, and the like. Without the *Réflexions,* there would be no *Nouveau,* and although not many care, there would also be no *Regular Guy, Bitch Girl, Buddy on Uncle Ned's Farm, Up Missoula Way, Air-Conditioned Marriage, How Can We Talk about Quietly Calling When We Really Feel Like Buying Tickets?,* and God knows how many other instantly classic masterworks. Ask Michelle Caccatanto! If she hasn't got her nose in a book of short stories what make you feel meaningfully alive, or maybe look like they're alive, or maybe that we're all alive if we only took the time to really be alive, or maybe speak to us of the author's aliveness despite the haunting fact that he was once a drunken short-order cook on a hardscrabble ranch, yowza, well, anyway, why then, she's got a book of short stories on her lap, and she's reading with the avid perspicacity of a thin-skinned muskelonge rising fast and sure for the crappies! *That's* loving books, or I defy you else!"

"Right," Sol agrees. Together they ease toward the air-conditioned ambience which has never ceased to beckon. Perhaps, rather than "ease," their "gait" might be thus described: Together, arms linked, they clumsily amble toward, and et cetera.

May we note here that the crappies abide. Not only abide, but though flustered, flourish, and, flourishing, prevail.

"Hots" Reilly is still more or less contentedly married, so they tell her, and still more or less reconciled to the alias she can't quite remember acquiring, "Humps" Daly, although she vaguely remembers knowing a lot of other women, closely related to her, or so it now seems, with equally improbable names. Her real name is Bárbara, of that she is quite sure. Someone who says that he is her husband is sitting with her at a sticky table in the recreation room. He may well be her husband. These things are clearly a recreation room and a sticky table. They say. Who is this man again? He's astonishingly homely and very old, probably too old to fuck her and that's what she could really appreciate, the hell with the orange juice! Bárbara "Hots" "Humps" asks him again who he is, and he tells her. She wonders why he reminds her of the holy syphilitic in Roberte's poem "Renée Pélagie: The Ecstasy of Her Agony," and he smiles stupidly. She wonders if he ever picks up hot women to fuck in the Reno Tavern and he shakes his intolerable head and offers her a Lifesaver. She asks him to bring her a copy of *La Révocacion de l'Édit de Nantes* by Pierre somebody, find out for Christ's sake, now there's an elegant piece of erotica. She pulls her breasts out of her nightgown and tells him about somebody, Dick Otto or Otto Dick or Ricardo, he loved to suck on them, and why is he staring at her, didn't he ever see a tit before? She reminds him that when she was young and beautiful, *sultry,* he was interested in every *other* skirt but now that she's old and tired and sick all he does is try to undress her and play with her tits and pussy. She reminds him of some friend of his, Richard, or maybe she's thinking of Ricardo Dick, who was always surprised at how cool he was toward her, but not *everybody* was so cool. For instance, Biggs Richard, who was happy to drop in during the week, in the afternoon. And, for instance, the guy who was always talking to anybody who asked about anything, he'd drop in too. And Father Richard, oh yes, she smiles, I imagine it was a sin even though he'd only sit there and stare at me, his pants all bulging, his mouth open, just the way you're staring at me now. She sobs, you're always here, always, with your sticky table and Lifesavers and orange juice and your pop eyes on my old sagging tits, and trying to feel my pussy. Staring the way you stared at those little well-bred tits on Jane Richardson, you remember her, with her clothes and teeth and hair and money. She talked like she had a banana up her ass and a Ping-Pong ball in her mouth. And, she says, she yells, she shouts and screams as two attendants hold her and wrap her robe around her tattered, shredded nightgown, she screams at her husband as he walks toward the door, he's her *what?*, this balding, grey, stooped, addleheaded, drunken syphilitic, this faggot cocksucker, this sticky-table lover, she screams that he was also a goddamned fool for Jane's younger sister Punkie, the one who could have married somebody but ran off with a Cuban or something. "Humps" Bárbara "Hots" is still screaming at her disgusting cruel rotten husband who ruined her life as she's taken back to her room. The Richardson sisters are still a constant source of irritation, although at present their beautifully mannered stupidity poses a threat only to couturiers, sailboats, and high-strung horses.

"Clearly, automatic writing," Florence Claire scoffs. (Indicates transcribed sample of slipshod prose.)

"I reckon it mighty strange that Normal, who seemed such a capital fellow, 'pears to have lit out 'fore dawn," Dick remarked spiritedly to Buddy as the two chums sat shivering in the biting, early-morning mists of the ancient forest.

"Indeed it *is* odd, Dick," Buddy answered with his wonted, almost blunt sincerity. "Our newfound acquaintance seems to have exited with all the speed employed by Richelieu himself during the unspeakable excesses of 4 Germinal, although," and Buddy chuckled good-naturedly, "the famed Cardinal did not have to fret about a comely Saskatoon, eh? Ha, ha, ha."

But despite all, soon a hefty fire was blazing apace, and over mugs of blistering "java" the boys plotted their next move, which seemed to point to a necessary resupplying of their victuals-bags, bread boxes, and miscellaneous airtight containers in varying sizes. "We certainly have the *room* for healthful victuals, and so, away!" Buddy blathered, delightedly quoting the line made famous by Thompson Richie in *The Party*. "Away!" Dick echoed, his knobby fists raised toward the distantly louring sky.

"I loved that moving picture," Buddy mused enthusedly aloud.

"Even when I had no true idea whatsoever of the responsibilities of a key clerical position, Richie, as 'Ridie,' the gallant Lord Ridingcrop, seemed to embody all the manly traits of a titled regular fellow, and yet he never gave the unfortunate impression of being the sort of nance who'd actually *live* in a snobbish town like Riding-on-Alum. Of course, there *were* a few explicit scenes."

"Yes, good pal," Dick interjected loudly, "and I can recollect that the tights he had a mind to doff on almost any pretext showed a powerful lot of his beziques, especially in the dripping-forest scenes, if a fellow is thinking correct."

"Partly true, my astute camerado," Buddy whispered patronizingly, for there was little he didn't know of Thompson Richie's career as a film star, committed naturalist, oenophile, diamond amateur, discreet algo-lagniac, and best-selling author of walloping good reads. "But if you'll think again, *carefully,* you'll recall, I'm sure, that Richie's beziques are revealed, yes, but not gratuitously. In a word, the aesthetically pleasing exhibition of the excellent fellow's manly equipment serves to further the plot! The actresses are, of course, perfect foils for this masculine display. And Dick," Buddy added waspishly, "please try to remember that an adjective does not perform the adverbial function, all right? One might think that you'd never delivered important papers swiftly and accurately!"

"As always, I'm powerful—powerfully—grateful to you for your seemingly endless corrections, Buddy," Dick hissed neurotically through clenched teeth, his hand fervently gripping a lead pipe he'd come across at the bottom of a tittering rill. "Thanks again."

"What's that in your weary hand, dear ruffiano?" Buddy laughed happily.

"Ha! Ha!" Dick echoed. "Ha! Ha! Ha! That's rich!" The trees bent, whispering, to the sere and yellow grasses of the hummocky glade, bee-drunk in the attar-laced haze.

"Well?" Buddy pursued, refilling their mugs with the caffeine-rich nectar of which the boys had grown weirdly fond.

" 'Pears it seems like a kind of worthless bagatelle given me by the Saskatoon, who I sort of hit it off with last night," Dick fibbed quickly.

"Ah," Buddy sighed in his superior way, "a love token! As Rilke put it, 'give me a garter of thy love, and I will move the world.' Wonderful!"

"I don't recollect I brought any garters with me on this trip, Buddy," Dick blushed deeply. "Charles Rimini-Bates, the fletcherizer representative and rassling coach who took me under his wing at the Holt Rinehart Legion Post, mentioned on garters being, well, right unhealthy to the developing boyish moral fibers. Something about them turning a feller into a fruity-boy. Anyways," he concluded almost smugly, "I threw them away in the degraded trash."

"How unbelievably rich! Garters! Oh, Dick, Dick, you are truly a jocular brick of a fellow," Buddy slathered gaily. "But now let's break camp and see if we can discover a humble thatch-roofed cottage or thatched-roof cottage, at which we may purchase some victuals and other provisionings. As the deathless Alger somewhere writes, 'A fellow needs a stew to speed his stride if he plans to get to Rio.' "

"Rio?" Dick queried ignorantly. "Alger?" he continued in the same vein.

"Don't concern yourself with it," Buddy sighed.

Swiftly the boys began to break camp, and as the last ember was smothered by the fire-resistant branches of the lumbago fronds which stood crookedly about the humid glade, the friends prepared their equipment, and with experienced motions of woodland know-how, *heaved* it in such wise that it landed squarely on their broad backs in an almost welcome involution. Such were their devoted skills.

How many hours they'd walked they did not know, how many rocks, pines, splintered items, quiet falls, and comatose forest denizens they'd passed, they were heartily ignorant of. Just as well! The sun burned down upon their youthfully plucky heads, and visions of their lost companions, of the Saskatoon, of craven Knute, of drear caves and the blubbery lips of the elusive dago, of the maddeningly insubstantial map, and of the comradely jocosity of Manly Normal passed before their fevered eyes.

"This exhausting hike and its exhausting accompanying visions smack of the literary, Dick, don't you think?" Buddy managed to gabble through cracked lips.

"I reckon so, Buddy," Dick rejoined, perspiration soaking his gabardine mashies. Then all was silence once more, save for the sound of the rocks and pebbles which fell from the looming jalousies of polished granite surrounding the boys like so many prison walls, like the ornate facade of the Ritz, like the cold darkness of impure and unmanly thoughts of, for instance, garters! Of a sudden, around a bend in the sylvan track down which they struggled, a small, worn farmhouse appeared, humble in the extreme, yet neat and well-cared for, despite the barren yard's grey dust, and the withered kitchen garden just beyond the sagging back porch.

"Thank Scott!" Buddy ejaculated, halting in his courageously blistered tracks. "This farmhouse, Dick, has appeared as surprisingly and abruptly as a shift in time in the novels of Alain Robbe-Grillet, whose books I've often urged you to read, to no avail."

"I seem to recollect on dipping into one book about the orange chifferobe, but darned if I could tell the men from the women and the furniture and chains and such," Dick laughed stupidly.

"You mean *La Robe orangée,* my thick friend," Buddy gibed gently. "The problem is that you do not read the French language, which makes for a bit of difficulty, n'est-ce pas? Ha! Ha!"

"Let's knock loudly on the blasted door!" Dick uncharacteristically suggested, wondering glumly what a "nezzpah" could be. Although he'd surely be vehement in denial, of late he quietly seethed over his chum's chortling, at his expense. He wasn't interested in those snotty frog books anyway! For a split second he thought, "Loyalty is one thing," yet he pushed the phrase out of his mind before he could think what *another* thing might be. But putting an end to this cultural discussion, both boys stepped boldly to the door and addressed its sturdy oak panels with an imperative tattoo.

After a moment, the door slowly swung open to reveal a furtively bent woman of decidedly unpleasant aspect, her clothes badly soiled with hamburger fat and unrecognizable culinary orts. Screwing her face up into a grotesque grin, she looked at the lads as if seeing them for the first time, and harshly spoke.

"What can I do for you fine boys?" she rasped. "Not much hereabouts a young feller'd be interested in, unless," she paused mysteriously, "he's the sort o' boy who relishes a hanker on sledding!" At this final word, she reeled into a gale of icy laughter, laughter so cold that it seemed almost frigid as it chilled the lads to the quick.

"We're of a mind to find the old blue mill on the other side of yonder Misty Crag if we can," Buddy said soberly, disregarding Dick's bewildered glance, "and we'd be extremely grateful if we might purchase some 'grub' from you. We may look disreputably rough and essentially unlettered, but I assure you that we have some money and are of honest middle-class roots." And with this, he introduced himself and Dick to the tattered scullion.

"My father is a streetcar conductor," Dick interjected proudly. In the strained silence which followed, a loon coughed idly in the bog.

"Well, come on in then, boys," the hag said. "My name is Zenobia, Miz Frome if you prefer, I reckon to be thinking. Don't pay no heed to these two danged fools setting in the parlor—one's my kitchen helper, my pot-walloper, my slop slob," she grinned foully through her shining green teeth. "Roberte, Roberte Ce Soir is her name—or so she fruitlessly wishes!" she cackled gently. "And this other's my husband, Robin, which is what I reckon I pleasure to call him. No need to know his true, Christian name which he give up when the devil crawled inter his overalls, heh, heh. Neither of 'em's good for spit," she laughed, hawking up a sliver of glittering yellow phlegm. "Robin hain't done his duty by me as a *man* for years, an' Roberte—pshaw!—it's all the French tart can do to light a yaw fire with a 'tater match." And with this, the shrew flung herself into a filthy rocker which seemed to shriek quietly with a horrible secret!

The boys stood uncertainly in the middle of the squalid, fetid parlor, thinking that a plunge into a cataract wherein razor-clawed grizzlies gather to bathe would be preferable to this interview, if such it could be called. But by whom? they wondered in unison.

"I-I'm powerfully sorry, Miz Zenobia," Buddy managed hoarsely. "I can see that we've come at an inconvenient time. I notice, for instance, that you're about to 'dig in' to your midday repast," and with this remark he gestured toward a potful of chemises boiling effluviously on the stove. This error occasioned general merriment, as might well be expected. Buddy then gestured to Dick with his eyes, frantically signaling to him like a lighthouse keeper looking for his wave-torn dory, signaling to his chum with winks and blinks that they should leave, and leave apace! But suddenly, a voice issued from the sober and tragic figure of Robin, collapsed, like a large bag, or sack of unidentifiable soft things, in his wheelchair, his hand resting pallidly on the hand of the twisted young woman in the wheelchair which tenderly abutted his own.

The young woman's name, Roberte Ce Soir, had filled Buddy with a curiously "electric" sensation when first Zenobia had blurted it out with her noisome spittle. That, and the way that her eyes melted when she gazed at Robin, seemed somehow important to him—more important, perhaps, than he knew or even dared understand!

In the tense silence, broken only by the buzzing of a fly against the windowpane, Robin's voice, which had, of course, already issued, now issued again. The boys leaned close, listening with rabid attention, for the message might well be an interesting one.

"Stay an' set fer a spell, boys," the disabled man cried weakly but hopefully. "We hain't goin' no whar. We're . . . *par'lyzed!*"

The lads staggered back as if struck by shards of offal.

Questions to be entertained.

In Betty Barker's collection of "adult musings" on life, *A Batch of Stuff,* o.p., the author states that Sister Rocco Portola "knew a lot of girls very well indeed." Did the female religious in question smoke Gitanes in the privacy of her Spartan room, and, if so, where did she get them?

What did David Rockefeller have to do with offshore oil drilling, if anything, and why do certain neohistoricists link his name with that of John Crowe Ransom?

Why did Berthe leave four complete summerweight uniforms, with extra caps and aprons, behind the bar in Rocky's Tavern, known everywhere as "a hotbed of gender insensitivity"?

How is it that the meter of Theodore Roethke's "My Papa's Waltz" is often blamed for the weak, warm Manhattans served at many wedding receptions?

Why does Professor Brian Rolex, the author of *Illusion and Absurdity: The Uncanny in the Works of Howard R. Garis,* insist that the visiting niblick authority, Fantoine of Brittany, is the "devilfish" of Assyrian mythology?

Whereas a Roman *person* may profoundly involve himself with Roman Catholicism because of its traditionally jewel-encrusted trilbys, garbos, shakos, fedoras, and tatting "sheds," Rome itself devotes much prized leisure time to pasta dishes recently invented in California. What, then, is a "garbo"?

Ronda the Crazy Gypsy (not her real name) sits perspiring in the hot shadows of the small Queens store, known to the local residents as RONDA READINGS AND CONSULTATIONS. Here and there may be seen decks of cards, tea canisters, a crystal ball, and, for atmosphere, some flyblown mystical texts. "I know it's hard to believe," she says, "looking at this ruined face (indicates face, which, while not precisely "ruined," is definitely the worse for wear), that I was once romantically involved with such luminaries and top-drawer people as George the Polack III, the backyard lark, 'Puppo' Chanko, whom I playfully called 'Manny,' and 'Tits' O'Rourke, about whom, as they say, enough said!—as well as with a big guy in green work clothes who had some kind of thing for motels and pool furniture and bears in parking lots—don't ask *me*. Anyway, here I am in Queens, sort of living behind the store with Billy Joe Selma, a barber who thinks he's an Indian brave, Blue Wind. Amazing! How the mighty have fallen, as I sometimes assert, not that I was ever exactly mighty, but there was a time when I called broads like Lady Bustier and the Countess O'Mara my friends. Anyway, Billy Joe just called a minute ago (indicates Princess telephone in popular pink) and said it's important that I tie a pair of my panties around my neck and walk around outside for a while. I may be Ronda the Crazy Gypsy here in Rego Park, but I'm not *that* crazy! Well, I never denied that Billy Joe has his kinks like everybody else, but I always told him fine, just make sure it's in the privacy of the bedroom, not that we actually have a bedroom, and that's just between us, O.K.?, now he wants sexual oddities in the street? No thanks."

Dwight tells Ronnie as the latter is going off his shift that he's goddamned sick and tired of Allen and Chet excluding him like they do, just *excluding* him, when he's normal just like everybody else when it comes to the eternal beauties of nature, the sunlight gleaming on the thatches or whatever they are, the soft breezes sloughing the wild grass, and like that, for Christ's sake. Ronnie surreptitiously picks little bits of licorice off his apron and tries not to stare at Dwight's blackened teeth and lips. He doesn't really want this forced intimacy. Well, he's going to go and see the Eiffel Tower after all, all by himself, maybe he can run into some French boy who won't think that he's an *athama!* But soon, despite these vows, Dwight is calling across Great South Bay from a small hillock in Bay Shore: "Allen!" he calls. "Oh Allen! Chet, Chet, say Chet, you bitch!" State Trooper Kimberley Butz parks her patrol car, gets out, and tells Dwight to get his fucking faggot ass on the sidewalk and keep the noise down, sir. She looks none the worse for her recent ordeal. Just then, a horrendously misshapen man appears out of the mists which forever cloak this small but somehow chic village of the "fog belt." He seems to be trying to smile, twists his hat worriedly in his "hands," then introduces himself as Mr. Ronobe, Master of Rhetoric, the twelfth Marquis of Earl, and asks, or so Trooper Butz records it in her notebook, "if anybody has seen some flying people in the vicinity of Gnatville or Agapa." As Ronnie edges toward a dripping copse of sumac vetch, Trooper Butz takes a step back and places her hand on the grips of her service revolver. As she looks, officially, at Mr. Ronobe, the space which is occupied by his deformed body is suddenly filled with nothing but fog. Ronnie is by now running full tilt toward the Fedora, a small, discreet leather bar catering to putatively straight politicians, wherein his ex-roommate, Guy Ropes, is the waiter-bartender. "Some *flying* people?" Ronnie shudders, and picks up speed. Meanwhile, Ronobe is walking quickly across the bay toward Fire Island, wondering, for the hundredth time, how he, the twelfth Marquis of Earl, managed to get stuck with this shit detail.

But reading *Blackjack* is not soothing to Dick, and he feels a momentary letdown, which he prefers to think of as a "depression." The one positive thing about the book, with whose spine he is idly rubbing his crotch, is that Alice reminds him of Rose Marie, a girl he almost married after he and April went *kaput,* as he likes to say. "April and I, well, *kaput!*" is how he puts it. Occasionally, this remark will inspire someone to throw a chair at him, but for the most part he gets away with such things. He dials Rose Marie and waits.

Isn't Rose Marie's full given name Rose Marie Karen?

Right, of course!

Rose Marie says hello and Dick tells her this and that, *Blackjack,* depressed, thinking of her. So many years and so much water and so many bridges, *kaput!* "Yes," she says. What might have been, his old workshirts, April the bitch and April the cunt, he really tried, well, they really tried, he and she, well. But when he thinks of her wantonly bent over the kitchen table, does she remember that? "No," she says. *Black-jack*, Alice, didn't know her when he wrote it but amazing that she should *be* Alice, doesn't it strike her as strange? "Sure," she says. Rose of Washington Square, he called her if she remembers but does she remember why? "No," she says. Washington Square because they met in the Village, in the Village! She *must* remember. "No," she says. But all the different roses, he means her name and Washington Square and they went to see some play, right, *Odd Number,* in the old Rose Theatre, she must remember? "No," she says. Well then, she might agree that she's a cunt bitch whore cocksucker? Doesn't that sound about right to her? "I'm too old for this, Dick, and so are you," she says, and hangs up. Dick begins to cry, realizes that he is wildly aroused, and goes into the bathroom so that he can watch his face as he masturbates over the sink. "Motherfucking bitches all of them!" he says to the grey-haired old man looking into his eyes.

Horace Rosette sits in an armchair and listens to his joints creak. He pulls a shawl around his shoulders, then continues looking over the typescript of *New and Selected Poems* of Gilberte Brie, from which "Spanning the Azure" has been ruthlessly excluded by Horace, the book's editor. What no one knows, and has never known, is that Gilberte Brie is Horace himself, Horace in, we might say, his Creative Mode, In Touch With A Deeper Reality, etc. Horace is also the Dante Gabriel Rossetti, his little joke, of "Household Tips and Repair Wrinkles," a column syndicated in 137 newspapers, and, too, the Dante Rossini of the Rossini Veggi-Talian restaurant chain. He thinks of himself, however, as an abject failure, for there is no point in being any other kind of failure, or so he thinks, or, in any case, he thinks at this moment that this is what he thinks, although he doesn't actually think the phrase "abject failure." Credit where credit is due. He puts the typescript on the coffee table, leans back in his chair, closes his eyes, and begins to recite, from memory, and with amazingly few mistakes, poems by Rupert Brooke, Wilfrid Owen, Ernest Dowson, Laurence Binyon, Alfred Douglas, Walter de la Mare, A. E. Coppard, Harold Monro, Lascelles Abercrombie, and James Elroy Flecker. On he goes, yet each time he finishes a poem and opens his eyes, he is still alone, wholly bereft of youthful companionship. Alone! Alone! "Alone!" he cries, melodramatically but sincerely, then launches into

> When you have tidied all things in the night,
> And while your thoughts are fading to their sleep,
> La da la da la da la da la light,
> La da la da la sheep.

Well, he never liked Monro anyway, and besides, he can't ever remember this one, ever, he can't remember, well, he can't, it seems that he can't remember what he can't remember, nothing strange about that at his age, he remembers.

Then too: Rostaing's "Vapors" Theory Causes Rift in Decorative-Phallus Sect; Neo-Historical Post-Marxist Deconstructionist Theorist Claims Mark Rothko "Only a Painter"; Round Lake Inn's New Owner Will Revive Lost Glamour of Strip-Tease Contests; Royal Manual to Play Poet Frost in *Natchez-Mobile* Remake; Orthodontist Jack Rube to Change Name to Dr. John Rube, Endodontist.

Rupe stands, arrested, next to the garbage dumpster outside the A & P's sidewalk freight elevator. He is certain—because of (a) the modestly arranged skirt; (b) the Red Moon nail polish; (c) the confessed delight in leafy burgs and shady volumes; and (d) the small metal shoe buckles—that the woman recently "profiled" is his ex-wife, Ann Taylor Redding. "I maintain that Dr. Redding is still one of our loveliest scholars," Rupe blurts deftly, looking shyly away. " 'Loveliest' may be a strange word to use in reference to a woman who's gained a pound or two, but lapidary prose, despite these decayed foodstuffs (indicates shopworn food), symbolic of a degraded urban environment, is my cynosure and flense." He savagely brushes a tear from his rude cheek and disappears, as usual, into echoing nostalgia.

Cornelius A. Ryan sits back in the wicker porch chair and looks out onto the blazing, empty street. He is so wonderfully drunk that he feels cool and softly distant, far away from this wholly unreal Bay Ridge neighborhood. He drinks half of the Tom Collins at his elbow and lights a Camel. His old sister, older than he, is pottering around inside the house, picking up newspapers and muttering about wet garbage. He takes a deep drag and closes his eyes, and within a moment he inadvertently recalls an almost unbelievable night of love he had, some thirty years before, with a woman who fucked him with a wholly abandoned energy, with a girlish hilarity and joy, with tears in her eyes, until he gasped for breath in sobbing passion. Five minutes later, she sat in black, silent depression, and then he dropped her off, at her insistence, at the Kings Highway station. What was her name and where did she live and how did it come about that she picked him up and why did he never see her again? He finishes his Collins, lights another cigarette, pours four ounces of gin into the glass, adds a splash of mixer. The smooth, cool whiteness of her inner thighs, her candidly sexual language, her enthusiasm, her sudden bleakness. What was her name and where did he take her? Where did he meet her? What was her name? Will time tell?

Who should Ronobe meet on Fire Island but Sabnack, Marquis of Wounds and Worms, his battle gear safely hidden away, and his grim visage softened by his decision to—how does he put it?—"give his orders a new interpretation." It is, of course, outright mutiny if not desertion on Sabnack's part, and such reckless conduct reminds Ronobe of the one-time book-review editor of the *Sacramento Bee,* who supposedly recommended, during one holiday season, divers works of the Marquis de Sade's as "stocking stuffers with a festive twist." Suffice it to say that this eccentric editor now calls such notables of the demimonde as Sailor Steve and Patience St. James (aka Ronda the Crazy Gypsy) his dear acquaintances. Thus business "bends its 'frighted glance 'pon the orbèd world," and "mincing mows pricketh th' ebon Saracen!"

"When said yokel book-person was last seen," Sabnack says from his sunny deck, "he was rolling around on the floor of the emergency room at St. Vincent's, chain-smoking Salems and claiming to be Ho Chi Minh. You should have heard his version of the 'Communist Manifesto'!" Sabnack begins laughing so hard that he forgets to infect the wounds he's given a hapless stray dog who has got just a little too close to the beach house which the infernal sprite has occupied. Perhaps "occupied" is not quite the word.

"Wasn't it Saleos, the pander, pimp, and crocodile-fancier, who gave the poor chump the idea back in sleepy, steamy Sacramento?" Ronobe asks. He glances at the dog and sends him flying into the side of the neighbor's house.

"Probably," Sabnack says. "Anybody who'll make the Salvation Army indulge in a nude bebop festival outside Macy's on Christmas Eve—well, *nothing's* too crass for him."

"By the way," Ronobe says, "have you seen a couple of my colleagues, maybe flying around, or disguised as callow high-school boys or middle-aged ladies in cute pink dresses with puffy sleeves? Gusion *and* Glasyalabolas are apparently AWOL after coming over this afternoon to chastise some fake goddess. Don't ask!"

"No. I would have *noticed* two fruits like that," Sabnack says. "Would you look at that dog!" He points his tongue, which has the form of a cancer cell, at the dog, and the animal begins burning brightly within an enveloping sheet of jaundice-yellow flame. "I'm here to, let me see," he says, looking through his notebook, "right, to find some guy who wrote a movie or something, a poem maybe, they're all alike, titled *Two Gentlemen in Bonds.* I'm supposed to get him to collaborate with the guy who wrote *Lace Me Tighter!,* a corset-lovers' extravaganza. Whatever the hell a corset is. Why don't you stay a while?"

"I think I will," Ronobe says. "I'm sick and tired of always pulling the shit details."

"That's how I feel," Sabnack says. "You hungry?"

Let's not even *think* about the dog.

A certain rather familiar Sam rushes out of Crown SuperMart despite, so he claims, a "truly refreshing and enlightening" discussion, to which he has been privy, between two young women about the salutary fantasies of empowerment created by the ingestion of freshly ground peanut butter. (Indicates Crown SuperMart's peanut-butter machine.) "Do you remember one of the questions recently asked?" Sam says. "About Sister Rocco Portola and her Gitanes? Remember? Well, Sister Rocco is now, and has been for some time, Sister San Antonio Rose! She doesn't smoke at all, but is partial to self-flagellation with a cat-o'-nine-tails every Friday night. O.K.? Take it easy," he concludes, and rushes back into the store. This information is, of course, welcome, yet it seems spurious at best, since the Sister San Antonio Rose with whom we are casually acquainted does not know Betty Barker, and has lived at the San Francisco All-Natural Wine Factory and Cute Place for years, as a member of the Order of Sangre de Cristo.

"We of the Order believe in Santa Claus," Sister San Antonio Rose beams, her mouth filled with raw vegetables and nutritious things made of beans and redwood shingles. "And smoking should be punishable by death, of course. Did Christ smoke? No! But Judas did, the nicotine-crazed roustabout!" So long, Sister. Don't take any wooden clappers.

Father Debris, in one of those remarkable accidents which are so often at the root of mathematical innovation and discovery, finds that Girolamo Cardano's formula (q.v.), when applied to texts other than Lange's, yields information which the priest has long desired. For instance, when the formula is applied to Sappho's Ἀστέρες μὲν ἀμφὶ κάλαν σελάνναν, the name of the female star of *Blaze over Pago-Pago, The Hot Countess, Tongues at Midnight,* and *December* is revealed, almost miraculously!

"Indeed it is," Father Debris winsomely smiles, looking up from his rumpled desk. "The same wonderfully attractive and vivacious young woman starred in all four films. You quite possibly know her by the name she later made famous, but in the days when films were films and stars were stars, she was the oval-faced, silk-complexioned, flashing-eyed Sarah Lawrence—'America's Mystery Co-Ed.' Subsequently, she starred in *Sargasso Sea* with Douglass B. Satan, as the blind girl crippled for life when her pure love made her zooming sled crash into a tree, and in *Satanism on Saturday,* a film many critics think her best, and in which, as the 'Saucy French Maid,' Fifi, she was required to display her knees in direct contradiction of her religious beliefs. The forever fickle and puritanical public immediately abandoned her, and her career, in a few years, hit rock bottom. Sound familiar? It wasn't until Bill Saunders, a wise, and, I suspect, grizzled press agent, convinced her to star in a small-budget musical under the name Jeanne Popcawne, that Sarah once again tasted some of the sweets of fame. Of course, things would never be the same; her toilets, for instance, would no longer be flushed with champagne. Well. Her last film, *Sazerac,* was a musical version, ironically enough, of her first silent starring role, that of Madame Vermouth in *The Orchid Boat.* This remake is a drab item, wholly uninspired, its only bright spot Sarah's—or Jeanne's—triple-tongue singing of 'Jade Mountain,' which she performs while treading water in a pool filled with giant chartreuse 'lobsters.' After that, she faded into obscurity, yet they say that on still nights in the Hollywood Hills, one can hear her sobbing over rotten scripts." Father Debris falls silent, and sits, bemused, his face a mask of convoluted thoughts on life's bitter mysteries.

Sarah Lawrence? Jeanne Popcawne? *Sappho?!*

It makes him happy. Leave him be.

It's perfectly all right with me! Don't forget, I didn't have a word to say when you decided to tout that rotten short story "Scale Model of Splendide-Malibu in the Lobby of Splendide-New Haven" as one "attuned to how we now live." *Not-one-word.*

Duly noted. Do you think it's getting any cooler?

Hotter.

The disgruntled and footsore Scandinavian, Knute, at length reaches the old Dodge in Scone Canyon and with a great, fearsome oath crawls inside. Although Knute is still defiant, the ceaseless pressure of being a dour woodsman as well as a mysterious Lutheran is beginning to wear down his morale and vaunted pluck.

"Those damned pantywaist sissy-boys, Buddy and Dick, don't help none either!" he says, unhooking his coarse wimple from the heavy granola-canvas apron to which it is attached. "Whew!" he at length bellows. "That old-style wimple, even though it offers mighty fine protection from coochybugs, will *do* for a fellow, and that's for certain. But soon I'll be in Schenectady again and dearest Lars will take me into his brawny, felonious arms!" Then, a smile suspiciously playing about his calloused lips, Knute settles in among the still piles of yellowed newspapers which contain the mute records that speak silently of the quiet desperation of the voiceless throng of dumb humanity.

Lolita Kahane suddenly remembers, standing there on the kitchen sink, that she was once Lolita Schiller, "Dumb Lo" or Lo-Lo, as a few people hatefully addressed her. That seems right to her, although the name of her first husband, Richard Schiller, which comes to her in acute clarity, neither conjures up his face nor anything else about him, save for the memory of his whining voice complaining, as always, about the black grease under his fingernails, oh God, *fuck* his fingernails! "Fuck your fingernails," Lolita says, and is, in the great tradition, "startled by the sound of her own voice." She'd do well, she supposes, to get back to *The Girdle Story,* which is apparently about cold, cruel men doing it *fast* and *hard* to complaisant women, all of whom remind her of Lena Schmidt, white canes or German accents. It's a terrible book, in truth, even though many of "our" most respected journals of literary opinion think otherwise. For instance, some Joe Schmuck writing for, it must have been *Sciacca, Scootch Review* or *Christian Arts Monthly,* had this to say: "Pretty darned good, and even though there is a slight falling-off of narrative ability in the last third of this compelling novel, who else is doing such and knowledgeably writing hauntingly of whatever he is with a courageous power that is politically conscious, sensitively aware, projectively intuitive, and with this and with that passion, too, and also very compassionate and caring? Who indeed?" Lolita climbs down from the sink, showing "a lot of leg," although there is nobody to show this "lot" to. The novel reminds her that Conchita, a hazily familiar name, never wore a girdle in the days when *everybody* wore one. That doesn't mean, however, that Lolita can't remember— not by a long shot!—a few depraved evenings in the Score Motor Inn, Scotch on the rocks or "Scotch," who, although he liked pink on grown women (indicates pink cocktail dress with puff sleeves on attractive mother of three), was, in other ways, well, *all right.* "I'm Scots-Irish," Lolita remembers him saying. "That's *Scots,* not *Scotch,*" he'd say. What a glittering card he then seemed! It is now clear to her that he was yet another boring lout, interested, basically, in doing it *fast* and *hard* to her. At least, *fast.* Despite the banal decor of the usual Scranton motel room, "Scrapple from the Apple" or *The Secrets of the Bottom Drawer,* that was what "Scotch" *really* cared about. That, and the occasional smutty story about the whorish Amelia Sedley and the strange, mesmerizing things that she could do with place settings, cucumbers or wet bath towels. Lolita sits in an easy chair, picks up *The Girdle Story,* and starts reading where she left off on page 92, at a reference to Kansas City, a toy airplane or a perverse Continental gentleman. But before she gets too comfortable, maybe she should climb into the cupboard over the sink. That might be a good idea. Just take care of it now. While it's on her mind.

Not even that mighty prince, Seere's, fellow spirits of the aether know
that he is thought to have posed for the famous frontispiece drawing in
Segundo curso de español. The picture represents a beautiful man on a
strong, winged horse. His sharp eyes seem to be ferreting out evil and
chicanery, although students, to this day, joke that he's merely trying to
conjugate "ir" in all tenses.

"The drawing was done—I remember it as if it were yesterday—in
September," Horace Rosette reflects, gently tossing an anthology of
Georgian poets to the floor. "I had just finished editing *Set Pieces,* my
third collection of Great Short Stories from, ah, Dixie, when I was
suddenly transported to Annie Flammard's studio—dear Annie was
not yet *acting*—and there, in the most delicious sort of Iberian outfit,
with boots and silk shirt and little buttons and fringe and a wide-
brimmed hat, oh, *everything,* there was this *beautiful man,* with
something really otherworldly about him. I was in Seventh Heaven."
Horace picks up his book, and sits in silence, his eyes closed on this
memory. He doesn't choose to remember that the model who posed for
the textbook drawing was not Seere, but a professional, Greg Purlson.

"Greg Purlson?" Lena Schmidt blathers, stumbling through her
apartment, her white cane wreaking its occasional havoc on dishes,
glassware, and what look, a little bit, like houseplants. "Greg Purlson
was a *beautiful* man! I could see that despite my fast-developing
cataracts. He was also a kind man," she continues, thrusting her cane
neatly through one of the living-room windows, "in that he introduced
me to the knowledge necessary to a young woman's peace of mind by
pressing upon me the classic pamphlet, 'Sexology: 100 Facts.' From
that day on—thanks to Greg!—I could hold my own with sophisticated
sexual beings like Sheila and April. Unfortunately, I soon became
vision-impaired, and that precluded a number of ocular-sex thrills
which sighted people may take full advantage of, the lousy bastards!
But 'a little drop of rain must splash on everybody's face' now and then,
as the old song goes."

N.B. Lena Schmidt's remarks are here "translated" and may not
precisely correspond with her actual or intended meaning.

Ann Taylor Redding no sooner begins animatedly talking about her dissertation, "Sexual Desire as Evidenced in Selected Phonemic Groupings in Virginia Woolf's *Mrs. Dalloway,*" than her interviewer excuses herself and, as they used to say, takes a powder. Dr. Redding mutters irritably that one would think that she'd offered to read aloud a recent article on the crisis in Israeli morality! Expeditious departure in such an oppressive case would be understandable, surely, she thinks. But what can anybody have against phonemic groupings and the cultural secrets which they often reveal? Especially when well-shaken! The doctor also knows that these groupings may be successfully plumbed only if one understands them to be representative of their maker's attitudes toward his or her contemporaries. In other words, or in other phonemes, as Dr. Redding often says in subtle jest, each grouping presumes a *possible* scene of tension and heartbreak, and *possible* voices from the other side talking a lot of "shit." (Indicates bursts of vocal malarkey.) Dr. Redding, weary now, goes to the window and looks down at Benita and "Chick" O'Hearn munching raw zucchini and strolling hand in hand toward a large assemblage of tofu admirers gathered about the apparently insensate body of Louis Condy, prostrate, and covered over with tar and several layers of feathers. This is life! she thinks, and then decides to take a bath. It may here be of interest to state that Dr. Redding, some years ago, was inspired by her dissertation to write a short work of erotica, rooted in a long-standing and profound phallic obsession which she vehemently denied. One of her admirers, aware of her growing devotion to the literature and cult of the phallus, said:

"It seems to me, Ann, that you're obsessed of late with things, well, phallic."

"What?" Ann replied, then added, "Poppycock! I deny that vehemently!"

Yet she began working on her erotic *récit,* "Shadowie Lumpe," even before her dissertation was approved and her degree granted. Her problem is—and we use the present tense because Dr. Redding is still "at work" on the piece—that she wishes to encapsulate the erotic feminine response to the omnipresent and tyrannical phallus in a language at once enveloping and penetrant, aggressive and passive, lustful and aloof, *non-erotic* yet everywhere vibrant with sexual longing.

This desire, which some hold responsible for the minor disaster which her life has become, is kept alive in her by the demon Shax, Destroyer of the Understanding, who makes her believe, whenever she sets to work on the huge, ragged manuscript comprising notes, notes on notes, bibliographies, false starts, emendations, additions, marginalia, inter-linear variants, canceled chapters and sections, pornographic drawings and photographs, etc., etc., that she is a man, possessed of a phantom phallus, the size, weight, rigidity, and very *presence* of which make meaningful work on "Shadowie Lumpe" all but impossible. For how can she create a legitimate work of erotica as true, dark, and brilliantly artificial as sexuality itself, and capable of arousing the deep libido of women, if the imaginary phallus "actually" rooted in her burning crotch drives her to write in the lying pornographic language of lying men? At the same time, such work becomes utterly necessary to Ann if she is ever to speak clearly to women of the lies which men perform in the name of literature, to speak, that is, as *cunt,* to women, as a *cunt* to *cunts.* She often thinks of Maureen Shea, one of April's oldest girlhood friends, whose sexual language is so remarkably childlike and sketchy, and who is so carnally naïve and transparent, that did she, Ann, have *her* sensibility "in reserve," so to speak, she might well compose "Shadowie Lumpe" as the erotically innocent yet anarchic work she can sometimes envision, but not effect. Envision, but not effect! At the moment, Shax is cruelly and gratuitously sporting with her, as she stands naked before the bedroom mirror, cursing and hissing with frustration as she tries, again and again, to roll a Sheik onto the erection which is so stiff that it pains her groin with its urgency. We feel obliged to add that Dr. Redding's sexual complexities have nothing whatever to do with "penis envy," an idea which may well have seen its day. Dr. Redding's complexities cluster around the non-existent phallus which she, at times, truly possesses, and with the fact that she can find no language in which to write either of her own or of masculine eroticism. Suddenly, she gasps and groans as she comes to her hot, spurting orgasm. She falls to her knees.

Lou looks at the picture again, the young woman is more than just familiar. She's a woman who changed his life. Modest, yet not really modest, something about Prospect Park. Long shadows, some big house in Locust Valley. Well, he can still take his car. He gets up, looks for his hat, his fedora, of course, despite the heat it's never really too warm for a fedora! A line from "Sheila Sleeping" unwinds in his brain, then another, then he's remembering huge blocks of the poem, what kind of a poem is it? Somebody in it named Sheila is sleeping. He is completely at home with the poem. He looks again at the young woman in the picture, her shift dress, her good legs, slightly apart, her breasts just suggested beneath the soft fabric. He looks at the picture. He puts it down, picks it up. The way she wears her clothes. "Sheila Sleeping." The memory of all that. Her dress. Sheila. He can't go out now, after all, he has no car, he has no moustache. He hasn't got his fedora! The way she stands. Sheila? Sheila?

Corrections of earlier errors.

Item: Annie Sheriff, long considered to be no more than a rather unconvincing character in Leo Kaufman's *Isolate Flecks,* is, in "real" "life," Mrs. Balte Brownie. When she is finally tracked down, flushed out, and hauled before Selected Literary Journalists, she will be asked some *hard questions* about her husband's affinity for prepared mayonnaise and his extended absences from home.

Item: Al "Whitey" Shields, recognized in certain quarters of Nuevo Laredo as "Pablito," "Happy," or "the lecherous one," is being sued by the Daughters of Durga International for, long years ago, naming his first wife, Bárbara, "Mrs. Raincoat." A spokeswoman for DDI contends that "the raincoat, as an adjunct to phallocentrism in all its many devious and insidious forms, is akin to the Ship 'n' Shore blouse, a demeaning garment with which women have been, for too long, tragically familiar. The governing board of DDI maintains that the insulting sobriquet was no small factor in Bárbara Shields's ultimate mental collapse."

Item: Gert Shitzvogel has not yet been *officially* informed that, had *The Orange Dress* been published under her name, it would have been reviewed in the *Montclair Co-Op and Lawn News,* the *German-American Family Gazette,* and *Your Art-Fun Weekend!,* and nowhere else.

"Hello! I'm Miss Shredded Wheat, or at least I was, more years ago now than I care to remember. It's terrific to me that my odd friend Sidney still likes to call on me once in a while, and one of these nights I'm going to surprise him by getting into my old Dixie Dugan costume, although I'll probably need a *shoehorn* to do it. Sidney likes twisted little things like that, as I sure found out when he took me last week to see a super-all-hot-action-classic-double-porno bill, *Silk Sighs,* and the sequel, *Silk Thighs,* both of them starring Annie Flammard. The things lubricious that girl could do! Anyway, that's about Sidney's speed, though he's not really a bad guy —a little bald, wears those tacky monogrammed shirts, likes the Boston Pops, and sometimes gets as mad as a Hindu with a raging tooth, but otherwise, he's just about right for me, at present. By the way, my name is, amazingly enough, Karen, *another* one, right?, although between Miss Shredded Wheat and Simone, another name Sidney calls me when we're, you know, being amorous, I barely answer to Karen anymore. Simone is the heroine from a book Sidney admires, *Story of I* or something, but it's a little too French-perverted for me. I mean, like fried eggs and things! Anyway, Sidney says that he knew a woman fifteen or twenty years ago who liked to fantasize herself as this Simone, something that I *don't* do, believe me! I get jealous when Sidney says things about other women but I try not to show it. I'm doing my best and keeping a cheery smile and a good thought and next week I'm starting on that new mineral-oil and lime diet. There's the phone, it's probably Sidney with a halibut or something!"

In this particular suburban neighborhood of small white "dream" houses, parched lawns where late the crabgrass sang, and splintery Adirondack furniture set carefully beneath trees almost totally denuded by the gypsy moth caterpillar, a woman whom her husband calls "Sis" strides purposefully down the street on her way to an assignation with her lover, whom his wife calls "Bro." We may conclude that dopey behavior invades even the most fragile dreams, and that the good life 'mid foliage and flowers is not exempt from the general madness of the day.

Michael Cullinan, who *is* Michael Cullinan, is roused from his disappointment at missing *Black Ladder* by the following question, put to him by an itinerant "populist investigator": "For what or whom do the initials S I S stand?" Such a question is Michael's special meat, or meaty specialty, and, laughing delightedly, the sunny-faced Irish pervert replies, with a gawm and a brogue and a dacent cup of beef tay till further orders, "S I S stands for *Sisters in Satin,* a courageous yet heartwarming film which does not shrink from detailing the secret erotic practices of the convent, high heels and all. Some ignorant film 'experts,' ha ha, continue to make the ludicrous gaffe of identifying the letters with *Sisters in Shame,* a film which, while of some interest because of its fresh use of the lost-brassiere motif, cannot hold a candle, if you'll pardon my ithyphallic figure of speech, to *Sisters in Satin.* The confusion seems to arise from the fact that *Sisters in Satin* is based upon the daily activities of the Sisters of Shame, commonly known as the Order of Sangre de Cristo. Most people wrongly assume that it is *Sisters in Shame* that is so rooted in the actual, but no-no-no!" Mr. Cullinane, excited now, gets up from his hoary desk and moves quickly, for such a small man, to his faded file cabinets, opens one, and begins expertly to scan its contents. "I have detailed descriptions of all the garments worn by the cast of both films, along with those of the garments regularly worn by the nuns of the Order, if you'd care to see them?" But the itinerant interrogator has simply taken his leave, allowing Michael to relax in the safe privacy of his harmless obsessions. No world leader he! He selects two bulging files, for the Sisters of Charity and the Sisters of Misericordia, and takes them to his desk along with a twenty-year-old issue of *Stella's Cellar: Public Wear for Private Occasions,* a biannual catalogue for a specialty business long vanished. To work! he says to himself, rubbing, yes, *actually rubbing* his hands together. Downstairs, May Cullinane is dialing April. It is indeed, yes, a sad old world.

Only Jimmy Blackhead's closest friends know that before he bought the moribund Black Basement he owned the Six of Diamonds, a restaurant famous for its bavette de boeuf chasseur, tomates grillées à la Provençale, poulé sauté beauséjour, and banane étonnement, the last the spectacular dessert of, some maintain, uncanny powers, and which has, of late, been responsible, or so it is rumored, for the sinister deaths of Percival Skeezix, the international bergamot; Cleerone (Slam) McTavishe, the Sneaker King; and "Slick" Jane Whitlock, author of the best-selling smasho courage-packed wallop, *Whores Bleed Red, Mom.* We don't quite know how this legendary dessert (or "sweet") can be held responsible for the demise of three of the people who made our pulsating city the excitingly electric dynamo of a hip thrill that it is, but perhaps M. Rimbaud has a thought or two in his louse-ridden *la tête.* Monsieur?

Rimbaud, clutching a copy of Monge's *Les Constructions métalliques,* momentarily and carelessly half-incarnates himself, his blue-white eye shining. "Sans doute," he says, "la débauche est bête, le vice est bête; il faut jeter la pourriture à l'écart." He smiles ambiguously and his pale image slowly fades. We never *quite* thought of Skeezix, McTavishe, and Whitlock as *pourriture,* but then we are not Arthur Rimbaud. Permit us to note, before angry letters and phone calls begin to come in, that this actual appearance, this *live* appearance by the famed poet whose books sell, year in and year out, in the thousands, was prefigured in Leo Kaufman's justly celebrated "Sleeping with the Lions," his astonishing piece of juvenilia. Jonathan Slug-Smith and Werner Smitts, in their "The Legacy of the Lions: Seminal Imagery in Leo Kaufman's Early Fiction," convincingly argue that the appearance in the story of the Rimbaud figure to a dissolute academic is recapitulated over and again in Kaufman's later fiction as well as in almost all of his mature poetry, finally occurring, in a daring semantic shift, along the cumulative "syntagma plane" as the "lost clam" and "rusted Chevys" of "Leo's Last Poem." Slug-Smith and Smitts also suggest, but far less authoritatively, that the "slime imagery" in Anne Kaufman's poems (see especially "Snails"), usually thought to be inspired by her early devotion to Roethke, is, in fact, a version of her ex-husband's bold employment of a crude yet robust magical realism. The scholarly pair argue that these phenomena suggest that truth is stranger than realism of any kind, and that Anne Kaufman was symbolically correct to enter the retail religious-supplies business.

Leticia Snap, a woman of impure thoughts and proclivities, remarks that "magic realism is like when ghosts and animals, like clams, put on clothes and dance and eat bananas and stuff and talk with real people, isn't that it? It sort of kind of makes you wonder about the meaning of reality in a big way and see like sort of under the surface? I've known a lot of men like that—ghosts, I mean." Miss Snap raises her skirt, and in the best tradition of meat-and-potatoes realism, *unnecessarily* adjusts her garters, showing *a lot of leg* while gazing at the *traffic far below* as if for the *first time*. "Now, for instance, if an exotic cassowary like walked out from under my skirt and started telling me the amazing history of the area in which I presently find myself," Leticia sighs, "that would be magic realism, is that about it?"

Close enough, Leticia, close enough. Nice *pair of shapely gams!*

Harlan Pungoe, still hobbling, scraping, and scuffling through the broiling streets, and dripping with malodorous and toxic sweat, is, according to a secret notebook, or "log," supposedly buried deep within an abandoned tungsten mine on Mystery Mountain, somehow close to the very center of *all* the activities of this summer day. Some citizens, quite recently interviewed, go so far as to insist that without Pungoe, none of the events presented to our rapt attention would even have occurred. That may be going just a little too far, although we have no way of disproving these opinions. It is time, however, now that Pungoe is on his way to what can no longer be disguised as a "casual visit" to Annette Lorpailleur, to indite here those oddities of his weighty presence which make him a figure to be feared even more than reviled, hated, or condemned.

Nota: At an earlier time, and in a very different place, Harlan Pungoe cynically represented himself as "Flem Snopes."

Nota: "The Snorter," a neo-impressionist-radical-pop-performance-feminist-rock-video artist, insists that her recurring bouts with paranoid schizophrenia, appendicitis, heroin dependency, coronary infarction, and chronic hemorrhoidal distress stem from the evening on which she responded coldly and contemptuously to Pungoe's casually "friendly" remark, to wit, "I like the cut of your jib and the lay of your luff."

Nota: Socks of SoHo, the custom-hosiery shop, is considered by the Buildings Department to have been in the process of spontaneous and irreversible self-deconstruction ever since the day that the owner quarreled with "a clubfooted man" over the price of a pair of nickel-plated opera stockings.

Nota: La Soirée intime, the erotic *récit* which figures in *La Bouche métallique,* a marvelous book filled with the subtle tips which literature alone can offer the pressured businessman, is said to exist, *in fact,* as the erotic *récit* entitled *La Soirée intime* by Léonie Aubois, as well as the screenplay (also entitled *La Soirée intime*) by a writer or writers unknown. The latter two "properties" are thought to be early-period creations of Pungoe's.

Nota: The famous Soirée Intime chain of lingerie boutiques is owned by Beshary Contemporary Ventures Inc., of which the principal share-holders are Annette Lorpailleur and Harlan Pungoe.

Nota: It is revealed in the *Thaumaturgic Experiences* of Éliphas Lévi, by means, it is said, of almost impenetrable late-Latin anagrams, that a man who walks with "a dip, stagger, and shuffle" and who favors the mystical color blue will come to be the familiar of Solas of Herbs and Stones, the bleak Raven of Astronomy.

Lincoln Gom is certain that "Some Fun," the translation of "Quelques choses par amusement," by his latest enthusiasm, Paul de Kock, does *precisely* what Ann Taylor Redding has been trying to do in "Shadowie Lumpe." Big talk!

"You'll soon be able to see for yourselves," Lincoln says over the phone, "because the story will appear in the next issue of *Green Sunshine.* Look, I like Dr. Redding, always have, she's got a lot of brains and a drop-dead pair of legs, also her English accent, wherever she picked it up, is charming. But literature is truth and truth is money!" Gom pauses to collect his thoughts, many of which have rolled behind the sofa, then continues. "I'm behind 'Some Fun' one hundred percent and I'm not too jaded or sophisticated, I hope, to admit that I fell in *love* with its nature descriptions, its characters, whose lives we feel we have participated in, and its amazingly sensitive adult scenes. In a word, they all work, gloves in hand, to pertinently wallop a reader! I appreciate Dr. Redding's honest attempt to tell a story from a man's point of view, of course, but de Kock *is,* if you'll pardon the expression, a man. The story may, oddly enough, remind you of *The Sound and the Fury,* or *Abalone! Abalone!,* or even *The Ballad of the Golden Hunter,* and other tales of the South. Or, if you prefer, you may recognize in it the rich gifts of sheer storytelling *just as sheer storytelling,* that we contemplate in

Southern Fiction *just as Southern Fiction,* all made even more stupen-
dously amazing, since de Kock is a French person, a kind of *homme,* I
think. Or he *was.* Anyway, one book editor I bruited about with some, a
fellow who lunches regularly here and there, remarked that he thinks
'Some Fun' has about it certain of the brooding niceties of the classic
fiction of the Southwest, for Christ's sake! He mentioned such classics
as the classic *Riders 'Mid the Silver Gorse,* and other classics. In any
event," Gom says proudly, "I thought I'd let you know so that you
might tell Dr. Redding that she's barking up the wrong lump. Ha! Ha!
Ha!"

We are puzzled as to how Lincoln Gom found out about Dr.
Redding's project, unless, of course, her frustration and her "block" are
common knowledge in the small but intimate world of letters and publishing, a world sometimes honored as "the media business," bless its
iron heart. In any event, *we* are not mentioning a word of this to Dr.
Redding, and of course, *things* are, for the most part, silent.

Unknown to Berthe, he has this day been befriended by Durga, the
Destroyer, the Serene, the Inaccessible. The goddess's benevolent
feelings for Berthe are no greater than her ire toward Edward Beshary.
She travels swiftly to Bermuda on her lion-dog, where she manifests
herself as the Albanian Lard Goddess in her incarnation as the sexually
enraptured young woman whose photograph bedevils the priest, and
many others, in the A & P. Her plans are to meet Beshary and by the
potent magic of her "personality" (indicates awe-inspiring body) and
the knowledge that those whom the gods wish to destroy they first infect
with greed, to sell the South West Development Company, a bogus
corporation, to Beshary Contemporary Ventures, Inc. What will she
not be able to present to the leering capitalist, as she leans lightly
against him at lunch, her pinstriped thigh brushing his? SWD, as she
calls it, is in the process of breaking ground for casinos, hotels, spas,
brothels, cinemas, boutiques, *everything,* in a desert currently as bleak
and barren as central Spain. Guests will be shamelessly pampered and
given everything from champagne and caviar to Frank's Orange Nectar
and Hooten chocolate bars. The decor, architecture, and landscaping
will range from Bauhaus to postmodern to '30s Grand Concourse to
fake Spanish moss. Everything will be available to the rich, including,

most especially, those things which they don't understand and so must possess. What does he think? Durga asks, sipping her cognac, her hand brushing the big strong handsome virile Arab's big strong handsome virile *batuta*. He looks at her, groggy with cupidity and lust, confusing, how wonderfully! how beautifully! one with the other, a common failing. Durga admires his skull, clearly outlined beneath the sweaty, yellowish skin of his face. "We've thought of calling the complex Nirvanadu," she says breathily, leaning her breasts against his arm. "It has a mysterious but familiar *donnée* to it, we think." Beshary blinks and blinks. He can't stop grinning his death's-head grin. We may be, at this moment, seeing the last of him, but time will tell. (Indicates clock, calendar, and gnomon.)

"Hi! I'm Karen Sperry! When I'm handing out tasty sticks of gum to unpop! the naughty, clogged-up ears of my passengers, my visage is friendly and caring, but hey! when I'm pitching and yawing on the bowjib with my conservative captain in his sassy white cap, I'm all laughter and unbridled admiration. And even though I'm working toward my advanced degree in useless-goods-marketing demographics, I can get with the idea of, like, wet things. Hi!"

Today, as on almost every day, the Splendide-Lincoln, Splendide-Malibu, and Splendide-New Haven are certain to report the disappearance of a number of what disgruntled policemen somewhat euphemistically term "thrillseekers."

And who are, actually. . . ?

Oh, the usual, mostly. Bergamasques, catamounters, thighbinders, mouthstrappées, concrete fans, featherkissers, shoepeople, garterboys, glimpsers, palmfondlers, partyrubbers, and so on.

Among the scores of "regular people, so-called," who have so far disappeared this year are the "Briefs" editor of *Sports Action;* "Jitters" or "Cheesy" Staffel or Stuffit, names employed by the plain Lucía Lewison, who arrived at the Splendide-Malibu still trembling from her modish experiences in the Lido; Myles Standish, an appellate-court judge, given to strange practices in his chambers with *Family Circle;* a fellow known only as Stanley, carnally befriended in his acne-ridden and drooling youth by Joanne Lewis during one of her self-hating frenzies; Stanziani's Neapolitan Restaurant staff, all of whom thought, so the New Haven police report, that they were going on a "boat ride" to Rye Beach, New York; and a man identified only as Star Eyes, so-called from his startling resemblance to a singer who once performed the definitive version of the song of that title, if popular and crisply written tomes speak the truth!

It is an oddity that Guy Lewis's "death by misadventure," among a number of other strange events on this day, was foreshadowed in Elizabeth Reese's undergraduate poem, "Starry Night, Bronxville: With Orgasm." The pertinent lines are:

> Some Guy, sore tempted by the fire escape
> —His dull bedlamite's vulgar patio,—
> Tilts there, then falls, his fall a last coarse jest.

We have so far been unsuccessful in trying to contact Miss Reese, who presently lives in Staten Island and teaches English Composition at a State Teachers' College; we'd very much like to ask her why the word "Guy," in the cited fragment, is capitalized, and how she decided, long years ago, on the "fire escape" as this despairing act's location. We will keep trying. (Indicates women, their sleeves rolled up, at unintelligibly blinking switchboards.)

"Wait a minute!" Cox says, "wait just a minute. That poem was stolen from one of the poems in *White Bridges,* I'd swear to it."

"I am forced to agree with this badly dressed yo-yo," Buddy Cioppetini nods. "The odor of plagiarism hangs over Miss Reese's 'poem' as surely as *E. coli* covers the known world."

"What the hell are you doing following me?" Cox demands. Well, he doesn't actually *demand.*

"I still think that you may know something of my missing *Homo Ludens,* and also you're plenty cute for a guy in real fake honest work clothes and careless coif."

"You noticed?" Cox blushes.

Like the doomed yet really aware polymorphous-perverse lovers in the Paul Whiteman Award-winning opera *Steel Orange,* the eminently singable work based on Wilhelm Stekel's "boot" monographs, Cox and Buddy head quickly toward a known shoe store. Forgotten on the instant are the irritations concerning missing books, sartorial acumen, plagiarism, inspissation theory, etc. As Dr. Johnson Mulloon once drunkenly remarked to Baron Sternhagen on the occasion of that nobleman's tenth-anniversary *hommage* to his miniature Stetson hat collection, "So you see, my dear Baron, that despite a clear and complete index, exemplary notes, and a mercifully brief introduction, no literary intelligence may long detain a yearned-for *jouissance!* Take it from me, I'm a doctor already, I know the agonies to which writers like Robert Louis Stevenson were subject, although I use him as an example only and in no way do I intend to stigmatize him as a mere hunk of fleshly envelope. Right?"

An epiphany from *Treasure Island:*
   "Har! Har! Jim, me lad! Scupper me Stillson jib to yaw the snatch-fathom quadrant, if loose apples don't spile the swabs afore the to'gallants! Har! Har!"

Although a "Stillson" is, indeed, the jib once carried or "flown" on barkenteens, it is, more commonly, the wrench used by meerschaum miners as the favored tool whereby to harvest large blocks of the precious "stuff." Day and night, fog permitting, Daly City is the scene of prodigious efforts as the hardy, stunted folk—whose roots are planted in the medieval mists of Stilton-on-Baskerville—mine the elusive flora, or something. It has always been so, as Tadeusz Creon, one of the world's recognized meerschaum experts, regularly notes.
   "That is true," Creon says, his eyes hideously encased in wrinkles as he looks up from his solitary game of *hrschszt,* an esoteric variation on Big Lotto, and one which is as old as many really old things. "The mining has always been performed according to ritual, for without the pull of continuity, gathering operations always tend to go awry. For instance, you've heard of the Cracow Scandal? Without that pull, it cannot be fully understood." He puffs bestially on his aromatic, crust-encrusted pipe. "Some purists—always there are purists," he spits coldly, "have inquired about Sonny Stitt and his role in the big picture, but to bring music into a discussion of the meerschaum harvest is always a mistake, and sometimes a manifestation of 'love madness,' as defined by Hans Dietrich Stöffel, who, in 1884, recognized and

presented the morphology of the illness in *De praestigiis amoris,* an invaluable work, often incorrectly attributed to Anthony Denim. Hmph!'' Creon sniffs, slowly ripping the arm from his noticeable chair. "Denim was but a ne'er-do-well whose only claim to our attention is the role he played in the secular canonization, if that is not too strong a word, of the bulging shakos affected by the *actual* Royal Hussars.'' Creon lapses into a peaceful silence, his gums calm at last.

It might as well be mentioned, now that Tadeusz Creon has been once again hauled out and dusted off, so to speak, that he is prominently mentioned in April Detective's memoirs, *Strange Coincidences,* as one of the many unsavory men who took advantage of her temporary nymphomania, during what she rather cryptically calls her "Struttin' With Some Barbecue" period. The relevant passage begins, "Mr. Creon—we all called him Teddy—was always waiting for me in the stairwell with his pants off and folded neatly over his arm, in what my mother would have thought of as 'a state'. . . .''

Item: Yolanda Stuzzicadenticcio has not yet been *officially* informed that, had *The Orange Dress* been published under her name, it would have been reviewed in the *Italo-American Banjo News,* the *Scranton Arts Times,* and *Weekend Fox-Trot Hoots,* and nowhere else.

A certain Mr. Suave, which name he pronounces, for his own good reasons, "Sow-EEV," is in the process of "striking up" an "intelligent" conversation with the repulsive Balte Brownie, hoping, in this way, to get an introduction to the towering wreck of a man in thrilling plaids who seems to be his, ah, friend. Eros will stoop, as we know, to anything. "Oh, but certainly!" Mr. Suave says. "Certainly, dear, *dear* boy! 'Suck My Whip,' Sheila Henry's first—and only—short fiction was indeed published, and in *Nougat,* for that matter. But it was *never* included in any anthology." Balte sullenly aligns family-size jars of mayonnaise, wondering what this "fruit," as he quaintly thinks of him, wants. "You may be thinking of Regina Fury's *Suck My Whip,* published by the Sudan Press. Could that be it?" Balte shrugs and begins to straighten out the ketchup shelves. At this moment, in a wild and pulse-throbbing blur of terrifying colors, Bam sidles up to the pair, his large hands just quite naturally *there.*

"I read *Suck My Whip*," he offers, in his best Ivy League fashion, trig, yes, yet a little frayed from psychological aberration. He considers the four eyes which have turned toward him. "I read *Suck My Whip*," he repeats, with the wonderful patience of the elect, and then he drives it home: "I read *Suck My Whip*."

"How marvelous!" Mr. Suave cries, an odd tingle or two carelessly rippling through his once-wiry but now reticent frame. "My name is Sow-EEV," he smiles, his attention momentarily distracted by the sight of a tortured-looking man, in apparent mufti, who crawls swiftly past them on his hands and knees. "Sow-EEV, yes, and I'm delighted to make your acquaintance. My! How very big you are!" At this remark, Balte walks disgustedly to the next aisle.

"You know, of course," Mr. Suave says toothily, "that Regina Fury is the *nom de plume* of Esther Summerson, whose works on obedience, discipline, organic beverages, and the homely virtues of the birch have gained her the affectionate title, 'the simmering spinster.' It's delightful that in *Whip* she gives us a glance at her lighter side, don't you think?" Bam, who long ago laid down the burden of thought, makes the sound of a cork popping, and says, in a friendly but determined way, "Twenty dollars."

We have just been authorized to tell you what day of the week it is. It is Sunday. For the record: This is Sunday, August 29, 1982. It seems to us that certain of the events, occurrences, adventures, conversations, and dramas—bathetic and otherwise—taking place today are more suited to some other day of the week. But we only work here, speaking of bathos, and our occasional suggestions, comments, and complaints are rarely acknowledged, let alone acted upon. However, if we learned one thing at Suntan University, one thing which has allowed us to look at "the human comedy" (indicates breathtaking canvas displaying Comedic Panorama) with an observant, cold, yet not pitiless eye, to inform, that is, the long look with all that is in our power, it is that misogyny recapitulates entelechy. A hard discipline, yes, but one fraught with the morality of shaky ethics and brimming over with food for thought. A hard discipline, yes, but one fraught with . . . oh. Sorry.

Especially forceful and rigorous in this time of namby-pamby folderol when ideas are especially annoying, when people of decent background are considering that maybe history, for instance, never happened or something. You get what I mean.

Wholeheartedly. I mean yes, right.

However, it's also why we're constantly getting yelled at.

"Well, actually, *I'm* the Sun Twin," Saul Blanche says. "Look at my varied illnesses, for Christ's sake."

"No, I'm the Sun Twin," Sol Blanc replies. "You'll notice how I'm limping gamely along, even though my life is practically flashing before my rheumy eyes?"

"Does said 'flashing' include the weekend debacle at Sun Valley when your companion, Miss Languish, glanced at a catered buffet and scarcely a moment later was performing unspeakable acts with Mel Proud and each and every last Melodic?" Saul tragically leans on a handy crutch. "Including the *accordion* player?" He shudders as if for the first time.

"Such a scene, yes, I admit it, also flashed," Sol weeps. "I definitely deserve to be the Sun Twin. We're talking diseases, maladies of the spirit here."

"But I'm the chump of a gazabo whose reckless wager on the Super Bowl lost me my wife of forty years, Susan," Saul groans, looking about for medical solace, none of which, as usual, is in the vicinity.

"I thought the excellent Mrs. Blanche's name was Hettie," Sol remarks.

"You're thinking of the other Mrs. Blanche. You know, the *other* one," Saul smiles. "So, am I the Sun Twin or what?"

"Let's take turns," Sol offers. "I have a hunch that that's what Mr. Beleth and Mr. Halpas intended. God knows, they *looked* serious enough."

Fist's current interview with Lorna Flambeaux reveals that *The Sweat of Love,* her famous book of poems, and a media event of the early '70s which, in Michelle Caccatanto's words, "gave women of all stations, classes, professions, races, and persuasions permission to get proudly and properly 'hot,'" was almost entitled *The Sweet of Love.* "Yes," Flambeaux says, coolly casual in her and with her feet up on the and occasionally sipping from a glass of, "it was definitely going to be 'sweet,' but a dear, dear friend of mine at that time, Sweaty Patsy, seemed deserving of *some* recognition, since it was Patsy who freed my thinking from the prison of bourgeois-liberal phallocentric ideology." Flambeaux frowns for a moment and reaches, yet again, for a. "Patsy, dear Patsy, as Ronda the Crazy Gypsy, now provides spiritual guidance to those currently buffeted by life forces beyond the control of, *perhaps,* generous credit allowances." She toys with her and pushes restlessly the around on the coffee table.

Knute suddenly wakes to the natter of Lorna's voice, amazing though that may seem, and draws his pawlike hand roughly across his deeply weathered lips, muttering "pshaw!" as he performs this essentially masculine act. "Some years back," he says at last, the repressed anger barely detectible in his voice, "I was advised by Ronda the Crazy Gypsy to throw off the insults of those who would impugn my heritage by calling myself 'Swede'—*not* 'Knute the Schmuck,' *not* 'the thick Norwegian,' *not* 'the Scandihoovian tree trunk'—but 'Swede,' an honest and accurate name." Knute shifts about amid the piles of yellowed newspapers, and pulls out his large clasp knife in order to display it to a curious woodland creature, perhaps a beaver. Or a vixen. "So I did, and soon I was married to a woman who read my diary and then refused to perform her lawful conjugal wifely duties, as well as some that seem, now that I think back on it, unlawful," he concludes merrily, his enormous, rumbling laughter —the ruggedly individualistic laughter of a man whom no mere woman can ever tame, a man who, like a great lonely oak, is destined to hurtle off scarps and crash heavily into chasms, and even arroyos!—echoing off the scarps, chasms, and arroyos with which Scone Canyon is so tediously endowed, as geography teaches.

Then too: *Swedish Lust* Producer Denies Film Is "Extravaganza of Lewd Blondes"; Gold Dust Twins Charge Swee'Pea "Ate Things" during White House Performance; Birth-Control Panel to Reveal Contraception-Efficient Findings on Sweet-Orr Overalls; Gstaad's Residents Irked at Government Silence concerning Their Reality; Director Claims *Blushing Nuns* "Symbolist Dialogue" with Church; Publisher Will Publicly Burn "Misogynist" *Synthetic Ink* despite Author's Tearful Apology.

According to possibly specious information proffered in the strictest confidence, Lydia Languish's infamous behavior at picnics, barbecues, cookouts, etc., is *not* the result of her victimization by "the vapors," as has long been supposed. It would seem, on the contrary, that Miss Languish is the special target of Sytry, the Leopard Prince, who assumes among humans a human form, sometimes that of a beautiful man, sometimes that of a handsome woman. This glinting demon's special powers procure love between the sexes and make women show themselves naked. The sexual chaos which results when Lydia strips can *only* be explained by the intercession of some perverse power remote from the social, ethical, and moral concerns of civilized men and women. This hypothesis is further strengthened by a tape recording, received along with the possibly specious information already mentioned, which allows the listener to make out Lydia's voice, chanting, as she tears off her clothing in the usual way:

> Jussus secreta libenter,
> Fabric razed!
> Detegit feminarum,
> Quim naked!
> Eas ridens ludificansque,
> Wonderful guys!
> Ut se luxorise nudent,
> Use my hot sex!

Lydia, it should be pointed out, knows no Latin, and the syntax of the English "lyric," it will be obvious, can be thought of as strained.

"Actually," Horace Rosette says, "I say as much, about women in general, of course, in my critical introduction to *Tableaux Vivants: Selected Poems of Pamela Ann Clairwil.* Pamela, although certainly not one of our great poets, yet who *is* one of our great poets, or, for that matter, who are two?, certainly has her finger on an important erogenous zone—if I may be forgiven a small *mot*—of women, and understands their concupiscent relationship to outdoor dining. Something about the wheat, or corn, of course. I point out, in my small but scrupulous way, as you'll doubtless remember, that in such poems as the early 'Tahiti,' the remarkable 'Tarot: A Sequence for Waite, Wirth, and Marseilles,' and the fully developed 'Charcoal Drama for Allen Tate,' Pamela clearly suggests the strangely libidinous yet yearningly puritanical tension which develops within those scenes—some quite economically posited—which touch upon the sexually charged politics of contemporary *al fresco* feeding rituals. Oh yes indeed." Horace settles back amid scattered furbelows and tries to remember what Pamela Ann looked like, long years ago. Was she the one who wore the notable pink dresses with the *outrageous* puffed sleeves? Astonishingly bad writer!

Dear Nancy,

I've read in the paper that you are waiting with a sense of tragic heartbreak for the unexpected moment when you might explode. I too live in daily fear of this ever since scientists discovered the idea. Few who know me can sense the horror of what my days have become, especially since I seem to have everything that money can buy including a stockbroker ex-husband who my lawyers took to the cleaners, thank God, he was fooling around with some floozy bimbo tramp slut of a whore stewardess with big knockers, if you'll pardon my frankness, named Karen. For some reason it's always a Karen it seems. Anyway, Nancy, I want to let you know that as a Nancy, when I pray for myself not to suddenly explode, I'll also pray for you even though you are probably not like us, that is, my circle, at all.

With noblesse oblige,
Buffie (Nancy) Tate

Lucy Taylor is thinking of Lorzu Fashions and her ex-partner, Lee Jefferson, thoughts she has not had for years. Lucy is very much alone in her little pre-fab house—actually, a bungalow—in Teaneck, and has been very much alone for years, ever since the day that she was ordered to leave town and keep her big dyke mouth shut by Harlan Pungoe and Annette Lorpailleur after the boutique fire. But the story is well known. (Indicates well-thumbed, creased, and dog-eared story.) But *Lee* is still in town! Lucy thinks, bitter again after all this time. *Lee* can still have a drink or dinner or whatever with all the young women she wants to! It is *not fair,* she thinks, erroneously. Sad to say, exile has not improved Lucy, who looks, dresses, and, in general, presents herself in much the same way as she did when young. For instance: baggy cardigan sweater; flat-heeled shoes, badly scuffed; wrinkled, semi-opaque stockings; thin white anklets; hairy legs; pasty complexion; mousy brown hair streaked with piss-yellow grey; and etc., etc. Not even the most fanatic nature fans would, as the phrase goes, "make a move" on the woman. Teaneck may very well be the perfect locale for her, although certain areas of Northern California could easily absorb her without a murmur. The unprepossessing waif can and does blame her lack of feminine society on the fact that she doesn't know a female soul because none is worth knowing. And also because life, as we know, *is not fair.* She walks into the bedroom and lies down on her—but of course!—lumpy bed, and feels the musty, moist heat envelop her. On the dresser she sees "Big Yank" and her Large Economy Family Bruiser-size bottle of Prell. Which? She is sweating a lot, especially under the arms. In this, it will be remarked, she is like Lee. Perhaps I should remove my baggy cardigan sweater, she thinks, as she reaches for, what the hell, "Big Yank," always, when all is said and done, a summer favorite. As she begins to "dig for gold," to use the Mormon phrase, she thinks of Sara Teasdale's lines,

> Oh, beauty, are you not enough?
> Why am I crying after love?

Teddy, a *boulevardier* who occasionally, and without warning, asks pointed questions, wants to know why the Mormons, of all people, use such a phrase, what "beauty" there is in Miss Taylor's life, and what position in the canon is currently occupied by Sara Teasdale. Thanks, Teddy, great questions, really *great* questions. We'll get back to you. By letter. O.K.? How's the wife? Still at it?

"Hi! I'm Karen Teeth! When I'm streaking through thin air, which those in the know sometimes call the 'either,' in a gleaming silver tube, a rhetorical figure which those in the know sometimes call a 'monotony,' I usually do my pseudovirginal best to steal the probably well-off hubbies of 'mature' women who live in fear of sudden explosion, fatty thighs, and bimbo tramps. But when I'm on my hands and knees in an impersonal hotel room, I throw the demure act to the winds—all four of them!—and rely on the burning flesh. Hi!"

It doesn't seem possible, but Frieda Canula, who but recently was "chatting," so to speak, with Bunny Lewis in Gnatville, is reported to be in Tel Aviv. Surely, there is a mistake? Let's listen to a lately unearthed recording of Frieda herself, "talking" about her wanderings, shall we?

"I tears up my close, like bobbykoo people. Good fun but wet! Then, take train, is very nice. Here I am! I look for others of like thinkings and food bents. Here in Tellevauk is the home of many Albanian folk, as so often I shall have had read."

Frieda has reached her destination by train, so she cannot possibly be in Tel Aviv.

"Could be a sinister code about a secret kike weapon we know nothing of," Knute calls from his fastness. "Like the cannonballs of the idlers of Zion."

What, then, does she mean by "Tellevauk"?

"If I may interrupt?" Father Debris interrupts. "I couldn't help but overhear your remarking on the difficulty of 'placing' Miss Canula? I may be able to help?" The priest takes from his soutane a slide rule, a small calculator, a pad, pencil, and a geographical dictionary. "Now," he grins, displaying, by mistake, a small piece of what looks like François of Fargo's asparagus bread, which he swiftly, to his credit, caches. "As Riemann writes, if there are given in a plane a line L and a point P not on L, there are at least two lines through P parallel to L. So far so good?" the canny Jesuit asks. We nod stupidly, a, as they say, gog. "Then," he says, figuring, sliding, jotting, riffling pages, and so on, "I must conclude that Miss Canula is, as you surmise, not in Tel Aviv, but is currently enjoying the activities offered by either Ten Eyck Walk, in historic Brooklyn, or Terre Haute, in fairest Indiana." Father Debris puts his tools back into his soutane and leaves.

What? What did he just do? Ten Eyck Walk? Whoever heard of such a place? In Brooklyn? Just then, the phone rings. It is Joanne Lewis, hoping against hope that the rumor which has put the Albanian woman in Israel is true. We can, unfortunately, but assure her that all we know is that Israel is having a crisis of morality.

"What a refreshing change!" Joanne says.

"So, if we're actually going to get married, Terri," Terry says, chuckling wisely, "you can tell me anything, really, *anything.* We're no spring chickens, and hell, I've been around a little, seen a few things, been in the Navy, by God," he chuckles wisely. "That sojourn of yours, as you call it, and I like that word, in New Mexico? Those parties? Old boyfriends? Hell, don't bother me a damn bit," he chuckles wisely. Terri smiles at him, or, to be more precise, her shimmering, snowy plates do, leans back in her porch rocker of chaste Shaker design, clasps her arthritic hands in her still-attractive lap, and begins to speak, remembering. "Biff and Harlan and Teddy and Joanie and Marlene and Sam and Georgette and Dolores and Liz and Chester and Max and José and Ed and Kate O'Neill and Ricardo and George and Connie and Louie and April and Johnny. And me. And, oh yes, Terry, like *your* Terry is spelled. I almost forgot him because he'd only come every couple of weeks, you know, when he could get ahold of some really *big* pooches." She picks up her crocheting. "Is that all right, dear?" she smiles. Terry seems to be rigid, his eyes wide beneath his Coors baseball cap, his wise chuckle stuck somewhere in his throat, his eyes frantically signaling "amok! amok!"

Billy Joe Selma is telling Ronda this and that, the injustice, the misery that his people have suffered. His Indian accoutrements, or what he thinks are Indian accoutrements, lie on the table before them, wet from the sweating beer bottles clustered there. There is no justice. The asshole son of a bitch insulted him. Nobody cares about the wily buffalo or the great flame or the holy spirit or the wampum pipe or the smoking coup stick. The swift sun dance! Ronda is laying out the Tarot deck and not really listening to what she privately thinks of as Act Two, Scene One. Barnett Tete, senile old bastard, he's behind the damn movie with its crass remarks and shitty script, just like he backed that turkey *Thames,* who was in it? That old idiot-faced fuck with the jet-black hair and the wrinkled neck, should have put him in the old ham's home years ago? That's the one where the Sioux chief turns out to be some faggot child molester? Disgusting. And he also produced the one about the halfbreed Kiowa who spits on the flag, what's the matter with the fucking swine? And if truth were known, he's behind this disgusting freak film *Lace Me Tighter!,* where a dirty rich broad asks some other filthy bitch to treat her like a savage Indian brave would and, like, torture her, you dig? It's always the same old shit! Ronda sees herself in the Tarot with surpassing clarity, dead at last, wishful thinking. Billy Joe says that we should never have let the bastards know a word, not word fucking one, about Thanksgiving, Indians have always been the goddamnedest fools. He looks over at Ronda then and asks her if, hey, she went out today like he asked, with her panties around her neck, he has his reasons, and Ronda turns over The Tower and says that of course she did. What was he saying about some rich broad with jet-black hair?

" 'That's for Me' is thought of, with a kind of enervating regularity, as Our Song, by Janet and Tom Thebus, although in the midst of the sweetness and light which is their life together, Janet occasionally has unexpected visions of Tom's body, bloody, broken, and quite satisfactorily dead at last, at the bottom of one of the ravines which crisscross Mystery Mountain, upon which their living-room windows mercilessly look. Oh well. Tom, to give the devil his due, is often startled awake by a recurring dream in which a young woman sits, naked, on a large flat rock in the middle of a field. She looks at him as he passes in the coach of a commuter train, and smiles ambiguously. Sometimes he sees the title of the book she holds so tantalizingly in front of her private parts, *There's a New Sun in the Sky,* but he can never make out the author's name. As the girl begins to raise the book, he eagerly brings his face closer to the window, in order to see her sex, then knows, with a shocking certainty, that she is his mother. At this point, he wakes, sweating, fearful, terrified of sin and yearning for grace. At such times, Janet touches him tenderly with her knees, puts her hand on his shoulder. After all, well, after all. He's a good old wagon. The one thing she cannot abide, however, is his craven praying, after which come his altar-boy stories, followed closely by a detailed accounting of how he broke his parents' hearts and crushed their spirits, and all because of— oh God!—a married temptress who forced him to—oh God! Janet thought, and thinks still of Tom's parents as two vicious, greedy hypocrites, but has not mentioned this for some nineteen years now. However, in moments of overwhelming ennui, usually when Tom tearfully gets his battered Baltimore Catechism out, she accuses him of wallowing in his own stupid and impossible gloom, and says that *his* song should be 'They Can't Take That Away from Me.' Or is it they *won't* because he won't let them? Or is it, they can't, *thank God*? He looks at her, at such times, with the sort of pitying understanding which fills her heart with rage and her eyes with stinging tears. I know these things," Fred concludes, "because Thebus often confided in me during the many hours we spent as fellow commuters, oh, years and years ago now. Also, I drew a few conclusions on my own. I was in accounting then, as I may have mentioned, and some think that when I went into the re-insurance game, I died. But no. Here I am!" The old man attempts what gifted authors call a brave smile, despite the ultra-casual leather straps which embrace his head. It would seem, contrary to all expectations, that Fred has survived, intact, the "Queen of Sheba," much to the Frankenstein girls' amazement and delight. And there's *still* some zip in the old coot yet!

"Wooo!" one of the girls gasps. "I'm pretty much all enthused again! Loosen his ropes, will you sweetie?" she says to her sister. "It's that *dream* he told got me!" Her sister nods, clucks uncharacteristically, and tests the consistency of the hot fudge sauce, then adds another spoonful of cayenne pepper. She is startlingly and vulgarly provocative in a black lace version of an SS uniform. "Slide the *cannoli* over it right *now,*" she laughs. "This fresh old guy is ready *again!*"

"SS?" Himmler barks. "Who are dese people? I vant to zee dair paperss! Black lace? It zounts like mongrelized Choo corruption. DAIR PAPERSS!" he screams. The redoubtable chicken-fucker is lucky that he is, so to speak, "on the outside looking in."

The wind, stronger now, as if taking its tragic cue from the mood of tension and heartbreak which grips the humble agricultural area (indicates "farm"), is bending the tender young burgeon almost to the ground, yet its force can do nothing to set the demoralized cow on her feet again. Troy cradles boss's great, cockeyed head, trying not to look after his Helene, oddly dwarfed by her considerable luggage, as her feet kick up the choking, clayey dust formed by the effects of sun and drought upon the brick-red clay which covers the bleak, clay roads and offers shelter to naught but the papery cloche-bug, summer scourge of the alfalfa gin. Troy stares sightlessly into his cow's huge, liquid eyes, and croons, in an untrained but pleasant alto, his heart wild with pain, "Thinking of You," the show-stopper from *Thoreau,* the last musical that he and Helen "took in," or was it "took to"? Durned if he could ever get fancy city-talk right! But that was in happier days, before tragedy fell heavily, like a large, drunken boondocker, on the simple family of the rich alluvial bottomland. From a flask, then, he pours an ounce or two of Three Feathers, one of our finest blended whiskies, "smooth," as testimonials confess, "as silk," down the gentle Guernsey's big throat, which Troy, despite a year of college and a proud stint in the National Guard, humbly persists in thinking of as a "thote" or "thoat." So, one never knows! Boss is coming around, and is, in fact, scrambling to her feet! An unfettered cry of bitter joy rises from Troy's own distended "thote" as he understands, and completely, again, yet again, that certain things have actually happened after all! And despite everything! And then, in his reverie, he hears Helen's voice calling him from the sun-blasted porch, calling, calling out the news that a Three Stooges film, one of their very best, is about to begin. When *was* it that Troy first realized that the zanies were brilliantly surrealistic? God! he thinks, what a strange maze life can be, in all of its odd occurrences, and even adventures. Supporting the youthfully lovely cow with a perhaps overly solicitous hand, Troy leads her toward the house and Helen's reassuring, matronly presence. He refuses to glance, even insouciantly, toward the road, where now the only sign of his lost daughter—O lost! and by the lost wind lost, lost!—is a thin puff of reddish "whiffle" dust on the trembling horizon. He cannot see, as he reaches gratefully for the icy tumbler of Thunderbird proffered him by his wife, his wife and Helene's mother—O lost! lost!—the big guy, sad and portly in his green work clothes, who awaits his daughter. Nor can he know that just two weeks from this coming Thursday, his slightly built and sadly undernourished girl will realize that there is no money to repair the large crack in a motel swimming pool, that certain patio umbrellas are torn and quite disreputable, and that Tillie, a cruel cashier who hates the dusty heat of a small town, will fill herself to bursting with cynical doubts about a number of fairly important statements. It seems that *everyone* knows how things are.

We have on hand the *Times* of London and the *Times* of New York, or, correctly, *The Times* and *The New York Times;* we subscribe to and read both newspapers. This information, while of a private nature, is here tendered in order to lay to rest certain objections of which we are currently in receipt—obviously the concerted effort of a vulgar cabal— as to the accuracy of some of our statements concerning, among other things, literature, the plastic arts, theatre and cinema, music, science, mathematics, philosophy, psychology, medicine, horticulture, cuisine, linguistics, and sexuality. All of our statements are checked and double-checked with *the facts* as these two "newspapers of record" possess them. Any errors are, of course, our own, but we do make every effort, really, to verify all remarks. We are, of course, wholly responsible for our opinions concerning events and "personalities," but we insist, over and over again, that said opinions are scrupulously objective. For instance, and briefly: We still maintain that Emmanuel Chanko, quite possibly the leading authority on the life and art of Jeff Chandler, is wrong in his blanket condemnation of *Tin Pig,* the novel on which *Chorus Orgy,* a pioneering film of the "montage-dialogue" school, is based. We believe that *Tin Pig,* rather than being the "literary equivalent of faeces," is a sensitive, delicate treatment of the impact of marital spats on a gourmet cook and real-estate "whiz." Mr. Chanko holds that we really know nothing of California, but he is not only a morphodite who likes to wear half-slips, he is also a *cetriol'.* (Indicates large specimen of the latter.)

"On the other hand," Knute says, wiping great tears of bitter laughter from his exophthalmic eyes, "I also despise those names given me by others, mostly wiseacre city kikes, who are always trying to ravage sweet Christian girls so that they can put their blood in matzels—everybody knows that. Names like 'Shambling Galoot,' 'Two-Bit Hitler,' 'Boy Scouts' Revenge,' and 'Tin Woodman.' I was even called the last name in print, for gosh sakes, by that mockie drunk pervert, Leo Kaufman. Yes indeed! In his 'Tit Poem Number Five,' which is supposed to be, or so I've heard from talk bandied around by the Cambridge 'Rowdies,' a disgusting gloating over how many sweet, clean, Christian sorority girls in pink dresses and cotton underpants this Jew befouled! 'Course, the 'Rowdies' is all namby-pamby English sissies, but they talk good sense." Knute suddenly stretches his arm out the car window and signals wildly to a lurking Scandinavian silhouetted against the eastern sky. "Lars! Lars!" he calls hoarsely, his weathered brow abruptly wrinkled with creases of wilderness wisdom, yet not, be it said, *unhappy* creases. "Lars!" he calls again, floundering helplessly amid the shifting piles of yellowed newspapers. But it seems as if the distant figure in filthy parka and fur-trimmed chockablocks hears nothing, nothing save the wind through the sere leaves of the towering ouzels. But Knute will not, he *cannot* give up, it has been too long, too long since that careworn moment when he first set out on what he now knows is a fruitless quest for his lost Zuleika! Clawing his way to the window, he places his rawhidelike mouth as close to it as he dares! Then he cries, piercingly, keeningly, hoarsingly desperate, "Tommy! Tommy! Over HERE, Tommy! In the old DODGE!" But the silhouetted figure moves implacably on, somewhat like Fate, or Time, toward the "tree line." (Indicates some half-dozen representative citations in Southern fiction.) Finally, his gumption at its lowest ebb since the morning, years ago, when he realized that his beloved Invisible Scarlet O'Neil was, quite probably, a Roman Catholic, he makes one last effort, so-called, to attract the plodding Northman's attention. "Tonia!" he screams bodaciously. "Tonia! Tonia!" But the distant hiker, of whatever identity, has disappeared into the sulky forest. So it ever is at such times.

Questions to be entertained.

John Hicks, while writing a weekly column for *Toujours Gai,* fell in love with Jackson "Jack" Towne, who had, at the time, something to do with the Buildings Department, wherein Hicks was then also employed. John, as we know, is now Adelaide Hester's "guy." Is this current amorous attachment an indication that the Homosexual Rehabilitation and Behavior Modification Society program which he was "urged" to participate in by Dr. Mona Girls, "the Turkish scourge," was successful in terminating, or at least, abating certain vicious practices, e.g., pumpkin-beating, scrimmaging, horsing around?

The *Tractatus,* a difficult and demanding wallop of a reading thrill, on which Berthe Delamode patterned the specialities offered by her spectacular brothel, Creations Tastefully Designed, Inc., boldly asserts that one picture is like one word, or any word, or that a word is like seeing things, or *something,* or some *things,* or something like that. Why is it, then, that the once marvelously trim and handsomely coiffed Mme Delamode currently suffers from a "maladie nerveuse," one which is exacerbated by the sound of galloping horses?

Raulin's *Traités des affections nerveuses du sexe* and Lange's *Traité des vapeurs* are, of course, two of a mere handful of classic medical texts upon which all modern knowledge of "the vapors" rests. Yet Professor Solomon Traxy claims, in the current issue of *Science Fads,* that "Raulin and Lange were a pair of perverted nances, given to unnatural practices, and, as my research reveals, they were also culturally misogynistic." But can Professor Traxy be called an *authority* in Vapors Studies, given his admittedly superficial familiarity with the "neurasthenia papers" of Jean Ingelow?

Dexter Gapoine, Karen Gash, and Berta Garrett are laughingly speeding toward Misty Crag's only clam house, but Berta's husband, "Hap," is nowhere to be seen. Why has the technique, by judicious use of which Mr. Garrett has been excluded from the party, been called the "Tremont Avenue Toodle-oo"?

The shifty-looking man finally controls his quivering and weeping, and decides to destroy his raincoat, disturbing as this may be to the unwritten code which binds the large, and for the most part, nameless as well as tortured band of American perverts together in a rigorous camaraderie of need. Need and desire. And hope. Need, desire, and paralyzing fear. Fear of discovery and the wish to be helped. The fear of being helped. The wish to be paralyzed. The paralyzing desire to—

What code is that? Hello? Hello?

Now the raincoat is finally blazing, and two charming Consciousness Scouts from the Tribade Conspiracie converge on the subject on the roof, the scene of painfully joyous confession, and the need to be discovered. Trixie, one of the Scouts, is speaking. Hard to keep one's eyes off Trixie! The other Scout simpers a little.

"The subject is filled with remorse for his debauched deeds, and here, on this rough-hewn, semidesolate roof, a roof as anonymous as a Trojan condom, or, to those of you who have more than a few grey hairs, a Trommer's beer, we are privileged to witness what attractive, body-conscious, slender, college-educated couples who feel that keeping up with current fiction is essential, call an 'extravaganza of wholesome despair.' But here's State Trooper Kimberley Butz to share some of her thoughts with us, despite all. Trooper Butz?"

"Thank you," Trooper Butz asserts, a mysterious smile playing lethargically about the full pout of the lips which have, in the past, been known to cause the toughest male troopers to spill their large glasses of

Three Feathers whiskey—a *man's* drink if ever there *was* a man's drink, and there was! "Thank you again," Trooper Butz smiles again. "I've been involved in pervert arrests before. Not pretty, I can vouch for that. When they begin to tear up their decks of obscene playing cards, well, it's not too much to say that there's a kind of rapier pertinence about it, and it almost attains the indefinable perfection which is at the heart of all great dining experiences, an unexpected analogy, I agree. My sister, Karen, however, insists on staying in the back room, mostly, of the Tropical Bible Aids Shoppe in North Miami. Touch of neurasthenia. She wanted, of course, *so* much to be a stewardess, serving mankind and all, then, one day, she had a vision which she now rather deftly describes as being like 'an editorial hand guiding clumsy prose to a lapidary finish.' Whew! Now there's a turn of phrase, and with women like that about, it makes one feel that the perverts *will not win!*"

"Hi! I'm Karen Butz! When I'm in the back room of the shoppe, I dream of terrible men burning their raincoats on rough-hewn wooden roofs, the rain pelting down on their pasty, look-at-me faces. It's then that I understand how articles like 'They Lived by the Bible—But Wallowed in Lust!' can actually appear in magazines of quality like *True Action.* Although little if any decency is shown, even if requested politely, I've come to realize that there really *are* people like Elmont Truro, who talked to his own sister's pantyhose, and 'Legs' Tubetti, who, when possessed by his depraved other self, 'Sucks' Tortoni, described morally offensive movies to helpless vagrants to whom he'd promise cigarettes and fortified wine for their attention. How many saintlike bums he enflamed and doomed to perdition I can't even begin to imagine! Here in North Miami we don't have anything *like* that, and some old-timers say it may be because of our rather famous skyline, which *is* a wonder. Of course, there's a man who lives nearby, by the name of Tucci, or Tuccio, or Tucco, an Italian film mogul, but he seems very nice, loves children, food, wine in moderation, games of chance, and noise. I don't think that *he* can be held responsible for those other dagos who sully the very name of strictly private individualistic interpersonal intimacy with real emotional attachment thrown in. Which is *our* middle name."

Thanks! Karen, is it? Thanks a lot, Karen!

"Just a minute! A good friend of mine, a lovely woman who has a really nice parking space, tells me that Tucson, in Arizona?, is just *filled* with dagos, but according to the hotline columns of *True Action, Actionworld,* and *Action Monthly,* there are very few incidents where, for instance, undies are stolen from clotheslines for Satanic rituals, or regular, manly guys go bowling in their wives' high heels, or porno kings laugh in the face of the law which is helpless before them and their sleazy, big-shot lawyers filled with talk about free speech and the rights of these inhuman flesh-beasts! who desire to make us want to jump all over each other and *do* things! It's one thing to talk about the power of the objective correlative and the current needs of the business world, and quite another, *I* think, for drooling perverts to be able to ogle gorgeous gams and shapely jugs wherever they turn, be it here or be it there! So you really can't blame the honest dagos, can you, whatever people say?"

Not at all! No indeed! And thanks! See you soon, Karen, is it?

"That's Karen for you," Trooper Butz laughs sincerely. "If you ask me, she's got a crush on Delilah Crosse, even though she's never met her. Has had for twenty years. Well, it's all in what the dissolute painter in *Hellions in Hosiery* calls the 'spirit of Arthur Rimbaud.' "

Rimbaud? *Hellions in Hosiery*? What?

Shh. It's not important. And it's getting late.

"My heart fell instantly into a fairly disturbing irregularity of rhythm," Buddy expostulated thoughtfully, "when I realized the misery and horror permeating that wretched cabin. Or perhaps bungalow. As far as I'm concerned, I'm only too dratted happy to put plenty of rough trail between it—and *us.*" And so saying, he began to take even longer strides into the hushed, dripping forest. Dick needed no inducement to keep up with his doughty chum, and, at times, even rudely elbowed Buddy out of the way in order to demonstrate his own virile disgust, coupled with wise compassion.

Soon, huddled together on a barren plat of fenestrated moraine, the lads watched the dawn rise, their arms linked, their differences, such as they were, settled for the moment. "I 'low that what burrowed deep into my quick," Dick said, the morning mists almost totally engulfing his awed face, "was when the terr'ble hag asked us what 'grub' was, and was it some type of 'flywheel tool.' My blood just about up and give a curdling yell then," the boy remarked.

"I agree, ingenuous pal," Buddy nodded, disturbingly squeezing one of Dick's tumid biceps. "But what, too, of the addiction the trio obviously shared—that to Tudor beer? There were moments when one could virtually see their chances for meaningful, productive lives frittering themselves away into some sort of bad Janus-like paste of shame!" With this odd remark, Buddy helped himself to one of the stale biscuits which Zenobia had finally been prevailed upon to relinquish for what Buddy would later call "a beautiful cent."

"Is this Tuesday, Buddy?" Dick nonchalantly asked with a sadly fleeting smile. But then, quickly recovering, he said, "Forget Tuesday! How is it that you've gone and locked up the food lard? A small biscuit and some sparkling stream water'd, I powerful 'low, go down pretty fine about now with *this* feller! How come only your mouth is stretched gluttonously out of kilter with victuals? Amn't I too made of red flesh, or blood?" At the conclusion of this uncharacteristic speech, Dick fell into a sullen dump, the sparkling moraine silt flying up about him in nervous clumps.

"Oho!" Buddy exclaimed, almost unpleasantly, his hands, filled with biscuit, held high above his head, out of his friend's reach. "First of all, and although I expect the question was only the badinage of smoke-screen on your part, as you rather lamely admitted yourself, this is not Tuesday, according to my pocket astrolabe, an ingenious navigational surd made in the manner of the common tachometer. Are you listening? *This is not Tuesday.*" But Dick was rolling about on the ground in a semblance of Protestant anguish, his web belt and cordovan brogans creaking with their superbly wonted dash.

"Secondly," Buddy continued, as his eyes amusedly searched the skies, "I reject the term 'food lard,' even though certain linguistic trend-setters claim that since it once appeared in the *Tulane Drama Review* when drama was drama, it smacks heavily of the permissible." Buddy paused to sneer freely. "Perhaps such a barbarism is allowable in *Tunisia,* where the poppies encarnadine and the enervating heat prevent fellows from doing hardheaded and productive business. But it is not so *here,* I vow to you, where traffic hums far below busy hotel windows and communication is the life's blood of important executive messages! Where, by gosh, nylon was invented, as I've related!" His eyes were moist with excitement, and his back twitched against a spiny bung, whose half-eaten crown seemed almost labile in the matutinal haze.

"Buddy, dear comrade!" Dick blurted wetly. "Forgive me, please, if'n I got you on a worry, for, darn it to tarnation, I sure as thunder warn't a-fixing to. It was just a hunger pang what fixed to make me want to feel like fixing to rile you. Are we all square now?" With this, he and Buddy shook hands like two half-frozen Mounties meeting unexpectedly while strolling in the Yukon tundra wastes.

"Great Scott!" Buddy presently screamed, "what can I have been thinking of, heartlessly to deny you food, you, my hiking buddy, my assistant in arcane yet practical chemistry experiments, my farm companion when adventure takes us to the lands of wheat, corn, puling hogs, and scattered outbuildings?" The lad, with a muted cry of youthful exuberance, opened the padlock on the bulging food bag, and handed Dick a small biscuit. The latter's hand closed on the homely morsel, so redolent of grease spots and linoleum, and suddenly the sun burst through the haze to reveal what seemed like Roman candles joyfully streaming in the sky!

When the youths awoke, the sun was high in that same sky, and the chichi beetles were drumming madly in the hollow logs which seemed to yearn almost hospitably. How absurd! And yet, it *was* time to leave, and suiting action to a few obligatory words, late morning found the boys crashing, as always, through silent acres of bitter vetch.

"Oddly," Buddy panted loquaciously, "I dreamed just now of Joe Billy Tupelo, a young file clerk I was acquainted with some years since. He wore wonderfully knotted bow ties in crackerjack patterns and muted colors, but was, I fear, fated to a brutally demeaning career in lower management because of his ruffian nickname, which was 'Texie' or 'Taxi,' I can't quite remember. That, and, of course, the fact that he recklessly, and in despite of his starched white shirt, exposed himself one afternoon, and during *inventory!*, to Elisa Hess, the department-supervisor's wife. It was a full-blown scandal, and mortifying to all parties concerned," Buddy concluded, veering slightly to his left so as to trample a nest of tarantula eggs cunningly attached to a discarded fender. "Nature's camouflage," he marveled, as he did a practiced "jig of decimation."

"What does 'expose himself' mean, Buddy?" Dick queried, joining in the spirited assault on the potential monsters. "Is it kin to, say, a gal showing off her attractive legs in creamcake poses, kind of like Lana Turner? Or the current Miss Tutti-Frutti?"

"Ha! Ha!" Buddy roared wordlessly. "How wondrously amusing a companion you truly are, Dick, dear, clumsy dope! Showing off one's attractive legs and exposing oneself are not precisely alike, even," and Buddy began quivering beneath a new wave of barely repressed mirth, "when taking *creamcake* poses into account! Creamcake!" And with this, the husky youth fell to his knees, his body helplessly twisted in abandoned hilarity, his eyes dropping tears as rapidly as if he had just consumed a handful of mastiachi peppers.

"I'm obliged to you, Buddy," Dick grumbled quietly, racking his brains to remember the correct word for partially clad, leggy women in indecent poses. Goldurned if he hadn't *seen* enough of 'em! The problem, as the churl well knew, lay in his avoidance of reading those items useful to a young man intent on wearing a crisp white shirt and quiet tie each day, a young man entrusted with bills of lading, rubber stamps, a desk calendar, and various pens and pencils. What *had* he read, really *read,* recently? He twitched in shame! *Twilights,* a best-seller, which, while being a staggering wallop of a riveting read, was light and frothy and, well, *cheap* in its libidinously candid descriptions of the degradation of more than one female body. He buried a violent fist in his open palm so loudly that he startled the surrounding chirps. That, yes, and "Two Guys from Hackensack," which—but at the memory of this story, the boy blushed and fought free of the wild, dark temptations which often seemed to come along lately, usually *without warning.*

"By Cecil Tyrell, am I correct?" It was Buddy's voice, calm and quiet as a batwinged cat's paw among the legendary magnolia and honeysuckle of the South, O lost! Lost amid the red clay roads, O forever lost! lost!

"Wh-wh-what in tarnation, B-Buddy?" Dick said, taking a step backward into a small churn of viscid bonito. "Y-y-y-you. . . ?"

"Yes, I've read your mind," Buddy mouthed demurely. "I've been waiting for the right moment to try out this newfound wrinkle of mine. I hope I didn't give you too much of a turn, sock of a chum," the large-boned lad glowed fervently. "I feel that it's on the same intellectual level as sight-reading difficult piano music." He colored fetchingly.

"Tarnation take all! Lord a-mighty Goshen's sake!" Dick rejoined hysterically. "It's a blasted wonderment! To think that you're sort of two different classes of friend—a regular American fellow and a mysterious mind reader, sort of foreign and pizenlike. Pshoo!"

"Whooff!" Buddy tittered into a quickly waiting handkerchief. "I've never thought of it that way, possibly because I've never read anybody's mind before. Hmm. *Two* Buddies, you say? Or at least, imply? Rather like, if I may rapidly construct the classic analogy, two totally unlike and sternly opposed Janus faces on two otherwise identical coins!" He reddened uncomfortably, and fidgeted. "Ha! Ha! I should say, of course, rather like one Janus face, bisected on the lateral plane, on two coins of different size and value." Blushing ferociously now, the durable fellow fell to his hands and knees once again, and pressed his face to the dewy mallow, limp in the insipid sunlight. "Drat," he whispered to a leaf bud, "it is exactly, again, as if I've been listening to, as Dick has said, Nick Maggie, or is it Magger? When I entertain the difficult concept of the Janus face, I become a nattering fool, much like the effete Prince Poniatowski, his breeches tight as a bongo skin, in Chicharrón's *La Última despedida.* Dick *must* not cotton to this bookish likeness." With that, he scrambled massively to his feet.

Dick, a true-blue friend, ignored Buddy's outburst of gibbering idiocy, as always, and soon an efficient and seductive campfire had chased the grey chill which always descended from Misty Crag at this hour, and the delicious aroma of the biscuit stew which bubbled cheerily in the old rude blackened pot of seasoned oak filled the boys with renewed hope. The trees soughed implacably, the clouds heaved themselves into semi-recognizable shapes at times, the plashing waters made the comrades consider their departed friends, even now, perhaps, part of the great food chain. Time seemed to pass as slowly as if it were a thick, viscous liquid, like syrup or honey, or, perhaps, like molasses, yes, *molasses.* Time passes slow as molasses, they thought.

Sighing, some time later, in slothlike contentment, the boys fell into a discussion about the wisdom, or at least, the *conventional* wisdom, of leaving Mystery Mountain in order to return to the variegated panoply of urban life and the modernistic responsibilities which awaited them, the "humming electricity of the clerical," as someone had so neatly put it. Perhaps Abbagnano. At this point, Buddy softly said, his eyes darting toward the verdant screen surrounding, "I've been thinking, Dick, of your old Uncle Johnny, 'Mr. Tuxedo,' and what advice he might now have for us in our dilemma, outside, that is, the connubial," he gaily blushed.

"Uncle Johnny?" Dick almost perspired, yet gulped. "I reckon that I haven't thought on him for a month of Sundays' blue moons. Uncle Johnny," he uttered pensively. "You know, dear pal, that he passed away some five years ago?"

"Yes!" Buddy snapped genially. "You *told* me! Somehow, he was tragically struck in the temple at a wedding reception, as I recall. He was always the life of the party, the swell old chump!"

"He held a patent, you know, on the recipe for the Warm Manhattan," Dick weakly enthused, "and, even at his powerf'ly advanced age, keeping up his book of wedding-and-honeymoon jokes, stories, observations, and tips was a reg'lar daily task of his." He looked toward the verdant screen, heaving in the wind as slow as molasses. "There's a story, uh, banded about, you know," he muttered ruefully, his fingers nervously filling his mouth, "that his passing on warn't exactly an accident. That the bride was sort of, well, that the girl, that she was fighting the old feller off, and. . . ." The boy reddened profusely and hid his steaming face in his "java."

"Fighting him *off?*" Buddy queried relentlessly, his eyes, despite themselves, popping like a demented lighthouse keeper's clogged ears. "Then you mean that the dirty little rumor. . . ?"

"Correct in all partic'lars, I'm afraid," Dick confessed. "The *coupé da grace* blow to his wrinkled temple came from a violently snapped garter which he'd, in some kind of mad fashion, got his old face tangled up in."

"Lord!" Buddy breathed in horror. "And here, I've been sitting and thinking of the old fellow with mingled feelings of warmth and patronization. Yet, he died a common pervert, exactly like the fellows in the raincoats."

"I reckon so," Dick said in a whisper. "His funeral," he shuddered, "was picketed by the Porno-Death Kommando of the Daughters of Durga International." He paused, then passed a sweaty hand over his wiry stubble. "So, as far as *advice* goes, why, pshaw!, I 'low that any request, even if the duffer was still with us, why it'd be replied to with a risky story, that's what I 'low!"

"Live and learn," Buddy had a chance to say before a stranger burst quietly through the verdant screen. "How fine to see you young fellows," he said with robust simplicity. "My name is de Kock, novelist and correspondent. I trust that you lads are not unfamiliar with good letters?" And with this provocative remark, the gentleman made himself at "home."

"Hello! I'm Miss Tutti-Frutti of 1982. I just have a minute to say that this idea that Dick Witherspoon has that my creamcake poses are somehow who *I* am is just all wrong! As Miss Tutti-Frutti, I visit military bases, hospitals, battleships, wonderful and caring homeless kitchens, county fairs, amusement parks, mortuaries, and car dealerships. All right, so I show some attractive leg now and then, but it's for a good cause. In real life, my name is, for the record, Karen, and I'm interested in a career in theatre, movies, cinema, or television, in stagecraft, you know? And, of course, being a responsible anchorperson. Because the news is important to everybody, not just to people who never ever look at creamcake glossies. I've never actually heard that expression, 'creamcake,' by the way. Is that a business word?"

"Hello! I'm Miss Understand. Karen, if you like. My current enthusiasms, even though I'm what many call middle-aged but I like to think of as 'older but wiser,' as in 'if you don't want my peaches climb my tree anyway,' include unashamedly revealing my attractive, hard-won body to the *right* man, and he doesn't have to be handsome, just caring and sensitive and with a sense of humor and a few bucks. I also right now just love the marvelous sequel, finally!, to *Unicorn Crimson, Unicorn Grey—The Duke of the Golden Prong*—and, let's see, Civil War Songs of the Union Army, and the poems of Rupert Brooks, especially the one beginning 'O little friend, your nose is ready.' The oddest thing about poetry, Rupert Brooks's or anybody's, is that I first got interested in the stuff after reading an article on it, in, of all places, my ex-fiancé's favorite magazine, *Universe of Action.* Really! I remember being so surprised that I called Fred's, that was his name, Fred's attention to it.

Fred, as usual, just grunted and went on doing some of that darn research
of his on some movie something or other. Thank God we never got
married! You don't think this skirt is too short for me, do you?"

What's this note here? U.P. What's this mean?
  No idea. U.P.? Up?
  Well, yes. But.
  No idea then. Sounds familiar, though. U.P. Up.

April finishes another bottle of the elixir which, in its wonted role as
a "changer of reality," is indeed changing the semi-comatose woman's
liver into something very like pumice stone. She thinks to get up, but
is peremptorily arrested by a vision, one so powerful as to seem, as
she may later phrase it, "trust Mike Smit's fuzz-hair" ["just like it
was there"]. April's vision is of herself twenty-five years earlier, her
hair jet black, her eyes clear, her figure slender in a miniskirt, sleeveless
crocheted sweater, and close-fitting suede boots, her lipstick a pale
pink-white. She is on the landing just outside the emergency-exit door
of the small company for which she works as a clerk-typist, engaged in
certain sexual activities with a tall, mustachioed UPS driver. Perhaps
Catullus may, once again, be called upon to describe the nature of
April's current adventures, of which this present one is fairly representative:

> nunc in quadriviis et angiportis
> glubit magnanimos Remi nepotes.

As the grinning UPS man, resplendent in his crisp chocolate-brown
uniform, reaches his climax, his eyes starting forth with surprise and
delight, and wait till he gets back to tell the guys in the garage!, April,
rigid in her sweated bed, a knuckle in her mouth, stares in terror at the
tiny, motile penises wriggling blindly in their thousands on the walls,
ceiling, floor, and bed. "Oh! oh!" she gasps, meaning "No! no!" Or is it
that she gasps "No! no!" meaning "Oh! oh!"? Whatever, the miniature
phalloi pay her no heed.

We are finally in possession of certain information which may serve to
clarify the occasional difficulties, ambiguities, problems, contradictions,

and paradoxes of the matters here under "review," as we prefer to say. There is, of course, given the shifting nature of information, the possibility that the aforementioned difficulties, ambiguities, problems, contradictions, and paradoxes may be compounded. With this caveat firmly in mind, the information follows.

Nota: Valefor, Mentor of Thieves, who appears to man as a thief, and who leads those with whom he is familiar into theft, is the fiend ultimately responsible for Norman's possession of Guy Lewis's painting *The Valley of the Shadow of Death,* sometimes called the "Moon River" of Abstract Expressionism. Valefor has told of the particulars of the theft—carried out, apparently, by Bart Kahane in return for a little black dress with matching shoes, hat, and bag—to Vassago, a mighty prince, "good" by nature. Vassago immediately visited Norman and told him the seamy story behind Bart's sudden offer of the painting. Norman was not especially pleased by the visit, since it was Vassago's fancy that evening to appear dressed in a suit of an eerie, shifting, shimmeringly iridescent blue of a shade "to look upon which," so declares Antoine de la Mothe Cadillac in his study of the *Grand Grimoire, Ventriloquists' Dummies,* "is to feel the wind of madness pass across one's face." Norman has since placed the painting in storage.

Nota: Vepar, Duke of Storms and Tempests, appeared quite recently to Mamie Morsett, the celebrated prizewinning poet of "meticulously exact traditional forms with a crisp modern punch!" as Michelle Caccatanto has, perhaps justifiably, often written. The demon, incarnate as a fetching mermaid, swam up to Ms. Morsett on her beloved wind-strewn, tempest-clogged beach ("the sea, the sun, and the quiet peace always seem to rejuvenate me," the poet has repeatedly claimed) to warn her to "lay off," as he carefully put it, his friends, the clams, and to find herself another subject, "like Vermont," the sprite reportedly said, "or potatoes," before heading back to sea. Ms. Morsett, in an admittedly stultifying telephone conversation, threatens that she'll be "in close touch" with prizewinner Peter Viereck concerning "new subject matter" and the ever-handy iambic pentameter, "the breath of heroes," sometime after Labor Day. Good news at last! In the meantime, she and her husband, a prizewinning instructor of Creative Writing and a fine poet in his own right, are having some repairs made on their little gale-buffeted cottage, or "shack," built in 1682 by the Puritan ecclesiastic and mystic Geoffroy Chandeler.

Nota: Vine, Monster of Witches, who is fond of making calm waters stormy, is the diabolical force behind the producer Virginia Vivaldi's suspiciously megalomaniacal plans to film, over the next ten years, a series of "operals" based on old Tom Mix classics—*Rifles on the Pecos, Rio Grande Leather Man, Guns of the Colorado, Claw Sky, Dude Chump!,* and others not so well known. In a tumultuous press conference marked by senseless violence and sexual innuendo, Ms. Vivaldi, pressed on her decision to commit hundreds of millions of dollars to an admittedly quixotic project fraught with risk, angrily denounced the legacy of economic frugality passed on by the late president of Jayvee Studios, Jerrold "Jambo" Vizard, calling him "a man with a mind like a Volvo owner's." The conference broke up soon after in a melee of angry shouts, threats, screams, wild punches, and indecent gropings, when Ms. Vivaldi's husband and business manager, Quirt Bimbeau, suggested that Mr. Vizard had been "a sexual slave and dupe of Minna von Hattiesburg," characterized by Mr. Bimbeau as "a big whore, like."

Nota: A long-awaited letter from an actual professor whom we occasionally employ to do scutwork informs us that *The Voyage Out,* attributed by some scholars to Jack London, was "probably" written by Guillaume Apollinaire under the pseudonym "Virginia Stephen." The professor also takes the opportunity to give us some excruciatingly complete details and academic anecdotes concerning his latest TRIP TO EUROPE, which, as far as we can discover, was "wonderful" and "exciting." He notes that he "hated to come back" and that there is "nothing like Europe." He is a heck of a guy, and let's indeed hope that he "got *some* work done."

Nota: Vual, the Camel, he who speaks Egyptian, he who excites friendship even between enemies, he who arouses the love of women for each other, was, in the early '40s, the original choice for the Women's Army Corps' (WAC) tutelary patron and guiding spirit. After revelations concerning the deity's true nature had rocked the youthful WAC to its very foundations, most of which were, in accordance with government specifications, lightly boned, a new spiritual leader, Lord Ridingcrop, the twelfth Earl of Terraplane, was named. Soon after the feisty nobleman's extraordinary recreational tastes became known to the Army, he was supplanted by the city of Waco, "Wedge of Paradise," for what the Joint Chiefs of Staff termed "obvious reasons."

"You could get a nice tattoo in Waco years ago," Walt says, strolling into the A & P. He's wearing plaid trousers, which, in a civilized society, would lead to his arrest and imprisonment. "A very nice tattoo, nothing gauche or fey, but redolent of the values of the Southwest. Fairly *smacking* of them. A lone star, a rattler, a scorpion rampant. . . ."

Walt? Who is Walt? What *is* this?

"Instead of being rude and making a fool of yourself into the bargain," Walt says, "you might tell me if the A & P has any copies of *Absalom! Absalom!* left amid the crisp, tangy apples."

Look for yourself. Whoever you are.

"And these trousers are not, believe you me, *my* idea," Walt grumbles.

Myrtle Wandajajiecowicz has not yet been *officially* informed that had *The Orange Dress* been published under her name, it would have been reviewed in the *Sheetmetal Patio Gazette,* the *Polish-American Accordion Intelligencer,* and the *Platform Workers' Crafts Weekly,* and nowhere else.

Item: War Action, the original and still *top* magazine for *nonstop combat thrills,* announces its intention to expand its coverage. Beginning with the BIG October issue, *War Action* will include stories of the WAR on CRIME, featuring a regular monthly "Crime Tips" column by State Trooper Kimberley Butz, author of *I Maimed a Rapist—And Learned to Laugh Again!,* and some hunk of woman!

But the strange foreign woman seems to have returned, and is standing again in front of the house, while Bunny peers at her from behind a yellowed lace curtain. She is at her wit's end, because as far as she can tell, her father has decided to stop trembling, quivering, shaking, gasping, and, for that matter, breathing. There is an excellent chance that he is dead. And now this stupid, ugly woman is back, she is not in Israel or Brooklyn, but here! And, oh God! What's happened to the chicken coop? It's smoldering, yes, but there are no flames! "Oh Jesus!

Oh Jesus!" Bunny says, "what good is *smoldering?*" She runs to the door, sobbing, as they occasionally say, "uncontrollably." Frieda looks up and stops feeling the sweat-soaked areas of her shatteringly homely dress, smiles in her friendly American way, and raises her smutty hand in imbecile salute.

"Go away!" Bunny screams. "I'm *not* Bunny Lewis! I'm *not!* I never went to the Art Students' League! My name is Joanne Ward! My father is, of course, Mr. Ward, one of the neighborhood's great barbecuers and machine-shop teachers, currently retired and perhaps deceased. My mother, *Mrs.* Ward, died some years ago of a sudden unexpected outpouring of bile, hatred, and despair centered on the celebration of the holidays, especially those 'robust' holidays having to do with colorful dried leaves, objects of warm earth tones, wrapping paper, and bushels of savage food! Especially defunct birds! My ex-husband, Guy, will come and tell you *bar stories* if I just give him a call, that's all it takes. *One call,* and he'll tell you movingly funny anecdotes of gin-mill life for a solid week! Now, get out! Get out! Go away! I can't stand it anymore." Frieda looks at her and begins, once again, to walk away, while Joanne sinks to her knees at the door, directly under the place where Mrs. Ward was wont, each fall, to hang sprays of Indian corn, dried leaves, deformed gourds, and other impedimenta of the harvest. This scene may represent, if we are not careful, that which is meant by the hoary phrase, "there's no escaping the past." But suddenly, a noise is heard from within the house. It seems to be, it is! Mr. Ward calling hoarsely for his barbecue implements! Apparently he is alive, after all. Time will tell. There's no escaping the past. Let a smile be your umbrella.

Item: Despite his odd method of "reasoning," Blow is correct in his assumption that he was conceived behind the bandstand of the Bluebird Inn. His father, Dave Warren, one of New Jersey's legendary fox-trot instructors and egg-seekers, speaks on his deathbed in Netcong: "Hello there, nice of you to come and see an old man. I'm on my deathbed in beautiful Netcong, New Jersey, a place in which the late Alexander B. Davis was once served an absurd mixed drink which he dryly dubbed a 'Brooklyn.' It is also the birthplace of Andy Warhol, who got his start in the exciting art business right here, as well as the architectural paradigm for much that is good and real and spiritual in our nation's capital, Washington, D.C. I thought I'd come clean and confess that I'm Blow's dad all right, although I'm afraid that I don't know *who* his mom is. Sniff. (Indicates eyes brimming with tears.) I'd guess it's either Sailor Steve or Werner Smitts. Whew! What a load off my mind! It's also kind of nice to cash in my chips wearing these really cool and comfortable all-cotton pajamas. It's a real killer-diller, gate!" In the background can be heard the familiar strains of "String of Pearls." Or is it "Skylark" or "Deep Purple"?

Duke Washington sits in his furnished room in front of a fan, drinking beer and listening to old bebop records. He's snapping his fingers, oop! He's tapping his foot, bop! He's scatting along with the solos, sh-bam! After all these years, Duke is the same boring lout. Though bald and sadly gone to seed, yet hath he his hipness entire. He wants to go out and sit in an air-conditioned bar, but there's a chance, a very *slim* chance, that Henri Kink, that goddam square jive-ass Jew mother-fucking turkey faggot, the producer of, among other hit shows, the long-time ratings leader among daytime soaps, *A Waste of Shame,* might call with an offer of a small part in *Mickey's Bologna,* the new comedy smash series. Duke hates Henri as he hates almost everything, for he is much too perfect, too hip, too smooth, too knowing, too well-dressed, too *streetwise* for all this poke-lip ugliness, too canny, collected, wary. He opens another can of beer. Smooth, wary, collected, canny. Oop-bop-sh-bam!

"What?" Fred says, struggling against his restraints. "There's no *real* Duke Washington! Duke Washington's a role once played by none other than the shadowy Baylor Freeq, one of my many interests, as you know. Remember, girls? Remember I told you in the restaurant of my research?"

"You are a funny cute geezer and a big old baby," one of the girls says, watching her sister begin the notorious *cannoli tremolo* on Fred's painfully alert body.

"Oh sweet Jesus," Fred gasps. Or utters hoarsely. "What in the heck is *that?*"

"You are just as *darling* as a ten-cent button!" his ministering angel laughs.

We were asked last month by an editor of our acquaintance if we'd be good enough to help in the "difficult yet rewarding" task of bringing a first book by "an unknown author" to the attention of the "reading public," *those* feckless sons of bitches! Well. We have tried to, how shall we say?, "put it off" in the hope that the unknown author might die, or that the editor might forget the essentially innocent ski weekend he delights in perversely recalling our reluctant participation in. (Indicates pile of incriminating photographs.) We insist now as we insisted then that *no one* was drugged or hypnotized or blackmailed (indicates pile of screenplays in which the line "blackmail is an ugly word" is underlined in each) into "doing" anything! Not the blind Scoutmaster, the Rosicrucian dental technician, the truss model, the thrill-hungry housewife whose lips were starved for soul-searing kisses of abandon, and certainly not the hook-and-ladder company captain with the big family and happy dogs! However, friendship worth keeping is friendship worth working for, or at. So, the following contribution to the life of modern letters. (Indicates wave of nausea.)

FOR IMMEDIATE RELEASE

Esther Waters, the dynamic author of *Odd Ends,* who humorously describes herself as being no more than a "fed-up housewife" just five years ago, tells, in her compelling book of personal and personalized essays, of her abandonment of her boring husband and restrictive family in order to "feel things I'd always wanted to feel right down to my shoes." Feel she did, as *Odd Ends* testifies. More than merely one sprightly, cool, intelligent, amused, and spirited woman's look at the strange, surprising, fascinating backwaters of American life, *Odd Ends* presents us with wholly possible and viable alternatives to what Ms. Waters calls "the rat race" of modern life, the "wasting of our natural powers through getting and spending." As she so eloquently puts it in her Introduction, "I wanted to be free, to fly again, to know what it was to make great discoveries in the laboratory and studio, as well as to star in the boardroom and the bedroom!" In this compelling and often shocking book, you will discover:

THE LITTLE TOWN of Webster Groves, Missouri, whose *entire population* learned conversational Greek in three days, and was soon chatting of *delissos, massgrevvi, soss, aybol,* and *spigtami* like the sons and daughters of Ulysses.

BILL WEEPERS, a highly respected tennis spectator, who unabashedly tells of his love for Adolf Hitler—the Man, the Moustache, the Myth behind the Meerschaum pipe.

THE DOOMED PATIENT who feels that the courteous yet hollow slogan "Welcome to Kansas City" is no substitute for the daily Popsicle now denied him.

THE SUBWAY MOTORMAN, Benjamin Welles, who disappeared in the Amazon Basin during a vacation jaunt and was rescued by a tribe of gentle ostriches.

EDGAR GRAHAM WEN, who speaks with startling candor of his horror of culottes.

RESPECTED APPELLATE JUSTICE Harold Wenj, who reveals the shocking practice of sexual self-abuse throughout the judiciary; "It's the robes," he says sadly.

THE WEST VILLAGE "character," J. Bartholomew Whammo, who has lived for three years in a tent set up in the kitchen of New York's finest *cabochon* restaurant.

AND MUCH MORE * Including * the sickening truth behind the steamy luncheon scene in the box-office gold mine *What a Girl!* * the hilarious story of how "Vomit and Die!" became the award-winning docudrama *What's for Supper?* * the "rodeo marriage" of "Giggles" Whinge and "Gallie" Bilge, judged by *Today's Genetics* to be the stupidest women in the world * the inspirational and touching story of E.B. White's invention of English grammar *

Odd Ends by Esther Waters. Available soon at your bookstore.

"As if Pascal's *Pensées* were written by St. Augustine and Sheila Graham."

—*Tamara Shicksa-Rabinowitzowicjiez*

His unseasonably heavy tweed jacket reeking of dried sweat, a despairingly seedy Vance Whitestone hesitates before entering his shop, The Good Company. The place depresses him, the costumes and uniforms depress him. His *bored salesclerks* depress him. The Florence Nightingale Camisole. Oh God. The Stern Stepmother Bathrobe. Oh God. The Ilse Koch Whip-and-Garter Combo. Oh God. He stands, smelling himself, fresh sweat soaking the rank, threadbare fabric. "Is it possible that I once wrote interoffice memos?" he says to his tie. (Indicates proverbially grease-stained tie.) "Is it really true that I once gave orders to Lee Jefferson, undressed Karen Ostrom, even unto her silken flesh, was a business partner of Lincoln Gom's?" He steps back from the shop and stands in an adjoining doorway. "Lincstone Productions was once half mine?" Vance starts to cry, then begins a pained, maddened dance, bringing his knees, in exaggerated prancing, almost to his chin, hurling his hands into the air, fingers opening and closing spasmodically as if in an attempt to catch flies. "Weird Widow Corset-Mask Set," he sobs. "Oh God, oh God." He would, quite possibly, whistle in his dementia, except that, as we know, he is a stranger to the art of whistling.

White Sun Talent Associates is, for all practical purposes, run by the scheming and cold-hearted mogul Edward Beshary. Janos Kooba, one of Beshary's partners, has been for some years now engaged almost exclusively in his literary pursuits, and Albert Pearson, the third partner, has privately disclosed that he is not averse to selling his shares to Beshary. "Who needs the aggravation?" he often says, slapping his knee, or, when at home, ogling his still-attractive wife of thirty-eight years, Ruthie. Beshary has ruthlessly, cruelly, and coldly stepped up his efforts to absorb those companies "ripened up well for a simple plucking," as he puts it in his still-uncertain English. So, besides being a trifle, ah, *tapette,* he also scorns the language of the great nation that has made him rich! As we know. Among his recent acquisitions are Contemporary Ventures Inc., White Sun Village, White Sun Cabanaland, the Black Basement, Crescent and Chattaway, Marvelous Magazine Management Corporation, *Scranton Arts Times,* and Daughters of Durga International. Yet, for all his success, soon the dear, stubbly face of Berthe—as well as his hairy gams, calloused feet, bloodshot eyes—will be gone from his life forever. Of course, if Durga, the Serene, the Relentless, the Unknowable, has her way, *everything* will be gone from his life forever. *Telex bunt impetigo, trio gator.*

At precisely 4:00 P.M., Whitey enters Village Victuals to spell Bud. It is not too much to say that this hapless young man despises his emotional problems and is also getting sick and tired of the severe beatings administered to him by enraged and insulted women shoppers. "I can't help it," he says at times to a pal with whom he likes to share an orange-colored "drink" and a bag of crunchy things. "I'm not like, you know, a *sex* fiend. I don't even have a big one like Bud! I *really* hate it when the ladies laugh and call me 'Teeny Peeny' before they beat the shit out of me. What a life being a despised pervert!"

"Hello! I'm Miss Whole-Grains, although I don't feel too darn healthy standing in this dirty, drafty hallway listening to Sylvie howl in what the English language, rising to the occasion, calls 'exquisite pleasure.' Well, I don't know about exquisite, but more power to her! And let's hope the poor horny creep with the raincoat looking in the window is having a little fun too. I'm *actually* Karen Ostrom, *really,* and it wasn't *my* body they found twenty years ago at The Red Swan. My God, was that twenty years ago? Anyway, I heard it was Sheila Henry they found there, but Sheila just died *today.* At the beach, I hear, that's what I'm here to tell Sylvie. Oh hell, who cares about us anyway? Incidentally, I've been looking for Vance to see if I might borrow some money from him, but people—well, *people*—say that he's just disappeared. I could use a decent winter coat, I mean that's why. God, I don't know why I'm sniffling. Something's wrong with me."

Then too: *Whores in Heels* Picketed by American Fellatio League as "Demeaning to Working Women"; Rupert "Roger" Whytte-Blorenge to Open First Shoefreex Store in Wichita Falls; Mme Marguerite Wig Denies Ties to Wilkes-Barre Banana Orgies; Scholar Suggests "Sheldon Feinstein" William the Conqueror's True Name; Freddie Willingmouth to Direct "Win a Bundle" Great-Fiction Promo Drive; Latest Research Shows Windsor Knot Cause of Unwanted Body Hair; Newly Discovered Papers Reveal Yvor Winters May Have Thought Wittgenstein Author of *Tender Buttons;* Marie Louise "Chinks" Wong to Star in *A Different Slant to Love;* Emma Woodhouse, 58, "Beach Babe" of '60s, Dies of Lust; Furor in GOP as Senator Katie Woodward Claims Husband "Wears the Skirts"; Leonard Woolf Invented "for Lark" by Virginia Woolf, Experts Argue.

"You'll excuse our startled appearance and unfriendly demonstrations of a perhaps boorish nature, I trust," Buddy said, flushing hotly with the memory of the crude language and shocking bodily contortions with which he and Dick somewhat unfairly greeted the distinguished author Paul de Kock. "We've had a number of right unpleasant surprises these past few days, or weeks, or so, here in the merciless brush, eh Dick?" the sincere lad softly queried of his friend.

"Tarnation o' sakes!" Dick shouted in an excess of nervous

prostration. "You say 'a number'? Pshaw! Seems like onto more'n a zillion on 'em, tol'able more and then some, or so, to me!"

"Pay my staunch companion Witherspoon's somewhat disabled language skills little or no heed, Mr. de Kock," Buddy inveigled desperately, the firelight leaping still toward the soft black sky studded with numberless, shivering astro-quarks. How far away they seemed!

"I understand completely," de Kock pensively grimaced, "being an author with profound insights into human nature and all. I half suspect," he laughed richly, suddenly helping himself to some more biscuit stew and "jamoke," "that you fellows may be feeling the effects of *mountain fever,* caused by rarefied, ozonified air, half-raw chuck, voracious hicks, the frustration of one's dearest plans, and the absence of the gentling abilities of female companionship. Sound familiar?" the scribe added, uncannily.

"I *say,* old man!" Buddy spat in surprise. "That's extraordinary! It's almost as if you've been dogging our steps, listening to our chats, fair undermining, I might say, our varietal impetuosity, at least performatively, for days on end!"

"Tut-tut," the wise author imperiously choughed. "It's simply that I've seen many cases of the ailment. One of my dearest friends, Lord Woppie of Azania, almost lost his *gules sinister* because of the devilish malady. Incidentally, old Woppie served as the model for Hubert, eleventh Earl of Worcestershire, in my *Gus Takes on the Mauve Sachet*—perhaps the most popular of the 'Gus de Toite' series. You've read it, of course? Or perhaps you've read *Georgette,* which, I dare say, would be more to *your* liking," de Kock smirked.

"I'm afraid not, old man," Buddy remarked, his eyes apologetically agog. "I find modern literature much too *drastic.*"

"We kind of cotton onto classical authors with uplift messages of the caliber of your Jean Ingelow, whose clean, muscle-toned verses helped us considerable just a day or two yonder back to search out a powerful cool and laughing freshet rill!" Dick proudly breathed.

"Jean Ingelow?" de Kock blustered, inadvertently kicking a glowing ember into a nearby primitive potting shed hulking darkly in sad disrepair. "You're better served reading Wordsworth and his leech-besotted doggerel of nostalgic blubbering! Better served with *World of Signs* by Derek Tights, 'the housewife's tamale.' Why, boys, *nobody* has read Jean Ingelow since before World War I. She's thought of as a large cardboard object, no more!" The embittered author heatedly spat into the blazing shed, meanwhile flinging his arms about in an excess of literary ambition gone to seed, and envy unfettered. Unpleasantness was manifestly palpable!

"So," Buddy lightly declared some time later, "you're on your way to the village of Misty Crag for some seafood, eh? Isn't it odd, Dick, that *we* thought Misty Crag but the *nom de forêt* of a beetling scarp, as shown on reputable, up-to-date maps?"

" 'Odd' is the gimcrack, gewgaw, tin-plate word for it, Buddy," Dick concurred in a subtly moronic voice, baring his teeth at their arrogant guest. Although the boy could not countenance the notion, the truth of the matter is that he had been sorely smitten by Miss Ingelow's poems, and, through them, by the poet herself. Goodness only knows what the lad would have done had Buddy shown him the frontispiece engraving of the poet in a lace snood! But the future tormentor of a number of resentful clerks took care not to let the well-fingered tome out of his sight or his hands!

"This stupid, wayward conversation follows closely on the feet of the dialogue between Mary Siffay and Thoresen Gossard in my *Lamond and the Loony.* You've surely read it!" de Kock hissed malevolently, his eyes gleaming in the firelight that danced as lightly as do slightly demented lighthouse beams. But Buddy and Dick pretended to whisper to each other, tittering vapidly, a surefire tactic, which, most often, drove craven adversaries into the blind bewilderment of the beaver trapped in the rude basement of his woodland home by a sudden watery onslaught of spring bilboes. Finally, after what seemed an eternity of fake confidences, Buddy remarked, "No, my literary friend, we haven't read *Lamondada Loony. Write and Be Happy,* the premier handbook for the budding author who longs to tap into the vibrant electrodynamics which inform the sizzling world of the pulsing media business, places your book in the DONT'S section, I'm happily forced to admit. Your *My Voice in Raymond* also languishes there," he boyishly whooped in triumph.

" 'Pears a feller might be 'lowed as how a certain *other* feller maybe won his own self the booby prize in the world of big-money *power* literature," Dick snapped, flinging a rock at a group of curious ferrets that just then shambled swiftly by.

"Why, you impudent, nondescript rubes!" de Kock exploded shame-lessly, his avid muscles straining toward a nameless lost—O lost!—perfection of once-glowing youth, now gone, gone! Gone forever! "What can you two petty clerks, shambling about like those ferrets who just passed by, know about this pathetic mountain, owned, yes, *owned,* I say, in proud manumission by the University of Chicago, huddled there below? What, I say, also, can you know of the agony of creative-prose composition, its blank pages, its typos, its faithful clichés?" Suddenly, the excited author was on his feet, and in his gnarled right hand, his typing hand, a hand as powerful as the arm from which it naturally protruded, Buddy and Dick glimpsed, with some alarm, the flash of a clasplock-switch lamprey!

As the boys prepared to flee in terror into the saturnine, fog-choked bosk, an attractive young woman, in some sort of figure-flattering uniform, strode proudly into the clearing on lustrous pumps. The boys paused in their potential career, and de Kock, thoroughly chastened, smashed his weapon with a slab of calcimine. As all three goggled, the woman spoke.

"Hi! I'm Karen Wyoming! I'm *really* sorry to impinge so unex-pectedly on your rugged, manly interlude, but this secluded site happens, like, to be on the path to Chinatown, whither I'm headed, to convince our Oriental compadres that the delirious skies would be, like, *moreso* if they'd just sort of *fly* more! They seem to prefer to poke around with their mu-shus and gai-goos and noodle things. Anyway, I want to get down there *sometime* before the Year of the Snail, for gosh sakes! I know that you fellas suspect that I'm all business because of the really intense sales-persuasion mode I'm in, but believe me, when I'm closeted with my guy, a frozen-dessert engineer, we really *work* at having an imaginative, fulfilling, pleasantly kinky, and guilt-free sex life, despite the odd chancre now and again. We also love good histor-ical novels like *The Dame from Troy's Corsets.* Hi!"

Then she was gone, and with her intelligent and winsome "Hi!" echoing in the miasmic mists, the lash and sting of the trio's late dis-agreement seemed to dissipate like a lightning bolt. The three embraced fondly, and the boys loudly proclaimed that rarely had such a fine fellow as the noted author stumbled upon their camp. Or even camps! For his part, de Kock, in an explosion of stunning humility, passed up the golden opportunity to call attention to the obvious fact that *he* had authored the novel spoken of with undimmed praise by the comely airline employee. He was proud, and rightly so, of his virile modesty, as were the boys. They were, in a manner of speaking, *all* proud.

"We're deuced proud of your enchanting modesty, de Kock, old cruller," Buddy confessed sheepishly, as the three set out in a cold drizzle. "Such silence, as my dad, Old Buddy, once put it, is 'golden chaff that gilds the chinks of paupers' cells.'" The lad wept bitterly into his faded tallboy for a moment, then recovered his storied aplomb.

"Thank you, dear boy," the portly author blushed innocuously, draping his neckerchief over his abashed face. Some time briskly passed, and then came the inevitable moment for the boys and de Kock to part company. A rustic signpost at a gale-whipped crossroads proclaimed that MISTY CRAG lay some few miles to the north. With a furtive display of snots and half-hidden tears, there were embraces, embraces and kisses, yes!, rough, manly, stubbly, crude, brutal, painful, and effluvious embraces, and wet, hairy kisses all 'round! Then, almost oneirically, Buddy and Dick watched de Kock plunge, at first lurchingly, then "ass" over teakettle, down the steep, mud-clogged road which led to the secluded town's legendary clam house, hidden, as devotees discover, to their peril, amid mounds of aromatic furze. The boys, crying openly now, blindly adjusted their moocher-pack web-sling straps and walked on in silence, their garments merrily steaming in what was surely the blazing sun!

"I reckon how that de Kock feller is at bottom *all right,* Buddy," Dick carefully enthused, "though for a spell I plumb thought on right walloping his head something fierce to learn him to get on with plain folks."

"Hm," Buddy noted with thoughtful alacrity, "I agree, Dick. A capital fellow, yet I too had a bad moment or two during which I rather basely thought of assault and battery and imagined his crushed body at the bottom of a yawning gravel pit, many of which, as you can quite easily see, hereabouts hazardously abound." Buddy paused, his eyes fixed on his steadily tramping feet. "I'm half-persuaded that much of his choler and imbroglionic actions are directly related to his unfortunately suggestive surname. A fellow comes in for a deuced hazing when he has to bear the burden of a depressing monicker like that, don't you agree, Dick?"

"I . . . I guess . . . so," Dick said uncertainly. "Sure. I . . . reckon so."

Buddy stared at his companion in amazement, and was impatiently about to recall to him, as an analogy and reminder, the tragic, depraved fate of their schoolmate, Herbert Shitface, when Dick spoke again.

"Say, Buddy," he blushingly droned, apparently dismissing de Kock's appellative problems summarily, "is there a picture of some sort or type of, uh, Miss Ingelow, uh, somewhere in her poem book of verses? It seems I reckon I thought once to have got a flitting glance at summat like," he shrieked at last, in barely controllable passion.

"Ha! Ha!" Buddy cackled nervously. "I fear not, Dick." The last thing he wished, now that they were well-nigh home, saving, of course, a brief detour at the great university, beetling quietly in the shale bluffs and devastating sunlight at the foot of the precipitous yaw of scuppered hills, was a lovesick gangle of a chum, panting and sighing and grappling with unbecoming and repeated tumescences, instead of keeping a sharp eye out for flash stook-blazes and psychotic carnivores. "No indeed, Dick," he lied expertly, his handsome face taking on the unforgettable qualities of a mass of dampened, unresponsive cheesecloth. "That's a steel engraving of Yasmine Danscul, Miss Ingelow's constant, ah, her constant, ah, let me not say companion, rather, as the French so suavely put it, her *femme entretenue,* or 'entertaining lady friend.' "

"Oh," Dick pouted sullenly, and in a flagrant excess of venereal pique he threw away his lightweight aluminum mess kit. Clang! it went. At that moment, they topped a crude rise, and before them, dazzling white in the sun, hulked Ye Olde Red Swanne Inne, empty now save for the bygone glories of half-stifled memories, still barely flickering in the hearts of older folks, the vast majority of whom were probably dead.

"What's thet?" Dick said ungraciously, lapsing clumsily into the rube-like twang which Buddy well knew would doubtless preclude a chief clerkship for his stubborn friend.

"*That,* old man," Buddy trilled fruitily, "*that* means that we've somehow come down on the other, some might say the 'wrong' side of the mountain, and now stand at the border of Yonkers!"

"Do you mean to tell a feller that, that, that. . . ?" Dick burbled stupidly, lowering his suddenly heavy torso to the cracked concrete, or asphalt, of the attractive city's outermost street. Perhaps he remembered that in Yonkers, "jewel beyond the Bronx," all streets lead implacably to what the townspeople dub "urban life."

"Yes!" Buddy said, joining his comrade on the ground. "The great university has apparently been, in some remarkable manner, moved to Yonkers! This is indeed Yonkers, for that ancient pile is the world-famed Red Swanne! This is the sort of capital suspension of the laws of nature which gives pause even to hard-driving chief executive officers who brook no nonsense and work twice as hard as their underlings! Great Scott! On the other hand, now that I am somewhat calmer, I realize that neither the university *or* Chinatown, its exotic neighbor, is visible. Hm, perhaps I err in my loose and easy, not to say glib talk of miracles," the boy concluded, thoughtfully placing his knuckles into his mouth, which seemed quietly to await them.

And so they wonderingly sat, drinking in the sight of the friendly town, birthplace of Andy Warhol; warmly dopey in the enervating sunshine, each knew, in his quietly pounding heart, the strong, somehow good feeling that would not leave, that would perhaps *never* leave; each knew the wonderful feeling of having confronted the strange secret of Mystery Mountain, and the even more wonderful feeling that the fog-enshrouded nights of the mountain no longer held their wonted fear, their wonted Janus-faced dichotomy of both fear and excitement at the same time, and in, of course, the same place, or two places at once! Soon, the boys would probably rise and attempt to find their way home, home, where a hot supper waited on the groaning table of a cozy kitchen. Home! they thought as one.

Yet somewhere, somewhere amid the clammy winds of the highest peaklike tors and crevasses, Ned Blutwurst, his altered features shockingly like those of the aging Elizabeth Barrett Browning *couchant,* was, even now, in the macabre process of destroying, without leaving a trace, Knute and the damaging knowledge he possessed of the Cambridge regatta scandal. *Whooshhh!* the mere shell of a car roared, as obliterating flames engulfed it.

We have been, in a word, *besieged* by informants complaining of and correcting certain errors in the foregoing episode—apparently the final one—of *Buddy and His Boys on Mystery Mountain.* Although we doubt the importance of such complaints and corrections, much as we doubt the importance of the narrative itself, let alone its necessity, several brutal threats persuade us to include the received data, without, we hasten to say, any commentary of our own to temper their inconsequentiality.

(a.) None of Paul de Kock's novels has ever been translated into English, although certain sections of *La Dame aux trois corsets* were included, in translation, in the anthology, *Modern Midwestern Sex,* edited by Horace Rosette.

(b.) Paul de Kock's "breakthrough" stories, which caught the attention of Virginia Woolf, "the overbred scribbler," are, unaccountably, not mentioned in the episode. They arc "Mon Hochepot, hein?" (trans. "You're the Top") and "Je suis bien content d'avoir terminé cette dissertation d'anglais" (trans. "Yours for No Down Payment Easy Terms").

(c.) Yasmine Danscul was not yet born when Jean Ingelow died. She is, in fact, an old friend of the boys' florid and debauched Dean and a sometime lecturer on "Odd Costumes and Business Success."

YoYo seems to have lost control of herself and is calling for her father, whoever he might be, to come out of the saloon in which, drunk or sober, he cuts something of a "fine-figured job of a man." After some half-hour of tears, threats, and pleading, John Greene Czcu, staggering slightly, emerges from the New Rensselaer Bar and Grill.

"Where is the Chief?" he unexpectedly asks. "My great, noble, redskinned savage of a blue chief?"

"You ain't my pa!" YoYo screams, falling quickly into a sodden heap of out-of-style garments. Czcu reenters the saloon to sporadic, albeit somewhat drunken applause.

Janos Kooba, noting this sidewalk playlet from the limousine which is speeding him toward the airport, whence he will depart this evening for a fete in his native Yugoslavia, shakes his grizzled head. "And the fools thought for long and exceedingly difficult years that *The Curse* was too melodramatic! It is enough to make a lesser man than I threaten to sough interminably." With this, he sinks back into the plush upholstery, his eyes, which but a moment before had darted about like the demented lighthouse-keeper father of a jilted daughter with Heinrich Himmler's baby in her womb, peaceful at last.

"Vot? Vot? Fair iss hiss paperss?"

Despite the fact that Fred's mind is curdled, if not devastated, by the indefatigable ministrations of the Frankenstein girls, it appears that he is correct in his opinion concerning Duke Washington's "actuality." The proof may be found in the small bedroom of an apartment situated somewhere in the midst of the semipulsing borough of Queens, where sits Chico Zeek, raconteur, experimental filmmaker, director, dogged admirer of *The Orange Dress,* and borrower of trifling sums. He turns the volume down on his radio so that he may hear his neighbors, Gladys and Angelo Zeno, go to it like the wren and small gilded fly. As he settles back to listen to the shouts, screams, splintering furniture, breaking glass, threats, curses, and wild laughter of the rutting couple, his eyes fall on the photo of Barry Gatto, who, as Baylor Freeq, played Duke Washington in *Hellions in Hosiery.* Those were the days! Chico thinks. When he could afford to live next door to svelte, educated, attractive vegetarian couples with numerous interests, rather than these two Yahoos. Suddenly, an enormous crash is heard—surely the dresser again! "I love you! *Darling! Baby!* PUSSY! WHORE!" follows, a predictable coda. He doesn't know whether to laugh, cry, get drunk, masturbate, or kill himself. Such, such are the joys.

Zet arrives at the A & P and walks directly to the melons, not that he wants to be anywhere near the melons. He doesn't particularly care for melons, and wonders, in his rattling brain, why the store doesn't have a Thomas Wyatt section, or at least a John Crowe Ransom section. He stands sullenly yet dutifully next to a giant bin of honeydews, and as Marcella Butler, who has returned to the A & P for her own good reasons, passes him, he looks at her and says, somewhat rudely, "Me lusteth no longer rotten boughs to climb." Marcie cracks him sharply across the face and continues on. It is apparent that Zet, an unpleasant, unemployable youth who recognizes an objective correlative when it's pointed out to him and is wholly aware that cocktail dresses have suddenly become hatefully gauche, has been "assigned" to the A & P. This has probably been done, for ineffable reasons, by Baal, the Cat, who has an unseemly interest in the retail-foods business; certainly not by Zepar, whom some have incriminated. Zepar, the Crimson Duke, who drives women mad with lust, has other fish to fry. At this very moment, with the shades of night threatening to fall, and soon, Zepar, in black tie, is rushing about city and suburb, looking for small parties to enliven with his presence. Enliven and, shall we say, *surprise?*

"Absolutely!" Zepar says. "I have no interest in *melons,* and have no wish to meet the crude fellow who seemingly *lives* for them. My word!"

Exhausted by the bourgeois, phallocentric attention paid her new aluminum diet ("Fat Poetess Hopes Metal Regimen No Fad"), Olga Begone decides, in her anger and ennui, to read her old, never-mentioned, and almost forgotten novel *Zeppelin Days.* She takes it from its hiding place behind the bathtub and beneath layers of dried polygonum and dense, thickly wadded clusters of greisen and shards of raw meerschaum. It must be thirty years since she's even *seen* the typescript. She sits by the window and begins to read, amazed, after a time, to discover that the novel is quite possibly the worst thing in the language, after *The Duke of the Golden Prong,* of course, that puerile exercise in penis worship. Perhaps worse! How wonderful that it was Sister Rose Zeppole, of all people, who saw with such clarity that Olga's true talents lay in poetry. Dear Rose. The soft night she came directly from the set of, what was it?, *Sisters in Shame?,* her face flushed and her eyes bright with love, still in her habit and wimple. God! She was beautiful, even if she was a little overweight from all those Hershey bars. She wanted to be thin, like Olga. "Like you." Ha and ha. Dear, dear Rose. Who was it who recently told Olga that Rose is now the companion of that insufferable bitch Tania Crosse? Well, she has to eat. Olga puts the typescript into a brown paper bag and places the bag in her garbage can. That is that.

There's a Zippo lighter in Zippy's hand. The latter is a young psychopathic delinquent with a special interest in arson, and his tool of choice, the Zippo lighter, has given him his nickname. At present, he is setting the paper-goods products in the A & P's basement afire, after which he will torch, in probable order, Crown SuperMart, Rudy's Superette, and Village Victuals. He thinks, as he watches a carton of Scott tissue catch nicely, that he can't really help it if these stores happen to be in the "Zone," *his* "Zone." Nobody has ever been able to discover what Zippy means by this, but it seems that it changes, sometimes from day to day. Whatever or wherever it means or is, Zippy obeys its call to action unquestioningly. There go the Bounty paper towels.

As this cruelly hot Sunday draws to a close, the fact is not lost upon us that many other curious and noteworthy things have happened today, involving people whose lives are, perhaps, as interesting or bland as those to which we have been constrained to pay heed, however superficially. Some of the other arresting and even intriguing incidents so far reported have been made so, perhaps, by the very paucity and sketchiness of the information surrounding them; for instance, we know of the reprehensible actions performed by Deirdre Angelica, a glittering zipper opened by George Zaremias, divers benisons conferred on Melissa Butte, the weathered yacht scuttled by Jurgens Yurplatt, unusual consternations caused by Sydelle Cooze, the robust xylophone sounded for Morton Xenon, the huge debts incurred by Monica Delizioso, a venal wit joking with McDonald Webfoote, restless energies expended by Prudence Echevarría, a muscular vagina clasping Smitty Vandoosian, various frivolities indulged in by Charlotte Funze, the despairing ululation heard by Barry Ugh, spectacular gaucheries committed by Zoe Guitarra, the concupiscent tootsie provided for Caspar Tittlenose, juvenile hilarities perpetrated upon Wanita Hutchins, the weird string bean eaten by J.J. Stinsonberg, assorted imbecilities retailed by Lona Iacozzo, the impudent rodeo attended by Edwin Rodgers-Wales, sophomoric japes pulled off by Ella Jacaranda, an appalling queue waited on by Jeremiah Quentin, licentious kudos lavished on Olivia Kincannon, a svelte pannier woven for Marcus Peterpeak, the jocular lectures delivered by Mary Ellen Lemonade, a paper oil well sketched by Teddy O'Mara, scandalous memories treasured by Dolores Melanzana, the aloof nylons gift-wrapped by Bill Nemo, eschatological nuances suggested by Betty Newport, the curious machine invented by Guido McMac, gloomy orisons offered by Norma Okeechobee, the filmy lingerie stolen by Bert LaLane, troublesome psychoses suffered by Shauna Psaltery, a blustering knight dressed down by Ingemar Knauss, facetious queries asked of Ella Queynte, a loose jib secured by Ralph Jocelyn, querulous ripostes aimed at Mimi Ragazza, the crippled iguana nursed by Emil Ippolito, amusing situations stumbled upon by Agatha San Remo, an enormous ham carved by Moise Al-Raschid

Hillel, improper transactions made by Dorothea Trigridd, the new gymnasium buffed for Jamie Georgeton, vainglorious undertakings undertaken by Jennifer Ulalume, a bloodthirsty fly smashed by David Farquhar, startling visions encountered by Angelique Vanilla, a stuffed eagle ogled by Jackie Endicott, hollow welcomes extended to Jane Weir, the unabridged dictionary perused by Cecil Densmore, the crippling xenogamies endured by Eileen Xanthos, a gigantic cucumber sliced by Jerry Corfu, stultifying yearnings hidden by Berta Margolies, the sacred broom plied by Welles Banjo, illegal zealotries championed by Marjorie Sciszek, and the toy airplane dropped on Robert Armbrister, but that is all we know.

Lee Jefferson, whom we have been reminded is sometimes called "Zooz" or "ZuZu," nicknames given her years ago by one of her lovers, is exhausted. She beats some of the dust from the files off her skirt and blouse, wipes her sweaty, streaked face with a tissue, and sits, sprawled, at the crammed and cluttered desk. This anthology business has awakened a lot of memories, most of them unwelcome. Lee lights a cigarette, and realizes how desperately, how completely, how deeply tired she is of all these "contributors," of, really, hell, everybody. Old friends, lovers, acquaintances, all the fools, all the enemies, the darlings, the dears, the predators, the manipulators and the manipulated, the victims, the sweethearts, the mad, the disappeared, and the dead. Tired of all of them. Herself as well. There's been a lot of laughs, anyway. Usually at somebody's expense. Well. A job is a job. Life is life. And life, as they say—and *say*—goes on. The office is very dim now. The sun is low over New Jersey. Twilight is approaching, yet another twilight. Soon it will again grow dark.